KOSMOS OBSCURA

A COSMIC HORROR ANTHOLOGY

KOSMOS OBSCURA

A COSMIC HORROR ANTHOLOGY

CONTENT NOTES

Please note: because this is a horror anthology, it should be assumed that the basic horror tropes will apply.
These include death, gore, and violence.

For a list of potentially triggering subjects, please refer to page 354.

FOREWORD

BY J NEIRA

Originally, I was hesitant to submit a story for *Kosmos Obscura*. The reason being though I personally thought of cosmic horror as stories dealing with existential dread; it seemed like most people I met defined the genre as synonymous with HP Lovecraft and his tentacled deep-sea or outer space deities. None of my stories fit that definition. But then I read the guidelines posted at Graveside Press's website and at The Horror Tree, excerpted from nofilmschool.com:

"Cosmic horror, also known as Lovecraftian horror, is a subgenre of horror that emphasizes the terror of the unknowable and incomprehensible. It favors these psychological horrors more than gore or other elements of shock and awe. … The core of all cosmic horror is the protagonist being absolutely terrified of the unknown or the future and what's going to happen to them. … There should also be a contemplation of the human experience and the humanness of the struggle. They usually don't have a lot of blood and gore, and instead thrive on the ideas that are scary."

Turns out I *did* have a story that fit this definition very well. Because even though Lovecraft is cited here, the themes of the unknown and fear (often included in his stories) would be valid enough to be included for consideration in the anthology, regardless of whether an author wanted to use elements from Lovecraft's canon.

I submitted a story partially inspired by my own germaphobia and my desire to see the perspective of germaphobes treated respectfully rather than ridiculed—the latter of which happens way too often in recent pop culture.

So, I submitted it, hoping for the best, and was honored and excited when it was accepted a little while later. Then, a month or so after my story was accepted, Hannah (Graveside's Acquisitions Manager) invited me to help narrow down the finalists to help determine which other stories would appear in *Kosmos Obscura*. Because of this, I got the unique opportunity to read many of the stories found in this anthology during the submissions process.

One thing that impressed me the most about the stories submitted was how original everyone was while still following the theme. I was not the only one who chose to create my own characters rather than re-using Lovecraft's. In fact, most of the stories were original in this way. And of the ones that did use Lovecraft's canon, they mingled it with their own styles and characters, crafting stories that were original in how they dealt with the established characters. (Of course, I was reading through the finalists, so these were naturally going to be the best!)

You will find all sorts of cosmic horror within these pages, from classic deep-sea, eldritch monster tales to interpersonal dramas where families are hiding terrible secrets. There are stories of the world coming to an end and stories of daring treasure hunts. Tales of bugs and tales of seagulls, accounts of rituals gone wrong, and reflections on self-discovery. Some stories are set centuries ago, others are set today, others in different worlds completely.

Sometimes, oftentimes, humans are the real monsters. If I were to write a story using Lovecraft's canon, I've often thought I'd have written one portraying the Innsmouthers in a positive light. After all, they're the victims of a genocide in Lovecraft's own works, which he justifies due to his own despicable racism. *In Kosmos Obscura*, there are several stories that tackle the real-life horror of bigotry head-on. In some cases, this bigotry has a supernatural component, while in others, the supernatural turns out to be a solution in how to fight back against white supremacists and other wicked humans, and in others still, the existence of worlds beyond our comprehension provides an escape from the cruelty of society. These kinds of stories are especially important today, but really, they're universal.

The writers in *Kosmos Obscura* come from a diverse range of backgrounds and from all over the globe. You'll recognize some authors from previous Graveside Press anthologies, while others are new. At least a couple of the authors in this book haven't been published in any anthology until now, while others have appeared in dozens. I became a fan of several of them just from the stories in this anthology, and am eager to read more from them.

Of course, not every story is for everyone. Thankfully, there is a full list of trigger warnings near the end of this book. I myself am a cozy horror fan (often the opposite of cosmic horror!) and some of the stories might be too disturbing for me to read more than once, though I admire the skill of all of them. One of the many reasons I love being part of the Graveside Press author community is every book has trigger warnings for anyone who wants them.

Thank you very much to Hannah Rebekah Graves, Kelley York, and Steven Radecki for welcoming me into the Graveside Press community and for putting together this terrifying collection of tales. Thank you to our talented team of editors (Kelley, Lauren, and Kala) and Syd, our awesome Graveside Press assistant!

Several stories I read for *Kosmos Obscura* were disturbing enough to cause nightmares. Not all of them are as scary as that, but more than one ranks among the top ten scariest short stories I've ever read.

They're waiting for you.

—J. Neira

SUMMONING CALEB

MARGO PECHA

I THOUGHT I UNDERSTOOD loneliness before I summoned Caleb. I really thought I knew. Stories about men like me filled every type of media; we couldn't form friendships, we didn't know how to interact with women, let alone other men. We couldn't regulate our emotions. We were toxic and suicidal and dangerous. I didn't think I was any of those things, but after a while, I started to believe that maybe there was some truth to it. Why else would this constant sense of despair and yearning hang over me?

The blue light of screens bathed me in a ghostly glow day and night from being glued to my phone, my laptop, my work monitors. I kept the blinds tightly shut and worked on marketing projects in the dark. I sent pointless emails and kept my second monitor filled with 24-hour news coverage, my gaze yo-yo-ing between work and hysteria. Bodies burned. Hospitals turned people away. Something hard felt permanently lodged in my throat.

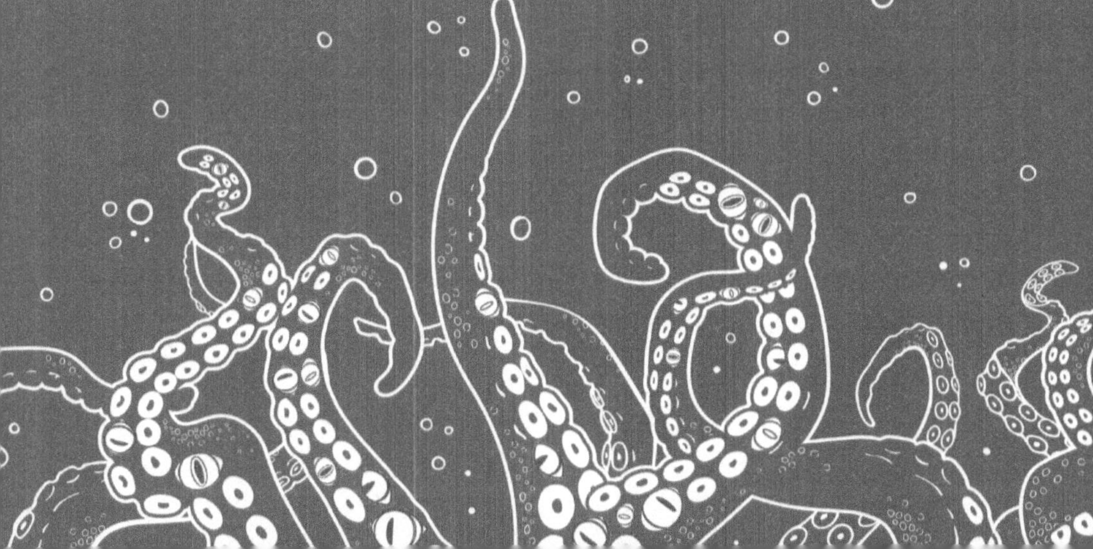

I couldn't remember the last person I'd spoken to. Was it the barista on my way to work on that final morning before isolating? Hadn't I exchanged a few apprehensive words with the grocery store clerk when I stocked up on food? I racked my brain, but I truly couldn't recall.

After work, I lay on the floor and stared up at the cracked ceiling, feeling small and insignificant. If I contracted the plague and died, would anyone even notice? I tested out my voice, worried I'd forget how to talk. It sounded hoarse and foreign, like it belonged to someone I'd never met.

"No one will know your name when they find you," I said to the ceiling.

I closed my eyes and imagined roots emerging beneath my body, sinking into the floor as I languished and withered away, becoming something else entirely. Something unrecognizable.

Some couples and families endured the isolation well. They had gardens to tend and backyards to escape to and pets to care for. I saw it all through the fluorescence of my phone, through square pictures and quick bursts of video. Songs and dances and skits. Fear and heartbreak and love. I connected to everything, all of it, still cloistered in my own personal hell: a studio apartment in the middle of the city, no balcony, no pets allowed. I was a caged animal, violently angry one moment, then despondent and curled in on myself the next.

I tried dating, but it was even worse than before. Virtual dinners were depressing affairs. No one wanted to attempt small talk with a guy who had no hobbies or friends. My eyes grew red-rimmed and bloodshot from endless hours of screen time. I guzzled beer to fill the days and the emptiness. I looked ill. I *felt* ill. An ache had settled deep in my stomach and nothing eased it.

I needed a hobby, but hobbies cost too much. I could barely afford my rent as it was. Still, I put on a mask and walked to the store, but the shelves were bare. Upon the looming threat of lockdown, all the puzzles were gone, the Lego kits were out of stock, and every movie had been hastily snatched up.

Too cheap to subscribe to Netflix, I watched *American Psycho* over and over again. It was the only DVD I owned.

I found the instructions on a subreddit late one night. Lying on the floor once again, I scrolled and swiped endlessly on my phone until my brain began to gelatinize and my eyes glazed and unfocused. A can of Pabst sweated nearby, its condensation puddling in watery rings on the floorboards. The summer heat was oppressive and stifling.

Lonely? Here's how I summoned a ghost to keep me company.

I clicked on it. I had nothing better to do.

Are you feeling alone in these trying times? I was, too, until I learned how to summon a ghost for companionship. My grandmother was into the occult before she died, and I found the instructions written in one of her old books. My ghost is named Lyra, and she's been a great friend to me. She keeps me company while I work from home, and we surprisingly have a lot in common despite having lived centuries apart. We even play backgammon together!

I snorted. How dumb could you be?

Here's what you do: Place a cup of water outside when the moon is full and let it charge in the moon's energy all night, at least eight hours. The moon must be full, otherwise it won't work. While the water charges, go to the cemetery and find a grave. Walk around for a while and see if any particular headstone calls out to you. You'll know when you've found the right one. This will be your ghost. Take a handful of dirt from the grave and go home.

The next night, mix your energized moon water with the grave dirt until it becomes a slurry. Do not heat it up under any circumstances. Draw two overlapping moons on the floor in ash. Take half your slurry and mark the runes (depicted below) in a counterclockwise fashion.

There was a drawing inserted into the post. Two circles overlapped like a Venn diagram, and a series of unfamiliar runes encircled the two rings. The circle on the left had a crude spider drawn within it. The one on the right had an arched door.

Place six candles along the outermost rings of your sigil, one at each of the cardinal points for each circle. Light them and stand in the middle of your sigil. Drink the other half of the slurry. (Yes, you have to drink it all.)

Close your eyes and speak confidently:

Bring to me of the ageless three
from Eye of Eye and ancient tree

of lunar light and graven soil,
a threshold breached to mortal coil.

Shroud of darkness, release thy bond
of One confined and abiding beyond.

Enduring One, oh come to me,
I beg of you to hear my plea.

Eidolon, eidolon, I summon thee.

If you've done everything correctly, your ghost will appear. Happy haunting! ;)

I dubiously scanned through the many comments. The general consensus was that it actually worked. People alleged they'd experienced a magnetic pull toward a particular grave, elaborating on how their ghost had appeared after reciting the summoning spell and how interesting they'd found their apparition. One person had even done the ritual twice and claimed to have a set of twin ghosts occupying their guest room. Others maintained that they'd had deep, meaningful conversations with their new companion, and that they weren't afraid of death anymore. The specifics varied from person to person, but the one thing everyone agreed on was that none of them were lonely anymore.

An aching need welled within me. I scrolled back to the top and carefully read each comment. A hunger grew with each one I consumed, the ache ballooning and swelling; by the time I'd gone through them all, I knew I would attempt the summoning myself.

A nagging little voice in the back of my brain still lingered from my cast-off Evangelical upbringing, warning me this was dangerous—forbidden even—but another larger part of me thrilled at the thought of doing something as illicit as contacting spirits. The agonizing chasm in my chest gaped wider, and it soon dwarfed the intrusive thought.

I glanced out the window at the full moon. Could I find everything I needed at this late hour? My resolve steeled from the challenge.

For the first time since March, I pulled up my blinds. I set my cup of water on the windowsill, hoping enough of the moon's light would reach it, and then I set off for the cemetery.

I chose Venerate Grove because it was the oldest cemetery in town and would therefore have the most interesting ghosts. I wandered along winding paths bordered with crumbling, leaning headstones and ancient trees dripping with moss. I didn't really know what I was supposed to feel or how I would even recognize it. My flashlight beam bounced from headstone to headstone, from marker to mausoleum. Aimlessly roaming the large cemetery, I searched for that elusive feeling. All was quiet and strangely still, my surroundings illuminated by the silvery sheen of moonlight.

And then I felt it: a sort of beckoning, a tugging toward the opposite side of the cemetery. I followed as if pulled on an invisible line. Soon enough, I ran, flying past vacant-eyed angels and stone lambs as the urge propelled me onward. I leapt over headstones, the beam of my flashlight bouncing erratically. I didn't need the light anymore, as I knew exactly where to go.

Tucked toward the back of the cemetery, a nondescript headstone said simply CALEB. A large crack rent its surface, splitting the name in two before snaking into the ground. A wave of glossy-leaved ivy crept toward it from the nearby fence, and goosebumps skittered down the backs of my arms at the thought of those vines surging forward, smothering and choking everything in its path.

I scooped a handful of soil from the gravesite, probing my fingers down beneath the damp grass and peeling it away in chunks. The earth below was soft and cool in my palms; shiny black beetles scurried out of sight and glistening worms writhed and wriggled away, fleeing my intrusion. It smelled musty—ageless and enduring. I filled an empty jar with the soil and tried to rearrange the chunks of sod as best I could. A small spark of excitement ignited in my chest.

I tucked the jar into my shoulder bag and sat down, leaning against the headstone. The summer night was muggy, but the stone leached cool relief through the back of my t-shirt. While I rested, I Googled "house fire near me" from my phone and searched through the most recent news articles until I found one on this side of the city. It was ten blocks out of the way, but it would provide the ash I needed.

Anticipation compounded in me as I walked the ten blocks. By the time I arrived at the charred remains of the house, I nearly vibrated with excitement. I hardly noticed how sticky with sweat my clothing had become. I scooped some ash from the ruins into a second jar.

The two vessels clicked against each other in my shoulder bag with every step home I took, like some dark metronome counting down to a great unknown.

I slept late the next day, exhausted from my excursion the previous night. I spent some time sketching out the sigil while I nursed a steaming cup of coffee, wanting to make sure I had it correct before staining the floorboards with the ash. The post didn't specify what time I should perform the summoning, other than "night", so I waited until darkness had settled softly in the corners of my apartment before rolling back the area rug and getting to work.

I made huge, sweeping motions with my hand along the floorboards, pressing the ash into the dings and crevices before marking some of the finer details with the tips of two fingers. My hands were dirty and dry when I was done.

The drawing took up the majority of the room. I placed candles along the appropriate points of the sigil and lit them, then I combined the grave dirt and moon water in a bowl, forming a dense sludge. Grimacing, I scooped up the muck and carefully used it to draw the runes before situating myself in the center of the symbol.

I choked down the slurry in gagging gulps, nearly vomiting when the thick slickness of a worm passed over my tongue. I leaned my palms on my knees, breathing heavily as my stomach churned. Sweat trickled down my temples. I wiped a smear of mud away from my mouth and stood up to begin the incantation.

The candles' flames danced brightly as I recited the words; I'd read the post so many times throughout the day that I'd memorized it by now. I closed my eyes and let the emotions evoked by the strange phrases carry the cadence of my voice. When I'd finished, I found I'd lifted my palms to the sky at some point, and an oppressive silence hung heavy within the room. I shifted from foot to foot.

Nothing happened for a moment. Then the candlelight guttered as if something giant approached. I held my breath, every muscle tensed.

A hot wind blasted through my apartment. I shielded my eyes with a forearm as the wind roared around me, pelting me with grit and nearly bowling me over. It couldn't have lasted more than a couple of seconds, but it felt like an eternity. When it ceased, it did so abruptly. My ears rang from the sudden silence.

I lifted my head, rubbing the grit from my eyes. A pyramidal shape of hazy dark matter filled the corner by my bed, monolithic and dense. The immeasurable black seemed to leach all the color from the surroundings, sucking it inward. Seven pinpricks of cold white light shone from the uppermost part, arranged in no discernible pattern, which gave me the distinct impression of a calculating, spider-like intelligence. Whether the thing hovered or rested upon the ground, I couldn't tell.

My heart quickened, and I stepped back a few paces. "Are you Caleb?" I croaked. My mouth felt grainy and dry.

The void said nothing, only stared at me with those pinhole eyes. I noticed then that it had no mouth. I edged away until my back bumped against the opposite wall, staring at the thing before me.

In a panic, I returned to the Reddit post, quickly scrolling through all the responses; my gaze toggled between the thing and the phone screen as I searched for any mention of a dark shape. I couldn't find anything.

"I think I did something wrong," I typed into the comment box. *"Do any of your ghosts look like evil Grimace?"*

I pushed "reply" but was met with a new message: "*Commenting has been turned off.*"

I uttered a guttural cry of frustration and chucked my phone onto the mattress. What the hell was I supposed to do now? I sat on the edge of the bed and regarded Caleb warily. He made neither noise nor movement toward me.

Well, I reasoned after a while, no one had actually *said* what a ghost was or wasn't supposed to look like. Maybe this was it, and humanity had it all wrong the whole time. I moved uneasily through the apartment, keeping an eye on him. He abided, silent and motionless.

The first night with Caleb passed unremarkably. He remained in the corner, watching me. His gaze made my skin crawl, but I tried my best to converse with him as I cleaned up the sandy substance coating every surface of the apartment. I thought it would feel good to talk to someone finally. All I felt was a rising sense of anger and frustration.

Eventually, I put on *American Psycho* again and let Patrick Bateman's droning monologues lull me to sleep. At some point, I woke in the night, Caleb's constellation of eyes shining cold and harsh in the dark.

A week passed. Caleb still lingered in the corner. I checked the Reddit post nearly every hour, but comments were still locked and the author hadn't responded to my direct messages. I spent a lot of time lying on my bed, watching bars of sunlight bleed through the blinds to pinstripe shadows on the opposite wall. The lines disappeared, abruptly cut off, where they fell across Caleb. He hadn't moved an inch over the course of the week, and I didn't know how to send him back. He both angered and frightened me. I tossed empties at him, then guiltily gathered them up.

Tears welled in my eyes at the absurdity of it all. I scrubbed my face with the heels of my hands, chiding myself for being so upset. This was what I'd wanted, wasn't it? A confidante, someone with whom to pass the slow drip of daily life? The hollowness inside me widened, festering. I couldn't understand how my liminal companion could make me feel even more alone, like the last soul in all existence. I'd clearly done the ritual wrong and would now live with the consequences, since I couldn't figure out how to reverse it.

On Saturday, I needed to do some grocery shopping, so I donned a jacket and prepared to venture into the world. A small pearl of hope assured me I would feel a little less solitary while doing my errands. The masks we all wore lent anonymity to the mundane, leveling the playing field—I was just like everyone else, and we all suffered alone together. We were all suspicious, casting furtive glances at anyone who got too close. I wasn't the guy with no hobbies or friends. No one had friends, right?

I patted my pockets, double checking I had my wallet and my keys, and reached for the doorknob. I was so absorbed in my circling thoughts about Caleb and the sad state of the world that I somehow missed the handle. I glanced over my shoulder at him and groped for it again. When I turned back, still not feeling it, I saw my hand pass right through.

I tried again and again. My hands seemed to grow fainter and more transparent with every sweep of my arms. Panic rising, I careened through my apartment, attempting to open cabinets and drawers, trying to pick up various objects until my hands resembled indistinct outlines so opaque I could barely see them.

I choked back a sob and turned toward Caleb. Two hazy hand-like shapes were taking form, one on either side of his silhouette.

"Is this you?" I cried, holding aloft what remained of my hands. And then they dissolved, vanishing entirely.

I tried using the nubs of my wrists to open the front door, but I couldn't get a good grip on it. By the time I'd given up and turned toward him again, the hands—*my hands*—had fully materialized. They hung suspended at his sides, seemingly attached to nothing,

He stood in the corner, fingers tensing and flexing, rediscovering the sensation of touch, of movement, all the while watching me with his horrible pinprick eyes.

I thought maybe my hands would reappear, but when I woke up the next morning and couldn't make coffee without breaking all of my mugs, I knew they weren't coming back.

I tried to call my mother. We hadn't spoken since the election. I dialed her number with the tip of my nose and waited, hovering over the phone's screen.

"Mom, something's happening to me," I said when she picked up. "I need your help."

"Oh, you want money?" she sneered. "You finally call after all these years and expect a handout?"

"No, I—"

"You kids think you're so entitled to everything," she ranted. "You have no work ethic."

"I work full-time!" I shouted. "You know that!"

"No, I don't," she sobbed. "You never call me!"

"This is exactly why I never call you!" I yelled. "You're a manipulative bitch!"

"And you're an ungrateful leech!" she screamed. "I don't know where we went wrong with you!"

My blood boiled, but I tried to calm myself. "Can you just *listen* to me for a minute? I need help!"

"From your bitch mother?" she jeered. "I don't think so. I think we've given you enough handouts. Whatever you've gotten yourself into, you can figure it out on your own."

The line went dead; she'd hung up.

I swiped the phone off the table with my forearms, flinging it across the room. What the hell was I supposed to do now? I'd lived in the same building for five years and didn't know any of my neighbors—and even if I did, it wasn't like I could get the door open to ask them for help, anyway.

I paced and fumed around my apartment, walking in endless circles. Caleb's glacial, effulgent eyes followed my restless treading. The hands at his sides twitched and spasmed.

Finally, fumbling, I used my elbows and wrists to push the buttons on the TV remote. *American Psycho* was still in the DVD player. I collapsed on the bed, resigned to solitude and desperately craving a beer I could not open.

Nearly a week later, I lost my feet. One moment I paced the four walls of my apartment and the next I felt like I'd been planted firmly in concrete. I looked down and saw nothing below my shins, just a gap of about four inches between where my ankles should have been and the floor. Somehow, I remained upright. Affixed to nothing but not exactly hovering, either.

Panic rising, I struggled and pulled, vainly attempting to release myself, but my not-there feet felt like they were stuck *beneath* the floor, rooting me in place. I couldn't understand. I'd lost my hands but could still move my arms; surely I should still be able to move the stumps of my legs?

Caleb stepped out of the corner, an amorphous vacuum traversing on bare human feet. *My feet.*

"Why are you doing this?" I yelled, jerking my knees up as if they'd somehow pull my feet back into existence. "I just wanted to be friends!"

He strolled leisurely through the room, touching and caressing my possessions, examining, curious. From time to time, he turned his many eyes on me and cocked his head to the side, as if something about me amused him.

I had the horrifying realization that the rules, as I thought I'd understood them, didn't exist.

Two days passed, and I was still rooted to the same spot. My lips had cracked and peeled from thirst. Every part of my body ached from standing for so long.

"I need to eat something," I pleaded. "Anything. Please, Caleb."

He heated up a frozen lasagna and left it on the floor before me, along with a bowl of water. I managed to crouch at an awkward angle and gobbled up the hot food like a dog, using the nubs of my wrists to pull it closer. Marinara smeared my face, and I burned my tongue. I slurped up the water as best as I could. Bits of noodles and beef slid down the collar of my shirt. I squirmed at the sensation, begging him to bring me clean clothing.

Caleb ignored me and settled into my office chair instead, preoccupying himself with my computer.

Days trickled into weeks; I lost track of time and even more body parts. I thought maybe when my stomach disappeared, I would lose all sense of hunger. I didn't. Regardless, Caleb stopped feeding me. The dull ache of phantom limbs and bodily functions settled into the lingering awareness I somehow still possessed. Sometimes my palms prickled and itched or my legs cramped, but I knew nothing was there anymore. I couldn't remember when I'd given up on crying, but now I knew it was pointless. I simply endured.

I zoned out most of the time, letting my mind wander and my eyes glaze over. Caleb kept the blinds pulled up, flooding the apartment with light. I vacantly watched the window for the flit of passing birds or the gentle shift and sway of leaves on the neighboring tree. My apartment was so quiet without the constant stream of news chattering in the background. A profound sadness settled over me, draping like a heavy blanket. Caleb no longer looked at me like I amused him; he hardly looked at me at all.

It must be close to November now. A cold wind gusts through the window Caleb left cracked, and russet leaves plaster the pane. He types away at my work computer, using hands that are no longer mine. He joins video calls. I don't know how my coworkers don't notice the black void on the screen. He's confiscated my phone, and he reclines in my office chair, swiping left and right on Tinder. He plays "Hip to Be Square" on repeat, filling the apartment with its poppy, upbeat chorus until my head aches. He answers the door and signs for packages I didn't order.

I keep asking him what he's doing, but he never answers. I know he can't until he has a mouth. My mouth.

Some sick part of me thinks it will be worth it just to hear another voice.

DARLA'S MONSTER

CASSONDRA WINDWALKER

"MAKE ME A monster, Mama," Abby whispered as Darla tucked her in.

Darla's heart seized up. She knew what Abby meant. Darla was Quartz Creek's resident monster-maker. A tiny town tucked up in the ancient, slump-shouldered Ouachita Mountains, Quartz Creek was little more than a speed bump on the rutted highway that a few brazen tourists took to get to the hot springs. Its survival hinged on its residents' ability to convince travelers to stop.

There was a "moonshine" diner, the requisite rock shop, an outfitter's cabin for the more adventurous, and Darla's own toy store. Not the sort of toy store that sold dolls and trucks and train sets, though. Darla made monsters.

Knitted from only the finest, silkiest, most brilliantly dyed yarns and luxuriantly stuffed, Darla's Monsters were a necessity for anyone daring to travel farther into the forested mountains. Or so the sign proclaimed, and most tourists happily chose to believe. It'd become something of a social

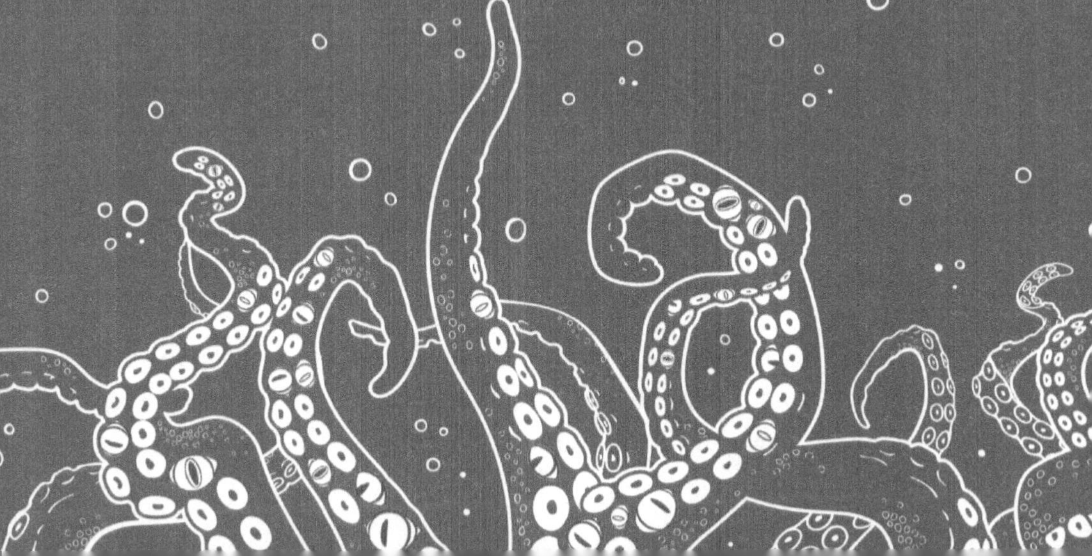

media craze, photos of their own personal Darla's Monster perched on the dashboard, guaranteeing their safe passage on a road haunted with massacred Native peoples, escaped slaves, unrepentant moonshiners, and even the more recent victims of a 1980s serial killer who'd never been caught.

And Darla knew why Abby needed a monster of her own.

"Okay, baby," she whispered back, forcing a smile she hoped looked reassuring. She tore a cotton ball in half and squeezed the pieces into her daughter's ears before kissing her on the forehead.

Maybe Dale wouldn't come knocking tonight, but maybe he would.

He still had a key. Darla hadn't been able to get away to the city to buy new locks yet. She couldn't afford to close the shop before tourist season slowed down. She had a deadbolt, at least, though she didn't think he'd hesitate to break a window or kick down a door if he really wanted in.

Of course, even that wouldn't really be necessary. She couldn't afford to run the swamp cooler twenty-four hours a day. Most of the time, the only relief from the sticky, oppressive heat was open windows and buzzing fans. Their only real protection against him was the rifle she kept over the door, but a woman had to sleep sometime.

And she was tired. So tired.

But it was only eight o'clock. Luckily, four-year-olds tuckered out early, which gave Darla time to work on building up her shop inventory. Folks rarely saw her without her knitting needles, anyway. She was always working— sitting behind the counter at the shop waiting for the next car to stop, in the hard wooden pew at church on Sunday, at the rundown town park watching Abby play on the rusted steel toys.

Tonight, though, her only task would be Abby's monster.

She turned on the television. She kept the volume down low, partly so it wouldn't disturb Abby, and partly so she could keep one ear peeled for anybody creeping around the house outside. The first couple of nights after she kicked Dale out had been awful. He'd prowled around the house like a polecat, screaming, banging on the door, throwing bottles, looking in the windows.

Darla had been putting cotton in Abby's ears at bedtime since she was tiny, because that was invariably when Dale got wound up and went off. Even that couldn't help with him circling around and banging on Abby's walls. The little girl had been terrified, though like any child who grew up in a house of violence, she hadn't permitted herself the luxury of hysteria. Darla had found her on the floor under her bed, soaked in silent tears.

It had almost been enough for Darla to relent, to tell Dale he could come back. After all, the bad nights weren't every night, and on good nights, Dale was as charming and funny and downright hypnotic as a snake-oil salesman. And he was Abby's father.

Once upon a time, Dale and Darla had been the sweethearts of Quartz Creek. Almost every day since the breakup, someone or other came into her shop to tut-tut or shake their heads sadly over her broken home. The preacher was coming over "for a good talk," he'd said, but she'd managed to be too busy so far.

Most of them, she told herself generously, had no idea what happened behind their closed doors. Dale was always careful not to leave a mark where it showed or break a bone. But them what knew—Dale's friends and her family—saw that scary flash in his eyes and had watched how liquor brought out his beast, didn't seem to care. Not enough, anyhow.

And that last night—Darla shuddered thinking about it. He must've seen the resignation in her eyes. She knew what was coming, and she only managed to summon dread instead of the terror that delighted him. So, he'd threatened to wake up Abby, to drag her out of bed and ask her what she thought of her whore mother.

That'd been Dale's fatal mistake. Darla could lie to herself as long as Dale kept his terrorizing to her. He'd always doted on Abby up until then. Darla had snatched down her daddy's rifle and ordered Dale out of the house. At first, he'd laughed at her—the thing wasn't even loaded, but when she screamed at him in a voice he didn't recognize that she was going to bash his head in with it, he'd retreated.

And it was loaded now.

Darla picked her yarns first. Blue was Abby's favorite color, so she chose sapphire and midnight, silver and aquamarine. She closed her eyes, resting her hands on the soft materials, and let her mind drift away, let the chatter of the television become nothing more than the ripple of a creek or the murmur of the wind. She waited for the monster to appear in her mind.

She didn't see the face that peered in the curtainless kitchen window, its glass set much too high above the ground for any person to reach. A face riven and creased and gray like the bark of an old cottonwood tree, its eyes burning like swamp-lights.

She didn't hear Abby, eyelashes smudged and shadowy on cheeks flushed with sleep, humming the tune to a lullaby Darla didn't know.

Darla started knitting.

Abby stared at the stuffed monster whose ridiculously long, spindly legs wrapped around her cereal bowl the next morning, her expression confused. The monster stared back, its X-shaped eyes and wobbly smile seeming to search for acceptance. A broken red heart was emblazoned on its blue chest, which was covered with lumps and bumps like tree burls.

"What is it?" Abby asked.

"It's your monster," Darla replied, fighting back tears. Dammit. Every little thing made her cry these days. There was no reason for her daughter's disappointment to feel like a kick in the belly. So what if she'd stayed up half the night making it? Abby was four. Maybe she'd pictured something different. Darla could just put this one on the shelf in the shop and let Abby pick the one she wanted instead. It wasn't as if her daughter was rejecting her.

Darla turned away to pour orange juice and swiped at her eyes.

"No, Mama," Abby said, speaking slowly as if she were a teacher explaining something very simple to a rather slow child. "I wanted you to make *me* a monster. Not *make* me a monster."

Darla definitely needed more sleep. "What?"

Abby beat her little chest emphatically. "Me! Me. I want to be a monster."

"Oh, Abby." Darla laughed a little, then straightened up quickly when she saw her daughter's earnest face. "Why do you want to be a monster, honey?"

"Monsters keep people safe. That's what your sign says. They keep people safe from baddies and make sure they always find their way home."

Oh, that hurt. Her poor baby. Darla crouched down by Abby's chair and pulled her into her arms. "I'm your monster, honey. I promise I'll keep you safe. And you are always home with me, wherever we are."

"Okay, Mama." Abby's voice was muffled against her shoulder, but Darla knew when a four-year-old was patronizing her. She gave her one more fierce squdge and let her go.

"Now, eat your cereal. I need to get you to Miz Lou's and open the shop."

Darla could have kept Abby with her all day at the shop, and she did have a little room set up there with toys and books. But she liked knowing Abby had friends her own age to play with, so last summer she'd started sending her to Miz Lou.

At least Miz Lou was one of the few folks in town who wouldn't give her any grief about kicking Dale out of his marital home. Miz Lou had always only ever been a *miz*, and everybody knew she was a little more "modern" than other Quartz Creek residents. God only knew why she stayed in the town. Although her roots went back deeper than most anybody else's, Darla figured. Miz Lou was descended from the freemen, the black slaves the Cherokee had brought with them on the Trail of Tears.

Darla wasn't even sure how old she was. Miz Lou might've been forty, or she might've been seventy. At any rate, children loved her, women listened to her when the preacher wasn't looking, and most men feared her. She lived her life on her own terms, and Darla had no qualms about leaving Abby with her. Dale's mama didn't approve, but that was nothing new for Darla.

Darla was surprised to see Abby tuck the new stuffed monster under her arm when she slid out of her chair to go brush her teeth, but she didn't say anything. Maybe Abby had decided to take some comfort in the creature after all. A little grin curled Darla's mouth to see the long silvery-blue legs trailing behind her daughter.

Twenty minutes later, Darla handed Abby's sack lunch for the day to Miz Lou. Abby had already squeezed past the older woman's broadly planted legs and raced, squealing, to join her friends in the backyard. Darla's heart lightened to see her daughter shed her fears so easily. Abby was going to be okay. She was doing the right thing.

But Miz Lou frowned, seizing Darla's chin to stare imperiously into her eyes. "You got new trouble, girl?" she demanded.

"No, Miz Lou. No new trouble. Just the same old trouble, and I'm getting rid of it. Everything's going to get better."

Miz Lou dropped Darla's chin and shook her head. "You ain't alone, Darla. The Old Mother's with you. That means new trouble."

Uneasiness skittered across the hair on Darla's arms, light as a water-skimmer dancing over a creek. "The Old Mother?"

Darla knew who The Old Mother was, of course. Everybody in these parts did. Some tangled combination of Irish and Cherokee folklore and modern-day superstitions, she was as likely to embody destruction as she was salvation. Impossibly tall, with a weirdly folding body that looked just like a cottonwood trunk in the moonlight. She was regularly spotted in the flashlight beams of folks stumbling home late from the diner or in the fog-bleared gazes of early-morning fishermen. Her appearances always seemed to coincide with some tragedy, so whether she helped or hurt, nobody wanted to see her.

Miz Lou nodded heavily. "Look behind you."

Darla drew a deep breath and turned. Slowly.

Her air whooshed out in an unsteady laugh. There was nothing behind her but the empty highway, its tar already melting in the hot summer sun, and beyond that, a stand of trees.

"Miz Lou, you scared the bejesus out of me! Don't do that to me."

But Miz Lou didn't smile back. "Trouble, girl. I'm telling you. Watch your back."

Darla was still chuckling at her own gullibility as she opened the shop. There was nothing new about the trouble she had. And while she might not enjoy it, at least it was familiar. She could handle Dale. Even he had his limits.

He was still the man she married, the boy with whom she'd grown up. He had an ugly side she wasn't going to tolerate anymore, and once he came around and accepted that, things would calm down. Dale loved his little girl, and in his own toxic, unhealthy way, he still loved Darla, too.

Love just wasn't enough anymore. She'd had years to think about ending their relationship. Every time he threw her against a wall or kicked in her ribs or screamed in her face. She was sure Dale had never considered leaving, so he would need some time to make his peace with it. She would wait out his bad side and appeal to his good side, and eventually they'd all get through this.

She'd drunk two cups of tea and sold three monsters and about convinced herself of her own happy ending story when the phone rang.

"Darla, I'm sorry, I'm so sorry."

The fear in Miz Lou's voice galvanized Darla more than her words. Darla didn't know Miz Lou was capable of fear. Before the woman managed her next words, Darla was already locking the shop door behind her and running the few yards down the street to Miz Lou's clapboard house, her phone pressed to her ear.

"What happened?"

"He got her. Oh, Lord, he got her. Took her right out of the yard."

Miz Lou's words were hardly comprehensible through her moaning. Darla didn't bother with a goodbye as she shoved the phone in her pocket and sprinted the last few feet. She banged through the front door without stopping to knock. Miz Lou was pacing the living room floor, the other three children she watched huddled close with wide eyes and tear-stained faces.

Miz Lou rushed to her, wrapping her in her soft arms and squeezing her tightly to her ample breast. But Darla didn't want comfort. She wanted Abby. She pulled back and put her hands firmly on the other woman's shoulders.

"Tell me exactly what happened."

Miz Lou gulped and nodded. "The kids were playing in the backyard. I came in to get some juice boxes, and by the time I got back out there, Abby was gone. The other kids said her daddy took her."

"He should've been at work," Darla argued futilely. Dale drove trucks for an outfit in the city, thirty miles away.

"I know, honey. I'm so sorry. Please forgive me."

Darla just shook her head, unwilling to countenance the idea that anything was happening that would need forgiveness. "I'm going home. I bet he took her home."

Miz Lou clung to her arm. "Maybe you should wait. I called the sheriff."

Darla snorted drily. "The sheriff? And what are they gonna do when a daddy wants to spend time with his own little girl? It's not like I have a protective order. We're not even divorced. He has every right to pick up his own child from daycare. They're not going to do anything. I'll be surprised if they even show up."

"Dale is dangerous. Take somebody with you, at least."

It should have been affirming to hear someone else acknowledge the reality she'd lived the last five years, but contrarily, Darla rebelled at Miz Lou's assertion. How did she know that, anyway? Gossip and rumors were all. Darla had never breathed a word of Dale's temper to anyone outside her own four walls.

"He's Abby's daddy," she snapped. "He won't do anything to hurt her. He's just proving a point to me. Don't worry. I can handle this."

She didn't wait for more protests from Miz Lou. She walked the half-mile back to her house with long strides that ate up the crumbling sidewalk. *No need to run*, she told herself. She'd gotten carried away by Miz Lou's melodrama, but this was no big deal. Dale was making a point, that was all. Abby was probably having the time of her life, on an unexpected adventure with her daddy. Playing hooky.

Maybe Dale was working on one of his make-up schemes. He could go overboard when he was in the mood to apologize. Maybe she'd get to the house and find him and Abby cooking up some fancy dinner, with flowers in the living room and a bottle of wine in the fridge.

Her heart rate was almost back to normal when she tugged on her own front doorknob.

Locked.

Her heart rate kicked back up.

Okay. She needed to handle this right. Needed to stay calm. Figure out what Dale was thinking and work on him until she had Abby safe in her arms, whatever that took.

She knocked lightly, clenching her fingers to keep them from shaking.

"Dale? It's Darla. Can I come in?"

"Mama!" Abby's scream was choked off as suddenly as it began.

Calm fled. Darla pounded on the door until it shook. "Dale! Dale! Let me in."

The curtain in the window beside the door shifted. Darla squinted against the sunlit glare on the glass. Her knees nearly buckled when she saw Dale standing there with her daddy's rifle draped casually over his arm, a lazy grin on his face.

"I don't think so, honey," he said. "Doesn't feel so good to be the one locked out, does it?"

She clasped her hands. "Dale? Dale, please don't do this. You don't have to do this. We can work things out. We've known each other our whole lives. We can figure this out. Just—just please come out. Or let Abby come out. I know she's scared in there."

The grin vanished from Dale's face as if it had never been there, and in its place, she saw something cold and hard and altogether unfamiliar. "I don't think so, Darla. I'm done being played by you. All these years, you made me feel like the bad guy. Like there was something wrong with *me*. And now you've convinced our daughter of the same thing. Do you know, she acted scared of me when I picked her up this morning?"

Darla's phone was buzzing in her pocket. Probably Miz Lou. More than anything, she wanted to pull it out, call 911, tell them she'd been terribly wrong, she needed help desperately, her baby was locked in the house with an armed madman, but she stood paralyzed at the thought of enraging him further.

He was still talking. "I can't have that. You know I can't have that. She's my little girl. I've never even spanked her. And now she thinks I'm what's wrong with this family."

"Let me see her, Dale." The words poured out of her mouth, unplanned. "Just let me see her, for a minute."

"Oh, sure. No problem." Dale turned and motioned behind him. "Your mama wants to see what she's done. Come to the window, Abby."

Abby appeared at the window, a silver strip of duct tape over her mouth. In her arm, she still clutched the monster Darla had made her last night. Her eyes, wide and swimming, were the stuff of nightmares; terrified and begging and still somehow hollow with a knowledge no child should have.

Darla stumbled up the porch steps and rushed toward the glass, her hands outstretched, but Dale tilted the rifle ever so slightly so that it pointed straight at Abby's head. "I don't think so. Back yourself up. Go sit down, Abby."

Darla scrambled back as quickly as she could. "Don't…don't point that at her, Dale. Point it at me. I'm the one you're angry with, not her. You love her. You don't want to hurt her."

"You're right. She's not the one I want to suffer. She won't feel a thing. You're the one who'll have to live with the knowledge of what you've done."

Behind her, Darla heard the wail of police sirens. Miz Lou must've convinced the sheriff to take her seriously, after all.

The curtain dropped, and Dale disappeared. Darla flung herself back up the steps and pounded on the door. "Dale, no! No! Dale, don't do this!"

She spun around, searching the yard. Her eyes lit on the border stones she'd piled along the edge of her choked-out flower garden. As she hurled it through the window, she heard the crack of a rifle over the shattering of the glass.

She howled, an inhuman sound, vaulting herself over the jagged pieces of glass to land in what had once been her living room.

Had been, because there was nothing of a home about it now. Blood and broken furniture drew the eye in a dizzying chaos that made it nearly impossible for the brain to sort the images it was seeing into anything like a cohesive whole.

The remnants of her husband lay strewn from one end of the room to the other, hardly recognizable as human body parts. The rifle lay on the floor, a hole in the drywall testament to its futility. Abby was nowhere to be seen.

Panting heavily from a crooked mouth and hunched awkwardly over long spindly legs, a broken-hearted creature the color of oceans and skies with knobby, burled skin watched Darla as she struggled to understand what had happened. Darla might have been afraid had she not looked into the monster's eyes and known in a breath whose soul burned inside.

"Abby?" she whispered, reaching out a shaking hand.

Two sparkling tears welled up and poured over the monster's blue cheeks.

Darla didn't hesitate. She raced across the room, over the debris, and wrapped herself as tightly as she could around the fat belly, the spidery legs, the bony knees. "I love you so much, baby. More than I can ever tell you."

The sirens were very close now. Darla nearly jumped out of her skin when a knock sounded at the back door. Had Miz Lou found someone to watch the children and hurried over herself? Darla unfolded herself gently from her daughter's strangely large embrace and unlocked the back door, opening it tentatively.

A creature Darla knew in an instant, though she'd never before seen, towered there.

The Old Mother bowed down so that her head could stretch inside the house, like the reaching limb of a willow tree. "It's time to go, Daughter," she rumbled, her voice at once birdsong and thunder.

To Darla's horror, Abby crawled toward the door, tucking her head so as not to bang it on the ceiling fan.

"No. No, she can't go," she protested. "She's my baby, my girl. Please, don't take her."

The Old Mother's cottonwood-bark face moved in something that looked like grief. "You know monsters aren't safe in your world. She'll be safe with me."

Car doors slammed outside. Heavy boots pounded the dry brown grass around the house. Someone on a megaphone was shouting something that didn't matter anymore.

"Time's up," said The Old Mother, taking Abby's long-fingered blue hand in hers.

"Such a tragedy," folks said, though no-one was sure what the tragedy was, exactly. A gravestone in the Quartz Creek cemetery read Dale Evans, Beloved Son, 1998-2023. Miz Lou hung a flowered cross-stitch in her kitchen whose trailing stems spelled the name, Abby. Darla Evans still kept her shop open for the tourists, though every monster she knitted now came in shades of cornflower and azure and lapis lazuli. Cops in their cups told stories of a giant tree with a woman's face who walked away into the mountains holding the hand of a knotty blue monster with long spider legs.

And on moonless nights, a little indigo girl curls up outside her mother's bedroom wall and listens to her tell stories of happy families and forever love and other fairytales.

NORTHERN LIGHTS, TOO FAR SOUTH

MICHAEL KELLICHNER

"You ever see anything like this before?" Sean asked.

Justin took a few drags off his cigarette, less to ponder the question and more to push down the vomit sneaking up his throat. He didn't consider himself squeamish—he'd hunted his fair share of deer, gutted them, skinned them, and prepared them himself without so much as a gag, even when he accidentally cut right through a scent gland the first time—but the mess in the chicken coop was something else entirely.

"Nope," he said when the feeling had passed.

In the fenced-in patch of grass next to the coop, the bodies of ten chickens were strewn about, burst like overripe melons, their entrails slopped across the ground. Most were deflated, empty sacks of skin, but a few had turned almost completely inside out. Feathers caught in the grass and fluttered where they stuck to the chicken wire.

"Bobcat?" Justin suggested around a stream of smoke.

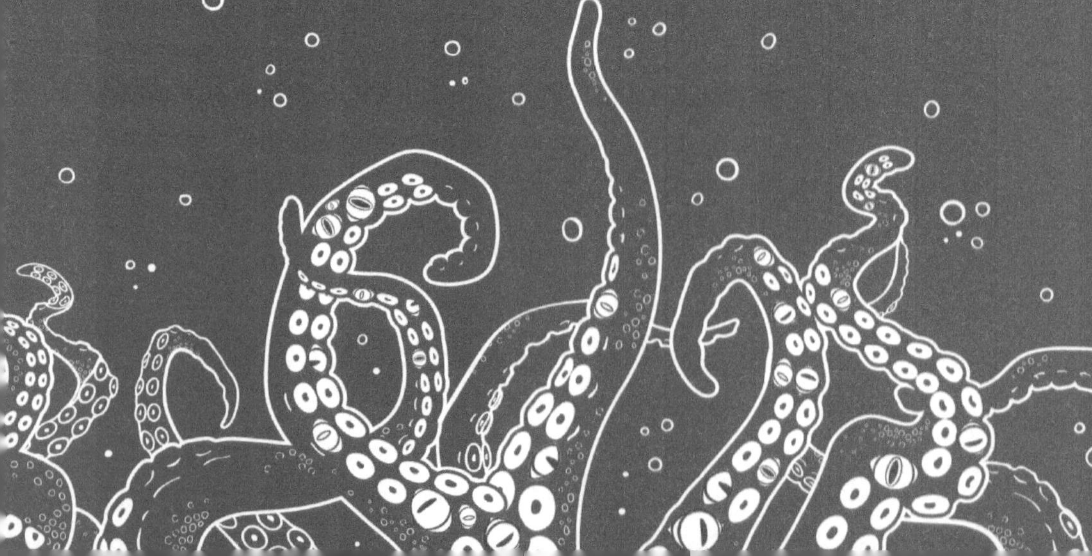

"You ever see a bobcat get a bunch of chickens and then just leave the meat uneaten? I sure ain't."

"No," Justin admitted. He scratched his beard with his thumb. "But they're sneaky fuckers." He hiked up his pants a little over his gut and stepped into the pen, easing his boots around the blood and viscera just inside the door. He crouched down next to the nearest chicken and waved away a fly that buzzed past his ear. The skin didn't look torn or ripped. Every edge was smooth, as if snipped with scissors. No teeth marks or chunks missing. It was like the chicken's insides had suddenly wanted to be on the outside.

He stayed, finishing his cigarette; the longer he waited, the louder the buzz of flies grew in his ears. A swarm of them gnawed and crawled through every open crevice, feasting on the soft, mushy insides usually denied to them. It seemed like every single fly on the entire farm must have flown in for the chicken buffet, crawling over each other to burrow into the offal.

Justin swatted his hand to clear the air in front of his face and glanced back at Sean. His old friend looked paler than he'd ever seen him, and he just stood in the same spot, staring at what was left of his chickens. He'd called Justin early that morning, woke him up from a hangover sleep and asked him to come over right away. Now, squatted among the chickens, Justin could see why Sean had sounded so panicked on the phone. In the end, however, it was just some dead chickens.

He was just about to stand up when a glint of color caught his eye. He stuck his cigarette in his mouth and shifted to the nearest chicken. It had fallen straight back with all its insides burst out through its chest. Head tossed back, neck limp, beak and eyes open. Instead of the usual flat yellow or blue or red iris, they had glazed over with a blurry, wavy gradient of green and lilac.

He waved his hand through the air again to keep flies from landing on his face as he leaned in closer. Sean was saying something behind him, but the loud buzzing drowned out the words until only a faint murmuring remained. Justin swatted, but the buzzing just grew louder.

"Where are these fucking things coming from?" he muttered and took a deep drag on his cigarette, the crackle of burning paper silent beneath the buzzing. He blew a thick cloud of smoke to scatter the flies, but through the haze, he realized there was not a single fly crawling on the chickens. Not on the entrails. Not on the bodies. Not slicing through the air.

With a shaking hand, he snuffed out the cigarette in the soil and stood, trying to back away in a normal manner. Once he took his eyes off the chickens, the buzzing vanished and the sound of wind through the corn and wheat rushed back in.

"Justin? What is it?"

Justin, the buzzing gone from his head but an itchy feeling of fly feet all over his scalp lingering, hawked up a thick wad of phlegm and spit it onto the ground. "Fucking fly flew in my mouth." He came out of the pen, shaking his head. "I don't know. Your cluckers there sure got it good, that's for certain."

Sean nodded slowly, but his eyes were distant. "Ain't never seen anything rip a chicken apart like that."

"Me neither. But unless some satanist is running around slicing your chickens up, it doesn't make any sense for it to be anything else."

"Satanists? You think there could be satanist 'round here?"

"Jesus, Sean. Look. It's probably some bobcat or coyote that broke in and got spooked before it could finish. Hell, maybe even a raccoon." Sean nodded, but just stared over Justin's shoulder. Justin sighed and said, "Hey, just keep everything locked up and the shotgun loaded, alright? If something's out here chewing up livestock, it's nothing a few rounds of buckshot won't put a stop to. Works the same for satanists."

Sean grinned a little and nodded. "Yeah, I suppose so." He looked away, but it seemed to Justin it required a great effort. "Thanks for coming all the way over for nothing. Want a beer before you go?"

"Well, if you're going to twist my arm about it."

They sauntered over to the barn, and Sean opened a mini fridge next to his toolbox. He took out two bottles and handed one over. Justin popped the lid with the bottle opener on his key ring, and they stood silently, drinking. Sean kept looking back toward the chicken coop. When he did, he got the same faraway look in his eyes he had before. Every time Justin noticed, he felt a pull deep in his muscles that made him want to turn his head, too. Look back at the fluttering feathers. Go back to look at the mess in the grass.

He shook his head and instead walked to the far end of the barn, past the tractor with the ripped out motor to look out over Sean's corn field. The morning chill was already fading away as the sun went up, and the wind was making all the stalks whisper as they swayed.

"You gonna get that corn in soon?" he called back.

Sean shuffled up next to him. "Pretty soon." He looked down at the bottle and turned it in his hands, like he was inspecting the label, and asked, "Hey, Justin. Do you believe in aliens and stuff like that?" Although Justin turned and gave him a look, Sean stayed focused on the label. "Some people talk about it. Seeing weird things at night. Lights in the sky, being abducted, you know?"

"You trying to tell me you got abducted?"

"No, no. Nothing like that." He tipped back his beer and emptied it. "Just thought I saw something strange last night, is all."

"Like aliens?"

"Shit, I don't know. Probably just some government crap no one wants to talk about." He looked back at the fridge. "Want another beer?"

Justin did, but a chicken feather tumbled across the dirt and drew his attention back to the coop. He thought he could hear the buzz of flies again, even though only floating hay dust filled the barn.

"I'm alright," he said. "Got some stuff to do today."

He went back to his truck, Sean following, and climbed in. He had never seen Sean looking so fidgety, wiping his hands on his jacket and glancing around, then down at his feet.

"Look, Sean, you have anything else weird happen around here, you give me a call. If you really want, I'll come over with my gun, and we'll both keep an eye on things if you think something's coming around again."

"Yeah," Sean said. "I'll give you a call."

That night, at nearly two in the morning, the lights started.

Justin sat in his trailer at the card table in the kitchen, smoking and drinking beer, which had become his routine in the past few months. He'd just finished up a pack of cigarettes and the smoke hung clouded around the dull yellow light. The rest of his trailer was dark.

Then, the smoke above the table shifted from gray ocher to vibrant indigo. He looked up and spent a moment glancing between it and the light, but no matter what, he couldn't make it make sense. When it then shifted into a deep lavender, he got up and turned off his light. The glow persisted, but now the color washed in through his window, the entire room taking on its subtle hue. He rubbed his face, the smoke from the still burning cigarette stinging his eyes, but the color remained, softly undulating like light reflecting off a moving river.

He went to the window and looked out. Lights reached down from the sky, rippling tendrils scintillating between greens and purples with touches of pink and crimson.

"What the hell?" Justin muttered to himself. He swatted at a fly buzzing near his ear.

He pulled on his flannel coat and shoved his bare feet into his boots, then went down the stacked cinder blocks for stairs and into the narrow patch of grass between his trailer and his neighbor's. Outside, shifting colors filled the night—only in the sky to the east, but near enough that they seemed liable to fall down on top of him at any moment. He'd heard about the Northern Lights, but he'd never heard of them being in Pennsylvania. Besides, he was sure they filled the whole sky, not just a narrow band stretching down and vanishing beyond the trees that hedged in the trailer park.

He walked out to the road for a better look, but the trees blocked the view of the horizon, so he just stood on the edge of the blacktop, staring up at the lights as they snaked down across the sky. They didn't look like the waves of colors he'd seen in pictures, more like slow-moving lightning bolts, undulating and flicking between colors.

With the lights off in all the other trailers, the windows became mirrors reflecting whatever color dominated. Justin didn't know how anyone could sleep with those lights in the sky and the buzzing of thousands of flies. He swatted wildly around his head, but the flies just kept coming. He felt their tiny feet pricking across his neck and ears, trying to get into his ear canal. When he turned to check the rest of the sky, the buzzing lessened and the pricking feet receded. All the stars were out with barely a cloud in the sky.

But to the east, the narrow band of colors continued to pulse. He kept looking at it, the buzzing in his ears growing louder until it was the only sound in the night. His mind filled with the burrowing of insects digging deep down into the soil, their tiny tunnels and labyrinths crisscrossing as they gnawed through anything in their path. Roots, detritus. Everything.

The next morning, Justin's beeping alarm stabbed like a knife into his skull. He slapped the clock so hard it flew off his nightstand, silencing abruptly when it hit the floor. Justin groaned and pressed his palms against his head, his arteries throbbing hard enough to burst. The sun wasn't quite up yet, his only blessing, and he staggered through the dark trailer toward the bathroom. He drank cold water from the sink, splashed some on his face, but the sting of icy water made the pounding in his head only more acute.

Swearing, he grabbed a bottle of aspirin and swallowed two pills. Then he went into the kitchen, made coffee, splashed in a finger of whiskey, and sat hunched at the table to drink it. A fly buzzed past his head. He swatted it away.

The coffee and whiskey and aspirin quickly took the edge off his headache. He rummaged through his drawers until he found his canisters of flypaper, ripping one open to hang the gluey strip in front of his kitchen window. Just to be safe, he put another over his sink.

"See how you like that," he muttered as he refilled his coffee and drank it down.

He dressed in the dark and went out to his truck. He drove through town to the highway and then out to the lumber mill. Rolling down the window allowed the frosty morning air to help clear his head. After a few minutes, he turned on the radio and listened to a morning talk show followed by country music. A few songs later, he pulled into the gravel parking lot just as the sun came up. He sat and had a few smokes until the rest of the first shift arrived and started filing in.

The noise in the mill was the same familiar, unending whir of machinery. Sawdust filled the air as the head rig saw went through the same ceaseless cutting motion while the rest of the machine drew a tree trunk back and forth, flipping it around until the last section was finally sawed in half and another trunk got hooked onto the conveyor belt. Justin waited to push each freshly cut board through the sander.

Justin had been doing the job for so long that his arms remembered the motions well enough, and he no longer needed to stay focused to ensure things went smoothly. As he moved the boards, his mind wandered back to the lights of the night before.

It had all possessed such a strange quality that he couldn't be sure it wasn't a dream. How the air had felt, the temperature, the sounds in the night were all hazy details that changed while he thought about them. He kept imagining crickets chirping throughout the night, as was always the case, but he couldn't quite remember if he'd actually heard any. There had been a kind of silence, but not the silence of being out in the middle of nowhere. A silence that was somehow also filled with noise, like the air itself hummed.

A fly buzzed and he swatted it away. The lights replayed in his head over and over again, enough to make him think they had a pattern. Not a repetition, exactly, but a purpose behind each arc and slither as they moved down the sky. Some kind of code.

His mind hummed with the idea, and he batted at another fly while he replayed the image of the lights snaking across the sky, trying to figure out what it was. But he couldn't focus because—how the fuck did so many flies get into the mill? They were everywhere, buzzing past his ears, and he felt their tiny feet landing on the back of his neck, burrowing beneath the sawdust caught in all his arm hair.

"Justin! What the fuck! *Justin!*"

The flies immediately vanished and the sound of the unnaturally quiet mill came rushing in. The saw had stopped in the middle of a piece of redwood. Most of the men in the mill gathered around to stare at him. Boards clogged the conveyor, and several had already run off, lying all around and even on his feet. He hadn't felt a thing as they'd dropped on him.

He opened his mouth to say something, but a rush of vomit came out instead. He doubled over, heaving a splattering of thick, yellow bile that stank of whiskey, beer, and stomach acid onto the freshly cut boards. He choked on the taste, the smell, then heaved up another thick mouthful. Cursing, he wiped his mouth. His glove came away with a string of bile and a streak of blood. He shook the glove off and wiped another thick smear of blood from his nose.

"Fuck, Justin," the saw operator said. "Get the fuck out of here with that."

A new wave of cursing came from the far end of the mill as the foreman stormed in, demanding to know why the machines were off. When he saw Justin, he shouted for him to get out of the way and didn't stop yelling until Justin had staggered to the break room and clocked out.

His stomach churned like something skittered around inside it. The pounding pain in his head came back, each heartbeat making the world waver a little bit. Justin sat at one of the wooden picnic tables where he usually ate his lunch and stared at the wood for a few minutes until he could breathe normally again and his headache had diminished to just a terrible hangover. He went out to his truck and drove home, squinting in the daylight, driving slowly while hunched up on the steering wheel.

When he made it back, he washed down a few more aspirin with a beer and put up a few more strips of flypaper, then went to bed.

When the phone rang a few nights later, darkness filled his bedroom, but the kitchen at the opposite end of his trailer was awash in emerald and mauve. The phone's ringing smashed like a hammer through the walls, reverberating right into Justin's head. Cursing, he got up and pushed his way through the sticky flypapers hanging throughout his living room. Only dust had stuck in the glue; Justin knew those damned flies were on to his plan, hiding anywhere they could, then coming out to buzz around while he tried to sleep.

Black circles darkened his eyes that were more bloodshot than white. Every time he had lain down to sleep during the past week, he heard the constant thrumming of flies. No matter where he looked, he couldn't find them. After a few hours, he'd resigned himself to sitting at the table and working his way through a bottle of whiskey until he couldn't keep his eyes open any longer. He'd then collapse into bed and manage a few hours of sleep before driving into work. He'd made it two days before the foreman had told him to not come back until he was put together. After that, he'd spent a few days in a cycle of drinking himself to sleep, then waking, sobered up a bit, to the buzzing of flies.

And now the fucking phone's ringing kept trying to split his head in two. He yanked the receiver off the wall and almost threw it, but a voice shouting on the other end made him pull the receiver up to his ear.

"Jesus, fuck!" Sean screamed on the other end. "Oh, God—Oh, the fucking chickens! The chickens!"

"Quiet down," Justin yelled back. "Sean? What is it, Sean?"

"The fucking chickens, Justin!"

"What about the chickens? Sean! Are you drunk? What are you on about?"

"Oh, holy fuck!"

"Sean?"

Sean's voice still blabbered and shouted and screamed, but the sound of it moved farther away. Justin shouted into the phone a few more times before he finally slammed the receiver down. He stalked back through the trailer, waving away the flypaper. When the strips stuck to his arms and tore from the ceiling, he ripped them off, taking out every hair stuck to the glue. In the bedroom, he scooped up the whiskey bottle he'd left by the bed and took a quick swig to ward off the headache he felt building like a storm front in his brain. He then lifted up his mattress and grabbed his shotgun from on top of the box springs. He opened his nightstand drawer and took out the box of twelve-gauge buckshot. Ripping through the fly papers again, Justin stumbled out of his trailer and into the night.

More tendrils of light filled the eastern sky. The moment Justin saw them, the buzzing of the flies came back. He covered his head with his arms and ran for the truck, laid the shotgun across the passenger seat, and tossed the bullets next to it. He slammed the door. A silence greeted him that he hadn't heard in days.

"What the hell is going on?" he muttered, staring at the dashboard. He started the engine, backed his truck onto the street, and drove eastwards toward Sean's farm. On the road, he stared straight ahead into the lights as they snaked down from the sky and vanished behind the trees. He did his best to focus on the road, but his eyes kept wandering up to the lights. Flies landed on his neck and arms.

"Where are you fuckers hiding?" he yelled as he slapped at them. His truck drifted over the center line. He jerked the wheel back into his lane.

When he licked his lips, he tasted blood. He wiped his nose, his hand coming away slicked with red. Cursing, he yanked old napkins from the cup holder and stuffed a few up his nose.

One of the curves in the road came up faster than he expected, and Justin wrenched the wheel into the turn. His back tires skidded on loose gravel, and he had a frantic few seconds of spinning the wheel back and forth, trying to correct the swing. The buzzing of flies and their tiny little feet skittering across the back of his neck and through his hair made him let go of the wheel and swat and smack and the truck careened off the road and tipped into a ditch. The crunch of glass and metal overpowered the buzzing in the brief seconds before the world went black and silent.

When everything came back, Justin had no concept of how long he'd been out. His head throbbed differently than before. When he reached up to his forehead, his fingers came away bloody. It took him a moment to get his bearings and realize the truck was balanced on the left headlight in the ditch. The engine was still running, and he gave it a few presses of the gas, but all he did was rev it up while the truck remained motionless in the shifting hues of a too-colorful night.

He rummaged around on the floor for the gun and the box of shells, then loaded it and put more shells into his pockets. He shoved open the door, climbed out, but his right knee couldn't support his weight and he stumbled down into the ditch. Pulling himself up along his truck, Justin dragged himself out and back onto the road, knowing Sean's house wasn't too far away.

The lights in the sky seemed to possess an entirely new brightness. Strange shadows tinged with the colors from the sky washed through the forest, making the trees and the underbrush seem like they swarmed with faces that kept changing. In all the time he'd spent in the woods, he'd never felt like the trees watched him. He kept a tight grip on his shotgun as he limped down the road.

When he rounded the last bend that took him out of the woods and onto the edge of Sean's cornfield, he stopped in the middle of the road and stared. The lights were plunging into the earth all around Sean's house. The roof was awash in colors. Columns of light connected the sky to the land, slowly drifting through the cornfields.

"What the hell?" Justin murmured.

He hurried on, the ache in his head and knee forgotten as he stared at the lights moving around Sean's property as if to musical accompaniment. Yet the night was silent except for the swarms of flies. Justin gritted his teeth, white-knuckled his gun, and kept limping along as fast as he could down Sean's gravel driveway.

"Sean?" he yelled, his voice lost in the buzzing. The air was still. Not even a stalk of corn shivered. The lights roamed through the fields, seeming to disrupt nothing despite their massive size. They spun down like tornadoes, but much more slowly. The longer Justin stared, the more it seemed they constantly changed shape. Sometimes like round whips, sometimes vast sheets, only to become a collection of pinpoints vibrating together.

"Sean!" he called out again, tearing his gaze away and heading for the house.

He got a few steps before he stopped. One of Sean's chickens strutted between him and the building, pecking at the earth and clucking. But its insides were still outside, wrapped around its body like ribbons on a terrible present, the flesh underneath all floppy and empty. The ropy entrails steamed faintly in the night. It turned its eye on Justin; in that eye, all the sky colors swirled and churned like a nebula. When it clucked, the sharp sound pierced into Justin's head like a proboscis that injected a swarm of flies. He could feel those flies inside his skull, skittering around with no way to get them out.

"Oh, Jesus," Justin breathed.

The chicken dashed toward him, head bobbing, each cluck shoving more flies through his ears. Justin backpedaled, terrified. The chicken's entrails slithered over its body like coils of snakes flecked with dirt and grass and leaves and twigs. He lifted his shotgun, pressing the butt against his shoulder. His eyes practically vibrated in his head, the flies stepping all over the backs of them. The chicken clucked, jerking forward; when it came just a little closer, Justin squeezed the trigger.

The chicken exploded. Chunks of viscera sprayed through the air. No blood, just shreds of meat suddenly caught in the turquoise and violet light before vanishing into the darkness. Justin expelled the smoking shell and chambered another.

Behind him, more clucking. He spun around, gun raised. Out of the corn stalks came the rest of the chickens, their entrails looped around their deflated bodies or dragging behind their limp skins. Their clucking gathered like pressure in a thunderstorm and thudded inside of Justin's head. Barely able to focus through the pounding, he took another shot, but the pellets whizzed harmlessly through the corn.

Justin retreated, expelled the empty shell, chambered another round, and tried to aim again. Behind him, another cluck. He spun around and saw the beak of the chicken he'd shot at his feet. It wobbled on the ground, still squawking. Justin leapt back, staring at the moving beak, and only when he got far enough away did he see the entrails slithering through the gravel toward the mouth.

Justin turned and ran for the house. The clucking pelted his back like stones as he threw open the front door and slammed it behind him. The interior of Sean's house was awash in the colors of the lights.

"Sean!" He clomped through the foyer and into the open living room. "Sean?"

"It's here."

Justin's attention went to the dark shadow of Sean's head silhouetted against the window, where he sat in a rocking chair. The chair remained perfectly still, Sean's hands gripping the armrests.

"Sean, what the fuck is going on out there?"

"It's here," Sean repeated. His voice came out dull and empty, almost hypnotized, everything spoken in the same cadence without inflection. "And now it'll just." His head twitched to the side. "Take everything."

"What's here?"

One of Sean's hands rose as if lifted by an invisible string. It limply gestured to the window, through which one of the emerald columns of light churned. "It's arrived. Finally. After thousands and thousands of years. Do you know how empty space is? How long it takes."

The fingers on his hand jerked hard enough that Justin heard the crack and pop of bone.

"To get from one."

His hand twisted with another pop of bone, his fingers almost pointing back down his arm.

"Massive field of nothingness."

His head jerked straight again.

"To another?"

Justin looked around the house, but everything was the same as the last time he'd visited. The flat-screen television on the wall. The overstuffed couch. Everything done up in old wood paneling. His mouth was so dry he could barely speak. All he could get past his cracked lips was, "Are you drunk?"

Sean gave a dry chuckle. "Drunk? No. Just." Sean slowly pushed himself up from the chair. "Finally seeing things clearly." He turned around. The lights that came from the sky, the same ones inside the chickens, shone and swirled in Sean's eyes. So luminescent it made the rest of his face look slack and haggard, sagging and hollow.

"Jesus," Justin muttered, backing away.

"Don't be afraid, Justin," Sean said. His head started to loll to one side but then snapped back up. "I was afraid, too. At first. But there's nothing to do. Now. It'll burrow down into the ground. And just." His arms jerked out straight. "Spread. It will get into everything. The plants. The trees. The animals. Just." A creaking, cracking step forward. "Seep in. Settle in."

"Stay the fuck back, Sean," Justin said. He pressed his back against the wall and slid along it toward the door as Sean kept shambling closer.

"Just stay a while," Sean said. One of his legs buckled and he almost went down, but it jerked straight again to keep him upright, cocked slightly to one side. He shuffled forward, managing an uneven step with each disjointed pause in his speech. "It's all. Inevitable anyway. We'll all become. One. One wonderful nourishment. It's so. Hungry. After the long trip."

Justin reached the door and fumbled with the handle.

"We're just. Food, after all."

Justin aimed his shotgun. "Get back, Sean."

Sean's head lolled to the other side. "That won't solve." Another step. "Anything."

Justin squeezed the trigger, and Sean flew back, his chest turned into a hole of ground meat. Inside, somewhere beneath the chewed up flesh, a faint pulse of green and violet seeped out like smoke. As it quickly dissipated into the air, the colors coming in from the window seemed to deepen around Sean's motionless body.

"What the hell is going on here?" Justin muttered.

"A great binding," Sean said.

Justin jumped. He brought up his gun and squeezed the trigger, but the firing pin clicked uselessly against the expended cartridge. In his panic, he couldn't do anything else but try to fire again.

Sean sat up. The light emanating from his chest reached out for Justin, coiling into hook-like claws. "Soon it'll be. Everywhere."

Justin reached behind him for the doorknob and managed to twist it and get out of the door before Sean regained his feet. Outside, the lights had grown brighter, washing the entire night with their colors. At the bottom of the porch stairs, all the chickens had arranged themselves into a line that blocked the way. Their clucking brought back the stabbing pain in his head. Buzzing now vibrated from the pillars of light and made the entire porch shiver like the boards themselves—and maybe even the rest of the house— would shatter into glassy fragments, and then a fissure would split the land completely in half.

Wavering, bile rising in his throat, Justin managed to cock his shotgun before lifting it again. He aimed at the chickens, but the empty click sent him fumbling in his pockets for his extra shells. A thud rattled the door behind him. He heard Sean's muffled voice saying something unintelligible as the shells slipped from his fingers and clattered against the porch. When the knob jiggled and the door started to open, he ran to the side and launched himself over the porch railing. He landed in the rose bushes, tangled up his feet, fell, but kicked himself free without losing his gun. The chickens were coming, so he took off. He charged into the cornfield, ignoring the leaves slapping and slicing his face and arms. He ran, leaving the clucking behind, the shouts of Sean quickly fading to nothingness. Just the rustle of corn as he tore through the stalks.

When Justin ran far enough that the only sound left was the buzzing in his head, he stopped, and with trembling fingers, managed to reload his shotgun. He gripped it in his sweaty hands, trying to catch his breath as he listened for any sound of Sean following him. He swatted at the flies trying to land on his face and brushed them off his beard, but they were in his clothes, crawling over his skin. The buzzing sounded louder now, and he tried to look around, but the corn leaves blocked his vision. He couldn't tell where the pillars of light had gone.

The corn crowded in, and Justin waved his arms, trying to scatter the flies and the corn, but the stalks suddenly pressed against him, wrapping around his body, caging him in. He grabbed one stalk, twisting and bending it until it snapped clean and emerald light oozed out from the broken ends, which then reached for him, buzzing; Justin threw himself back against a lattice of stalks and leaves behind him.

He flailed, swinging his shotgun's barrel, grabbing anything he could to rip and tear it apart. Each broken stalk bled light. Corn cobs snapped off and stomped beneath his boots revealed glassy kernels of turquoise and fuchsia. He threw himself to the ground and crawled between the stalks. Leaves bent over him. Stalks leaned in, suddenly forming bars all around. He scrambled back and tried to go another way, but the stalks bent into a dome, each tear and crack from his struggle bleeding color. He tried to look away, but the color reached down and brushed against his eyes, showing him the infinite space between stars.

Then came cold, desolate silence, and the silence somehow seemed worse than the buzzing. Justin squeezed his eyes shut against the light, but it burrowed underneath his eyelids and he saw impossible shapes, spaces between dimensions, and the colors burrowing deeper and deeper into the earth.

He lifted his shotgun and fired up through the corn. Leaves ripped away, stalks shredded. Light fumed out from the wreckage. But the lattice of leaves and stalks slowly closed in again, and in the silence, he heard the clucking of the chickens coming through the field.

DOSSIER #KR-042: THE VEIL CANTORS

SUBHAM RAI

FIELD AGENT LOG: THE HOOK

March 9, 2025, 09:17 MST–Kressler's Veil, Montana

This is Agent Mara Cole, Echelon Group, badge 1429, starting my log for Case #KR-042. I'm sitting in my truck on a ridge above Kressler's Veil, staring down at a valley that I would swear is holding its breath, waiting to spit out something ugly. It's rural Montana—nothing but fog, scraggly pines clawing at the sky, and a silence that presses on your ears like a heavy hand. The air smells damp and metallic, like wet coins left in a drawer too long, and the horizon's swallowed by a thick, gray mist that clings to everything.

HQ pinged me yesterday about anomalous radio signals spiking from an old Cold War listening post down there. Some concrete bunker shut down in '78, abandoned to rust and rot after the government pulled the plug. Locals call this place "the whispering bowl" because sound does strange things here, bouncing off the hills like it's caught in a snare—old-timers swear they've

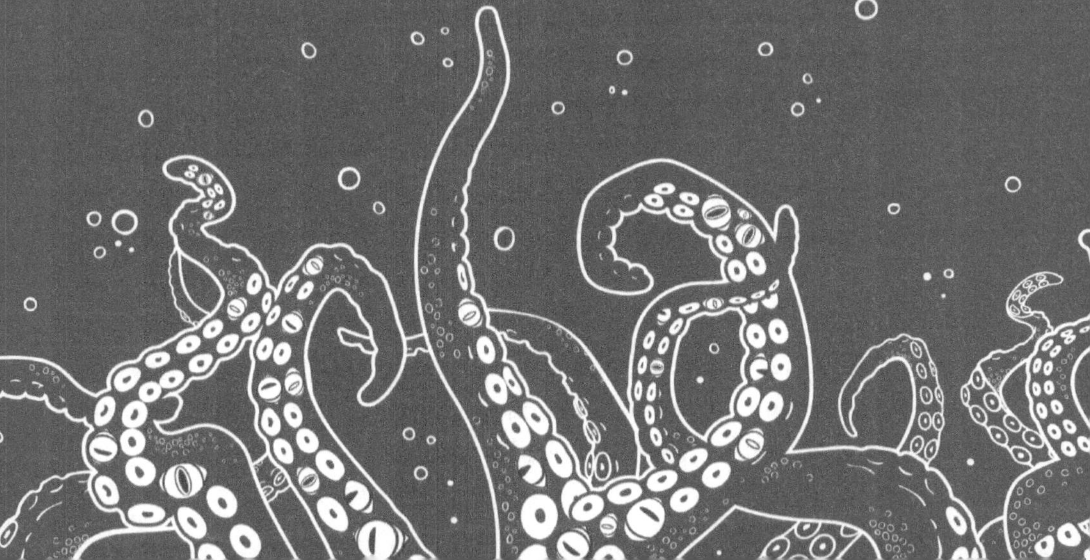

heard their own voices calling back from the fog. Lately, though, it's more than echoes. They say it's been humming, soft and low, like a choir with no singers, rising up from the valley floor.

A hiker named James Pelton went missing last week chasing that hum. Sheriff found his truck parked on the valley's edge, radio blasting static, keys still dangling in the ignition, driver's door flung wide open. My orders are straightforward: figure out what's broadcasting and why it's hitting frequencies we haven't touched since the '70s. Dead channels from a dead era. Should be a quick in-and-out, but something about this place is already gnawing at me.

I start the descent at dawn, tires crunching over a gravel road that's half-collapsed into a sinkhole, jagged edges poking through the dirt like broken teeth. The fog rolls in thicker the lower I go, choking out my headlights. I'm driving half-blind, wipers smearing wet streaks across the windshield, the engine's growl muffled by the damp air. I park just outside the station's sagging, rusted chain-link fence and grab my gear: a portable recorder, a signal tracker, and a flashlight that barely cuts through the gloom.

The bunker looms ahead—gray, cracked concrete stained with moss, antennas snapped like brittle bones, windows as dark and hollow as empty eye sockets. Inside, it's a tomb; empty consoles stripped to wires, shattered glass crunching under my boots, a faint drip echoing from somewhere deep in the walls, steady as a heartbeat. The tracker's picking up a pulse. Low, rhythmic, not like any machine I've ever heard, more like something breathing.

I switch on the recorder, let it run while I scan the room, shadows shifting in the corners. First, it's just a hum, soft and hollow, no more than wind whistling through a cave. I lean in, tweak the gain, and it shifts to my sister Ella's voice, singing "Hush, Little Baby." She died when I was eight, taken out by a drunk driver on a rainy night outside Boise, her car crumpled like tinfoil. I haven't heard that lullaby in twenty years, haven't let it cross my mind since I stood shivering at her funeral, rain soaking through my coat. My stomach drops. I check the log time—09:22 MST. I hadn't spoken, hadn't hummed, hadn't done anything but breathe. But there it is, clear as if she's sitting next to me, looping over and over. I play it back, hands trembling, and it's not just Ella—there's a faint edge to it, something glassy and wrong, like a second voice hiding underneath, sharp and cold as a blade.

Whatever's out there, it's not a memory dug up by chance. It's alive, it's here, and it's already got my number.

AUDIO TRANSCRIPTS & TEXTS: THE INVESTIGATION DEEPENS

Audio Transcript #KR-042-B

March 9, 2025, 14:33 MST

[Mara, voice steady but clipped]: "Cole here, inside the listening station. Walls are crumbling—concrete's split wide open, like someone took a sledgehammer to it in a rage. Old consoles are stripped down to wires and dust. Signal's spiking now—40 hertz, pulsing like a heartbeat you can feel rattling your teeth."

[Pause, faint static crackles]

"There's that hum again, louder this time, seeping through the walls like damp rot. Listen close—it's not just background noise."

[Recording: A layered drone swells—dozens of voices weaving together in a messy, haunting tangle. Ella's lullaby threads through, soft and eerie, her pitch wobbling like a warped cassette tape stretched too thin. Then James Pelton's voice cuts in, ripped from a voicemail the sheriff dug out of his phone last week: "It's beautiful, gotta get closer," looped tight and frantic. A high, glassy tone overlays it—not human, like crystal shattering in slow motion, sharp enough to make your ears ache and your skin crawl.]

[Mara]: "Something's moving out there. The fog's shifting, curling against the wind like it's got a mind of its own. Setting up a motion cam by the east window, lens pointed at the tree line where the pines fade into gray. If this is a glitch or some kid screwing around with a speaker, it's one hell of a trick. I'm not buying it for a second."

TEXT EXCHANGE
MARA TO AGENT DANIEL REESE, HANDLER
March 9, 2025, 15:02 MST

Mara: Dan, audio's picking up voices. Pelton's, my sister's, even mine from this morning's log. It's not echoes. It's happening live, right now. Something's in the fog out there, and it's not just sound bouncing.

Daniel: Could be interference from the old arrays bouncing off the hills. Valley's a natural amplifier. Cross-check with weather data; fog might be playing tricks.

Mara: No arrays left. They're twisted scrap, rusted out years ago. Cam caught shapes in the mist. Small, flickering, like bugs made of static or light, darting in and out. They're singing, Dan, and it's not random noise. It's targeted, personal.

Daniel: Hold position. Pulling station files. Might be leftover tech acting up, some Cold War relic gone haywire. Keep logging everything, don't touch anything you don't understand. Get me visuals if you can.

AUDIO TRANSCRIPT #KR-042-C
March 9, 2025, 17:19 MST

[Mara, voice tightening, breath quick and shallow]: "Cam's rolling—got it angled out the window, lens is fogging up already. Fog's so dense I can taste it. I see them now. Calling them Veil Cantors, for lack of anything better, something to pin this on. Hundreds of them, maybe thousands, drifting in clusters like fireflies gone wrong. Wrong color, wrong rhythm. They're translucent, wings buzzing like TV snow, bodies flickering in and out like bad reception."

[Rustling, boots scraping concrete]

"They're closing in—sound's hypnotic, tugging at me like a current pulling me under. Ella's voice is everywhere, filling the room, but it's off. It keeps whispering, 'Come home, Mara,' over and over, soft and insistent. I never said that to her, not once in my life—she was gone before I could."

[**Recording:** The hum surges—Ella's lullaby warps, stretching thin and brittle, blending with Pelton's desperate, "Don't leave me," and a kid's laugh. Mine, from some birthday party I can't pin down, cake smeared on my hands, balloons popping in the background. The glassy tone rises, sharp and alien, cutting through like a knife through silk. A faint rustle—like wings beating— grows louder, closer, rhythmic.

[**Mara**]: "They're right outside now—swarming the glass, tapping at it. My head's swimming; it's like they're pulling strings I didn't know I had, unraveling me.

[Cough, hoarse]

"Fog's seeping in—cracks in the frame, curling up the walls. I'm staying put, but this isn't normal, not even close. Dan better have answers, because I'm running out of guesses."

SURVIVOR'S LETTER: THE DESCENT
Letter found in Mara's backpack, Undated

If you're reading this, I'm probably gone—or worse, part of whatever's out there now. I'm Mara Cole, Echelon Group, badge 1429, and I messed up worse than I ever thought possible. It's been hours since I logged. Maybe a whole day, maybe more. Time's slipping through my fingers down here in Kressler's Veil, and I can't keep it straight.

I went deeper into the valley last night, chasing the Cantors after that last audio cut out, after they started whispering my own words back at me through the fog. I had to know what they were, what they wanted, even if every nerve in my body screamed to turn back. They're not insects, not animals. They're something else entirely, alive but not alive, flickering in the mist like ghosts carved out of static and light.

I found a logbook in the station's basement, half-rotted under a pile of moldy crates, ink smeared across yellowed pages, but legible enough to piece it together. Project Echo, '73, DARPA screwing around with radio waves to trap sound in the valley, some harebrained Cold War scheme to eavesdrop on the Soviets or God-knows-what. It went wrong, tore something open—a crack in the air, maybe in reality itself, a wound that never healed. The Cantors came after, spilling out like a bad transmission bleeding into the world. They've been here ever since, waiting.

They don't kill you fast—they sing you apart, piece-by-piece, until there's nothing left to hold on to, nothing left that's you.

Pelton's voice was in the hum when I hit the valley floor. His words from that voicemail the sheriff pulled, "It's beautiful," over and over, but warped now, pleading, "Don't leave me," like he's still out there, trapped in it. I tracked his truck a mile in—still parked where he left it, doors flung open, dust thick on the seats, gray and fine like ash that won't settle. No sign of him, just his echo bouncing through the fog, louder with every step I took.

My voice is fading too. Every word I speak, they snatch it, twist it, sing it back louder until it's not mine anymore, until it's theirs. I'm hiding in the bunker now, back where I started, scribbling this with a pen that's running dry. The fog's thick with them; Cantors everywhere, their light pulsing in time with the hum, a rhythm that won't let go.

It's in my lungs now, that fog. Bitter, heavy, coating my throat like oil. Making every breath burn. I can barely talk; every sound comes out rough, like sandpaper scraping bone, and even that's slipping away.

They're seeping through the cracks—little tendrils of mist curling under the door, up the walls, carrying that damn song into the room. Ella's lullaby is the loudest. Cutting through the drone, but it's not her—it's *them*, twisting it into something wrong, something that pulls at me like a hook in my gut. I keep seeing flashes; her face in the fog, smiling like she did that last summer before the crash, braiding my hair by the lake, but her eyes are blank, her mouth stretched too wide, teeth glinting like glass.

It's not a memory; it's a lie they're building out of me, stitching it together from pieces they've stolen.

I tried the radio an hour ago. Static, then my own voice came through, begging, "Get out, Mara," like I'd already given up, like I'd already lost. I smashed it with the butt of my flashlight, shards flying. But the hum's still there, louder, drilling into my skull until I can't think straight.

My hands are numb, shaking too hard to hold this pen much longer. Ink's smearing, paper's damp from the mist. If you hear this valley hum, run. Don't look back, don't listen, don't even breathe too loud. They've already got you mapped out, every word, every thought, every scrap of who you are, and they won't stop until they've taken it all.

Tell Dan—tell someone at Echelon—this isn't just a signal gone rogue. It's alive, it's hungry, and it's been waiting a long damn time.

TEXTS & MOTION CAM TRANSCRIPT: THE BREAKING

Text Exchange: Mara to Daniel

March 10, 2025, 06:12 MST

Mara: Dan, voice is almost gone. Barely a whisper scraping out Cantors are everywhere, humming my logs back at me. Made it to the truck somehow Don't know how I got the strength, legs shaking the whole way

Daniel: Extraction's eight hours out. ETA 14:00 MST. Status? Can you hold position until we get there?

Mara: Status is I'm falling apart. Memories jumbled, mixing up like a bad dream They're singing my life, but it's wrong. Ella's alive in it, calling me home, her voice so clear it hurts. Get me out, Dan please… I'm begging you.

Daniel: Hang on, Mara. Station files confirm Project Echo breached something. Might be extradimensional, not just tech gone bad. Team's gearing up for containment, full lockdown protocol. Stay put, keep texting me, let me know you're still there.

Mara: Still here Fingers slipping on the keys, can't feel right. Ella's laugh, my laugh, all twisted together. I'm losing it hurry they're in my head

MOTION CAM TRANSCRIPT #KR-042-F
March 10, 2025, 07:33 MST

[**Visual:** Mara leans against her truck, fog swirling thick with Cantors. Flickering forms tighten around her like a living net, closing in step-by-step. She claws at her throat, nails digging into skin, mouth open in a silent scream, eyes wild and bloodshot, darting side-to-side. The swarm pulses, light strobing like a heartbeat—fast, erratic, flashing in bursts that paint the mist red and white. Shadows twist in the fog; shapes that might be faces, might be hers, stretching and melting into each other, too fast to pin down.]

[**Audio:** A symphony erupts—Mara's logs from yesterday, clipped and distorted: "It's alive," over and over, a broken record stuck on repeat, layered with Ella's lullaby, warped into a keening wail that rises and falls like a siren. Pelton's cries, "Don't leave me," stretch thin, unraveling into threads of sound, swallowed by a low, throbbing pulse weaving underneath, growing louder, deeper, shaking the mic until it crackles. Her silent scream cuts through for a split second—raw, human, desperate—then drowns in static as the hum swallows it whole, burying it under layers of alien noise.]

ECHELON REPORT: THE AFTERMATH
Echelon Group Classified Report–Case #KR-042
March 12, 2025

Agent Mara Cole (Badge 1429) unrecovered after investigation of Kressler's Veil, MT. Entity cluster, designated "Veil Cantors" (Class-C, mnemonic-parasitic), documented via recovered gear—motion cam, recorder, partial logs.

Traits: amorphous, luminescent, capable of vocal and memory assimilation, forming a collective auditory phenomenon. Incident linked to Project Echo (1973), DARPA experiment to manipulate acoustic containment—suspected non-terrestrial breach, origin unverified.

Cantors exhibit coordinated behavior, possibly sentient, targeting auditory and cognitive data for unknown purposes. Cole's equipment retrieved March 11 from valley perimeter; vocal capacity compromised prior to loss—texts indicate progressive deterioration. Audio evidence suggests entities reconstruct victims' identities within their chorus. Integrating stolen fragments into a sustained harmonic field.

Valley quarantined—hum detected five miles beyond initial site, expansion rate accelerating. Containment escalated to Class-B pending isotopic analysis of Cantor residue, recovered from truck interior.

Addendum: Final transcript includes non-human frequencies matching Echo anomalies, peaking at 12 kHz—beyond terrestrial biological range. Purpose unclear. Hypotheses include predation, communication, or archival of assimilated data. Activity intensifying; civilian reports of distant humming logged in adjacent counties. Operatives: avoid auditory exposure, deploy silent protocols.

Personal Note from Agent Daniel Reese: Mara was one of the best. She deserved better than this. Whatever's out there, it's not just a signal—it's a predator. And it's still hungry.

THE BOOK OF HOWARD

ALEX HUNTER

IT'S THE STRAPS that I remember more than anything.

Leather, old and faded. And the sound of them as they were tightened. They *creaked* like one of those heavy old doors in an old Roger Corman movie. You know, the ones with Vincent Price. Except the doors in those films were fake and fashioned from balsa or something.

These straps were real.

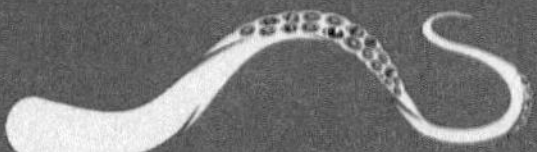

My mother sipped champagne throughout that whole service like she was at a wedding or something. She must've been in her late thirties at the time. I know now that sixty would've seemed a long way off. It isn't.

I was nineteen and living my best life at Oxford. Getting stuck into philosophy. And enjoying the company of a fair few girls—boys, too.

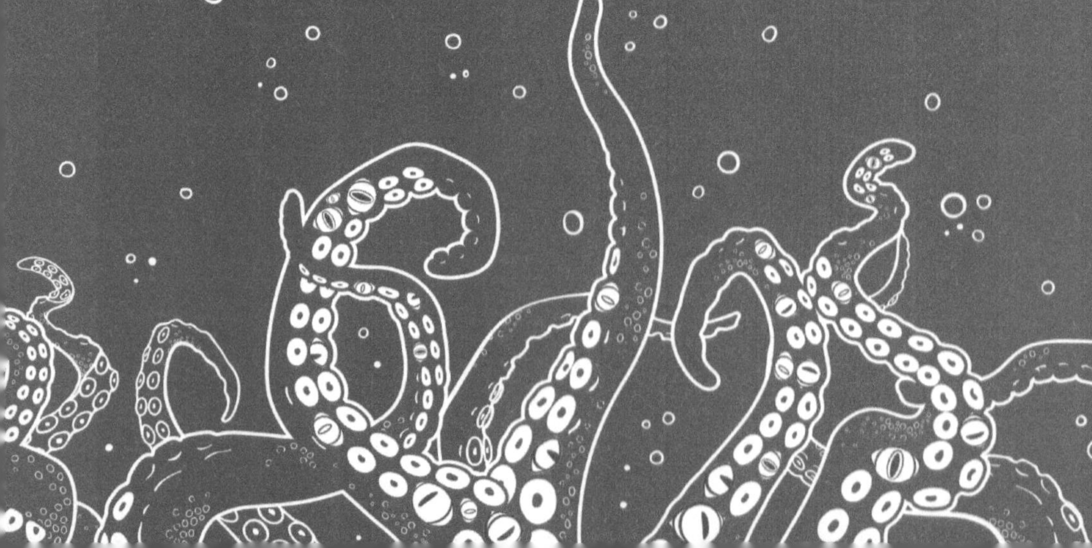

I'd tried to avoid the ceremony, but my parents weren't having it. It was "*family*" my father intoned, dismissing the notion of my staying at college rather than returning to the ancestral home with a wave of his hand.

Ancestral home. *Ha*! How they had drilled that into me over the years. The Howard family had been there for as long as anybody knew. Could never leave. Those were the "rules".

The rules were written in faded ink, held within the pages of a thick volume bound with something which looked alarmingly like desiccated flesh. On that particular night, the volume was on display, perched on a dais from which the celebrant (yet another distant Howard cousin) intoned in a language which I didn't understand. Most of the twenty or so people in attendance ignored the strange invocations, which formed a backdrop to the burble of conversation and occasional laughter.

Those straps, though. I heard them, *craaacckkk*.

The volume was known, I think with tongue in cheek, as the Book of Howard. The book didn't reside in the manor. It was kept in a temperature-controlled environment in the family lawyer's office. And, yes, the firm was Howard & Howard.

Never let it be said that we don't keep it in the family.

I won't pretend to know all the secrets contained in the Book of Howard, although I know more now than I did at nineteen, that's for sure.

What I did know, and had since childhood, was that sixty was the age at which power was transferred to the eldest of the family line. That person would abdicate at the point at which the next heir reached their sixtieth birthday. Abdicate being a euphemism, of course.

Oh, you might wonder how those marrying into the Howards stood for it. How they kept the secret. Well, as you may have guessed, we keep *everything* in the family. My parents were cousins of one sort or another, which was normal. To hell with the gene-pool.

My father and mother were considered beyond the pale by some of the more fundamentalist Howards for having only had one child. The heirs—such as yours truly—needed a spare to create even more little Howards, but none had ever been forthcoming. This was a bone of contention at family gatherings but, by that night, angry voices that had rung out over the years about my status as an only child, had dulled to the occasional muted tut or side-eye.

I wonder if my mother, who would be heir after that night, was afraid. As she stood sipping her drink, her dark hair spilling down her shoulders, ivory silk gown shimmering in the candlelight, she appeared relaxed. She was radiant.

As a future heir myself, it had been made clear to me from an early age that siring children outside of the extended family was not an option.

It was this that had spurred on my early forays with other boys while I was away at boarding school. What better way, I reasoned, to avoid unwanted pregnancies? As I'd matured, I found myself indulging my desire for female company as well. My parents, concerned, had insisted on meeting me at the Oxford offices of Howard & Howard, in order to remind me of the rules.

In the event of an unfortunate girl finding herself "with child" (and yes, I had to stifle a laugh at this point), she would be encouraged to "deal with it". Failure to do so would result in the poor girl and her precious cargo being "eliminated".

"Douglas," my mother had said, placing her teacup on the venerable oak desk, "rest assured, we will do it. As a family, we've built up unlimited resources over generations. Fallen girls from outside of the family will be dealt with and nobody but us will ever know."

"If you insist on penetrating anything that moves," added the lawyer, "I suggest you wrap it up. Save all of us the headache."

Those damned straps.

As you might have guessed, my relationship with Pater and Mater was not something other families would consider healthy.

Yes, I had a gilded childhood in many ways. Howard Manor was huge, with plenty of space in which an only child could let his imagination run riot. I had the finest education money could buy and, if I asked for a new bike, toy, or whatever, it would be delivered.

But love? Not a bit of it. From the point of conception, I, Douglas Aaron Howard, was an *heir*. That was my purpose, whether I wanted it or not. Yes, I could build a storied career. Yes, I could marry and sire children of my own (if I couldn't choose a cousin, one would be chosen for me) but, upon reaching sixty, my purpose would be fulfilled for however long I was required. For this reason, I was discouraged from personal relationships, even friendships with those outside of the family.

Despite the lack of genetic diversity, by fifteen I realised I looked pretty good. While many of my peers at school were suffering the indignities of adolescence, voices like rusty gates and the need to slather themselves in daily vats of acne cream, I made a smooth transition from boy to man. I was pleased to enjoy the Howards' dark hair and blue eyes and these, combined with my years on the rugby field, gave me physical maturity beyond my years.

Looking back, I realise I was a shameful flirt. Other boys, however straight, were more than willing to share my bed. As far as the staff were concerned, a flutter of dark eyelashes could get me out of any trouble.

Perhaps I was looking for companionship, even love?

They were happier times.

At fifty-nine, and with just a few days to go, I don't know if I'm ready. If I will ever be ready.

Various other branches of the Howard family will arrive over the next few days, although The Book itself won't be brought to the manor until just before the service.

My daughter, the next heir and brimming over with unseemly anticipation, is around here somewhere. My youngest, Philip, will be back from school on exeat in the next day or so.

I've rather shuttered myself in the bedroom. I have been avoiding the Sanctum for months—I have no desire to see my mother before the ceremony. The Manor is large enough for my daughter and various staff to get lost among the dark hallways and beamed rooms. I have asked to not be disturbed.

As for my father, both he and my cousin-wife, Annabelle, are gone these last twelve years. Why he had got behind the wheel in his state, I'll never know. How he persuaded Annabelle into the passenger seat is destined to become a Howard mystery.

It's unsurprising they found themselves at the bottom of the lake, but they did. By the time anybody realised, they were gone. It was one of the happiest days of my adult life.

My father, by the point of his death, was little more than a desiccated husk. As for Annabelle, well, she'd been *chosen* for me. I'd done my duty and pumped a couple of kids into her before closing, without ambiguity, the door on any further marital relations. My wife had kept the manor going while I'd taken up residence in an apartment overlooking the Thames. While there, I'd fornicated away to my heart's content.

My daughter, Susan, takes after her mother. *Insipid.* The perfect heir, perhaps. I rather envy Philip, for I sense he enjoys himself as much as I did at his age. Good for him.

I can't help it. I am afraid of those straps.

Back then, at nineteen, I had thought little about being a future heir. It all seemed too far off, barely relevant. After all, I had a life ahead of me.

My parents weren't speaking on the night of the service, as I recall. I am unsure which of the many conflicts might have been to blame. Mother flirted with various male family members while my father brooded in the corner. Bored, I suspect.

The voice of the celebrant had been getting louder, all the better to be heard over the general hubbub. In fairness, these services were the only time many members of the family had to socialise with one another face to face. Numerous Howards who lived overseas, and whose existences were a mystery to me, had flown in to attend.

The celebrant reached a crescendo—taking the hint—the voices quietened until there was nothing to be heard beyond the *craaacckkk* of the final strap as some minor Howard or another tightened it.

Our attention focussed on my grandfather, who had arrived here from Kent in time for his sixtieth.

I've covered all the mirrors in my suite.

I cannot explain, but I don't want to see myself. Yes, objectively, I remain handsome (I'm a Howard; we do) but I hate that my eyes look *haunted*.

As a young man, my parents, the lawyers, and the wider family told me how proud I would be to ascend. What an honour it was to be the heir. To serve. And perhaps it is. I know Susan cannot wait; she's told me often enough, but it's a long time off and she might feel differently when the time comes.

This is *my* time. The day that I prayed would never come. Should I have considered ending it? A bottle of pills or a rope from the rafters? Oh! Would that it were so easy.

The Book is clear. The heir will ascend on the occasion of their sixtieth birthday. Death will not come to them in advance of this, natural or otherwise.

Family legend tells of one Seth Howard. This was back in the 1700s. Fearing ascension, he attempted, more than once, to hang himself. Each time, the rope, rather than his neck, snapped. When he tried to cut his wrists, the wounds knitted back together.

The Howard heir has two purposes—to continue the family line, and to ascend.

There are no other options.

Tonight, I will finally fulfil my destiny. And, yes, I know that makes me sound like a character from a comic book.

Before that decades-ago ceremony, my grandfather's mother had been removed from the sanctum. As her son was prepared for ascension, she, little more than skeletonised remains by this point, breathed her last.

I overheard one cousin whisper to my mother that a single tear had fallen from one of the empty sockets where my great-grandmother's eyes used to be. His mother's remains taken to be interred in the family crypt, my grandfather was the focus of attention.

In the hush that descended since the celebrant had fallen silent and the final strap was cinched tight, the new heir had become the centre of attention. I could hear his breathing, his bare chest fighting against the leather straps that would hold him in place until it was my mother's turn—more than twenty years hence.

Grandfather looked to be in a state of shock. His vivid blue eyes darted around the sanctum as if searching for something in the flickering candlelight. From time to time, he pressed himself against the back of the ancient wooden seat that was to be his home.

I registered, with distaste, that he was erect, the tip of his penis twitching against the coarse grey hair of his belly. I pulled at my bowtie, desperate for some air, as the realisation dawned that I was seeing a vision of the future; *my* future.

Grandfather's eyes sought, sought, and then locked on something to my left. Instinctively, I looked, knowing that I would see nothing. It felt like everybody in the room, many of us who had never attended an ascension before, was holding their breath.

My grandfather did not blink. Could not blink.

"They are held," he whispered.

And with that, it was done. There was a polite smattering of applause as the celebrant lifted The Book of Howard from its place on the dais, led us from the room, and closed the door behind him.

The rest of the night went by in a drunken blur. I think I must have collapsed in a stupor. I know I awoke lying barefoot and trouser-less in the grass next to the pond where my demented father and my cousin-wife would meet their ends many years later.

The knock on my bedroom door is soft, but brooks no argument.

A new celebrant, I do not know which branch of the family she comes from, walks into the room without invitation. She's young, no more than twenty-five, and wears robes of a navy so dark it's almost black.

I know what's coming. "Douglas," the celebrant says, "your mother has ended her duty. As her heir, it is time to ascend."

She walks with me to the sanctum, its door closed but never locked. This is a door that seems to require no locks.

I see no one on our route, and for this I am grateful, but I hear voices and laughter from behind closed doors. The celebration has begun.

Inside, the sanctum remains as it always has. Unread books—many ancient—line its walls. Its wooden floorboards are painted a deep blood-red. The only illumination is from candles dotted around the place, the light guttering in the draught from the open door.

In the centre of the room, the Howard Seat. Its ancient wood is almost black; those terrible straps hang from it like skin shed by nameless serpents.

The celebrant has been joined by two others. They wear black robes with hoods and look like dark monks. They say nothing and look straight ahead. I know these monks have a simple role to play at this stage—to get me into the Seat, should I seek to resist.

I want to resist, but know I must not.

"Remove your clothing," the celebrant instructs. I do so, and the garments are placed in a wooden box in one corner of the room.

I stand for a moment, vulnerable in my nakedness, hands cupping my manhood. I am shivering, whether from fear or the chill, I do not know. I say nothing.

"Take your seat," she says.

The wood is hard, unforgiving beneath my backside, and I shuffle in a fruitless attempt to find comfort.

The celebrant gives me a thin smile. "You are ready."

I remember little of my mother's ascension. Perhaps my grandfather's has seared itself into my memories because it was my first time. All these years later, I still dream of it, still hear the *craaacckkk* of those straps as they bound him to the Howard Seat.

Perhaps my memories are so vivid because I sensed my grandfather's fear. In contrast, Mother couldn't wait to ascend. The weeks leading up to her sixtieth birthday were a whirlwind of dinners and parties, where she revelled in the attention. I did my utmost to avoid it all, wanting as few reminders of my duty as possible.

All I recollect of the service itself was my mother's smile. It had an insane quality to it, joy in the face of unspeakable terror. Whatever secrets it holds, The Book of Howard is silent on what happens once the ascension has taken place. Mother, with Father's wholehearted agreement, always described it as a "miracle". I wondered who she was trying to persuade.

In the early years, particularly after I married and moved to the manor for a time, I would sit with my mother in the sanctum. It's ironic that I spoke to her on those days more than I ever had as a child.

Of course, she said nothing back. Those unblinking blue eyes staring at a fixed point by the door, until time rendered them nothing more than crust-filled sockets. During the decades in which she fulfilled her duty, Mother's body, of which she had been so proud, wasted away. It didn't rot so much as *harden*, her fine breasts drying to sagging bags, her limbs becoming nothing more than bones wrapped within leathery flesh.

But still, she breathed. From time to time, various cousins had the task of tightening the straps that had loosened during her slow decomposition.

One time I walked into the sanctum with a mug of coffee. As I sat down next to my mother, I saw the small brown teeth which had fallen into her lap. I didn't visit her again.

One of the Howard & Howard cohort walks in wearing white fabric gloves and gently places The Book of Howard on its place on the dais in front of the celebrant. As if on cue, the rest of the family file in and the silent monks take their places alongside me.

My daughter walks in without glancing in my direction. She's done the best with what she has. Her squat body and plain face have nothing in common with the Howard beauty, and this makes me sad.

As my son Philip enters, he gives me a wide smile and a thumbs-up. I am ashamed for him to see me in my nakedness and cannot help but avert my eyes.

Once everybody is in, drinks in hand, door closed behind them, the celebrant opens the Book and begins to speak.

"H'aar, mah'ire! Howar'de rem'ns h're. En f'll 'gs. 'Ct' n's s'e!

The monks place straps around my wrists and ankles, and I can no longer shield myself from the idle gazes of those present. These bonds they tighten, without gentleness, and I hiss in a breath as the aged leather pinches against my skin.

I cry out as more straps, the straps I have feared since my youth, are pulled across my torso and cinched tight, restricting my breathing. The leather burns, and I fight against the tears which spring to my eyes.

Why do I have to do this? *Who* decides my fate, my duty?

Craaacckkk, more straps over my shoulders, pinning me down into the seat. At the edge of my awareness, I hear someone laugh. The Howards getting the party started.

The celebrant drones on. After a few minutes, my tears falling freely now, I realise I can understand what sits behind the forgotten tongue for the first time.

"The duty that falls upon the Howards, the chosen, will be hard. It will be long and arduous. It is both your honour and your tragedy.

"You, and you alone, can hold them back."

I can hear the words, but I don't understand what they mean. In my fear and confusion, I become less aware of being held down, strapped in, unable to move. I am trapped and yet, somehow, I am not. My job is to hold them back, but I do not know who, or what, they are.

My field of vision shrinks. My extended family, many of whom I have never seen before today, become dim and distant in their celebration of my ascension.

In my blindness, I can *see*.

The sanctum stands empty, and the voice of the celebrant recedes into the distance. I test my bindings, and they hold true. I am trapped and will remain so until the day of my daughter's ascension—her sixtieth birthday, some thirty years hence.

A spider crawls over one of the books which line the walls. It's large, larger than any spider I have ever seen. Its black carapace winks at me in the candlelight as it drifts upon its web to the floor. The spider scuttles to the front of the Howard Seat and looks up at me. It is so large I see its many lidless eyes.

The hated straps begin to pulse and undulate. Instead of cracked leather, they feel slick, thick tentacles locking me in this terrible chair. I feel something like suckers puckering against my flesh, as if seeking to draw something from me.

The spider, surely the size of my hand, skitters onto my bare foot. Wiry hairs on its legs irritate my flesh as it makes its way up my shins. I want to move, to shake it off, but I cannot.

The tentacles shift and slide, tightening themselves around my body and restricting my breaths. The spider, slow now, continues its exploration of my leg. I unleash a thin spurt of urine, fearing that my family somehow remain in this room, revelling in my shame.

The books look to be alive. They seem to breathe in their cases, pushing away from the walls from which nobody ever takes them. Thick volumes fall to the blood-red floorboards, revealing that which wants to escape. From the empty spaces left by the fallen books push tentacles as wide as a man's leg. The tentacles are pink and translucent, and blood pumps through thick veins while they waver as if probing the air.

Many insects fall from the bookshelves. Cockroaches tumble over one another in a frenzy of movement, while huge millipedes spill from unseen cracks in the wall.

As I watch in horror and confusion, I feel the spider reach that part of myself I have always held most precious. Impossibly thick arachnid legs cup my scrotum like the obscene memory of a lover, and I imagine, with horror, the spider using the warmth of my manhood as a receptacle for its eggs. It locks on tight, the pain like a bolt of lightning in my groin and stomach. My balls shrink into my body to escape the assault.

A tentacle waves wet and pink in front of my face. As I watch, unable to tear my gaze away, the tip begins to split and tear. Thick fluid, ichor, oozes from the wound while smaller tentacles, which were once straps, hold my body ever tighter.

Something begins to birth from the ruined tissue.

I hear a scream. I think it comes from me.

The end of the ruined tentacle bulges and becomes distended. The whole thing vibrates, and I am sure that it would join me in its screaming if it could find its voice.

Crowning. That's what they call it. The top of a head, thick with black hair, pushes through a torn slit, recedes and then pushes once more. The spider's legs cup my scrotum impossibly tight. It feels as if it is fossilising against my body.

The entire head emerges from the tentacle. I press back in the Howard Seat, its wood punishing my spine as my mother's face, wet with blood and unnameable fluids, stares at me from where it emerged through the wreckage of the tentacle.

The head—whether it is my mother or a facsimile, I cannot know—takes a shuddering breath. She pokes a tongue from between bloody teeth as if tasting the air. She smiles that mad smile.

"Hold them back," she commands. "It is your duty."

The head recedes, as does the tentacle from which it emerged, snaking into the darkness. Amidst the guttering candles, I see things that no living person should ever witness. Great insects, some with human faces, crawl over one another. Some mount their dismal companions, thrusting wildly, locked together, while others still gorge on their unholy brethren.

I shout in shock and pain as the spider locks its mandibles into me, piercing the delicate flash of my scrotum. I feel it feed.

As I watch through my mounting delirium, I see other things, things I cannot understand.

A multitude of shadows bleeds out of the wall and surrounds me. These are human in shape and ill-defined. Despite this, their eyes flash red in the candlelight. I can *feel* their hunger.

I know, in my heart of hearts, that the shadows and the creatures of this awful place hunger not for me. They want to consume it *all*, the world and everything in it.

I, no longer the heir but now the reigning Howard, am the only thing that stands in their way. Deep in my psyche, passed down through countless generations, I know what I must do.

I battle to look away from the shadows, to focus on anything other than their hunger. I do not allow myself to be distracted by the insectile carnality before me. I stop blinking and stare at the sanctum's oaken door and think of one simple word. One word, a word which will prevent the unleashing of a terrible, insatiable hunger upon the Earth.

"Lock," I whisper. "Lock."

As I utter the word—my world, the world of the Howards—comes back to me. My son and daughter, assorted cousins and distant relatives, stare at my naked body strapped into the chair. I maintain an unblinking stare at the door.

Champagne is being sipped, and there's a sense of anticipation in the air. They are waiting. For me.

"They are held," I whisper, to a smattering of applause.

The Book is closed, the service complete.

From time to time, the monks, dressed in civvies now, come to me. They wash my body with rough sponges and tighten the straps, in order that I should never break my vigil.

I have grandchildren now. My children never visit, never enter the sanctum. The little ones, a boy of around eight and a girl a few years younger, have no such reservations.

Sometimes they dash into the room, barely looking at me. At other times, they point and erupt with childish laughter. It's hard to know exactly what they do in the room because I cannot focus on anything other than the door. I cannot blink, for I am the Lock.

One time, the boy began prodding and poking me. I have no voice now and could say nothing. The indignity culminated when he punched me in the scrotum. I felt the unseen spider tighten its purchase and heard something wet hit the floorboards. My granddaughter burst into tears, and the children ran away.

Sometimes I hear the shadows screaming and I feel their hunger deep in my soul.

My purpose is being fulfilled.

They are held.

THE FAIRY FIELD

R. WREN

The first thing that worried him was the possibility of muddying his shoes. How would that be explained? The meadow grass was *visibly* damp. Just walking through it would leave damp streaks on his trousers. He knew he could roll his trouser legs up to his knees, but then, the field itself could be marshy. There could be sinking pits, and he could sink. That could not possibly be explained. The earth outside the farmer's gate was secure. He stamped it underfoot, to be sure.

Leon decided he would go no further.

But Rhona—who had been his encourager in all parts of this—said, "What are you waiting for? A check-in desk? A bellhop to carry your bag? A mint for your pillow? Actually, here, I've some polo mints in my pocket. Take one." She pressed one into his palm. Fresh from her pocket, it was noticeably warm. "If I'm going to kiss you, we don't want your breath smelling like sandwiches."

"I've changed my mind," he said. "What if we're caught?"

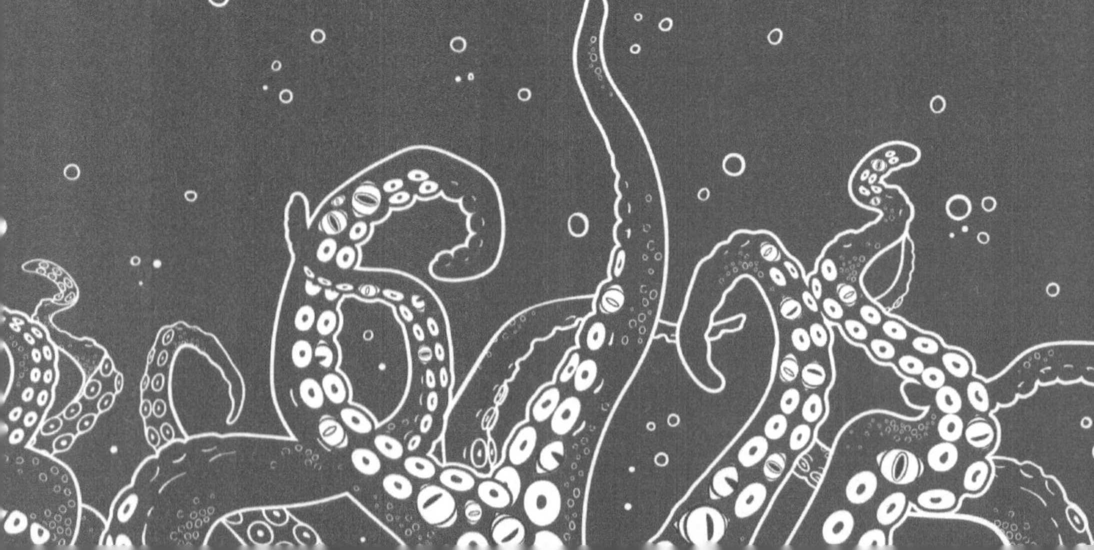

"This is the one time we won't be," she said. And that was true.

Until now, they had had to make do with half-way things, as they thought of them. If they were at Leon's house, they could sit no closer than knee-by-knee, because they were never alone. At most, he could give her a dry kiss, awkwardly chaste and with thinly pressed lips. If at hers, on the other hand, they would have to tidy up, quickly, at the end of the day—wipe clumsy slobber from his chin, reach around and help Rhona line up the hook and eye on her bra-strap—but he would still have to limp off home, hoping the cold air would ease the painful and shameful ache in his groin. They could never trust when somebody might barge in.

"Come on," Rhona grumbled. "Before I go off you."

She went over first, the picnic blanket under her arm. He watched her scaling the gate while it shuddered with her weight, twisting her hands around the slippery metal railings, coming away with chips of paint on her palm. He followed. His legs were already trembling by the time he mounted the top of the fence.

From up here, Leon could hear the rumble over the hedgerows where, down in the town centre, the market festival sounded with the distant thrumming of speakers. This was a once-a-year carnival. Nobody stayed home on such a day. Probably not since iron came. Even Rhona's Gran would be out today—rolled into the light to tell her old-style stories of the *daoine sidh*. There would be cider served sticky and foaming over in disposable plastic cups. Routine cast into the wind. Sullen, untended children running between sweet shops.

It was the one day of the year where they would not be watched.

Atop the fence, the furthest corners of the field were revealed to him. The tall grass was tallest where it grew in the shadows. Beneath the hedgerow, the top of a wooden stake just poked above the surface. Something flapped from its end, like a snag of black bin liner.

He looked into the far corner, said, "Rhona, what's that?"

"How should I know?"

He dropped himself down into the field. His feet squelched but did not sink. He doubled over, fastidiously rolling up his cuffs to bare his shins. The stake was not visible from the ground, because the swaying, wild grass had hidden it. He strode towards the stake, brushing aside the coarse, wet grass.

It was only up to his knees. It squeaked uncomfortably against his skin. He could not imagine himself undressing here.

He placed a foot down blindly. It squelched and filled with water. He yelped, staggering forward towards the stake. Rhona laughed the sweet, cutting laugh which always drove him on. The grass was growing higher, tickling his thighs.

"You want to go further in?"

"No," he said. "Just, there's something."

Growing over him as he neared, seeming to spread in real time across the sky, was the dark and knotted hedge. It separated this field from the next with sharp red thorns, each the size of erect thumbs. At its feet, there was undoubtedly a wooden stake. On that stake, with each step he became surer, there was unquestionably something lashed.

"Are you trying to run off on me?"

"Just come here," he said over his shoulder. "There's something."

He stopped abruptly as he collided with unsteady wood. He found himself standing before the stake. He pulled aside the long grass. The stake displayed the snapped, strung, and crucified remains of a dead crow. Rhona came to his side and fell silent, too. She also saw how its delicate neck had been efficiently wrung. They stood in silence for a moment, looking down at the top of its glossy black head, which hung at a morbid angle. The wings had been tied back with wire.

"Serial-killer stuff," he said.

"No." Rhona inclined her head. "Just a scarecrow. Gran told me about these. Farmers put up dead crows. Like displaying trophies. Scares the rest off. They're smart enough not to come back. Still—it's weird that you'd display it here. What's it protecting?"

Behind the corpse, there was a slim path beaten through the thorny hedge. It looked like a fox spoor. He wondered what stubborn or desperate creature would force a passage through such thorns. Teenagers looking to drink in peace, maybe. He thought he could probably wriggle through, with a bit of manoeuvring. If you panicked, though, you'd be torn to ribbons.

He glimpsed the still and placid field beyond. He found it strange how neat that field seemed in comparison to the one he stood in. The far field looked like nothing more than a patch of wild grass, with the far threshold just out of sight behind a slight hillock. The grass grew paler and taller there. He could not judge how far the field stretched.

It was over this path that this dead bird had been erected.

"We should go back," he said with his heart pounding. "I've changed my mind. I'm not going to be able to get it up with him watching."

"I'm not too hot on him, either. Want me to turn him to face the other way?"

He blanched.

Rhona only laughed. "Take my hand," she said.

She led him, tramping to the opposite hedgerow. Her palm was warm and sweaty. There were some hanging branches here, and the shadows floated over them both. Where the sun winked through, it sparkled on the wet grass. Rhona unstrapped the foil-bottomed picnic blanket and spread it out on the grass. It crackled and creased as she did.

He wiped his palms on his trouser legs. "We can still see the fence from here."

She stretched her neck. "Only a corner."

His knees knocked together and he felt vaguely nauseous. He knew he ought to feel excited. He did, in fact. The feeling was in him, somewhere, but it had gotten lost. It was buried somewhere deep in his belly, suffocated under a tangled, fizzing bundle of nerves.

"If whoever put up that crow comes back… I mean, if we get caught…"

"We could go into that other field."

"Past the crow?" He shook his head. "I've made my mind up. I want to go back."

"But you already stole the condoms," she said.

That stopped him. She was right, of course. He had stolen them. After pacing the aisle for ten minutes or more. He'd made closer and closer passes, studying the boxes with little glimpses, and from the corner of his eye. Finally, he snatched one up. He'd held that little cardboard box, plastic-wrapped, in his hand. He had never stolen a thing in his life. That had been the moment to back away or to commit, and he had committed.

Even now, he expected a firm hand to come suddenly down on his shoulder.

"Sit down," Rhona said gently, patting the blanket. "Come on."

Leon sat down awkwardly.

The fabric cover was the colour of bog moss. There were crumbs on it. The earth was bumpy beneath it. He decided that he must avoid letting his shoes touch the soft fabric. For this reason, he turned awkwardly, turning his body like a numb thing. The blanket shifted beneath him.

He looked over at the fence. The fence was still and quiet. It was only painted steel, hung between fenceposts. Distantly, the festival drummed on. Nobody to watch them but the crow.

Rhona called his name, and his eyes came away from the fence slowly, so that when the hem of her top rolled up, sudden alarm overcame him and he had to look away. His mouth went dry.

Rhona laughed sweetly and punched his arm. "Don't leave me the only one shivering."

He laughed hoarsely. His own fingers were clumsy and unresponsive, trying to unpick the prong of his belt-buckle. It lifted. He shuffled his trousers down to his knees. The others with it.

He watched Rhona fumbling with the cheap plastic hook behind her back. The tip of her tongue found the corner of her mouth as she manoeuvred it. It was all too much, and his ears rang, and he felt the absolute urge to look away again. In a moment, the bra, too, was collecting crumbs on the blanket.

"Will I…?" Rhona offered, pulling a condom out of the box.

"No, no, I'll…"

Rhona took the wrapper in her teeth and tore. His nostrils filled with the smell of cold latex. He breathed. He took it from her. It was like dead flesh between his fingers. He tried to remember how it worked. The pinch and the unrolling, did it go this way or that? He panicked, momentarily—there was a snag—it was a mechanical issue, the thing half-on. His heart was pounding. He could feel it in his back, where he lay against the blanket.

"Are you okay?" she asked.

Again, he nodded.

"Uh-huh," he said through gritted teeth. "Just as second."

"You going down, lads?"

A man's voice cut suddenly across the field and they froze. For a moment of pure animal panic, Leon felt weak. Rhona pressed a finger against her lips. "Wait, it's probably just…"

But the rattle and creak of the latch silenced whatever reassurance she had. He heard the thud of a work boot on the hardened earth beneath the gate. He imagined himself through another's eyes. Scrawny and pale and half-undressed, with timid eyes and grass-stains on his palms. He might as well have been lashed up for display.

He turned his head towards the crow.

"That field," he hissed.

"Don't!" she hissed back.

"What's that?" came an older man's voice. "Is there someone in there?"

So overpowering was the fear, then, that he pulled himself out from Rhona's arms and ran. He staggered and nearly fell on his face into the soil. His underwear was caught around his knees. He pulled it up while he fled. A man in a low flat cap was inside the gate. He closed the latch. The metal clanked with a penitentiary ring. There was nowhere else to go.

"Leon!" Rhona cried immediately behind him.

He brushed past the murdered crow, disturbing its oily feathers. He fell onto his belly into the snaking branch-pathway through the hedge. The thorns tugged his skin, drawing thin ribbons of blood along his thighs. He pulled himself through by his fingertips.

All he could hear was the rabbits-foot thumping of his heartbeat.

It was agony.

The briars had him hooked.

He felt like a scrawny sheep impaled on a wire fence, its tangled wool still ensnared around the barbs, its scalped pink flesh running with pale blood, sweat-diluted. The bonded sheep, so stranded, will die of thirst if it is not first found and devoured. The wolves were at his feet. So he strained on through the thorny passage. When he came free, it was with a splitting of a seam. That's how easily the skin slipped off him.

It fell away, off his shoulders like a loose gown. He left it to hang there, from the sharpest point of the thicket. It draped like a deflated, empty thing, like a discarded bin liner, like sagging rubber. It was not him—he shuffled on from it. As he did, he became lighter, freer to spread like mist through a sun-gold field. And being free, he felt a great coolness fill him. He felt how, without a heart, there would be nothing to clench fist-like behind his ribs. He felt that without lungs, there would be no breath to catch in his throat, no tightening vice to strangle him. There was nothing now to wrap him or to bind him.

Skinless, he knew he was unconstrained.

THE HARVEST

HANNAH REBEKAH GRAVES

"YOU ARE PROOF that rock-bottom is not the end," Miranda says to her reflection in the mirror. It sounds stupid, and she feels ridiculous, but it's a line her sponsor thinks is important to drill into her.

Letting out a breath, she reaches for the bottles on the counter. Three pills—one from each bottle, gulping them down with tap water. One of the meds—the one for depression—always leaves an awful aftertaste on the back of her tongue.

She runs through her mental list of daily tasks. She's gotten up, washed her face, brushed her teeth, dressed, and taken her medication. What comes next? Oh, right. Breakfast. Her recovery is still young enough that remembering to eat is a task: the shit she was taking *before* always killed her appetite.

On her way to the kitchen, she stops by her bedroom again to grab a pen and pad of paper. Might as well kill two birds with one stone, right?

Breakfast is easy—a bowl of cereal, nothing fancy. She chews thoughtfully while staring down at the pad of paper. It's interesting, doing her steps

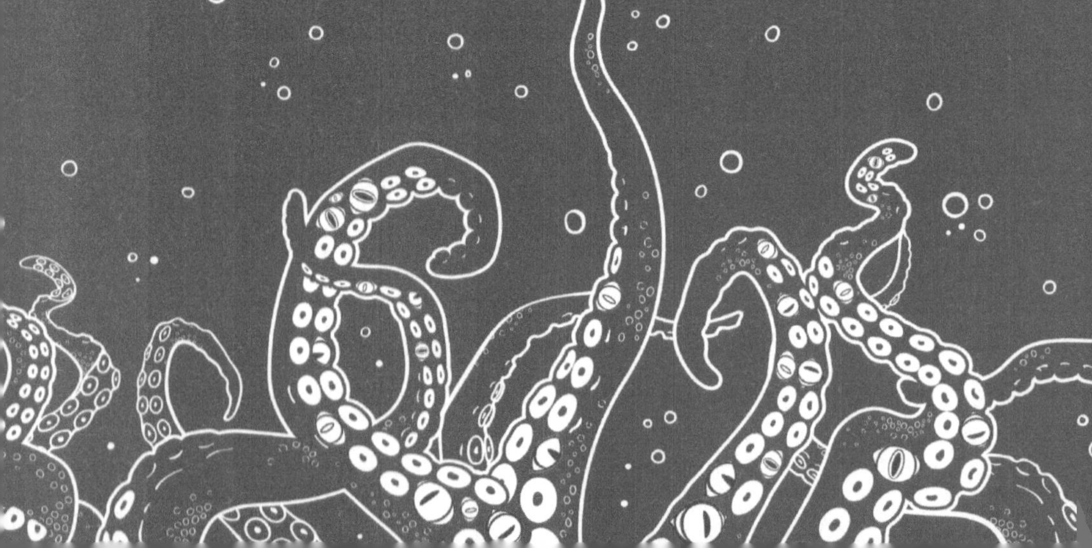

and being in therapy at the same time, because sometimes the advice is so different. Her sponsor believes writing letters to those she's harmed needs to be done much later down the line; her therapist thinks it's a good idea to work on them now.

Not to send them out, of course. God, no. She may be freshly sober, but she understands anyone she'd care enough to write a letter to would be *most* unhappy to receive one from her. She burnt a lot of bridges, and she's painfully aware of that.

After a few moments of thought, Miranda takes the easier route— *coward*—and writes a letter to a friend she stole from to get drugs. They weren't even *close* friends, but it's enough of a trespass to be put on her list.

She's halfway through it when she finishes her bowl of cereal. Pausing in her other task, she takes the bowl and spoon to the sink to rinse them out. That's one of her new rules. Taking care of things as they happen and not putting them off because of laziness or *I don't feel like it.*

As she does that, though, she notices something in the right-hand corner of the sink. It's small, but it's clearly a spiderweb. It looks a little strange, too, like the spider thought one web wasn't thick enough for its purposes and built over it several times.

She makes a face and immediately scoops up the web to wash it down the sink. It's not that she's *scared* of spiders, but she doesn't like them. The last thing she wants is to be a spider haven, so she needs to send a message. *You're not welcome here.*

Her night-time routine is like her morning routine but in reverse. She's ready to snuggle up in bed and read the latest horror novel she picked up at the used bookstore.

("Horror? Wouldn't you want to read something more upbeat? More positive?" her therapist had said. Miranda had laughed.)

She climbs under her blankets and reaches for her novel but then pauses, blinking. Her closet door is standing completely open.

That's strange, she thinks. *I know I closed it this morning, and I haven't been in it since.*

But maybe she's remembering things wrong. Her medications—especially the nighttime ones—can make her brain a little foggy, and she *still* sometimes feels like she's coming down from all the drugs. Maybe she forgot to close it. Maybe she opened it again for some reason.

It doesn't matter, she tells herself. *It's just a closet door, what difference does it make?*

Her sponsor has been telling her she worries too much about things that aren't important, and she's heeding that advice now.

She reads for a good hour before finding herself nodding off, so then it's lights out. Thanks to her meds, she falls asleep quickly and easily. Usually, she sleeps right through the night, though she has the occasional odd dream here and there.

A dream is exactly what Miranda thinks it is when her eyes snap open a few hours later. She blinks blearily at her clock—2:30 a.m.—and rubs her palms over her eyes. At first, she thinks she's awake, but when she settles back on the bed and gazes up at the ceiling…

Her heart stops in her throat.

There's a nest on her ceiling. Made of the same thick webbing she found on the sink, only it's much larger…and holding something.

Or *someone*.

Dark, matted hair hangs free, and a head slowly turns at an impossible angle to peer down at her. That face…that awful, awful face. Where there should be eyes, there are only deep caverns, and where there should be a mouth, there's only a gaping, bloody hole. There's still enough to the mottled skin to show that it's a young woman. Or used to be.

She tries to think of what to say, what to do, but before anything comes to mind, a raspy humming noise hits her sleep-addled ears. The girl-thing moves her mouth as though she's speaking, but all Miranda can hear is that humming, sounding more and more like it's internal rather than external, like something buzzing right against her eardrum. She doesn't know what to focus on, and the girl continues to talk animatedly, a long line of spit and blood dripping slowly from her mouth and landing right on Miranda's face.

It's enough to shake her from her frozen state, and suddenly, she's—

Screaming, sitting up straight in bed, heart and breath both going a mile a minute. She immediately fumbles around to turn on her bedside lamp and forces herself to look up, where there's nothing but the white popcorn ceiling she's come to know over the past three months.

A dream, then.

What the fuck kind of dream was that? I know the pills give me some weird ones sometimes, but that was…that was just awful.

And it still feels real. Real enough that she touches her face to make sure there's no blood or spit on there. Real enough that she shivers and curls into herself. Will she even be able to go back to sleep? She can't shake the image of the abyssal holes in that woman's face, the way it seemed like she could see forever in that darkness.

Miranda finds the second spiderweb the next day in the smaller second bedroom she converted to an office. She's a freelance editor with a couple of gigs she needs to be working on, but when she steps into the room, she almost backs right out.

Her desk is small and has two monitors set up on it, and the left one is…well, it's completely covered in spiderwebs. That same thick roping that suggests the spider went over its task again and again, unsatisfied with its work.

"What the fuck?" Miranda asks.

It's not like she has huge monitors or anything, but she was just in her office the day before last; there's no way a spider could've done this much work in so little time.

Unless it's a huge spider, she thinks, shuddering inwardly.

This time, she doesn't touch the web with her bare hands. Instead, she gets probably more paper towels than she needs then glances all around her monitor to make sure the spider in question isn't lurking nearby—it got the *back* of the monitor, too?—and wipes off the webbing as quickly as she can.

"This is ridiculous," she mutters. Should she call the landlord and ask about a spider problem?

No, she doesn't want to rock the boat. She was very lucky to get this apartment—and her sponsor put her name on the line to help her—so she won't make waves. Most spiders are harmless, anyway, right? Just creepy, and she's certainly lived through worse than creepy.

She turns with the wad of paper towels in her hand, intending to head to the kitchen to dump them in the trash—and she freezes. In the hallway, out of the corner of her eyes, she spots a darkened figure. Its edges are blurry, almost like static, and when she tries to focus on it, she wobbles on her feet, stricken by an overwhelming dizziness.

"Hey," she calls out weakly, not able to muster more than that. "Who's there? You have no right to be in my apartment. You'd better leave now or—"

Almost as quickly as the dizzy spell came on, it's gone. Blinking, she realizes the figure in the hallway is also gone, though she takes a moment to work up the courage to step out of the room to be sure. After discarding the paper towels, she goes over the entire apartment to make sure she's alone.

She is.

So, what the hell was that all about?

Instead of working, Miranda spends her morning searching the internet for side effects of her various medications. Mainly, she's trying to figure out if any of them can cause hallucinations. Results are all the same, though: *this medication does not result in any visual or auditory hallucinations.*

So, what was it, then? It's not other drugs, because she's been clean as a whistle for the past nine months. Was it because of that horrible nightmare? She was up for a while after that, and she *is* tired today, so maybe…maybe that's it. She's just exhausted and seeing things. That's a thing, right? The internet says that's a thing. Though usually after more sleep deprivation than one night, but she's going to ignore that.

Positive thinking, she tells herself.

The rest of the afternoon and most of the evening, she focuses on her work as best as she can. She works late enough that dinner will have to be something easy, but that's okay. She got a good amount of work done, and the important part is that she's eating at all.

Routine, then. Food, brushed teeth, washed face, medications, pajamas. Back into bed, blankets pulled up, reaching for her book, and—

The closet door is open.

No, I definitely *shut it this time,* she thinks. *I made a mental note this morning because of last night.*

She swallows, and instead of ignoring it, she pushes back the blankets and crawls out of bed, going over to pull it shut.

The moment she does, she startles at the reflection in the door's mirror. That figure from earlier, the darkened one with static-y edges, is standing a foot or so behind her. The dizziness hits her all over again, but this time she tries to focus through it. She wants to get a good look at what she's seeing, but her eyes won't cooperate. The form looks human, but maybe there are… too many limbs? Maybe there are things waving around that shouldn't be there. None of it makes sense. The longer she looks, the worse the vertigo gets, and it almost feels like she's being sucked into the creature, being pulled backward to be devoured.

Miranda forces her eyes to slam shut.

Immediately, the dizziness and that devouring feeling disappear.

She takes a few deep, shaky breaths and wills her heart to calm down. Then it's a matter of forcing her eyes back open, which she does slowly and carefully, one at a time, half-expecting the figure to be inches behind her when she opens them, but—no. She's alone again.

Just like last time.

The next day, the spiderweb she finds is on her toaster oven. The one she used last late night to heat up garlic bread. Like with her monitor, it's completely covered from front to back with those endless ropes of webbing.

"Can't you at least be good at your job?" Miranda groans. "You know, get it right the first time?"

She discards this web just like the two before it. Even though getting rid of the webs is supposed to send that *you're not welcome here* message, it's obvious the hint isn't being taken. It's also pretty strange that she hasn't even *seen* a spider around, and something that can work this fast and do this much…it has to be big, right? Her apartment is a small space. There are only so many places to hide.

Whatever. Deal with things as they happen, right?

The mess is gone, and hopefully, there won't be another today, so she starts her routine.

The rest of her day goes as it usually does. As it should. No more webs, no more weird visions. Just work, lunch, therapy, a meeting with her sponsor, and then a shower before dinner.

She's in the middle of rinsing the shampoo out of her hair when she notices a barely audible sound floating in from outside the shower. It almost sounds like…humming? She strains to hear over the rush of the water. Yeah, that sounds like humming. She can't hear well enough to make out the tune, but it's definitely someone humming quietly to themselves.

Before she can think, she throws open the shower door. Never mind that this could be an intruder, never mind that she's completely naked and her vision is a little blurry from the heat of the water. No thoughts tonight, boys, just action.

She spots the source of the humming and falls back against the shower wall, her spine smacking into the lever.

Still hanging upside down, but this time attached to the back of Miranda's door instead of her ceiling, is the woman-thing from before. Miss No-Mouth-No-Eyes.

The woman-thing stops humming and somehow that gaping hole twists itself into what Miranda thinks is supposed to be a smile. She opens her mouth to speak, and that humming starts up again. Her feet slip and slide on the bottom of the shower as she tries to get away, like she has anywhere she could even go. When the humming turns into a droning buzz rattling in her ear canals, she desperately wants to dig her nails into her eardrums to block the sound out. It grates down her bones, scrapes her raw. How could it be that this woman-thing is making that noise *inside* her head?

Miranda is screaming before she realizes it, and in the time it takes her to blink, the terrifying image is gone. She quickly reaches behind herself to turn off the water, but she has a feeling that a thorough search of the apartment will lead to nothing. She'll be alone, again. Just like she has been every time before.

During her next therapy session, she finally breaks down and admits she's been hearing and seeing things that aren't there. Every day for the past week now, there's either been that creature who makes her feel sick or the woman-thing wrapped endlessly in spiderwebs and her incessant humming. (She doesn't mention the spiderwebs she's found every day—on a single dress hanging in her closet, all over her makeup brushes, on the book on her nightstand—because that doesn't seem related. Spiders are spiders; hallucinations are something else.)

Her therapist is concerned, of course. Anyone would be. She talks Miranda through these episodes, trying to see if perhaps they could be the work of her subconscious trying to tell her something. When that fails, she asks Miranda if she feels safe at home or if she would feel better being monitored. (Miranda *quickly* says no to that. She's done her time in facilities, thank you.)

Her final suggestion, then, is to talk to her psychiatrist as soon as she can. Maybe the meds alone don't cause hallucinations, but perhaps the mixture might be the key she's missing. Miranda feels stupid. Why didn't *she* think of it? Of course. Medications can act strangely together, right?

Miranda leaves her session with a promise to call her psychiatrist to book an appointment. Which is exactly what she does when she gets home, but her spirits are dampened to learn that the soonest appointment he has available—even for an emergency—is two weeks away.

"Okay," she says to herself after she's hung up, taking a deep breath. "Two weeks. I can do this. All of this? Just my medications mixing poorly. No one's really there. Nothing's going to happen to me."

When she finds yet another spiderweb—this time on the little stand she puts her phone on while she works, "And this is just the work of some obnoxious spider who can't get weaving right."

On the second day of waiting for her psychiatrist appointment, something new happens. She gets itchy. Like her chest and abdomen are covered in bug bites. (She checks; they're not.) She gets some of that anti-itching cream and lathers it on, going as far as taking off her shirt so it doesn't wipe away, but even that brings minimal relief.

The real strange thing, though, is that it isn't constant. She tries to figure out if something's triggering it—a certain time of day or something in her routine—but each time it happens, something different has come before. It just seems to itch when it wants to and stops when it's done.

It even wakes her up a couple of nights with her skin almost bloody from how hard she's been scratching at it in her sleep. She resorts to gauze and cream, but sleep-her always manages to get it off and leaves herself a bloody mess all over again.

If Miranda is completely honest with herself, as she's supposed to be, as she's promised to be, she's getting overwhelmed. Between the spider(s?), the hallucinations, and now this itching…it's driving her batty. She just wants to live her life, to do her steps and her work and her therapy and continue to get better, get back to the person she used to be before drugs came into the picture and ruined everything.

It's difficult, though, when a part of her knows she could likely numb most—if not all—of this out with a few simple phone calls. She could make the itching not matter; she could make her brain unable to focus enough to even come up with the hallucinations…

(She's so goddamned tired of that girl and her buzzing.)

Another thought is to just stop taking her medications. If that's causing the hallucinations and the itching and she doesn't know which one it is, just stop all of them, right? Wrong. The internet quickly tells her that most of her medications can cause seizures when stopped cold turkey. So much for that idea.

Instead of doing either of those things, Miranda calls her sponsor to see if she has some free time to talk. She does, thankfully, and Miranda lets her know she's having a rough night, that she's thinking maybe life would be easier if she went back to the drugs.

It's an uplifting talk, one that lasts several hours, and gives Miranda the reassurance she needs. Her sponsor's always good at that; that's why Miranda adores her. She makes her feel ten feet tall and just as strong, as though she can do anything she puts her mind to.

She feels good enough, in fact, that when she goes to bed and sees the young woman back on the ceiling, buzzing so loudly in her ears that she just wants to drive something into her ears, she tells her, "You know what? I don't care. I'm going to bed."

It's three days before her appointment with her psychiatrist.

Miranda is a wreck. Her routine—her new routine—seems to be winning despite her best efforts. She's so tired of goddamned spiderwebs appearing in the oddest of places and having to clean them up. So tired of the shadow that may or may not be a man who leaves her feeling so sick, so much like she'll be vacuumed up into it if she looks too long. She's tired of the girl and the stupid itching that's created wounds that scab over, only to be torn open again.

Three days, though.

Three days, and she can talk to her psychiatrist, and he will hopefully—*please*—have an answer for her. He'll have a medication change for her to try or, hell, even a new one to add to the mix that will make this all stop.

Three days. She can do this.

Numbly, she cleans up the spiderweb on her vanity mirror and goes about her day. Counting down the hours until she can go to bed, doing her best to ignore the figure when he appears in the corner while she's trying to vacuum, the static of him snapping in and out of her line of vision. The itching is especially bad today and occupies most of her thoughts.

She does her best to remind herself that three days turns to two turns to one turns to that day.

Soon.

By the time she crawls into bed that night, she's exhausted. She doesn't bother putting a top on because it will just get bloody, but the blankets—well, they're a lost cause. She tries to read for a while as she absently scratches at herself, wincing now and again when she hits a particularly tender place.

Eventually, thankfully, her medications overpower the itchiness, and she falls asleep, her book still in her hand.

She wakes in terrible pain.

The itchiness is still there, but it's muted next to the fact that her chest and abdomen feel like they're on fire. She groans and tries to force herself to get up so that she can get some pain medicine, some of that prescription Ibuprofen, but she finds she can't move.

She tries again and still can't move.

Her vision finally comes into focus, and she realizes, with growing horror, why—she's covered, from the neck down, in those thick ropes of spiderwebs that have been haunting her house for the past couple of weeks.

When she looks around wildly, she sees it's not just her; her entire room is covered in those spiderwebs from floor to ceiling. *Really* like a nest now.

She lets out a scream and immediately receives a disapproving *hummmm* in return.

Her gaze drifts slowly, despairingly, to the ceiling.

There she is again, the woman-thing. That blackened maw twists into something that looks almost like a pout, and she says…well, whatever she's trying to say. To Miranda, it's the most uncomfortable buzzing sound so deep within her ears she can feel it in her soul.

"What the fuck is going on?" Miranda asks, voice quavering. "None of this is real. None of this is real…"

The woman-thing stares at Miranda for a long moment before the buzzing suddenly dies to a low roar, then a voice, just as raspy as the humming, finally says something she can understand.

"What are you talkin' about? This here's the realest your life has ever been and is ever gonna get."

"What the fuck does that even mean?" Miranda snaps.

"You still don't get it, do you?" When the woman-thing speaks in that broken voice, a mixture of blood and spit drools down onto Miranda's face, just like the first night. It makes her want to vomit, and she fervently wishes she could wipe it away. *"You've been whinin' and cryin' about how the meds are messin' you up, but, girl, don't you see? They're helpin' you."*

"How is this helping?" she cries, struggling against her bindings. Her imaginary bindings. She just has to break free of the spell her mind has cast on her. She has to focus on reality. None of this can be real. None of this makes any *sense*.

"It's helpin' you see the truth of things," the woman-thing answers in an almost whisper. *"Why, if you weren't on them, you wouldn't even have had the pleasure of watchin' the Harvest. Of gettin' to experience all this. You'd just be going about your day, drugged up or hiding behind your meetings, and then,* wham, *you'd keel over and know nothin' better. Them pills been helpin' you see the light of day, that's all. Lettin' you see what the truth really is."*

"Keel over?" Miranda's voice is tiny now, desperate.

"*You feel it, don't you?*" the woman-thing asks, the buzzing growing momentarily louder. "*Down below, beneath that itchiness, beneath that burnin' pain.*"

"What am I supposed to be feeling?"

"*The* movement, *silly. All the little flutters of life, the ones you been nurturin'.*"

"What the *fuck* are you talking about?!"

"*Hush your mouth and pay attention,*" she growls, more of that blood and spit dribbling down onto Miranda's face, into her left eye this time. She immediately closes it, squinting up at the woman-thing with her one good eye. God, she's going to throw up. "*Feel them. Know them.*"

And, for some reason, Miranda finds herself…doing just that. Like she's just a good girl who naturally follows instructions from strange spider-dead-creatures when given them. She tries to feel beneath her panic, beneath the itchiness and the pain that threatens to tear her in two.

At first, it's no good. She can't concentrate well enough. There's nothing there. It's just pain and itchiness, panic present but unrelated. No matter how many times she tries, no matter how many times the woman-thing encourages her… But then again, why would there be anything there? This is all a figment of her imagination and—

No.

She feels the first squirm deep in her abdomen, as though something is curling and stretching. Almost like a fluttering.

"No," she says, horror filling her voice. "*No.*"

The first squirm rapidly turns from one into many, until she feels like all the itchy, painful places are alive, with a mind of their own. Her internal organs are being shoved around, being picked at, and she screams again, louder this time. "What…what the fuck is this?"

"*The Harvest, girl.*" The buzzing in her ears almost deafens her as the other smiles widely at her. "*How many times I gotta tell you that?*"

"What is the Harvest?" Miranda manages, panting, still trying so desperately to break free of her restraints.

"*It's a time when our masters come into being,*" she says. "*Now, I know what you're thinkin'. 'How can they be our masters if they're so little?' Well, you should know better than to judge a book by its cover. These children exist far beyond our imagination and have abilities we couldn't even dare to dream of.*"

"You're fucking crazy."

And of course this is when not-a-man shows up. If she were capable of reasonable thought, it might occur to her she's never seen the two of them in the same room before, but right now, he just buzzes at his unknowable edges, and she thinks, *It fucking figures.*

The webbed monstrosity is still speaking to her. "*I've been so nice to you, and you've been nothin' but mean to me, you know that? I don't think you deserve the Harvest at all. If it were up to me, and it ain't, someone else would've been chosen. Someone more* grateful."

"Someone like you?" Miranda asks, teeth gritted.

"*Oh, I've already done my Harvest, sweetheart,*" she answers. "*Did that back in… No, I can't remember. It's been too long. Hundreds of years, at least. They only need to birth every now and again, you know? Probably on account of there being so many of them.*"

Miranda doesn't respond this time, too distracted by all the squirming going on inside her body, in how she feels she's literally being torn in two, like she's being picked clean from the inside out. Everything seems so real to her now, so vivid, that she's having trouble believing she ever thought this could be a hallucination.

A section of the webbing tears open and—with a pain that makes her scream again—a tiny being pops out from inside her.

This thing…this thing came from *inside* her? How many more are there? She feels like there are many, like there are far too many, like her body isn't big enough to handle what is yet to come.

She tries so hard to get a proper look at it, but both her brain and her eyes are fuzzy. There's too much going on to take it all in. What she does make out, though, is horrifying. Countless legs as thick as rope, covered in what looks like the softest webbing. *It looks almost like a mop head*, she thinks deliriously. Orbs glow throughout what must be the creature's body—or perhaps it's not a body, perhaps it's all legs—bright red, only glimpsed when it moves a certain way.

And the face… There are a million tiny eyes staring at her above a giant maw that takes up the rest of its face. Just a gaping mouth filled with rows and rows of teeth that are bright red from it eating its way out of her. That mouth is full with pieces of her. The dizziness she gets when looking at the blurry not-a-man hits her now, staring at this thing.

Like she's looking into the abyss.

She can't tear her gaze away from the creature, even as the pain intensifies. All she can do is buck against the webbing, pleading inwardly for the pain to stop. It doesn't. What did the woman-thing say about there being a lot of them?

A second one tears its way to freedom, and then a third, and then like a faucet turning from a drip to a gush, there are so many of the creatures crawling out of her all at once, leaving her shredded and broken. Each one emerges with a sick, wet tearing sound as the webbing—and her flesh—falls apart.

Delirious, she watches as the spider creatures crawl around, some of them nosing for more scraps of meat, some of them going to the static man, who's appeared next to her without her being able to say when he moved so close. He's just there *now*, and he's gathering some of the many-legged creatures into his arms so carefully, so gently. As though he were their caretaker, their creator.

Miranda is entirely forgotten. The woman-thing on the ceiling doesn't so much as glance at her with those endless voids, and the not-a-man moves away, seeming to take one step and then three and then one again, like a bad recording that skips.

In that moment, she finally gives up the last of her hope this is any kind of hallucination or nightmare. This entire time, this entire thing that she worked so hard to brush off—it was all very real. She'd been an incubator, her days counting down without her even knowing it. Her medicine had been trying to help her like it was supposed to, not hurt her at all. A warning she ignored.

And what good is she now?

A nest no longer needed.

The last thing Miranda hears is the webbed woman-thing giggling, her ears still thrumming with that buzzing sound. "*Oh, look how precious they are. Aren't you all so big and strong!*"

BERRY JUICE

BJ THORAY

WHEN MOTHER TOLD me I'd have to spend the day with Cousin Jack, I couldn't help but kick back. "Do I have to? Why me?"

Mother reminded me he was family and that he needed someone to help him to his appointments. Cousin Jack hated his appointments. He had a rare medical condition none of us could ever remember the name of. Even without knowing the exact condition, we all knew there was something wrong with him. He couldn't go ten-goddamn-minutes without being weird.

Like at Mary's BBQ, when he freaked out after a group photo.

"Delete it! Fucking delete it!" he'd raged. "Don't fucking let them see my face."

"Yo, Jack, who's lookin' at photos of you?" Cousin Kam joked, but Cousin Jack pretended he didn't hear and started kicking and smashing. That's how it was with Cousin Jack; you couldn't know what would set him off until it was too late. He was too much fun to wind up, though. Sure, the meltdowns were horrible, destructive, ended in us cleaning up after him. But it didn't always

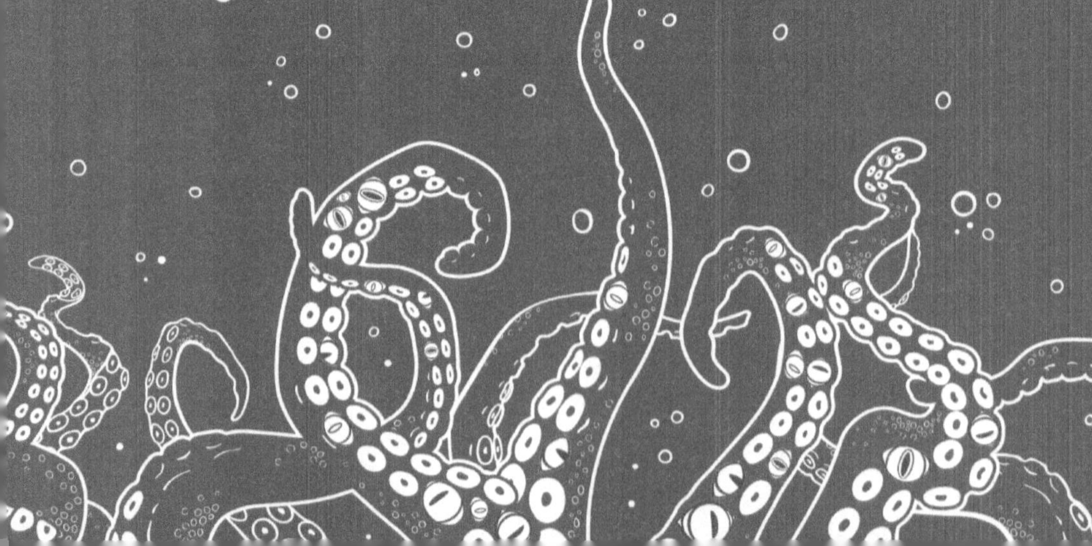

get to that and seeing him squirm at our jokes ("Hey Jacky boy! Give us a smile," or "Jack Jack, show us them pearly whites!") was the best part. He just didn't know how to hide that face.

In a group, it was easy for one person piggybacking off what was just said to push it too far and not realize a line had been crossed. Then the next moment Cousin Jack would be smashing up the yard like some kaiju, wailing and shrieking and being a terror until the elders surrounded him, exchanging looks while wondering how much of a beating it'd take to calm his ass down.

For instance, take Cassy's birthday party. Cass is just a kid, so it was supposed to be a tea and princess type thing, but us older fam couldn't help but have our fun with Cousin Jack. We knew he had one of his appointments coming up. Some of us youngers were looking forward to the party because we knew Jacky was gonna be a lot of fun, but too many of us were in on it and too many of us were hungry, and Cousin Jack sure-as-shit blew up right in the middle of Tommy or something's turn to go all mockingbird.

Cousin Jack smashed his arm into the cake and kicked at the gift pile and fell to his knees and just started fucking wailing in pain. Some people thought he'd go for Tommy, make his face into cake and what-not. But Cousin Jack didn't like to be dangerous. He didn't understand that his outbursts were scary. It didn't matter if he didn't get violent until he'd totally disassociated.

Anyway, us younger-olds were giggling and shooting looks, but the older-olds just surrounded and shook their heads. Cass's mother came up next to him, gently put her hand on his shoulder, and told him it was all right. After a minute or two, the wails became whimpers and she asked him something softly, and he sniffled and nodded and took her hand, following her inside. We were all grounded and had to apologize to Cass. Some of us insisted it was worth it, but seeing Cousin Jack be calmed down—I guess seeing the other side of the process—made me sad. I felt bad for Cass, too. Maybe someone had noticed my…my sympathy, and now I was paying for it.

"Why do I have to do it?"

"He's got an appointment coming up, and someone needs to take him," Mother answered.

"Why me?"

"Because you're responsible."

"What?" I say in disbelief. "That's not fair."

"We can trust you to take care of him. He likes you."

"Well, that doesn't mean that I like him," I said. "What if he hits me?"

"I've never seen him hit anyone that didn't deserve to be hit," Mother said. "Except that one time. Anyway, we're going over tonight. You can hang out and make sure you two get good."

"I'm going to be too tired for that," I said.

"Good," Mother said. "Then you can just listen and not stir shit, like your cousins. Now hurry up before you're late for work."

I hated going into the office while knowing that my evening wasn't going to be mine. I struggled to be productive for most of the day, dreading going to Auntie's and having to endure Cousin Jack's tone-deaf ramblings and clumsy attempts at jokes. It's like he was living in a different world. He was constantly talking about stuff no one cared about or knew much about. If not that, he was just straight-up saying crazy shit. I cottoned on to the fact that you could tell who the kids, the adults, and the olders were based on how they looked at Cousin Jack when he was allowed to keep talking with no one else butting in.

When Cousin Jack rambled, the adults, like me, most of the time we would grin or nod along as we bit our lips to stop from bursting out laughing. That's how it was when there were more of us around. It was a party, y'know, and Jackie, bless 'im, never caught onto when he *was* the joke. So, he never realized that sometimes you should stop talking or not tell everyone everything.

But the olders? Well, when Cousin Jack talked, they did a better job at listening, or pretending to, at least. They looked him in the eye, and then once Cousin Jack flinched, they continued staring at his face, in the general area of his eyes, where you'd look with a normal person. Then they'd listen attentively and nod patiently. They never let it through that they were just waiting for him to finish. When he finally did or they got called away and Cousin Jack actually acknowledged and said *bye*, then the olders made this face like they were sorry they couldn't do more or that something truly unfortunate had happened. I don't know if it just wasn't as funny for the olders or if they were better at hiding it.

Now, I've never seen Jacky go at a kid. It's not like he was some *doesn't know his own strength* galoot. He couldn't always help his rages, but as Mother said, he didn't hit anyone who didn't provoke him. And he didn't ever, even during the rages, go at or even near the kids. And the kids aren't always nice. They catch that he's weird. They see us—or rather, how we handle him—and they want to act like us, but even when they say some mean shit or talk about his weird head, Jack doesn't mind. Maybe once or twice, he winced or cringed and then made out of there quick. You could tell by the look on his face he didn't like it and wanted to get away, but that was generally it.

"Yo, sugars, you coming out tonight? Gonna watch the game at the local," Tommy asked from the desk over. We were all hot-desking now, but the crew generally kept together.

"Nah, can't boy," I said.

"Shit, what's got you?"

"Gotta hang with the fam tonight. Going over to the cousin's."

"Aw shit," Tommy said. "*That* cousin? The wilding one?"

"That's the one."

"Man, so you got work *then* work today."

"You know it," I said, not trying to hide my disappointment. "Get this, my mot—I mean, Mother wants me to take him to his next appointment. Like, why the fuck I gotta do it, y'know?"

"I know," he said, then we tapped, and he went around to see who else could chill with him tonight.

I left for work and took my time on the commute home. When I walked in the door, Mother didn't say anything about my timing.

"I laid out a shirt and jacket," she said after I'd taken my shoes off. "Please get ready and we'll go."

As we rode over, I looked out the window, taking in the neighborhood and enjoying my time alone before the night became all about Cousin Jack.

They were happy to see us. Cass opened the door all excited and her mother, Auntie J, came out and told Cass to go wash her hands. Then Auntie J saw us all in. She hugged me tight and thanked me for coming after work. Behind her, lurking in the hall and trying to look without looking like he was looking, was Cousin Jack. My eyes caught him, and Auntie J must've seen the reflection. She turned around and said, "Hi Jack. Go wash your hands, then come and say hello. Your cousin's here to see you."

"Hi Cousin," Jack said after he'd washed his hands. He sat next to me in the den. Just the two of us on the couch, looking at the blank TV screen. I thought about asking to turn it on, but Mother would just say dinner was almost on and we could wait.

"Do you like planes?" Cousin Jack finally asked. He was looking at the screen like he was watching a program.

"Sure, I guess. You? What's your favorite?"

"They're all right," Jack said. "I guess. I don't like things swooping down. Actually, I don't like them. Birds are okay. I guess planes are fine sometimes. I don't like sky planes though."

"Sky planes?" I balked. "Isn't every plane a sky plane unless we're talking some geometry shit?"

"Space planes," Jack said. "I meant space planes."

A long lull followed, one that went so long that I felt physically uncomfortable and started searching frantically for a way to break it. I wanted to say something to Cousin Jack, but I couldn't think of any conversation for him that wasn't really a wind-up. Finally, Mother and Auntie J called out that dinner was ready.

Cass said the prayers, and we all tucked in to dinner, but Auntie J interjected, "And thank you to Wayne for being a good cousin and community member by helping Jack to his appointment next week."

A round of disinterested *hear-hears* followed as the clan kept their gazes on their plates and mumbled out their commendations. Only Cousin Jack looked at me. I guess no one had told him. It made sense. The entire table looked exhausted, except for Jack.

After dinner, Jack and I sat in the den on the same couch together as before but with distance between us, the TV screen still blank, but the olders were there and mostly made the talk. Because it was a weekday and I had work tomorrow, we didn't stay long. We said our goodbyes, and I thought that the dinner had been good and the whole night wasn't as disastrous as I'd thought it'd be. I actually felt bad for pouting through my day over something that turned out to not be that big a deal.

The next week passed quietly. Cousin Jack's appointments were usually on Friday afternoons. I hadn't known this and appreciated being able to take the time off work. It felt like a little holiday, and because it was a family medical thing, I could claim it as legitimate away time. This lifted my mood, and I was thinking about my long-ass weekend ahead with Jack's appointment as just this small task to be accomplished before I could access all that happy. Given how he'd been at the dinner, I thought it wouldn't be much trouble.

I was wrong. When I got to Auntie J's, she greeted me warmly. Neither Cass nor the pets were anywhere in sight. Actually, the house sounded totally empty. Not a peep. Not a stir. Cousin Jack needed coaxing to leave his room.

"Please," Auntie J said, "you'll be late and make your cousin look bad."

"Helmet!" Jack raged from behind the door.

"Wayne, dear," Auntie J said, "go and get a strainer from the kitchen. The first cabinet to the right of the sink."

I found it easily enough, returning upstairs and handing it to her. She took it, opened the door, and went in. I heard shuffling. She came out. A beat later, Cousin Jack emerged in a pretty swish suit, with the strainer over his head.

"I'm ready," he said with tears in his eyes.

Auntie J walked us to the bus stop. "The route is simple. Just this for five stops, then off and straight ahead to the complex. I sent all of it to your device. If in doubt..."

"I've got the helper, Auntie," I said.

She hugged us both. When she pulled Cousin Jack in, he went limp, and the way his body plopped into hers made me think of a pillow being fluffed.

"You trust birds?" Cousin Jack asked on the bus.

"I dunno. I guess I don't need to," I said. *Trust birds with what?*

"I like the idea of birds, but I don't know... I just don't know."

"Y'know, Cousin," I said. "You don't have to know about everything. Sometimes, you're so set on impressing us or proving something that you know, but you don't have to. You can just chill."

"Yeah," he said, "because you guys like having me around."

I hadn't expected sarcasm. I was trying to be nice. "Well, we do, but sometimes, things get out of hand."

"Yeah. I doubt any of you would act differently."

"I don't know what you mean by that," I said. "This is us."

For a second, I wondered if Cousin Jack would act up. I'd have stood up and started to move to the exit, but he was still sitting. I turned back, expecting defiance. His face was blank. He was looking in my direction but past me, through me.

"Jack!" I said. "Cousin! Jack!"

He snapped to. His face shrank and I could tell he was uncomfortable. But he stood nonetheless and came out to the exit.

We walked from the stop through the medical complex. The buildings were tall and their sidings were glossy and reflective, even at night.

"What even is that material?" Cousin Jack asked bitterly. His mood was sour, like a child about to throw a tantrum. I followed the directions Auntie J had given, but with each escalator and elevator, I could sense Cousin Jack getting more anxious. He paused before taking the first step on or in, and when we stepped out, his eyes scanned the room, as if searching for a way to escape. On the final escalator, he started trembling. He noticed my noticing and turned to hide his face.

"It'll be okay," I said, putting my hand on his shoulder. His body heaved and his heart rate raced and his breath was absolutely gusting. He was sobbing violently.

"It's okay," I said again.

We were greeted with a big set of rust-colored doors. They looked heavy, but I opened them easily. I held one open and ushered in Cousin Jack. The crying had stopped, but the trembling—well—the trembling he couldn't control.

The waiting lounge was nice, I mean, like *nice*. It had comfortable seats and a crowd that looked—I don't know how to say this, really—but, like, cool. Like they were out of some advert or dance clip. I told Cousin Jack to have a seat while I signed him in.

"No," he said firmly.

When we got to the front desk, the receptionist looked up and greeted us with a warm smile. She looked down again at a small screen next to her main monitor and said, "Hi, Jack! Welcome back!" and then, to me, "You must be his chaperone for today?"

"Just here to support my cousin," I said, like it was nothing.

She smiled again, and I thought about slipping her my contacts. Her smile faded as she stared intently at the screen and typed, but it clawed its way back onto her face when she looked back up.

"Okay, you can both have a seat. We'll call Jack in just a minute or two." She reached back and opened a box, retrieving something wrapped in plastic from it. "And these are for you, while you wait."

I took the item. *Headphones.* The big ones that you put over your head.

"Have you ever used these before?" she asked with a smile.

"Headphones? Yeah."

"We ask that you only put them on after your patient—" she corrected herself, "I mean, Jack, has been called. They're augmented reality headphones."

"No way." I'd never used them before. Don't know if I'd ever actually heard of them, but I didn't want to show it.

"We know that this can be a chore. For both of you. So, we want everyone to enjoy their time with us as much as possible."

When I glanced at Jack as we sat down, I realized we were having different experiences. This was new for me. Surprisingly nice and comfortable. He stared at the receptionist with bald-faced hate. Jackie was as gentle as he could manage, but right then he looked like he'd happily smash that receptionist to a pulp if he could.

We sat down. Cousin Jack was a mess.

"Yo, Jacky," I said, trying not to sound annoyed. "Can you stop shaking? You're making the whole table vibrate."

"Sorry," he said minutes later, like he hadn't heard me. But he stopped for maybe, like, a minute. Then he started rocking back and forth. I eyed the headphones, wishing I could just put them on and be done with it.

"Jacky," I said after another minute. Several more passed. Then he looked at me with the same blank grin as if he actually *had* just heard and was ignoring me.

"Sorry."

Again, a minute of calm before Jacky was vibrating. It was a different motion, just his leg this time. Bouncing up and down like a jackhammer bopping into concrete. Just as I was about to lose it, the headphones lit up at the sides and a jingly sound came on over the intercom.

"Jack. Jack. A13Q."

Cousin Jack froze as a surge of people surrounded us. Uniformed security was near the doors like when we came in, but there were more. Two people in scrubs and skullcaps were now at Jack's side. The shorter, thinner one took him by the arm as the other scrub followed, and then the tall folks around us dissipated. I watched as Cousin Jack was gently ushered past reception and through the brown wooden door behind the desks. I thought he'd look back, but he didn't. The receptionist watched, and when she caught my gaze, she mimed putting the headphones on, mouthed "put them on," and smiled like she was advertising toothpaste.

I didn't know what to expect, but my reality didn't feel augmented. I felt pretty good, and the music they were piping in was nice, like my kind of stuff, but I guess my tastes run popular. It felt like no time passed at all. As if in a daze, I looked up after a few minutes and Cousin Jack was there again, looking calm but cowed. The orderlies—or whatever you call them— were at his side. I stood up and took off the headphones. Seeing the shorter scrub's hands already out, I gave them back. They escorted us to the escalator, watched us get on, and waited for the doors to close.

Cousin Jack was different, but I didn't know how. We went the way we came. He didn't speak a word, just whimpered softly. I wanted to ask what they did. I felt bad. I didn't like seeing him like that. It was like a more scared, more pathetic version of what we'd see at the gatherings.

"Looking good, Cousin."

Nothing.

"Hey, Jacky…"

Nothing.

"Jack, how bad was it?"

Nothing.

It wasn't like he was ignoring me. More like he lacked the strength. I was tempted to take him out for something, try to draw out his joy, but I'd promised Auntie and Mother that we'd make no stops after. Besides, he might've been sad, scared, pathetic even, but he was calm.

Finally, we got back to his house. I'd assumed I'd be over for dinner, but Cousin Jack stopped at the door.

"Thank you, Cousin," he said blankly, like he was someone else.

"What do you think your mother's got for dinner tonight?" I asked with a grin, imagining a chill evening with fam.

"We don't eat dinner after the appointments," Jack said. "At least not me. Not in front of me."

"Oh," I said, trying to hide my confusion. I laughed a bit in disbelief. "I'll just get going back to mine now. Bet Mother's worried."

"Hey, Cousin?" Jack asked once I'd turned to leave.

"Yeah?" I turned around.

"Maybe don't take so many pictures from now on. I mean, don't be in them. I know you're not that into photos of yourself."

"Oh, okay, Cousin," I said. I chuckled and left without looking back.

I didn't think much of any of that. A few weeks later, might've even been months, Mother again said we'd be going over to Auntie J's for dinner, just the two fams. I'd maybe been to one BBQ since the appointment. I couldn't actually remember the last big family or community gathering I'd been to, but I guess it was that quiet season.

Point being, I didn't think nothing about us going over to Auntie J's, except maybe that it was about time. I didn't see it as a chore. Was actually looking forward to it. I didn't grumble and groan through work that day, and I didn't stall when I got home. When we got there, I gave everyone a big hug.

Cousin Jack was his usual self: strange. We sat on the couch, listening to the kitchen, looking at the screen as clips played, followed by ads, followed by clips. When a plane flashed on screen, I remembered our conversation from the dinner before.

"Seen any space planes, Cuz?" I asked happily.

"Have you yet?" he shot back. I looked at him and realized he was being neutral. He wasn't kicking back or sassing me.

The call for dinner. We got up and sat down. Cass said the prayers, and we all started to tuck in to dinner, but Auntie J interjected, "And thank you to Wayne for being a good cousin and community member, and helping Jack to his appointment next week."

"What?" Mother said, looking at Auntie J. "I didn't know that."

"Maybe I assumed you knew. It was approved."

Mother and Father looked at each other, then down. I tried to catch Mother's gaze, but she was looking at Cass and then at Andie, my younger brother.

Conversation kept up for the rest of the night, but Mother and Father didn't say much and had to be drawn out. After we left, I thought back over the night. They only answered questions, and they talked, sometimes at length, but they weren't much for making conversation, and I dominated the table more than I'd ever had.

When we got home that night, Mother asked, "Why didn't you tell me you'd agreed to take him again?"

"I didn't agree. I didn't realize. I guess it makes sense that's why we went to dinner. Didn't you know? Didn't Auntie J ask you first?"

"Must've forgot," Mother said.

A week later, I pick Cousin Jack up. Like last time, he comes down with a strainer. Even has one for me. Like last time, Auntie J gently reprimands him and sends us on our way. The journey's even smoother than before, but after I sign Cousin Jack in at reception, they eye me strangely while I wait for the headphones.

"Sorry, the toilet's that way," the receptionist says, clearly annoyed.

"Oh, I was waiting for those headphones. Y'know, the augmented ones."

"Those are actually only for first-time chaperones. Please wait with your patient," the receptionist says. I sit down next to Cousin Jack. I feel uneasy. Jacky isn't exactly calm, but he also isn't shaking the fucking earth like last time.

"Jack. Jack. A13Q."

The scrubs show up, but the whole vibe is much less ominous than the last time.

Guess this is no one's first rodeo, I think to myself as they lead him away. I'm glad to have less of a crowd around Cousin Jack when they take him in, unlike last time. The thought that I'm maybe a responsible party here helps all of this go more according to plan and makes me a little proud.

It isn't a minute more until I hear Jack screaming from behind the door past the reception desk. It's angry, shrieking, pain-filled wailing. At first, I assume it's someone else.

"A13Q support," comes over the intercom. I look up. A gaggle of tall men, some in long coats and brimmed hats, stand over me. A scrub emerges from the door and walks over to uniformed security. The scrub makes a gesture and they both come over to me.

"Hi," the scrub says. "You're Jack's party, right?"

"Uh…chaperone, yeah."

"Well, Jack's having an adverse reaction to the treatment, and we'd like it if you could come in the room and help keep him calm."

"Um…okay. If you think it'll help."

The scrub, the security, and the tall folks all move with me as I make my way to the door. I look back and realize that while the scrub is next to me, everyone else is positioned so I can't move back, only forward.

The door opens, we go through, it shuts and locks. We walk through what looks like a dentist's office, and I can make out screams, maybe, but they're mixed with a din of drilling and jack-hammering. Once we make it far enough down the corridor, it gets colder and quieter except for the muffled screaming. The scrub opens the door, puts her hand at the small of my back without actually touching me, and ushers me into the room.

Except it isn't quite a room. Cousin Jack is there strapped to a gurney, screaming frantically, each howl loaded with pain. On one side is a scrub and on the other is someone in a lab coat. The room itself is dark and dimly lit. Only the side I'd entered from is a room with walls. Not far from where the gurney device is, the floor fades into a dark mass that ripples. The other end of the room is nothingness, pitch-black eternity.

Perched over Cousin Jack is something I can't make out. I stare hard and then something in my vision twists and it emerges, its head twisting as well and staring into me. Only for a second.

"He's here. I've brought him," the scrub says. Then, "Look at Jack, please."

I do, without thinking, and he immediately turns his head and looks deep into my eyes. Then the creature grabs his chin and turns Jack's face so it's looking ahead. Jack stops screaming. The man in the lab coat sticks a long, sharp white tool I've never seen before into Cousin Jack's cranium and scores it with a scalpel-like thing. He goes halfway around Jack's head. He grabs some flat, thin tool and wiggles it into the crevice, then starts shifting the skull until there's a *pop*. He shimmies the top of Jack's head then just sort of pulls it off. I'm staring at Cousin Jack's brain. He's staring at the creature, eyes wide with pain and fear.

The creature—I can't look directly at it, but from the blur it looks kinda like it's on two legs and thin. It leans over him and sticks something like a wiggling tongue out of its face. It licks the rim of Cousin Jack's skull around and around, making noises as it does.

Cousin Jack starts wailing again. He screams the whole rest of the time.

The creature does another lick around the rim, then pulls Cousin Jack's head closer and does it again. There's a flashbang, and I hear for just a split second the sound I'd heard the first time in those headphones, and I can now see a neon blue slime along the rim of Cousin Jack's skull that the creature slurps at greedily. The flash ends and the neon blue is gone. The creature continues to lap for a moment, then backs away. The doctor places Cousin Jack's skulltop back over his brain, then takes another tool I'd never seen before and starts lasering it back together.

"Thanks for helping us out," the scrub says, ushering me out of the chamber. "Now, don't think that talking about this is going to make things easier."

"What is that?" I manage to ask while shaking uncontrollably.

"I only know what I'm told, but *they're* here. That skull rim goop is a favorite snack, maybe a delicacy, I think, and we've agreed to provide it," the scrub says. "It's not a small industry."

"*We?* I didn't agree. Pretty sure my cousin didn't."

"I didn't either, but I'm guessing *someone* did. On behalf of your community. Your cousin didn't just end up here. Neither did you."

They sit me down in reception, and I stay until Cousin Jack returns, sad, scared, pathetic. Maybe not, actually. He's calm, more than cowed.

Once we're on the escalator, I try to say something, but it won't come out. Only once we're down and out of the medical complex and waiting for the bus does Cousin Jack look at me with sympathetic eyes and say, "Cousin, just so you know, the strainers don't help. Even if Mother doesn't take them away before you go. They've seen you now. Thought you should know. You're pretty much on the list."

INTRUSIVE THOUGHTS THAT ARE NOT YOUR OWN

T.T. MADDEN

MOSES AND LILY Green had just finished work on the nursery and were in the middle of celebratory lovemaking when they heard their neighbor spontaneously combust. They did not know that was the source of the sound in the moment, distracted as they were by one another's flesh. Mo laid on his back, Lily astride him. They held one another's hands, reveling in the contrast of their flesh, her white thighs over his dark hips.

They were shaken out of marital bliss when the enormous *KRA-KOOM* reverberated throughout the neighborhood, rattling their windows and shaking their bed. Mo's first thought was that it was an earthquake, and he pulled Lily, half-wrapped in their bedsheets, into the doorway. They both stood there holding their breath and each other, waiting for an aftershock.

"You all right?" Mo asked.

Lily nodded. "You?"

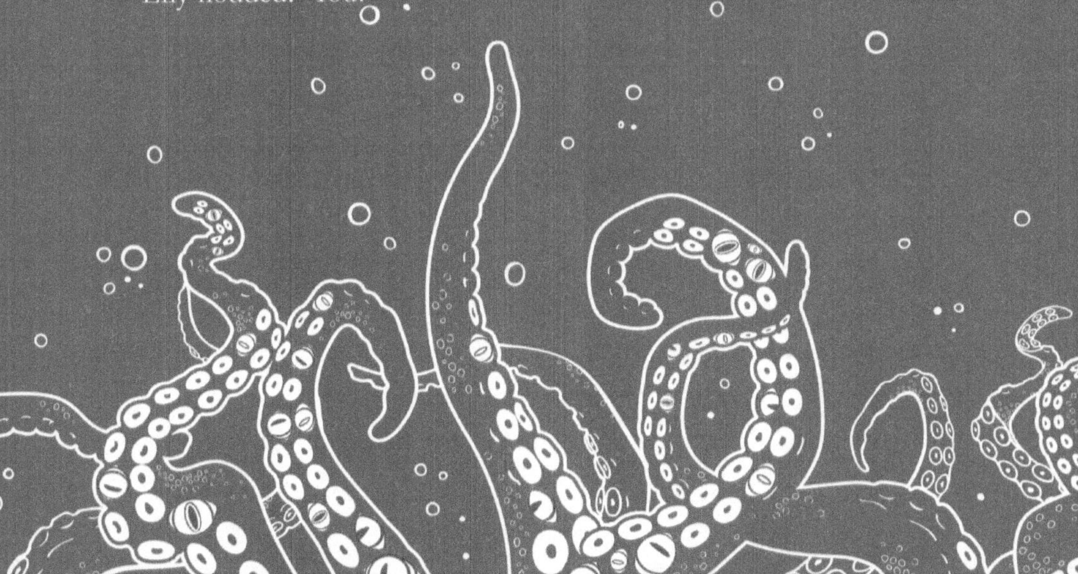

The follow-up came a moment later, when their neighbor, Arthur Jeremy, burst out his front door and onto his lawn, completely engulfed in flames. Mo and Lily heard the crash, heard the roar of the flames, and Arthur's scream as he came barreling out into the night, flailing wildly. They darted to the window, watched in horror as Arthur stumbled out into the street, his screams slowly dying away as he collapsed into a burning, charred lump.

The whole neighborhood had gathered around to look.

Despite the fact that they had to dress, Mo in a t-shirt and basketball shorts, and Lily in a nightgown that was hastily thrown over her head, they got there first. The fire had gone out quickly. Any traces of the individuality of Arthur Jeremy had burned away completely; his graying hair and glasses gone. All that was left was a charred, featureless husk. The fire had contorted him, shriveled him, left him looking like a corpse found in a tomb in an old adventure film. Most couldn't stand the sight for more than a few seconds. Even more could not handle the smell; a few neighbors didn't even make it over to the scene before they covered their noses and mouths, turned around or moved downwind, still wanting to *see*, but not really wanting to face it. Not wanting to *know*. Not really.

Mo and Lily had only ever known the man in passing. Enough to make the standard friendly neighborhood chitchat about the weather, or their respective gardens, or how Congress needed to get it together. Friendly, but never overstayed his welcome. But how well had they *really* known him, Lily thought, looking at his corpse. Was this an accident, or was it deliberate? If it was, who would do this to themselves?

"What happened?" Mo asked the rubberneckers at large, not really expecting an answer.

"We don't know," said Mrs. Olsen, a widow who lived a couple doors down. "You got here first." When she looked at Mo, it was with the same casual contempt he was unfortunately used to from her, as if she couldn't believe *one of them* was a part of her neighborhood.

Between them, Arthur Jeremy's remains smoldered and popped like logs in a fireplace.

By the time the police arrived, Mo and Lily had relocated to their front porch, away from the crowd, the corpse, and, more importantly, the smell. Largely, everyone had drifted away, content with a glimpse of the gore, but not to linger in it. Their morbid curiosity had been satisfied, and they needed no more of the truth of it.

Mo tensed when he saw the red-and-blue lights. Lily felt it and put a hand on his shoulder. The cop car had a presence about it. Something Mo couldn't quite pin down. It was like it brought a weight with it into the neighborhood, an oppression that sat across his shoulders and pressed him into the earth. The car itself was too shiny and polished, reflecting its own lights, the streetlights, the moonlight. A thing that demanded to be seen, to take up space in the world. It parked across the street, the crowd parting so it could illuminate Arthur Jeremy's corpse in its headlights.

When the officer stepped out of the vehicle, Mo felt that heaviness amplify, as if the car were merely a filter and that feeling was really coming from the man in the uniform. The cop sauntered onto the scene, into the crowd, and talked among them. After a moment, Mrs. Olsen pointed in the direction of Mo and Lily, and, as one, the crowd turned and followed the line of her finger right to them. The Greens could feel them, as if they were suddenly under a spotlight. They scooched closer, each feeling like their only protection in the world.

The cop approached.

"It's okay," Lily whispered into her husband's ear, her hands rubbing his stiff shoulders. "I'll talk to him." She was merely cautious before the police, where Mo was, very rightfully, afraid. He grunted in response, knowing from experience that a self-appointed shield did little to help in these situations, no matter what that shield looked like. But nevertheless, grateful.

The cop strode up the front walk, hands on his belt like a cowboy in a western film. At this distance, Mo and Lily could see the Thin Blue Line decal on the back of the phone clipped to his belt. Lily squeezed her husband's shoulders tighter. Mo's mouth went dry.

"Good evening, sir," the cop said.

"Hello," Lily said.

"Ma'am, I was talking to your boyfriend."

"My husband," Lily corrected. She tilted her hand slightly to display her ring. The cop didn't respond, just made a grumbling sound.

"Your neighbors said you discovered the body. Can you tell me what happened?"

Mo explained exactly what had happened. Nothing more, nothing less. He kept his tone flat, like he was trained to do, told the cop only the facts, kept his emotion out of it. Not that he had any emotion at the moment, he realized. His brain had activated some shut-off switch, something he needed in order to interact with the officer.

"Just ran outside," the cop said, mostly to himself. And then, to them, but really to Mo, "I'm not gonna find any signs of forced entry, am I?"

"How would I know?" Mo asked. "We weren't here."

"Where were you?"

"In our house."

"Doing…what?" the cop droned on, seeming to know the truth. What else would a newly married couple be doing, awake in their bedroom, in the middle of the night? The way he said it, though, it was like he was egging Mo on, like he wanted to hear him say it, to admit it. The look on his face was like a child's at such a realization: simultaneously disgusted and entertained. Trying to hide his embarrassed smile, like he wanted to hear more, even though he couldn't stand the thought.

The rumors started the morning after Arthur Jeremy ran burning out into the street.

What was inside his house?

In a room that one of the responding officers had accidentally stumbled upon.

Gary Holt from next door told Lily everything when she went out to get the mail. The Greens hadn't stayed outside, went back to bed, if not back to sleep, immediately after the cop released them. They didn't see the ambulance come, Gary said, didn't see the police officers go inside.

They didn't see the secret closet.

Gary could see the *whole* thing from his front yard, he told her; the angle was perfect. He watched as the officers pored over Arthur's living room, cataloging the burn marks and soot stains inside, trying to figure out how exactly he'd set himself on fire. One of them bumped into the wall, Gary said, hands animated, and that's when the wall slid away. That's when the secret door popped open and he saw what was inside.

The guns. Enough to start an army.

The flags of dead nations and lost wars.

The old, leather-bound books and the disturbing symbols scrawled on the walls, into them.

And the white suit with the capirote.

The Greens tried to resume some sort of normalcy after the night of Arthur Jeremy's immolation, but how did you ever go back to normal after that? After seeing your neighbor burst into flames and run screaming out into the street? After seeing his charred, curled corpse, melted, eyeless sockets staring up into the night? If some detective or medical examiner figured out how it happened, that news didn't make it back to either of them.

Mo tried to go for his daily jog, but something was amiss. He could feel the eyes of his neighbors on him, suspicious. An old woman he recognized but couldn't name shifted her purse to the other side of her body as she got out of her car. Other joggers crossed the street when he came by. From their gardens or front porches, his neighbors watched him, as if convinced he did not belong in this place. Mo lowered the music in his headphones, knowing he had to be more aware of the world around him.

At their house, Lily tried to weed the front yard. When she looked up and saw Mo returning from his jog, she screamed, completely sure he was some sort of interloper. Someone come to this neighborhood from a decayed city, bringing crime and violence with him. Someone intent on violating her (again?).

"It's just me," Mo said, maintaining his distance, holding his hands out before him so that none of their neighborhood witnesses could accuse him of doing anything untoward. Why, though, was he suddenly thinking that?

"Mo?" Lily asked, as if she'd forgotten not just his name, but him entirely.

"Yeah, Lil," he said. "Yeah, it's me."

They tried to paint the nursery but ended up simply standing in the middle of the room, looking at it.

"There's something…" Lily started, a paintbrush in her hand. There was a feeling she couldn't identify, something gnawing at the back of her mind, but not like it was part of it. A nagging, external thought. It reminded her of that left-the-stove-on feeling (she even thought she could smell smoke). Like she'd forgotten something, and she needed to leave this place immediately to attend to it, but couldn't figure out what *it* was.

"Yeah," Mo agreed. "Something…" He felt wrong being there, but in a different way. Struck with the sudden feeling that this was someone else's house, someone else's wife. That he wasn't supposed to be here in the suburbs, but in the city. With people more like him. It felt like he should run, like he should go back to where he came from. Before he was found out. What did *that* mean? Where had that thought come from?

"It's like…it's humid."

"But not," Mo finished. "More like smokey." There was a weight in the air, just like there had been with the cop and the car, that told them the mere existence of this nursery was wrong.

It was all she wanted. All they'd been trying for a year now. So, why, when Lily looked at the little pink stick that said PREGNANT, did she feel such sorrow? No, not sorrow. That wasn't an adequate word.

Horror.

Shame.

Like she'd been violated. She slipped off the toilet and curled up on the bathroom floor, sobbing silently. It felt like she had a monster growing inside her. If she told her family, they would be of no help. They would disown her.

These are not my thoughts. Lily remembered how much they loved Mo when she introduced them, how thrilled they were at the engagement party, the wedding. Those memories were real. They were her. So, what was this new feeling now? It couldn't be pregnancy hormones, not this early.

Lily felt that invisible weight from the cop and the car, from the nursery. She lay there on the bathroom floor, her hand over her mouth, trying to claw her way out from under that pressure, smelling not the cool, clean tile, but fire and burning skin.

Mo and Lily had inadvertently put off lovemaking since the night Arthur died. It wasn't deliberate. There was always a reason; they were stressed, tired, antsy. Some of them were precisely reasons to do the deed, but they had avoided it because of some nagging feeling in the backs of their minds. Some feeling they couldn't explain that told them they shouldn't. Neither of them had put together yet that every time those feelings arose, they were accompanied by that invisible weight. By the smell of smoke. The scent of burning flesh.

When they finally tried it, they opened their eyes in the dark only to find unexpected horrors staring back at them. Instead of her husband, Lily Green found a hairy, flat-faced abomination thrusting into her. In place of his wife's ecstatic expressions that he was used to, Mo saw a terrified face streaming with tears. The smell of the smoke, of the fire, of burning human flesh, was more powerful than ever.

"What's happening to us?" Lily asked later, after both their tears and screams had stopped. "Are we losing our minds?" They sat together on their marital bed, Lily's back against Mo's chest, wrapped in his arms.

"Is it Arthur?" Mo asked. Could Arthur's burnt corpse be the answer? Were they suffering from some form of PTSD?

"I think it is," Lily said, looking up. "But not because of how we saw him." She remembered what Gary had told her. "I think it's because of what he did."

They smelled smoke and burning flesh.

It was terrifying, it was impossible, but somehow it made sense. Arthur had done this to them. He'd made them feel insane. Made them distrust one another. Made them fear one another. This had all started the night after he died.

And they needed to find out how. And why.

They waited until the cover of night, and Mo wondered if the front door to the house was unlocked because Arthur lived in the neighborhood he did, or because he was dead. *No*, he thought, if Arthur was alive he would've locked it, but would've done so only because of the presence of Mo, right across the street.

Mo immediately knew Arthur Jeremy was a different kind of people to have not a picture, but a *portrait* of himself in the house; hanging above the fireplace was a stern-looking man with a large nose and ears, his short hair parted at the side. He wore thin, wire-framed glasses, and his narrow lips were sealed together, as if barely containing some curse, judging by the expression on his face.

He's mad we're here, Mo thought. A bizarre thought, but at least he was sure this one was his own.

"It's here," Lily said.

The secret room was right where Gary said it would be.

But what was inside was not exactly how he'd described it. He'd been far away, Lily thought, across the street and two large lawns. He saw the right shape, but the details had blurred at a distance, forming something recognizable, something he knew existed already. The reality was different. The flag, for instance, was a white circle inside a field of red, but the shape in the center, the black twist Gary had mistaken for a swastika, was actually a curl of dark tentacles. The white suit with the capirote was the same, but where Mo and Lily expected a red cross on the breast, they instead found a crest depicting some multi-headed serpent.

"This isn't..." Mo trailed off. He looked at the symbols written on the walls all around them. Esoteric glyphs he had no reference for.

"I know." She stepped further into the closet.

"What are you doing?"

"There's something back here," Lily said. A curtain draped over the back of the closet and, indeed, Mo saw it flutter as Lily approached it. She pulled it back and revealed a little nook. Within there was a small altar: candles, a thick, leather-bound book, and a picture. No, not a picture, it was older than that. It was one of those daguerreotypes, protected by a thick paper frame. It appeared to show an image of the sea. There was something inside it, something below it, a massive, dark shape, unidentifiable.

"This is where he did it," Mo said. The floor where they stood was very clearly scorched, as if someone had set a fire directly on the hardwood.

And then, a new voice, "See, that's the problem with you people…"

Mo and Lily turned and found a police officer—the same police officer—standing in the doorway to the secret room.

"Always sticking your noses where they don't belong." He looked at Lily, eyes impossible to see behind his sunglasses, but there was something back there. Something *writhing*. "Ma'am, is this man bothering you?" The smile he gave was too wide for his face.

Both Mo and Lily tried to step in front of each other, to protect one another, which made the cop chuckle. They settled for standing side-by-side, holding hands.

"Things were easier back in the day, you know," the cop said, stepping fully into the room. "Used to be the sun went down and we wouldn't have to worry about any of you. If you were even here at all. The ones who were foolish enough to be out when the sun went down, well, we could deal with y'all ourselves. Used to be—" another step, "—we wouldn't have to worry about our women being sullied by their evil magicks. Which is why we tried a little magick of our own." He gestured to the altar behind them.

"We," Mo echoed, and the final revelation kicked into place for both him and Lily. "This was all of you. The whole neighborhood?"

"And who said you people weren't smart?" Somewhere behind him, a door opened, and they heard more people shuffle into the house. Shapes appeared over the cop's shoulder, shapes Mo and Lily recognized as their neighbors. Gary Holt. Mrs. Olsen.

"You see, it always happens the same way," the cop said. "You people come in from the city, and the decay and all the trouble there follows you. It's only a matter of time until more follow in your wake. And then what happens to this beautiful neighborhood here? We all have to pick up and move somewhere else. And how is that fair? We were here first."

Mo had no idea how they were going to make it out of this. A cop, an entire neighborhood against them. He shifted slightly, moving in front of Lily, his hand in front of her stomach. Something dawned on him. He remembered the smell of fire, of burned flesh, but as a memory, not a spell.

"You forgot about one possibility," Mo said. He glanced at Lily only briefly. He had his hand on her stomach, twitched his fingers slightly, and she grabbed his wrist in response. She got it. It was enough to get her to understand, to follow his lead. Mo turned back to the crowd. "You forgot about what happens if people like me—"

"Like *us*," Lily added, for she was like her husband.

"When people like us start *breeding*." He said it with the vitriol he expected from their response, and he received it in kind. The neighbors all looked from him to Lily, to her stomach, and the realization dawned on their faces. They looked horrified, and he even saw a couple of them recoil in shock and horror.

He only smiled.

"What are you going to do, then?" Lily asked, holding her husband's hand tighter. They felt something tickle in the air around them, a pressure drop like before a storm, and their neighbors recoiled in awe of it, this invisible, intangible force. The force swelled and ballooned, growing stronger, coming directly from where Mo and Lily stood, and it made its way outward, crashing over the assembled group, sending a scream through the crowd. Mrs. Olsen lifted her hands and covered her eyes. Gary Holt began babbling incoherently. The cop reached for his gun, but his limbs suddenly stopped working, spasming uncontrollably. The crowd that faced them, that had once hemmed them in, scattered wildly, allowing Mo and Lily to walk right through them, unbothered. The crowd ran out into the house. They threw themselves onto the lawn. They bashed their own heads against the walls, trying to drive the images from their brains.

Their perfect world destroyed.

Their illusion shattered.

Their madness, their thoughts, entirely their own.

ELDRITCH MOON

JG FAHERTY

Their time is nigh.

I can feel it. Smell the stink of it in the sea air that reaches me through my window. Hear it in the distant primordial cries that sometimes shatter the silence of the night.

Soon, soon.

They're coming.

I know it. I try to tell them, but no one listens.

Just like they didn't listen fifty years ago.

There has long been a rumor among conspiracy theorists that the Apollo 11 landing on the Moon never happened, that the video was shot in a secret NASA hangar.

That rumor is both wrong and right.

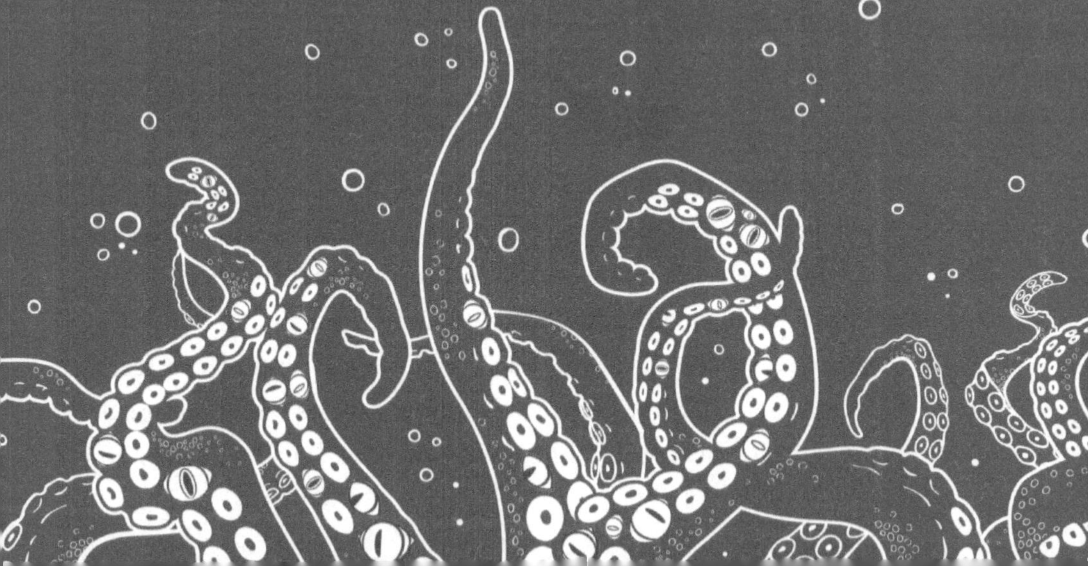

Mankind did land on the moon. More than once. However, the videos released to the world were fakes. All of them. I know this for a fact.

Because I was the first one there.

In 1967, while the rest of the country turned out and tuned in, celebrating the Summer of Love by experimenting with free sex and dangerous drugs, I spent my days and nights preparing to leave Earth for real.

Because we had learned we were not alone.

The first U.S. spacecraft to circumnavigate the moon was Lunar Orbiter 1, in 1966. NASA expected it to be a routine, if groundbreaking, mission. Map the moon in preparation for a planned landing a few years later.

Instead, it brought back information that turned NASA's goals of exploration and discovery into a top-secret military program. Suddenly, stone-faced men in dark suits ran the show. Funding NASA could have never hoped for poured in and research accelerated.

To the public, nothing changed. Mercury gave way to Gemini, Gemini to Apollo. The nation celebrated our rapid successes in spaceflight, never knowing the reason behind them.

On December 24, 1967, NASA launched a spacecraft. Officially listed as an unmanned satellite deployment, it was actually the first of the Verne missions, Verne 1. Its goal: conduct an ultra-low reconnaissance of the moon's dark side.

I was one of three people chosen for that team.

Although I'd studied the pictures from the orbiters, nothing prepared me for what I saw as our module, nicknamed Columbiad after Verne's *From the Earth to the Moon*, crossed the terminator and approached the Tsiolkovsky Crater at an altitude of three hundred meters. My co-pilot, Frank Dodd, and I operated the module. The third member of our team, Larry Piffner, remained in the capsule. Communications with the capsule were spotty at best; there were times we'd lose our signal to Larry for minutes or even hours. Still, we maintained a running commentary for the recorders.

"Coming up on the crater's edge," Dodd said, his voice tinny in my helmet radio.

"Roger that," came Piffner's crackling reply.

I looked up from my instruments and gasped, a sound echoed by Dodd on my right.

It was immense.

More than one hundred miles across and three miles deep. We'd timed our approach to just after sunrise, and the shadow of the central mount stretched on and on. While not tall by Earth standards—half the height of Kilimanjaro—it dwarfed the hills and protrusions around it.

"Beginning our descent." The plan was to circle the mount and then explore the crater. Our radios hissed and sputtered, Piffner's voice lost in the static.

Minutes later, we saw them.

Angular lines cut into the sides of the mount. And at the base, triangular shapes scattered in small groups.

"Jesus. Are those pyramids?" Dodd's voice mirrored my apprehension. The orbiter pictures hadn't lied.

At one time, there'd been life on the moon.

I glanced at Dodd. This was why we'd traveled nearly 240,000 miles in an untested tin can. He nodded, and I gave the order that sealed our fate.

"Let's take a look."

The pyramids were about one hundred feet tall—smaller than the structures at Giza, large as some of the Mayan ruins in Mexico. Staring at them caused a certain disquiet. They were wrong somehow, and I wanted to stay as far from them as possible, although if asked, I couldn't have said why.

"Not so close," Dodd said, and I wondered if he shared my uncertainty. My hand actually started to pull back on the joystick, and I had to force myself not to follow my instincts. We had a job to do.

So, despite my growing unease, I took us down until we were nearly even with the tops of the pyramids. From that height, every detail became visible. Gray and white stones carved with uncanny precision. I took us on a slow curve and we discovered another surprise. Dark areas at the base of the mount.

The mouths of caves.

"Signs of excavation at the base of the mount." I spoke for the benefit of those who would listen later. "I'm taking us in for a closer look."

"Don't," Dodd whispered. I wanted to comply. But we had orders.

We dipped another fifty feet while my entire being shouted at me to do the opposite. The feeling of dread grew to an almost palpable terror, a primal fear like what our ancient ancestors must have felt listening to howling in the darkness.

Dodd moaned and shook his head, but his hands remained steady on the camera controls, hundreds of hours of training winning out over instinct.

"Larry, are you getting this?" When Piffner didn't answer, I repeated my question. "Verne One, I repeat. Are you receiving our images?"

Space noise and static were my only answers.

"Another fifteen minutes before he crests the lip," Dodd said.

I weighed our options. Circle the mount, leave the crater and continue mapping, or land.

This is a military mission, John. We don't just want to know if something is there. We need to know if it poses a threat." General Roger Lear's last words to me before our departure.

"Prepare to land," I said. Dodd's lips tightened but he nodded.

We slowed the module and touched down with only a couple of bumps on the uneven surface, the closest pyramids two hundred yards to our left and one of the caves about the same distance to our right.

I unbuckled my harness, but before I could tell Dodd to prepare for an extravehicular walk, he pointed out the window.

"Look."

The surface of the nearest pyramid flickered in the bright sunlight. It took me a moment to realize the entire structure was swiveling on its base, revealing an opening in the ground.

"Shit." I lunged for the ignition controls. How long for a hot restart? Ten seconds? Eight?

Dodd gasped and my stomach clenched as an enormous, pallid, gelatinous creature burst from the hole and rushed toward us on dozens of multi-jointed, insectoid legs. Larger than our module, with bulging eyes scattered across its amorphous shape. I wanted to scream but my throat constricted, strangling my cries.

"Starboard! Starboard!" Dodd's shouts turned my head to the other window and now my scream escaped as more of the abominable monsters emerged from the caves.

The module rumbled beneath me, and I gave a triumphant shout. The engines had caught!

"Prepare for thrust!" I yelled to Dodd. "We have—"

The ship gave a violent lurch, cutting off my words and flinging me against the side of the tiny cabin. Red and orange lights flashed around me. I had time to see a giant, yellow eye staring in at us. Then the ship slammed back to the surface.

Something struck my head, and the lights disappeared.

I came to in Hell.

Stone walls surrounded me, their surfaces obscured by drawings of repellent creatures, images so unpleasant my stomach rebelled at the sight of them. Pseudopodial beings with bat wings and crab faces. Larval horrors with humanoid arms. Octopi with giant eyes that somehow conveyed a malevolent intelligence despite their crude depiction. A thing that resembled crawling entrails with dozens of mouths.

In those first few terrifying moments, I felt sure the vile entities were real. The primitive figures moved across the surface, lunging out at me with gnashing teeth and vicious claws.

At the same time, strange sounds filled my head. Antediluvian growls and rumbles and wheezes, as if I'd been transported to a prehistoric jungle. Strange words in a language I didn't know produced the most dreadful sensations in my body, aural knives carving bits of my soul away and filling the holes with poisonous slime.

"Cthulhu R'lyeh wgah'nagl fhtagn... Ch'yar ul'nyar shaggoth... ng'throd uh'e..."

Bizarre colors and shapes accompanied the depraved syllables: floating, twisting globules of sickly yellow and corpse green, more and more of them until I started to wonder if I'd never left Earth at all, if in fact I'd been dosed with LSD as part of the CIA's ongoing experiments.

I squeezed my eyes shut. With the images gone, the colors diminished and the whispers faded. My mind was my own again. I waited to see if the whispers reappeared. When they didn't, I opened my eyes.

Everywhere I looked, more of the offensive depictions waited to pollute my brain. The urge to escape them, to run until they no longer defiled my thoughts, brought me to my feet in a leap that sent me several yards into the air, thanks to the lower gravity.

My next steps were more careful.

Averting my gaze from the carvings, I examined the rest of the chamber, which was about a hundred feet in width and lit by an unknown source high above me. Whenever the drawings began to move, or the whispers started up in my head, I closed my eyes and counted until they disappeared.

Just thinking about the formless things I'd seen sent shivers through me. Where were they? What did they have planned for me? What about Dodd?

In this fashion, I navigated the chamber until I happened upon a square section of wall, twice my height and width, unsullied by any of the dreadful pictographs. I pressed my hands against it. The slab immediately slid open to reveal a long, dimly lit tunnel constructed from featureless gray stone.

My dread doubled as I crossed that threshold. I turned, expecting the door to close behind me, but it remained open. I resumed my walk, alert for any movements or signs of a trap. Not that I had any idea what an alien trap might look like. Their technology obviously so far exceeded our own as to make us cavemen in comparison.

How could Earth possibly hope to defend itself against such a threat?

I paused as my question birthed a different thought.

What evidence did I have of a threat?

Yes, the creatures we'd seen had appeared to attack us. But was it an attack or simply a detainment? Had they done anything my own government wouldn't have done if an alien vessel landed right in the center of a city?

And who were we to judge them as dangerous just by their monstrous appearance? After all, they'd been on the moon for a while. Maybe centuries. If they'd wanted to attack Earth, surely they could have done so already.

I resumed walking, suddenly unsure of my own species' motivations. Perhaps we were the ones to be wary of. Mankind had a history of violence. Countries poised on the brink of nuclear annihilation, missiles ready to launch at the first hint of provocation. Wars raging over petty things such as color or religion or invisible boundaries.

Perhaps the aliens should be worried about us.

Lost in contemplation, I almost passed the faint outline of another door.

Like before, I pressed on the stone and it slid back, exposing a chamber very similar to the one I'd awoken in, complete with arcane drawings.

Frank Dodd lay motionless on the floor.

I covered the distance between us in three twenty-foot strides, landing in a crouch next to his still form. A quick check revealed no visible damage to his space suit, so I shook him, gently at first and then with more force. I'd suddenly become convinced we needed to get away as fast as possible, despite my previous musings. Perhaps it was the return of the whispers in my head, and with them my nausea.

Dodd's eyelids fluttered and then opened.

"What…the hell…?"

"It gets worse." I helped him to his feet. "If you see anything…weird, or hear things in your head, just look away and think about something else. Counting works well."

Dodd gave me a funny look. "What kinds of things?"

Now it was my turn to frown. He couldn't hear them? It sounded like dozens of tiny demons had taken root in my brain, muttering and chanting

"Cthulhu-nyth…ph'shagg…gof'nn…"

Repellent figures danced on the walls again. It was time to leave.

"C'mon, there's a passage outside. Maybe it leads out."

Dodd followed me, walking in silence, his lips tight and his eyes focused straight ahead. My attempts to question him were met with curt shakes of his head, and I couldn't tell if he didn't remember or didn't want to say.

Ten minutes brought us to another doorway. By then, my low-grade dread had grown into full-blown fear. I wanted out of the tunnel, out of the entire edifice. I wanted to get the hell off the moon and never return. They could have it, these alien beings with their vile art and macabre science.

Benign creatures or not, at that moment I would have gladly given the order to drop a few A-bombs into the Tsiolkovsky Crater.

Just as a field mouse senses the danger of a hidden rattlesnake, so too did I sense impending peril. Despite the humid, stuffy air inside my suit, a chill danced along my skin and the sweaty bristle of hair on my neck stood at attention.

I glanced at Dodd. His eyes were closed, his helmet partially fogged from his rapid breathing. Remembering his panic in the module forced me to temper my own fright. We couldn't let ourselves lose control.

I palmed the door and stood back as it opened, revealing another chamber.

One that seemed to go on forever.

Confronted with that unbelievable expanse, I froze. Behind me, Dodd gasped. The idea that any beings could construct something of such enormity…

Once the initial shock wore off, I realized the room wasn't limitless. Perhaps a quarter mile in length and width, although with such distances and only a dim, dusk-like light, I couldn't say for sure. The walls were featureless, thankfully. Unlike the other chambers, though, this one contained something.

In the center of the giant space stood a miniature pyramid, an exact duplicate of the ones on the surface, only about twenty feet in height. I used the low gravity to cross the distance in long bounds, Dodd trailing behind.

The pyramid turned out to be metal. No lights or controls marred its surface, yet I got the impression of a device. A thrumming of intense energy reached me, like standing by a generator.

Dodd approached it with his hand held out. I grabbed his arm before he could touch the object.

"Don't," I said. "It could be dangerous."

"No." He gave me an odd smile. "They want us to."

He pulled free and placed his hand on the flat surface.

And the universe exploded.

How does one describe the impossible?

I was blinded by vivid, brilliant blackness, drowned in odors, smothered by sounds. It was the ultimate trip, a supernatural journey through insanity.

My senses revolted against this assault on rationality and my equilibrium vanished. I floated and sank at the same time; my thoughts ran backwards in my head. I screamed and tasted the cold, green sounds with my skin.

Then it all vanished.

Gravity re-asserted itself, and I fell to my knees on an oily beach bordering an ocean of sludge. Horrid creatures—part fish, part bird, part amphibian—rose from the foul, thick waters, peered at me with mad eyes, and then sank below the foaming waves. Man-shaped beasts with four arms and tentacles instead of legs crept across the surface, snaring tiny flying animals with long, chameleon-like tongues.

The stench of the alien world reached me despite my airtight suit, a heavy stink like seafood-filled garbage cans on a hot summer day. I had to look away from the disgusting waters. Behind me, an endless plain stretched to the horizon where a line of distant mountains poked at the bilious yellow skies, their peaks hidden by violent storm clouds.

All of this was bad enough, but far worse were the creatures populating the dreadful landscape.

Even now, so many years later, I still find it impossible to put their awful countenances into words. Just attempting it causes a sickness of the spirit, a contamination of the mind.

Giant maggots with vestigial legs humped and crawled along the beach. Formless masses of bluish jelly floated through the air, dozens of red eyes searching all directions at once. An eyeless lizard squirmed in the talons of a hairless wolf that soared the air on bat wings. Fighting the urge to vomit, I turned to look for Dodd.

And found him next to me, a maniacal grin on his flushed, sweating face.

He grabbed my helmet, and once more we transported through space. This time, we ended up at the base of those alien mountains, staring up at the miles-long tempests, gigantic swirls of black and gray and yellow forming enormous whirlpools overhead. Purple lightning carved jagged lines through the violent sky, yet no thunder sounded.

Dodd turned me toward the mountains, which in fact were not mountains at all.

They were pyramids.

Rising up thousands of feet, their apexes shrouded by mists and clouds, the smallest would have dwarfed most mountains on Earth. Some resembled the pyramids of Egypt, with their smooth sides tapering sharply to points at the top. Others had external stairs and distinct levels, such as those found in Central and South America, or irregular sections that created castle-like appearances.

All of them had one thing in common: cavernous openings at their bases, hundreds of feet high and wide.

"Look," Dodd said, pointing to the nearest edifice. Something emerged from the cavernous black hole.

Even from a thousand yards away, the creature was more loathsome than anything I'd yet witnessed. Hundreds of feet long and octopodal, its barrel-shaped body glowed with deep purples and violets; its one colossal eye, faceted like a spider's, burned with the fires of Hell. Three pairs of jaws opened, revealing wriggling, snake-like tendrils that ended with lamprey-like sucker mouths. It jetted through the air, trailing noxious black vapors.

The monstrosity reached us in seconds and came to rest close enough for me to see the pustules and scars covering its hide. Cat-sized insectoid things scurried over its skin, darting from one fold to the next in search of God-knew-what.

"Behold, Ythogtha." The voice in my brain was deep, wet, commanding— and painful.

"Ythogtha," Dodd repeated, his voice colored with awe rather than the pure terror coursing through me.

"You will return home." A new voice. Each syllable caused my bowels to release and blood to drip from my nose. I knew if I listened to it for too long, it meant death.

As if it understood my weakness, the creature extended a tentacle and touched my helmet.

And I *saw*.

Vast armies of grotesque abominations, the depraved images from the chambers come to life. Amoeboid creatures, giant crustaceans, vaporous things with poison fangs. Tentacled beasts large and small, their appendages lined with hungry mouths. Tall, bipedal organisms with bald, elongated skulls. Sea monsters large enough to grab a battleship with their spider limbs and swallow it whole. Monsters half-toad and half-lobster emerging from steaming swamps.

All this and more, a world populated by the most despicable things ever imagined in Satan's worst nightmares. Along with the images came words: *Iod, Kassogtha, Lam, Byatis, Coatlique, Hastur, Nyalarthotep, Shabbith-Ka, Yidhra.*

The inhabitants of a planet called Leng.

Information flowed into me. Their scout ships landed on Earth a millennia ago, when mankind had just learned to form communities and plant crops. The Lengians found the new world to their liking. Using humans for slave labor, they built structures unlike anything ever seen before on Earth. Towering edifices that harnessed magnetic and solar energies to power grids that ran machines and beacons. Worshipped as gods, they oversaw the rise of the first cities, where they intended to wait out the centuries until their signals reached their home world and the colony ships completed the long trek across the wide gulf of space.

And then the unthinkable happened.

The humans revolted.

The monsters had done their job too well, taught the humans too much. Slaves took up weapons—spears, arrows, swords, and even the aliens' own— and attacked.

Great battles waged. Entire armies crushed or devoured, cities destroyed or sunk into the oceans. Eventually, the tenacity and sheer numbers of humans proved to be too much and the invaders were killed or dethroned.

The surviving star lords scattered. Some remained on Earth, frozen in ice at the poles or slumbering deep in the oceans. Others retreated to the moon. As time passed, they became the stuff of legend on Earth, the basis for tales of extraterrestrial visitors or ancient gods, passed down from one generation to the next.

And while our species thrived in the bliss of ignorance, the Old Ones who fled our planet built a new outpost and waited.

All of this, I learned in mere seconds. When Ythogtha broke the contact, we were back inside the great hall next to the metal pyramid. A repugnant sensation lingered in my head. I shook Dodd's arm to get his attention. He turned away from watching the Ythogtha jet back to its lair.

"I know where the exit is," he said.

So did I. That knowledge, and so much more, now resided within us. We clasped hands and closed our eyes.

And found ourselves in the pyramid chamber.

There was no time to consider the magic of this, to wonder if we'd been in that room the entire time or transported by the mystical capabilities of the Lengians. We exited the chamber and found ourselves on the Moon's surface. Fifty yards away, the lunar module waited on its spindly legs. We covered the distance in four great leaps and entered the cockpit. I initiated the launch sequence and took us up, desperate to put as much distance between us and the monstrosities below as I could.

The moment we crested the Tsiolkovsky Crater, Piffner's voice burst from the speakers in an explosion of static.

"—*Columbiad! Do you read me? Gogarty? Dodd? Can you hear me?*"

"Columbiad here," Dodd replied, his voice surprisingly calm.

"*Thank God! What happened? We lost communications with you hours ago.*"

"We're okay," Dodd said, and that odd smile appeared on his face again. I liked it even less the second time. "We've got a story for you. Prepare for a rendezvous."

We docked with Verne 1 thirty minutes later and immediately left orbit. During the four-day trip back to Earth, we maintained near radio silence following a single coded message that indicated the situation was more dire than previously anticipated.

We'd just begun re-entry when Dodd went crazy.

Shouting *"Gnaiih nnn'y!"* he unhooked his harness and smashed his hands on the control panel, firing the front and rear guidance rockets all at once. The module went into a tumble and only my harness saved me from getting tossed around the interior until my skull got crushed.

Piffner wasn't so lucky. His seat came unbolted partway, just enough to slam him into the side of the capsule. He cried out once and then went silent.

The capsule spun again and Dodd landed somewhere in the back of the cabin. Red lights flashed and the frantic voices of Mission Control filled my ears. I knew we were coming in too fast by the way the G-force pinned me in my seat. The temperature rose quickly, hot even through my suit. Smoke billowed from several consoles.

Then a miracle happened.

Somehow, our chute deployed despite the electrical shorts and mis-orientation of the capsule. A shock ran through the ship as it decelerated too rapidly, but the chute cables held. When the capsule struck the ocean, I instinctively hit the lever to blow the hatch and release our life-raft. Then I unstrapped and checked on Piffner.

He was dead, the side of his head crushed. I turned to see where Dodd had ended up, expecting to find him in a similar condition.

To my surprise, he stood by the open hatch, seawater cascading over his boots. I couldn't believe he'd survived. He'd taken his helmet off and his eyes were wild.

His mouth opened and a mass of tentacles emerged, connected to a slug-like body with eight jointed appendages. The foot-long creature fell into the ocean and disappeared. Another emerged, followed by dozens more. When the last of them swam off, Dodd smiled and stepped toward me. I backed away, knowing what he—or the thing he'd become—had in mind.

The capsule chose that moment to give a sharp lurch that knocked us both to our knees. We only had a few moments before it sank, but I was prepared to drown rather than become something like Dodd.

A thundering roar reached us. Rescue copters. Dodd stared at me. For a single heartbeat, his eyes burned red. Then he jumped into the life-raft.

They had to sedate me to get me out of the capsule.

No one believed me, of course. The Air Force released a story about me suffering a breakdown. I ended up the scapegoat for everything: Piffner's death, the sabotaged re-entry, even the hours of lost communications on the moon.

At first, I tried to reason with them—the doctors, my superior officers. During the long weeks as a prisoner in a military hospital, I begged and pleaded for people to believe me. Until the day General Platte showed up. The man who'd recruited me for the mission, the one who'd first shown me the pictures of the secret moon base.

He entered my room and spoke a single sentence.

"Ph'nglui mglw'nafh chtenff ch'nglui."

When he left, all my hopes went with him.

Not long after that, I got transferred to a psychiatric hospital in Massachusetts. I've been here ever since. I have a nice room; through the bars on my windows, I can see the ocean on one side and Miskatonic University on the other. I get to watch the news every night and read the paper every morning.

Men continued to visit the moon. Space stations became a reality. Astronauts from all nations partnered on scientific missions. And not a word about aliens or moon pyramids ever came out.

I'm an old man now. For more than fifty years, I've waited for Dodd's vile spawn to come forth. Waited while his contagion, his unearthly seed, spread through the halls of power around the world.

Through all those long years, Platte's sentence haunted me.

"Ph'nglui mglw'nafh chtenff ch'nglui."

Dead yet dreaming, the brothers cross the threshold.

Waited, and wondered, in quiet terror. Not because of his dire promise, but from something far worse.

What sleeps inside me that I could understand him?

BLUEFISH

DOUG BRUNELL

"IT LOOKS DIFFERENT, doesn't it?"

Jeff turned at the sound of his neighbor's voice. After taking his garbage can to the curb, he had been staring at the stars in the clear night sky and thinking about tomorrow's chores.

"I don't know," Jeff said. He looked up again. "Does it?" Jeff was fifty-five, widowed, and lived alone in one of the two houses in the cul-de-sac. Corey lived in the other with his wife, Mallory, and teenage son, Brad. There were three more houses being built, but it seemed like the building projects had all slowed at the same time.

Corey nodded. "I think it does. When I was a kid, I used to be an amateur astronomer. Well…I could identify a few constellations. I don't recognize these."

Jeff shook his head. The stars looked the same to him. "Corey, you're still a kid to me."

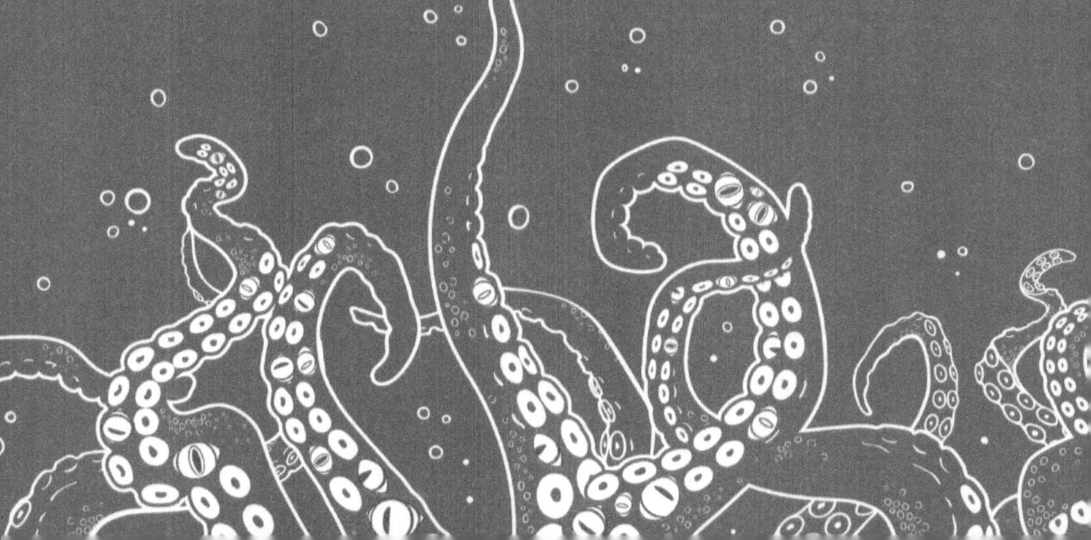

"Pushing forty," Corey said. He peered up into the sky and put his hands on his hips. "Yeah, they don't look right. I mean, the streetlight makes it hard to see some, but…"

"When did you notice?" Jeff asked.

"About an hour ago, I went to grab something from the car. I didn't think much of it, then I heard you take your can out and that reminded me to do the same." He looked around at the skeletons of the partially built houses around them and shuddered. "I don't like it."

Jeff changed the topic. "Wife and kid still visiting her folks?" He noticed the LED streetlight behind Corey's back flicker briefly.

"Yeah, they're back the end of next week. I have to clean house by then or a lecture *will be* delivered."

Jeff grinned. "You'd better, then. Look, I'm going to head in. It's going to be an early night for me."

"Sure." Corey looked up again and gasped. "Shit! Fuck! Look at that!"

Jeff tilted his head up and looked around. The stars and planets were gone. Not a single dot of light was visible in the night sky. He gave Corey a puzzled look. "What is that?"

Corey shook his head. "Clouds? Fog? I don't know." He looked up again. "What the hell is going on? It was crystal clear just a minute ago."

"You're the amateur astronomer," Jeff said. "Is this normal?"

The streetlight flickered again, and Corey turned to look at it. "That's weird," he mumbled.

Jeff dismissed him with a wave of his hand. "That's not that weird. Lights do that. *Is this normal?*" He pointed to the sky.

"No," Corey said. He had not taken his eyes off the streetlight. "It's not. There's no time the stars aren't visible at night…unless we are under clouds or fog, and those did not roll in that quickly. The sky was perfect for stargazing a minute ago."

"Stars don't just disappear," Jeff said.

"Nope. You got your cell phone?"

"I left it inside. It's been acting up the last few days, anyway. Dropping texts. No bars. Why?"

"I wanted to check the news."

"Where's your phone?"

"Inside. I've been having the same issues as you."

Jeff and Corey exchanged a nervous glance that quickly became one of surprise. Jeff asked, "Did you just feel that?"

"Like a small earthquake? Yeah."

"It got colder, too."

Corey noticed they were barely talking above a whisper. "I think we should go in."

The streetlight went dark, as did the one at the far end of the street. Jeff jumped. He looked back at their houses. None of the interior lights were on. They were in an inky darkness that filled him with unease.

Corey reached out and grabbed Jeff's arm. The absolute darkness made him dizzy.

"Do you have a gun?" Jeff asked. He tried to keep his voice steady.

"No. I thought you did."

"I got rid of it about a year ago. I was depressed after my wife's death. Didn't think it was good to keep around."

"Got it. I have a baseball bat by the bed. Knives in the kitchen, of course. You think we need them?"

"Well," Jeff said, "when we had those outages two years ago, we didn't have power, but most of Eureka still did. I could see the lights from the city over there. I don't see anything now."

"Everywhere is out?" Corey looked around and saw nothing that resembled a light source in the distance. His unease grew.

"I think so, and I really think we need to get the fuck inside."

"Okay," Corey said. "Let's go to my house. I've got candles and a flashlight that's easy to get to."

"Once they're lit, we better close the shades."

They sat at Corey's dining room table with a wide pillar candle lit between them. The baseball bat stood at Corey's side, propped up against the table. They'd tried several devices that ran on battery or house electric, and nothing had worked. Corey's cell phone was dead. The fridge was silent and the food growing warm, and the flashlight they found was a dud, too—though Corey admitted the batteries may have been old.

"So, what do we know?" Jeff asked. They were still talking in hushed tones.

"Stars are gone. Nothing electric works. Maybe something felt weird outside."

"It could have been nerves."

Corey nodded. "Maybe."

"Causes?"

Corey shrugged. "Terrorism? That's what it seems like."

"I don't know of any weapon that can make the stars disappear. Electronics shutting off? Sure. An EMP can do that. But the stars? What we felt?"

"We don't know if we *felt* anything."

"Okay. Let's discount that then. No odd feeling." Jeff didn't believe that, but he was happy to dismiss it for now.

"If not terrorism," Corey asked, "what?"

Jeff didn't know how to answer that.

"Hey, wait," Corey said. There was excitement in his voice. "Isn't there a big wildfire in Willow Creek?"

"Yeah."

"Maybe the smoke from that came over to our end and obscured the stars. That's possible. The smoke could be high enough that we couldn't even smell it. That *has* happened before."

"Sure," Jeff answered. "But that doesn't explain all the lights going out."

"PG&E shut the power down for public safety. They do that, remember?"

"We aren't close enough to the fire to do that. And what about your phone dying? You said it had eighty percent of its charge left."

Corey slumped in his seat. "Mallory. Brad," he muttered.

"You have to believe they're safe. Even if they're going through the same shit we are, they're safe."

Corey nodded. He wanted to believe that. He knew how Mallory felt about the dark, though. It terrified her and at that moment, he finally understood why.

Jeff tapped his fingers on the tabletop. The sound and motion of it helped him collect his thoughts. He did that whenever he needed to think.

"I didn't say anything earlier," Corey said. "I didn't want to sound crazy. I don't know, though…"

Jeff stopped tapping. "At this point, I want to hear everything. There is no crazy."

Corey pointed at the ceiling. "The stars? I said I thought they looked different."

"Yeah."

"I *know* they did. I *saw* them change."

Jeff leaned across the table. "*What?*"

"I didn't know what was happening. I thought I was seeing things or having a migraine. I don't know. It wasn't possible."

"How did they change? What do you mean?"

Corey ran his hand through his blonde hair. "I came out and initially you weren't looking up. I did, though. I saw the normal night sky, then all the stars sort of blurred and new ones started to appear. The old ones faded away and the new ones stayed."

Jeff leaned back in his seat. "Really?"

"Yeah. It was like a… What do they call that in the movies? A transition? One thing went out of focus, another came in. And then they were gone. Our sky got replaced." He gave a nervous chuckle. "Crazy, right?"

Jeff shook his head. "What if it wasn't the stars that were replaced? What if it was us? Our whole planet." He shivered. "It's getting colder," he said to explain away his reaction.

"Just because it's getting later," Corey said. He sounded like he was trying to convince himself.

"Or the sun is gone."

"Shouldn't we have frozen within a few minutes, then?"

"I don't know. This is new territory. I don't know the rules."

They sat in silence, watching the candle burn. Corey assured Jeff they had plenty of candles because Mallory had a "thing" for them.

Jeff finally spoke. "You know, I'm not tired. I'm not hungry. I'm not thirsty. I don't have the urge to go to the bathroom."

Corey shrugged and kept silent.

"You don't find that strange?"

"No. Stress does weird things to you."

"Are you any of those things?"

Corey thought for a moment. He started to answer, but instead just shook his head.

"Corey," Jeff urged, "don't get lost on me here."

Corey looked at him. "My wife and kid… I'm scared."

"I know. And they are probably scared, too, but they're with your parents. Your dad is an ex-cop. Hell, they're in better shape than we are. Assuming they even are going through the same thing. Everything could be normal there."

"It could be worse."

"They aren't in a big city. That would be worse if they had this blackout."

Corey nodded. "I'm going to light another candle."

"Why?"

"So I can take one out. I need to look around outside. I need to feel the bushes and grass, so I know they're there."

"Why wouldn't they be? The house is still here. I don't think going outside with a source of light is a good idea right now."

"Why not?"

"Because…it may make you a target."

"You think something is out there?"

"I don't know," Jeff said. "I'd rather we don't take the chance."

"Not 'we'," Corey corrected. "Me. I'm an adult. I can do what I want." He stood up from the table and grabbed a tall pillar candle from atop the hutch in the kitchen. He brought it to the table and lit it off the flame of the other candle. "Save matches," he said. "I'll blow this one out as soon as I'm back in."

A noise from outside startled them. It was a distant and faint howl like some large animal was in distress.

Jeff quickly blew out both candles.

"Hey!" Corey protested.

Jeff shushed him. "Quiet. No light."

"What was that?"

Jeff was breathing quickly. "I don't know. No light. And don't make any noise."

"It was far away," Corey whispered.

"It sounded so. I don't know, though."

"It sounded like a dying seal to me," Corey whispered. "I heard one of them before, down at the bay."

"Okay, let's ju—" He was cut off in mid-sentence by the sound of the doorknob at the front door turning.

They held their breath. Jeff began to sweat.

Corey stooped close to Jeff's ear. "Deadbolt is locked. Habit."

Whatever was on the other side of the door started to pull on the knob, rattling the door in its frame.

Jeff felt around the table for the matches. "Grab the bat," he whispered. He lit the candle. "We're going to need to see if it gets in."

Corey hefted the bat. "The light, though?"

"It knows we're in here."

"You sure it's an 'it'?"

Jeff shook his head. The door was being shaken violently now.

"Corey?"

Jeff and Corey gasped at the familiar voice.

"Mallory?" Corey called out. He started toward the front door, bat in hand and with Jeff holding the candle next to him.

"Open up. It's dark out here!"

"Tell us something, so we know it's really you," Jeff called out. They stopped walking when they got close to the door. Neither man wanted to get closer.

"Corey, *please*. It's dark. Cold. You know how I feel about the dark."

Jeff looked at Corey. "You feel something isn't right, don't you?"

Corey thought for a moment before nodding his head. Her voice didn't sound quite like Mallory's. There was a hint of something to it that sounded almost mechanical.

The doorknob rattled again. "*Corey!*"

"Go away, we're armed!" Jeff shouted. He turned toward Corey. "There's no way that's her. She could never have made it here in time."

"I was already on my way," the voice said. "I had to get back to you."

"Where's Brad?" Corey asked.

"He stayed behind. We all thought that was safer."

Corey took a step toward the door. Jeff reached out and placed his hand on his neighbor's arm. He shook his head.

"We're going to open fire through the door," Jeff said. "You better leave. And you better leave now."

There was a pause, then, "You don't have anything other than a candle and a baseball bat."

Jeff's eyes widened. He looked at Corey, who showed no emotion.

"Let us in."

"*Us*," Jeff whispered. "We need to get away from the door." He grabbed Corey's arm and started pulling him backward. Corey offered no resistance.

"*Let us in!*"

The demand seemed to come from all around, and then it was followed by pounding on the doors, walls, and windows throughout the house, including the windows upstairs. It was so loud that Corey dropped his bat and put his hands over his ears.

Jeff retrieved the bat. "Knives, kitchen!" He had to yell to be heard over the incessant pounding.

Corey grabbed a pair of knives from the block on the counter, shoving the handle of one into Jeff's hand without barely giving him the chance to set the candle down. The pounding grew—louder, faster.

And now it was coming from the roof.

"Stop!" Corey yelled. "Stop beating on my house!"

Jeff held the knife in front of him, ready to stab anything that made it into the kitchen. His hands shook with fear.

Over the pounding, they heard the distant howl again. Then the pounding ceased. Corey started to say something, but Jeff shook his head, holding his finger to his lips. Then he held one trembling finger in the air for him to wait.

Jeff silently counted to sixty. When he finished, he did it again. He heard no other noises. "It's a signal," he whispered.

"For what?"

"I don't know. At the first one, they or *it* came. At the second, gone."

"How did it know about Mallory and Brad?"

"It read your mind? I don't know. I really don't understand any of this."

It felt like hours since they last spoke. Jeff still didn't feel the need to eat, drink, sleep, or relieve himself. He assumed Corey was feeling the same way. Jeff stared at the candle in the middle of the table where they were sitting again, when he noticed something that he had not taken note of before. A shudder went through his body.

"Corey?"

Corey had been looking at his hands. He thought they were swollen ever so slightly. "What?" he asked.

"Look at the candle."

Corey glanced at it and then at Jeff. "So?"

"Look again."

Corey did. "I don't see anything."

"It hasn't burned down since you've lit it."

Corey took a closer look. "I think it is one of those slow burner ones my wife has. They last like twenty-seven hours."

"This hasn't gone down at all. How long do you think we've had it lit?"

Corey thought about that for a moment. "You know, I don't know. It's hard to figure out time."

"I can tell you this much, that candle should have burned down somewhat. Actually, I think the sun should be up by now."

Corey rotated the candle. "It hasn't melted the wax at all."

Jeff bit his lower lip. "That wasn't Mallory out there. That wasn't anything even close to Mallory."

"It sounded li—"

"It sounded nothing like her. You could hear it in the voice if you paid attention. It was close to her voice, and if you heard it over the phone, you would definitely be fooled, but that wasn't her. It sounded manufactured."

Tears fell down Corey's cheeks. "What the fuck, Jeff? What the fuck is happening?"

Jeff looked at the candle and then at his knife. "I…I don't really know."

Jeff had relit the second candle and was now standing in Corey's two-car garage. Mallory had taken the couple's other car, so there was a wide-open space that Jeff could utilize to put his plan in motion. All he had to do was find the items he needed.

It did not take long to get the torches assembled. Wrapped around the ends of a pair of rake and broom handles were old towels, which he secured with duct tape. A nearly full gas can sat between them on the concrete floor.

Jeff walked back into the kitchen. He was not surprised to see that Corey had not moved. "Corey, get up and grab the candle."

"Why?" he asked. His eyes were red from crying.

"Did you ever talk to the Bronsons?"

Corey nodded. "I think so. That's the old couple up on the street, right?"

"That's them. About four months ago, they had a teenage grandson on his way to visit and realized their air mattress had a hole in it. They asked to borrow mine, so I took it to them."

"Why didn't they ask us?" Corey asked.

"Doesn't matter, Corey. *Focus*. Mr. Bronson showed me his latest gadget. It was a hand-cranked AM/FM *and* shortwave radio." He waited for Corey to register what he had said.

"So? They run on batteries, right?"

"They do, but I have a feeling once it's cranked, the charge may stay, same way the candles don't burn down. Shortwave is what the government would use in case of an emergency if the AM and FM bands don't work. That's assuming they have someone to broadcast, and I'm figuring they do. Ed may already know what's going on."

Now Corey understood. He sat up straighter. "Okay. Yeah. So, how do we get there? These candles won't give off enough light. It's not the longest walk, but I'm not doing it in the dark out there."

"No. You don't have to. I made torches, and I have a feeling they'll stay lit, too."

Corey stood up. "And if that thing pretending to be my wife comes back?"

Jeff shrugged. "You have your bat. I have a knife. If that fails, well, we have to die sometime."

Jeff thought they had it well-planned. They had left Corey's garage through a side door. On the floor just inside the door were the candles, which they had extinguished, and matches. Outside the door was a bucket that had collected rainwater. They would dip the torches into the bucket once they returned.

The two men, weapons in hand, stayed on the sidewalk as they made their journey. It would normally be a five-minute walk to the Bronsons' house, but they were walking slowly. Corey was especially wary.

"I think they'll be attracted to the torches," Corey said for the third time.

"We gotta risk it. If we hear that noise again, we'll run. We'll run toward whichever house we're closest to."

"It feels different out here," Corey said. He kept looking around them. The light from the torches did not go far, but from what he could see—which was really the sidewalk, some of the street, and weeds from the undeveloped lots—it all looked as it did before everything went dark.

Jeff noted that, too. It may have looked the same, but Corey was right. It did *feel* different. The air was cold, somehow greasy against his flesh. It reminded him of walking into the kitchen when his mother was frying chicken. And then there was the taste. The air had a metallic flavor to it. It almost felt as if they were in the belly of some great beast.

Corey whispered Jeff's name.

"Yeah?"

"I had this feeling that something was following us. Parallel to me in the weeds."

Jeff did not slow down his pace. "Yeah?"

"There is. I saw a shape at the edge of the light."

"Should we run?" Jeff asked. He kept his voice calm.

"No. It's just following, like it's curious."

"What kind of shape?"

Corey glanced to the side. There it was, a mere shadow, but definitely keeping pace with them. "Small," he said. He did not take his eyes off it. "Like a cat, but with a really long tail that drags behind it."

Jeff nodded. "Does any light from the torch reflect off its eyes?"

"Not that I've seen."

Jeff thought maybe it did not have any eyes. If it lived in total darkness, what need would it have for them? His heart beat faster. He needed to relax. It probably *was* a cat, and the shadows and fear had skewed it.

"Alright," Jeff murmured. "If it gets closer or makes a move, we'll run to the Bronsons'. I think we're past the halfway point."

"Okay," Corey said. "Should I move my torch toward it? Kind of scare it, you know?"

"No!" Jeff hissed. "Don't antagonize!"

They turned right at the end of the cul-de-sac and continued heading toward the Bronsons' house. When they reached their paved driveway, Jeff gestured. "Halfway up the drive, there's a footpath on the left leading to the front door. I say we follow it, just so we don't get…lost."

"You think we'll get lost in our own neighborhood?"

"I think it's awfully dark out here. I also think that—well—this isn't our neighborhood anymore."

They walked up the driveway and found the flat stones that marked the path to the front door. Jeff looked down and cursed. Corey followed his gaze and asked, "What is that?"

"Blood. And lots of it." Jeff moved the torch toward the ground to get a better look. "It looks like something bleeding was dragged across the yard and walkway, and then across the driveway."

"You think all that belongs to the Bronsons?"

"I'm not going to assume anything right now. Let's go."

They followed the walkway, trying not to step in the blood, though it was quite difficult to avoid it. The closer they got to the front door, the more they encountered. At the top of the porch steps, there were large puddles of it. The front door was wide open.

"You can smell it," Corey whispered.

Jeff nodded as they stood at the bottom of the steps.

"We should call out to them," Jeff said.

"I don't like that. The noise may attract something. Besides, do they have guns?"

"I don't think so. They weren't into that, but I don't want to just walk in and get stabbed or hit with a shovel or something."

"Well, I think the torches are bad enough. I don't want to be yelling out. I feel like a big target out here."

Jeff looked around. "Is that thing still following us?"

"No. It left when we went up the driveway."

"Okay. How about we get up on the porch and quietly announce ourselves?"

"All right."

They ascended the steps, no longer able to avoid the blood.

"Ed?" Jeff called into the house. "Maria? It's Jeff and Corey from the cul-de-sac. You in there?"

There was no response.

"Ed?" Jeff called again. "We have torches. You in there? Maria? We don't want to just barge in."

Corey looked down. "There's a *lot* of blood here… Like, enough for two people."

Jeff moved his torch past the doorway. "There's some past the front door, but that's it. He or she…or both were taken here, I think. They answered the door. Probably thought it was their son or something. Same way you thought it was Mallory."

"Jesus." Corey shivered, realizing how close he had come to the same fate.

"Let's go in. Be careful with the torch. We don't want to burn the place down."

They walked into the house, their flames making shadows that danced along the walls. Everything looked as Jeff remembered it. He called out to the Bronsons again. When there was no response, Corey asked where they could find the radio.

Jeff led him into the living room, pointed with the torch and said, "That door over there leads to a home office. That's where Ed kept it, on a bookshelf."

Corey looked behind them. "We tracked blood in."

"I don't think they'll care."

With Corey on his heels, Jeff pushed open the door to the home office and walked in. "Found it." He went to a bookshelf, put his knife in his back pocket, and grabbed the small radio by its handle. He turned away from the shelf and then spun back. "What is this?"

It was two crank flashlights.

"Flashlights?" Corey asked.

"Yeah. Take one and put it in your pocket. I'll take the other."

They took the lights and Corey asked, "Should we listen to the radio here or at my house?"

Jeff thought for a moment. "I don't really like the idea of going back outside, but I also don't like being here."

"Yeah, this house feels creepy, like we aren't alone."

Jeff nodded. He sensed that, too. "We'll go back to your place and test the lights. Then we'll see if the radio works."

"Does it send messages?"

"I highly doubt it," Jeff answered.

They made their way out of the house and back to the sidewalk. "Keep an eye out for that thing that followed us," Jeff said. "I want to see if we can get a good look at it."

"Why?"

"Seeing all that blood made me mad. If we see it, and I can't identify it…"

"Yeah?"

"I want to kill it."

"It was kind of small to cause that kind of mess. What if that wasn't what got them?"

Jeff thought for a moment. "I don't care."

Jeff and Corey sat at the kitchen table by the light of the crank flashlights. Neither was concerned about the light attracting anything. What was on their minds was that they had powered up the radio and gone through all the FM and AM stations, only to hear static with the occasional odd electronic beep.

"This isn't good," Corey said.

"I'm going to try the shortwave band next. Ed told me it's sometimes used by spies for communication."

Corey laughed. "Really?"

"That's what he said."

Jeff made sure the radio was tuned all the way to the left of the display and then flicked the switch to change the band to shortwave. He slowly started turning the dial clockwise.

"Same shit," Corey said over the static.

Jeff kept tuning the radio.

"I think your idea is busted," Corey said. "Nobody's out there."

"I haven't reached the end of th—"

"…*fish.*"

Both men jumped at the sound of a man's voice coming out of the speaker. He sounded far away and had a slight accent that may have been French.

"*Status Bluefish. This message will repeat and be updated. We are in status Bluefish. Every essential and non-essential worker hearing this message who is able to make it to a safe haven must do so. Only two are active that we are aware of. Monument and Monolith. If you can make it to either, do so immediately. Have your passcode on hand or you will be shot. Proceed with the utmost caution. Do not turn off any devices that happen to be working. They will not restart. Do not drink any sources of water. This message will repeat in French, German, and Japanese. As updates become available, we will announce them. Again, we are in status Bluefish.*"

After the message repeated in the four other languages, Jeff leaned back. "What do we know now?"

"Nothing," Corey said. "All of that was code. It could even be old."

"It's not old," Jeff countered. "I'll tell you what I got from it."

"Beyond being in something called Bluefish?"

"Yeah. Some of it *is* in code. Can you get me paper and a pen?"

Corey got them from his kitchen drawer where they stored odds and ends, and gave them to Jeff, who wrote down the number from the dial. Jeff continued to turn the dial, and when he found nothing, he went back to the station where the announcement came from. Corey remained silent during the time, but finally had to speak up.

"Jeff, I'm sorry. That's all bullshit. It means nothing. *We're fucked.*"

Jeff smiled. "We may be fucked, but it ain't bullshit. Now, I'm going to take notes with any new announcements. Maybe we ca—"

"Well, what the fuck does it mean if it isn't bullshit?"

"I don't know," he snapped. "But I do know this. The group putting it out is multi-national, which means it's probably government or scientists. They also seem to know something about the situation we're in, hence the fucking Bluefish status. If they know about it, there's a chance they also created it, which kind of reiterates that we're talking about scientists. I don't know, though. I do *know* that these people who seem to know what is going on are putting out regular announcements, so I'm going to listen and take fucking notes."

Corey shook his head.

The announcement changed on its twenty-fifth repeat.

"*Status Bluefish. Update. Important announcement. Status Bluefish. Status Bluefish. Update at the end of the regular message.*"

Corey and Jeff eagerly awaited the update, Jeff ready to take notes.

"*Updated information,*" the man began after repeating the main announcement. "*Do not approach any children that you were not in direct physical contact with at the time of the event. If you lost physical contact with the child at any time, do not approach them. Even if it appears to be your child, do not approach. Even if the child uses your name, do not approach. Signs to look for that they are not normal children include using language beyond the scope of that child's age, such as an infant talking. Also, if they do get close enough to you, look at their eyes and tongue. They could appear to be abnormal. Again, do not approach any children you have not had continuous physical contact with since the event. They are dangerous. This message will repeat.*"

Jeff finished writing. "They should be saying the same about the adults."

"How much worse do you think this is going to get?"

Jeff shrugged. "I imagine they have people working on a solution. Probably the same people who caused it, but I have hope. Some hope, at least."

"I want to sleep and never wake up, but I'm not even tired. I don't think I could sleep if I tried."

Jeff chuckled. "You know what, I imagine if you were asleep at the time this happened, you'd still be that way. Assuming nothing got you, of course."

Corey smiled. "Well, that gives *me* hope. Mallory and Brad should have been asleep when it began. I hope they were."

"Me, too, bud. Me, too."

"How much time do you think has passed?" Corey asked.

Jeff shook his head. He didn't feel like talking. There had not been any new updates in eighteen rounds of announcements. It was depressing.

"It feels like it's been hours," Corey said. "Or days. I just don't know. It's weird not knowing the time. Not needing to sleep or eat. It feels strange."

There was a break in the static on the radio that always came before an announcement. Jeff put pen to paper and waited.

"*Status Bluefish. Commencing Operation Paradigm Realignment. Remain stationary. Attempt begins in minus sixty, fifty-nine…*"

The countdown had begun. Corey and Jeff looked at each other, afraid to be too hopeful, and unsure what they should be hopeful about.

"Are they trying to fix it?" Corey whispered.

"I hope so," Jeff said.

With ten seconds to go, Corey closed his eyes and began praying, something he had not done since he was a young child.

Jeff held his breath.

They jumped at the sound of the refrigerator humming to life and the light in the living room turning on. Neither man knew what to say. They just looked at each other with big smiles on their faces.

Jeff started to stand up.

"Wait!" Corey said. "Did you feel that?"

"It felt like a small earthquake!"

They made their way out the front door, not even realizing they'd left their flashlights on the table.

Corey looked up at the sky and yelled, "Fuck!"

Jeff tipped his head back and his stomach tightened. The sky was utterly black. Not a single star or planet was visible.

"They didn't do it," Jeff said. "They couldn't."

Corey laughed. "No! There they are!" He pointed toward the sky as the stars started to reappear. "That is… No. I don't recognize these constellations."

Jeff followed Corey's gaze. "I'm not an expert. I don't know."

Corey looked at him. "They aren't right. It still feels cold, too."

Jeff nodded. "But not *as* cold and not *as* greasy. This is good."

"It's not good. I don't recognize these stars."

Jeff shrugged. He knew it felt different outside. The streetlights were on, too, so electricity was back. He did not know why Corey was so worried about the stars.

Corey looked up into the sky again. "My bad. You know, I was far better at this when I was a kid." He pointed. "There's Ursa Major. Over there is Perseus."

"Well, the first thing to go…" Jeff joked.

"Funny. I forget the name of that one, but…yeah. That's what they are."

"Thanks for the astronomy lesson, Professor Corey."

Corey looked at his neighbor and laughed. "Any time. So, what brings you over again?"

"I… I… You know, I forgot! Weird. I just got this sudden feeling of *déjà vu*, and then I forgot why I came over."

"The first thing to go is the mind, as they *and you* say."

"Very funny." Jeff scratched his head and looked around. "I think, maybe…" He looked toward his driveway. "Yeah, I was taking out the garbage and then thought I'd… I guess come over and ask about Mallory and Brad. Are they back yet?"

"Not yet. Soon."

Jeff gave him a polite nod and started to walk away.

"I got that, too," Corey called after him.

"What's that?" Jeff stopped and asked.

"*Déjà vu*. I had that feeling, too, when looking at the stars. You know what causes that?"

Jeff shook his head. "I have no idea."

THE GORGE

TOM BLICQ

Halloween was over.

It was a glorious November afternoon in the small village of Red Springs, Minnesota. Farmers were out and about, tending to their livestock and preparing their pastures for the approaching winter. Every hour of sunlight would be put to use: a philosophy upheld not only in the minds of men, but in the hearts of children.

On a plot of land sandwiched between fields of sunflower and mustard seed, two young sisters were exploring the great outdoors. Both were in good spirits, for yesterday evening had afforded them enough candy to last well into the new year. Multiple pillowcases filled with sweets were shoved under their beds, just within reach—a temptation they'd found irresistible.

Earlier that day, their mother had caught them gorging on chocolates and licorice. She didn't take kindly to the discovery. "Out, outside! No more junk or you'll ruin your appetites." She shepherded them toward the backyard with the bristles of her broom; just like that, they found themselves running,

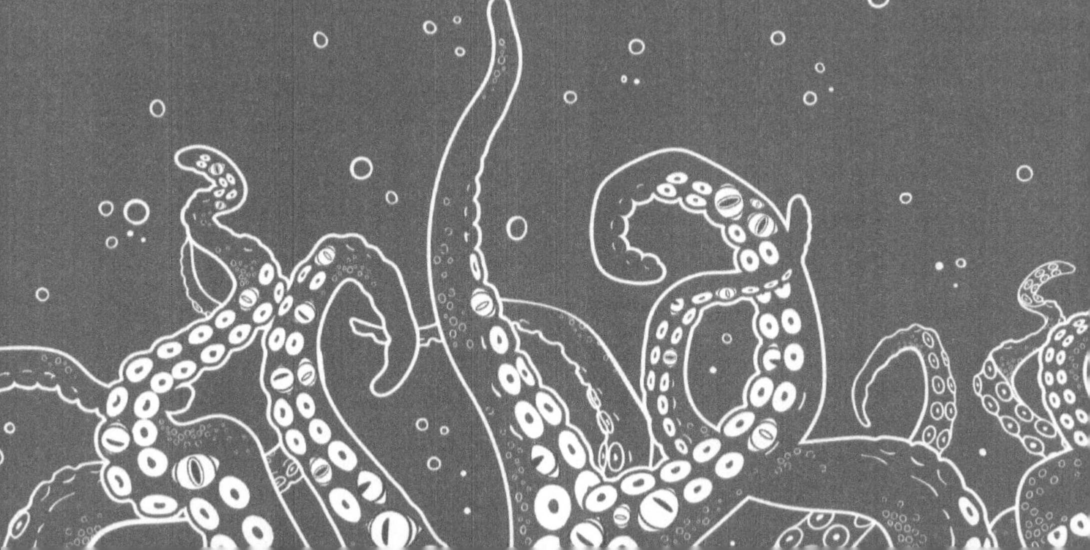

scurrying, giggling, and clamoring, their spirits intertwined with the majesty of nature. "Enjoy the weather while you can. We're in for a long, cold winter."

She was right.

November 1ˢᵗ was expected to be the last warm day of 1979. Subzero temperatures were right around the corner, meaning their outdoor excursions would soon be relegated to shoveling snow and helping stock firewood. With the darkness and freezing winds looming on the horizon, the girls made an unspoken pact. They needed to make every second count. Today, then, was a day for laughter and celebration. Their candy would last; the daylight wouldn't. What better way to commemorate their haul than with a game of hide-and-seek?

It was early afternoon when the game first began. Nearly half an hour had come and gone since then. Phoebe had managed to remain hidden longer than expected. *Much longer.*

Sophie was just about ready to give up searching. Her patience had worn thin, and her feet ached like never before. None of that seemed to matter, however, when weighed against the expectations put forth by her parents.

"Keep an eye on Phoebe. Make sure she stays safe out there. Don't let her out of your sight for a minute, you understand? You're almost eleven years old, so you're in charge."

Memories of the lectures resurfaced, inducing stabs of primal fear. Sophie chewed her lower lip. She knew the trouble she'd be in if any harm were to befall her precious little sister.

The girls were competitive by nature. Each had risked a bagful of treats, betting on who could stay concealed the longest. Such high stakes never failed to get the adrenaline flowing and the spirits of adventure soaring. It was a tradition they reveled in, dipping and frolicking together through the forested jungle of their enormous rural backyard.

But this time around, something was different. Something felt off.

Under ordinary circumstances, Phoebe's loss was inevitable. Sophie would stumble past her hiding spot, and a burst of uncontrolled giggling would give her away. Either that, or the vibrant colors of her costume (worn in keeping with the theme of trick-or-treating) would prove easy to spot amidst the browning foliage.

Sophie would find her sister in seconds, only to rescind their wager without a moment's hesitation. "How did you know where to look, *cheater?*" This accusation was met with the same answer every time.

"Lucky guess."

Today, it seemed as if her luck had finally run out. The woods were dead quiet, save only for the tweeting of birds, and the crunching of leaves and twigs underfoot. Phoebe hadn't made a peep, which was most unlike her.

Sophie was beginning to worry. "I swear, if she's down in that gorge again…" A twinge of bitterness entered her voice as she recalled the upshot of last year's game.

About a quarter-mile into the trees, the land gave way to a steep depression. Here, the girls loved to skip and scamper, heedless of the risk or danger. All that changed the previous autumn when Phoebe fell in and twisted her leg.

Dressed as a witch, Sophie was forced to carry her sister back to the farmhouse on foot. When questioned, she claimed they'd been attacked by a wild animal. This little fabrication proved a terrible mistake.

The girls found themselves separated and interrogated without mercy. Their story began to fall apart, prompting a series of tearful confessions. Both were grounded for longer than they cared to recall.

"Why weren't you watching her? Playing in a gorge? Do you have any idea how dangerous that was?"

Fearing a repeat of last year's disaster, Sophie swallowed her pride. "Alright, I give up!" In response, there came forth a distant cry, emanating from far deeper in the woods than the girls were allowed to venture. She broke into a jog.

Several twists and turns were taken amongst the trees before she came to the edge of an all-too-familiar clearing. There it was: the dreaded gorge. Sure enough, down at the bottom, she found her little sister.

"Are you kidding me?" Sophie shielded her eyes and squinted.

Something wasn't right. Phoebe had made no attempt to conceal herself. She sat out in the open, away from the shade of the nearby canopies, with the sun beating down overhead.

"Stay there! I'm coming to get you!"

Before starting her descent, Sophie surveyed the land with care. Something anomalous had caught her eye.

Climbing to the bottom, her suspicions were confirmed. A massive sewer pipe rested on the basin floor, protruding from the base of a sharp incline. Its surface was caked in rust, appearing decades old. Sophie's brow furrowed. As best she could recall, the gorge had always been vacant. An effluent line so large and ancient wouldn't have gone unnoticed all these years, surely.

Yet, there it was.

Phoebe knelt before the grille, resting mere inches from its framework. Nuts and raisins were being fed through to the other side, produced from the open trail mix bag at her feet. She was too distraught to notice the shadow approaching at her rear.

"Are you kidding me?" The question oozed with venom.

Phoebe jolted, alert. A muddy splash resulted, and some wildlife scampered away.

"God, you're filthy. Why are you wasting our snacks? Those are for hikes; you should've left them at home."

"I wanted more candy." Phoebe's response triggered an eye-roll. "You're so immature. Mom and Dad are gonna kill us, you know that? What are you doing down here, anyway? Hey. Look at me." Sophie tried to grab her sister by the arm, but she twisted away.

"There's a girl in the sewer," Phoebe insisted. "I—I wanted to help her."

Sophie shook her head. "It's just some animal, Phoebe." Her voice stiffened. "You didn't touch it, did you? Answer me."

"No, but there really is a girl. She needs our help."

"No, Phoebe. There isn't."

"Just look!"

Sophie heaved a sigh. Readjusting the tiara of her costume, she lifted her skirt and approached the pipe head-on. It was then that she noticed the black discharge.

Traces of raw sewage trickled outward, strained through a latticework of corroded metal teeth. She made a face. It looked and smelled like death. The spillover had tainted the shallow depths of standing water, and Phoebe, having sat down in the grime, had dyed her white angel dress a shade of sickly brown.

Covering her mouth to keep from gagging, Sophie maneuvered around the filth in careful steps and hops. A tenuous foothold was located. Her leverage obtained, she reached over and made several loud raps on the pipe's outer surface. In response, to her utter disbelief, there emerged a human voice.

"Please, help me."

Panicking, she leapt away and doubled-back. A glance was stolen over one shoulder. Once satisfied they weren't in any immediate danger, she turned and barked an order.

"Phoebe? Stay here and don't move. If I say to run, we run. Understood?" Her instructions were met with an anxious nod. "Alright. Alright, I can do this."

With that, she gathered her wits and stepped forward. No move was made to avoid the sludge pooling at her ankles like wet tar. Heart racing, jaw trembling, she cleared her throat.

"Hello?"

No response. Frowning, Sophie inclined an ear and listened. She could hear someone stirring on the other side. Their presence was punctuated by subtle disturbances in the murky flow of wastewater.

"It's all right. We're not going to hurt you. My sister and I are here to help. Are—are you hurt? It'd be great if we could see you." She paused, hoping her little speech might coax the mysterious stranger out of hiding. "Will you come a little closer to the light?"

Still nothing. Peering inward, Sophie studied the discharge line. Its innerworkings were dark and gloomy, but buried within that gloom, sequestered like a living shadow, there knelt a small figure.

It was a girl. *Phoebe was right.*

Sophie swallowed, but the lump rising in her throat refused to soften. "Wh-who are you?" she stammered, trying her best to ignore the rancid stench. "What's your name?"

"Help," the girl croaked, her voice thick with anguish. "Please, help me." She crawled forward. A small shaft of sunlight fell across her face, revealing the true extent of her predicament and eliciting a shrill gasp.

She was engulfed in sludge from head to toe. The same liquid darkness trickling from the sewer's open mouth had enveloped her like a second skin. Underneath all the grime and excrement, there were signs of severe malnourishment. Her limbs were gaunt as twigs.

"God. How long have you been down here?"

The girl's cheeks trembled as her lips peeled back, revealing a toothless mouth and gums tinged with rot. "Longer than the light," she insisted, casting a wistful gaze toward the heavens. "And far longer than the celestial atmosphere you know today."

Alarmed by her response, Sophie turned to address Phoebe. "One of us needs to stay with her. She's delirious. Phoebe, can you run for help?"

"No!" Her tiny features scrunched in distress. "I'll fall and get hurt."

Sophie cursed under her breath.

Phoebe was right; she stood no chance of making it out by herself. The incline would prove too much for her little legs, just as it had when she fell in the previous year. There had to be another way.

"Listen. I need you to stay here and keep this girl company, all right?" A small canteen filled with water was unclipped from Sophie's side and handed over. "Get her to drink this. Make sure she stays hydrated. If she can stomach it, feed her some trail mix."

Phoebe's bright blue eyes grew wide with terror. She started to shake her head.

"Phoebe, I'm serious. We can't just leave her here. This is life or death, you understand? It's an emergency. I'll go find help, and I'll come right back."

An acquiescent nod followed, slow, uncertain. "You'll come back before it gets dark?"

"Of course."

Sophie hugged her sister tight. Their embrace lasted longer than it should have. For reasons unexplained, neither of them wanted to let go.

A sloshing noise disturbed them, and they separated with a start. Stooping low, Sophie turned to address their new friend. "We're going to the police. They should be able to cut you out of there, so just hang tight."

"Please, hurry," the girl begged, her coal-black eyes radiating fear and desperation. "There are bad things down here. Awful things. I've begged and prayed for them to leave me alone, but they never stop their *gnawing.*" She let forth a sudden laugh, sharp and sustained.

She was referring to the wildlife, Sophie decided. Rodents, amphibians, insects, and God only knew what else. The unthinkable alternative—the idea that her mind had already snapped, and that nothing salvageable remained—pervaded, lingered.

How much of her was left intact? And was she still worth saving?

Without warning, the girl inched forward, raised a hand, and pressed her palm flat against the grille. The gesture induced a stab of pity.

Reciprocating with thumb and forefinger, Sophie reached through the latticework and stroked the emaciated flesh. It felt cold to the touch. "Don't worry," she breathed. "I'll be back before you know it."

She departed without another word. Along the side of the gorge she wound, struggling to find purchase along the craggy outcrops. Cresting the summit, she took one last look into the cavernous depths below. Her eyes narrowed.

Phoebe had moved. She now sat before the conduit and, by some miracle, had managed to squeeze her wrist through to the other side. To the girl trapped within, she'd offered a handful of food.

Moved by her compassion, Sophie managed a warm and tender smile.

What a little sweetheart.

The police required assistance locating the girl. With shattered nerves and a racing heart, Sophie guided them through the trees, pointing the way like a bloodhound on the trail of wounded game.

She'd tried her best to explain the gorge's location. Her efforts were hampered on two counts. The first was the sheer enormity of the backwoods. Landmarks were few, and the trails winding and labyrinthine. A second, more fundamental problem, lay in her refusal to mention her parent's address.

When brought before the officers at the station, she found herself delivering the vaguest possible answers. She then made the mistake of letting it slip that Phoebe was still with the girl. That cinched it. Multiple squad cars were sent out, with a not-yet-eleven-year-old girl indicating the way forward.

She made sure to take them through a neighboring field, several houses from her own. Blinds were lifted as they rolled past, and porch lights switched on as people gathered and stared from afar. Sophie crouched down low in her car seat. Her story would soon be made known to all the world. It was only a matter of time.

Onward they probed, zigging and zagging through the trees. Unexpected twists and turns were taken, yielding strange perspectives on otherwise familiar terrain. When they stumbled across the gorge at last, it was almost dusk.

"There it is! *There it is!*"

None of the officers shared in Sophie's enthusiasm. Upon arriving at the cliff-side, she found herself whisked away. Vehicle headlights blared through the trees farther back, their drivers guided by glowstick-waving cadets. Tripods of lighting gear were hauled into position.

After what felt like an eternity, one of the officers made his descent. He returned several moments later with Phoebe cradled in his arms. The instant she was deemed safe, the other members of the rescue team got down to business.

The sisters watched from afar as clusters of EMTs and shouting deputies fought to get the sewer main open. Both sat in an undercover police vehicle.

Looking after them was Officer Jenny Langdon. The regional authorities had introduced her as a member of their team who specialized in crises involving children.

Sophie had agreed to answer her questions on one condition. She wanted to stay and witness the rescue firsthand. This was, of course, only a ploy to avoid being taken home to her parents. She would have to face their wrath sooner or later, and of the two options available, later sounded better. *Much better.*

Officer Langdon turned to her colleagues for help.

"The station's pretty well empty," one of them said. "Probably better to wait until more of us get back, especially considering *the drive.*" Extra emphasis was placed on these last two words, and Langdon agreed. She was in no mood to shuttle her passengers back and forth along twenty-seven miles of open highway. "Just ask them where they live. Save yourself the trip."

And that's exactly what she did.

"Girls? Look at me, please." Her tone was condescending and artificial. "You did the right thing coming to us, but now I need your help in obtaining some answers, okay?"

A slew of questions followed. The girls found themselves relaying their favorite colors and describing the contents of their Barbie doll collections. Interlaced with all the casual banter were inquiries concerning their neighborhood and home address.

Sophie claimed she couldn't remember the street name or address number. An inquisition regarding the girl came next. *How did they find her? What were they doing? Did their parents know where they were?*

Getting the details was like pulling teeth. Masking her frustration, Officer Langdon forced a smile. "That's all right, dear. The names of your parents will be on file at the station. Your father's surname, you said it was Matheson?" A reluctant nod. "Perfect. We can work with that." She went on asking them all about their prettiest shoes and dresses; anything to take their minds off the grim matter at hand.

These efforts proved successful on Sophie's end. Believing they'd helped save a life, her unease began to ebb.

Phoebe's behavior was another story. She'd commenced blubbering the moment help had arrived. Her sobs were hysterical in nature, and punctuated by giddy, nonsensical mutterings.

"Finally free. I'm finally free."

Equal parts bewildered and unsettled, Sophie decided to intervene. She took Phoebe by the hands and gave a gentle squeeze. "Hey, you need to calm down. It's all right. We're safe."

"Free of that nightmare, free of that nightmare."

That's when she noticed Phoebe's eyes. The irises didn't belong to her little sister. They were pitch-dark, coal-black—identical to those of the mysterious girl they'd encountered earlier that afternoon.

Frowning, Sophie withdrew.

The thing wearing her sister's skin lifted a hand to its cheek. The flesh was caressed, and the stolen tongue worked across the lips, back and forth, back and forth. It repeated itself once more, just loud enough to be overheard.

"Finally free. I'm finally free."

There were voices echoing from the bottom of the gorge. Sophie caught the words "no signs of life" and, like a stone, her heart fell. Seconds passed like hours before a body was removed and carried out on a stretcher.

Officer Langdon enacted a quick diversion. "Come on," she insisted, starting the car engine. "Let's head back to the station. You girls can tell me more about your dollhouses on the way. Oh!" A series of quick beeps alerted her to the fact that the passenger side door remained open a crack. She shifted back into PARK. "Honey, can you close your door?"

Sophie wasn't listening. On the other side of the clearing, an ambulance had arrived. Without a second thought, she leapt outside and took off running.

"Hey!" The driver's side door was thrown open. Steel-toed boots pounded the grass and fallen leaves. "Get back here!"

Approaching the ambulance, Sophie took the paramedics by surprise. This afforded her just enough time to reach the gurney. As the EMTs struggled to grab her, she lifted the white shroud off the body, exposing the face.

There was the girl.

At first glance, everything seemed as it should've been. It didn't take long, however, before a glaring exception came to light: her eyes. They were open wide. The shroud was replaced over the corpse's head a moment later, and the gurney was hauled away.

Sophie had gone numb with shock. Her glimpse was fleeting, but in her mind, there lingered no doubt what she'd witnessed, nor would any doubt materialize in the years spent reflecting on that fateful autumn evening of 1979. It was a sight that would stick with her until her dying day.

Those eyes. The irises weren't as they should've been. The color was all wrong. They were bright, blue, and frozen in abject terror.

They were the eyes of the dead, and they belonged to her little sister, Phoebe Matheson.

HER SISTER, IN STARLIGHT

DEVAN BARLOW

"**W**HAT'S WITH ALL the green soap? I can't figure out what the smell reminds me of—" Leslie paused in the doorway, surprised to find her sister, Molly, standing on the screened porch with a strange woman who hadn't been there when Leslie arrived at the house. She had just put her bag in the guest room, changed her clothes, and washed her face after the four hours she'd spent in the car getting here.

Her sister and the woman shared a look that bespoke a long acquaintance—weird, considering Molly had stayed here only a few weeks. They posed on either side of a telescope, and Leslie couldn't help but think the stranger's stance was overly protective of the instrument.

"I make the soap myself," the stranger said. "One of my hobbies."

"Carol was a huge help after I moved in," Molly said.

"Moved in?" Leslie repeated.

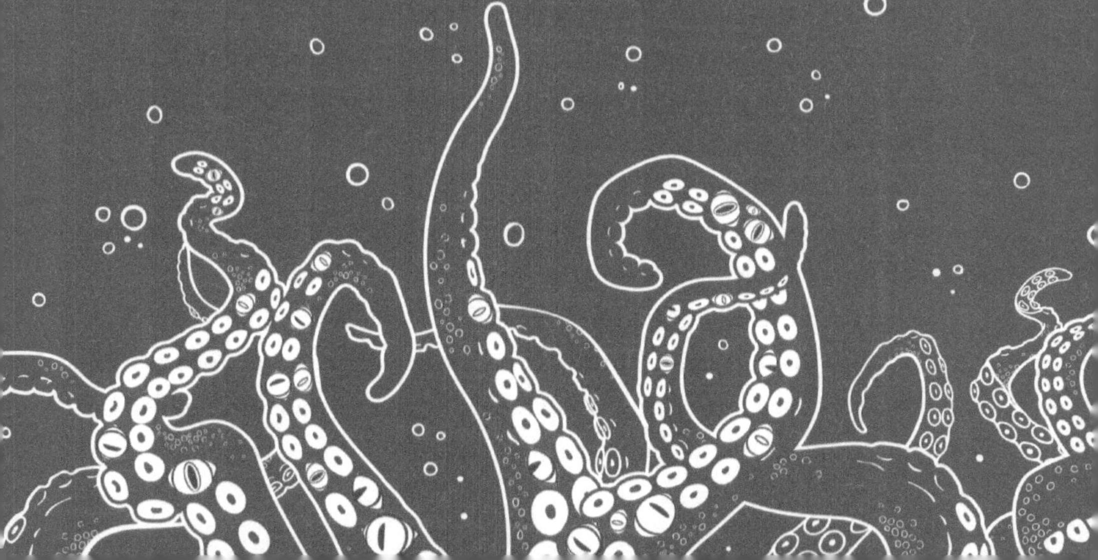

Molly's eyes flicked to a nearby end table. Leslie stepped close enough to read the envelope addressed to Molly at that address, sent by a utility company.

The stranger, Carol, rose. "I'm sure you two have loads to catch up on, so I'll get out of your hair." She gave Molly a nod, but her face fell when she looked at Leslie. "I'm surprised you haven't helped your sister before this."

"When was the last time you visited any of your siblings?" Leslie didn't realize she would sound so rude until the words came out of her mouth. Somehow, she didn't mind.

Carol's brows raised slightly. Before she left through the front door, she said, "I'll talk to you later, Molly."

The moment the door closed behind Carol, Leslie asked, "Does she realize I just slogged all the way out here to bring you home?" The drive had taken an hour longer than it should have, thanks to her phone providing very confusing directions. "Why does she think you live here now? Why are you getting *bills* here? You're just supposed to get the house ready to sell!"

"Because I *do* live here now. If you'd give people a chance instead of leaping at every opportunity to snark, you'd find the neighbors are actually very nice." Picking up the telescope, Molly retreated into the house.

Leslie followed, too surprised at first to respond, which gave her the first opportunity to really look at her sister and take in the fact that she didn't look…good. Molly had lost enough weight to make her cheekbones prominent, and her normally neat nails were now torn and flecked with bits of deep red polish. Without looking at Leslie, she picked up a sponge and started rubbing at a stain on the kitchen countertop.

"Molly, you can't stay here." Leslie sighed as she took in the house more thoroughly. It hadn't even been cleaned, much less emptied. "What have you been doing all these weeks?"

"Felicia left a letter—for Mom, I guess," Molly said, "but I was the only one here to read it, and I don't think Felicia would have minded. She was desperate for someone to continue her work."

"What work?" Leslie glanced at the living room, looking for some clue regarding their distant relative's profession. Unwittingly, her attention became snared by the telescope now perched in the living room beside a pile of books, as if the instrument might choose one to read.

Molly continued, "I didn't understand at first, but Felicia had left instructions, so I started using the telescope, and soon…" She stared at the instrument like it could lend her strength, then met and held Leslie's gaze, unblinking. "I saw it. The stars are changing."

Leslie frowned. "Isn't that a thing they do anyway?" She waved her hands. "You know, with the seasons?"

Would they have noticeably changed in the weeks since Molly's been here? Leslie didn't know, and she also didn't know why she suddenly felt so uneasy, like her sister's face wasn't the same face she'd grown up with.

"There's a new star, and it's coming closer," Molly said. "I think the other stars are running away from it."

Perplexed at the conviction in Molly's voice, Leslie stared at her sister and found herself suddenly reminded of a recent conversation: one that ended with both sisters agreeing they either needed to hire someone to help their parents, or one of them had to move back home.

Two months before, both sisters had visited their childhood house for a long weekend celebrating their parents' forty-fifth wedding anniversary. The entire time, their parents avoided all of Leslie and Molly's questions. They had awkwardly changed the subject to avoid discussing the house, which the sisters had never seen so dusty before, and their health, despite the pile of medical paperwork strewn on the kitchen counter.

The news that their mom had been contacted by the lawyer executing a distant relative's estate had finally distracted both sisters.

"I assumed she died years ago," Mom had said as she showed them the pile of documents. "Felicia was my…fourth cousin? I think? We only met once. I haven't heard from her in ages, so I don't know *why* she left me her house, but I suppose there might not have been anyone else…"

Hearing the unspoken plea in their mom's rambling, Leslie and Molly had promised to take care of getting the house emptied and sold, refraining from arguing about which one of them would actually *do* the emptying until they were out of their parents' hearing.

"Is this…is this because of Mom and Dad?" Leslie asked. "I know things aren't good, but you stressing them out like this isn't helping. Besides, whatever happened to using the money from the sale of this house to pay someone to help them? Mom and Dad are scared. You have no idea how many times they've called me…"

"And there we have it! You only care about what I'm doing when it inconveniences you. Well, this isn't about you or them!" Molly's voice became a small shriek. She cast about the room, twisting her hands together in front of herself. "This is *real*, what I'm doing here, and maybe you'll just have to be the one to worry about them right now." Her fingers knotted tight enough to make Leslie wince in sympathetic pain.

"You didn't even know Felicia existed until two months ago, and now you've given up your life for her weird obsession?"

Molly gave a humorless laugh. "Silly me. You texted you were coming and here I thought maybe my sister *actually* wanted to spend time with me! Maybe she'll be interested in what I'm doing!"

"What you're *doing*? You, what, gave up your job to sit out here and stare at the sky? Is the soap maker wrapped up in this 'the stars are moving' nonsense, too?"

"Her name is Carol, and do you have any idea how much there was to *do* when I got out here? She was kind enough to help out, make sure I had food in the fridge, and she knew Felicia well enough to help make sense of her seriously uneven record keeping. Hell of a lot more than you ever offered to do." Molly scowled. "I'm sorry Mom and Dad are worried. They're welcome to come visit—"

"Because that's so doable with the state they're both in?"

Molly's face softened. "I'm sorry about that, but I can't leave right now. The work is too important."

"Know what? Fine. I'll get out of your way, and you can just wait for the stars to fall down on you. I'm sure Felicia would be so proud."

"You shouldn't drive back tonight. It's already sunset. Stay the night."

Leslie knew her sister's words were meant as a peace offering, but that didn't mean they worked. She drew in a breath to protest, only for pain to snap its way across her lower back. She wasn't used to driving to begin with, much less for as many hours as she'd done today. On top of that, the nearby roads wouldn't be easy to navigate in the dark.

"Fine." Before Molly could respond, Leslie stomped back into the guest room. The overwhelming sensation of their argument coated her like a physical force.

Molly was always the one to reach out, ever since they were little. Always the first one to concede an argument or revive their text thread after months of inactivity. Leslie was always the one who refused to build upon whatever Molly offered. Maybe their parents were right about the sisters' shaky bond being Leslie's fault.

"If you would just include her more, we wouldn't have this problem. You've never worked on your relationship!" Dad had grumbled when Leslie had hesitated about coming out here to retrieve Molly. It was a variation on the theme both parents had barraged her with for as long as she could remember.

Was it Leslie's fault if Molly had entirely different interests? Besides, it had been the same ever since they were teenagers. Any time Molly tagged along with Leslie and her friends, she just went home early, and then everyone got all worried about her. Leslie always had to reassure them and risked looking like she was the mean one who didn't care about her sister. She was sick of it.

She scratched at her arms fruitlessly before deciding to take a shower. A very long shower. Let Molly deal with the water bill.

She washed her hair then figured she might as well shave her legs. The longer she bathed, the less she'd have to deal with Molly. She hadn't packed shaving gel, but there was more of the homemade green soap in the shower, and it foamed nicely. It would do.

A sharp, mechanical noise from outside the house intruded over the sounds of the water and the bathroom fan, startling Leslie enough that the razor slipped. A slender red line opened down her calf.

Swearing, she cleaned herself up.

She *was* trying, wasn't she? Wasn't that the whole point of her coming all the way out here? Clearly, it had been a waste of her time. If this place and its falling stars made Molly so much happier than anything the rest of her life could offer, let her have it. Leslie would move back home if that was the only way their parents would have what they needed...

So preoccupied with replaying every argument between herself and Molly, Leslie didn't notice that her spilled blood refused to merge with the soap foam. The two substances ran in parallel channels down her leg as if something about one repelled the other.

Clean, but still furious, she got into bed. It was a clear night, but the glow through the windows differed from back home in the city and only served to make her grumpier.

So she put on some music. Once she focused on the song instead of the obnoxiousness of her sister, she drifted to sleep.

A few hours later, a weird whining sound woke Leslie, the pitch jabbing the insides of her ears so pointedly that she felt it in her sinuses. It came with the overwhelming sensation of something being *wrong*.

She shuffled groggily through the house in search of her sister, but Molly wasn't in her room, the bathroom, the living room; all the while, the sound grew louder. Leslie reached the kitchen. Molly wasn't there either, but the front door hung open, and the sound came from outside—

Frantic, Leslie caught her foot on the threshold and stumbled forward onto the lawn. Despite the soreness in her back, she jerked herself backwards when she became aware she stood within a massive ring of floating, bright spheres. They hovered in every direction, blocking her path back into the house and off of the lawn.

The lights were *eyes*, she realized: bright points glowing within the shadowed forms of people arrayed along the street. Any color they'd once possessed was gone, overtaken by a gleaming gray hue. One of the shadowed faces split into a grin, and she recognized Carol, the soap maker. But where was her sister?

"Molly!" Leslie finally spotted her standing calmly in the circle's center, head tilted back to regard the sky.

And the *sky*—

Liquid light poured down so heavily that Leslie feared it would fill her lungs, squeeze out all the air until she became a vessel for this sickly brightness.

Pain seared up her leg from her shaving accident. When Leslie glanced down, the press of light intensified. The bandage had fallen off, and the cut had stretched wider and deeper. The surrounding skin unfurled, revealing not the red-pink of exposed flesh but a sickly, mold-like green. The scent of rot overwhelmed her, twisting her stomach as the green substance pulsed outward from within her leg, forming intricate patterns with impossible speed that reached out toward the circle of watchers.

"I told you a new star was coming," Molly said as Leslie fell to the ground. Her sister, in starlight, turned to her, fathomless eyes full of acceptance.

DESERT SILVER BLUE

JAY KANG ROMANUS

Always seein' 'wayoff dreams of silver–blue,
Always feelin' thorns that stab and sting.
—Badger Clark, "Roundup Lullaby"

"Y'KNOW WHAT I think he's up to?" Jake Carey asks me on our second day of driving the herd towards an unknown destination. The cattle are a dusty brown river flowing placidly through the ravine under our horses' hooves, but I'm still keeping an eye on them in case something sets off a stampede.

"Right now, or just generally?" I respond mildly, curious to hear what he has to say. We've worked together for four years, and I could count the number of thoughts he's had in my presence on one hand. He's got more muscle than sense, even if his eyes are slanted like a skinny Chinaman. I take a deep breath and let the dry Arizona air soothe my tortured lungs.

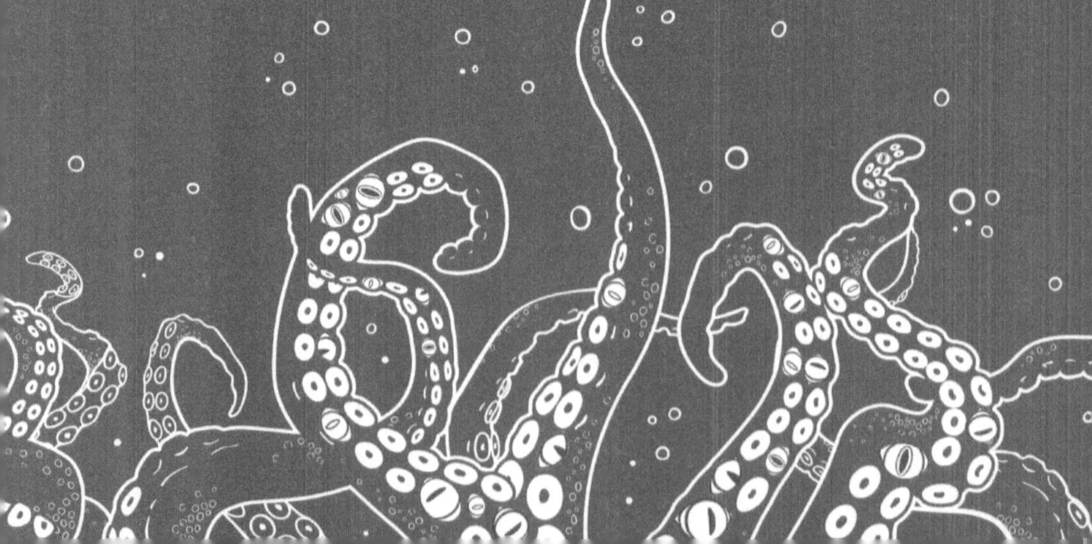

He waggles his eyebrows at me. "Generally, I think it's a present for his girl. He's off pissin' right now, though, if you're curious."

"That's none of my business," I say, hoping Jake doesn't catch the flush of blood to my face. Everything is orange under the setting sun, so I turn my face towards the west, letting it reach under my wide-brimmed hat and cover my face in light. "Anyways, a herd of cattle ain't romantic," I add. "I see why you don't got a girl if you think they want cows."

It's Jake's turn to be embarrassed; I can see it in his downturned lips. "I don't got a girl because the girls around here don't like chinks, even though I ain't one," he mutters. "All I'm saying is I don't know a man who'd spend this much on anything but a girl. You should see what they pay for the tightest ones over at my ma's place."

"Sure," I say, and pause; I hadn't meant to hurt his feelings, but he's wrong. Truthfully, I don't know exactly how much our mysterious benefactor is paying the ranch for us to drive the herd out into the wilderness towards nowhere, but it must've been a huge amount paid upfront. That's not whorehouse money, though I can see why Jake thinks so; being raised in one will do that to you. I open my mouth to say something about good business, but then our patron comes trotting out of the brush on his horse.

"Hey, boys!" he calls. I try to ignore the pulse of heat that flashes through me on hearing his rough voice. "Jake, Badger, how are we feeling about a few more hours until we stop?" The strange, round scars that pockmark his thin face crinkle as he gives us an excited grin. He told us to call him Vance, but something in me refuses to believe he could have such an ordinary name as that.

"Sure, boss!" Jake chirps and wheels his horse around to keep up with the herd. I trot after him, pushing down the urge to look behind me and check that Vance is keeping up. I know he is; he's the only one who knows where we're going. I know it like I know the reason I want to turn around is so I can see the way his strong legs guide the horse underneath him.

He rides up next to me with a smile that would feel like a threat if his eyes weren't so clear and gentle. "Sun's going down," he says, and I think it's a question, but I can't tell exactly what he means.

"Yeah," I agree. "I'm thinking we should stop once it's dark." Stopping at sundown is the only smart thing to do, but the cows have also been sluggish today, and I don't want to risk overworking them under the hot summer sun and giving them heatstroke. The last of the herd passes through the ravine below us and we both kick our horses into a trot that brings us to a low escarpment.

The desert stretches out below like a rumpled quilt, embroidered with explosions of brittlebush and saguaro. I take another deep breath, but some small piece of debris floating through the air catches in my throat this time, and I hunch over my horse's neck as my body is wracked with coughs so violent my eyes start watering. Jake waves up at us from the desert floor and Vance waves back at him.

"He wants to keep going for a while, you know," Vance says to me, like I haven't been here for the entire conversation. "Are you all right?"

We pick our way along Jake's path down the escarpment, me following behind Vance and trying to blink the tears from my eyes. I don't know what exactly it is about him that puts me on edge. It could be that he's paid an unbelievable amount of money to let a whole herd of prime beef become vulture food, or it could just be that I hate the way my body breaks out in sweat under my denim and leather when he rasps some well-cultured sentence at me.

"Tuberculosis," I tell him out loud once I've gotten my breath back. "I ain't dead yet though, and I'm tellin' you that if you start listening to Jake, you'll find yourself naked in a bar with three or four pistols pointed at you. That's the truth."

Vance chuckles in his throat as we catch up to Jake and the herd. "Could be fun," he says.

"I dunno," I reply. "Never happened to me."

"What's his story, anyway?" Vance asks me.

"Well, he won't admit it, but everybody knows his pa was one of them Chinese railway workers that still pass through Tombstone," I say. "That's why he looks like that." My lungs spasm one last time with a rattle and I swallow down the metallic taste of blood in the back of my throat. I'm not coughing the blood up like a fancy English lady yet, but it's only a matter of time.

"Are you sure this is the right job for you?" Vance asks, and he sounds genuinely concerned. I can't imagine why he would be; we'll only know each other for these few days while he guides us to guide the cattle where he wants them. The thought occurs to me that maybe he plans for it to be a much longer trip, but I have no real reason to be suspicious of that.

"The air down here's good for me, and I'm good for the ranch," I say. It's true, too. Every time I took a breath of the wetter air up North, it felt like breathing through soup, and I'm a steady worker who doesn't go out to drink as much as all the other boys do.

Vance is still watching me thoughtfully, something in his eyes like he wants to slip under my skin and have a good look around in there. I think I want to let him do just that; God help me.

"Hey, Jake!" I call ahead, trying to ignore Vance's piercing stare. "We're stopping here. Let's round up the cattle before it gets too dark to see our hands in front of our faces, yeah?"

The three of us each have our own tents, all snuggled up against the escarpment like we're hiding from something. It's a hot night, the kind that feels like you could snap your fingers and start a fire without even trying. I'm sweating through my underclothes from the beans we ate for dinner, and I can hear Jake tossing around in his bedroll a few feet away.

I watch the cattle's tails twitching at each night sound. Lightning flickers sleepily just over the horizon and illuminates the humped shapes of the herd in hazy silver-blue like a cyanotype. My ma and pa used to press prairie flowers on cyanotype paper, but I always preferred to see the living thing. Sometimes, a coyote will yap lazily a few hills away, and I expect one of the cattle to raise its head each time it happens, but the entire herd is sleeping like the dead tonight. I don't blame them for it; the heat can be a killer out here.

"Watch it," Vance's voice comes out of nowhere suddenly, and then I see his silhouette flashing between me and our banked campfire, followed by an unpleasant crunching sound. It all happens in less than a second, while I sit frozen in the opening of my tent.

He gingerly picks something off the ground and comes over to crouch by me. His hand is extended towards me, but it takes a second for me to realize that he's holding a fat rattlesnake. Its head is crushed, and its tail twitches limply as its nerves spasm for the last time. I've killed rattlesnakes before, but I didn't hear this one coming. My mouth goes dry as it slowly sinks in how close I came to being bitten.

"It was going for your ankles," Vance says.

"I'm wearing boots," I reply automatically, my mind still working through its shock. "Couldn't have bitten through them."

"Your wrists, then," Vance says, gesturing at where I have them propped up against the ground. He tosses the snake onto the smoldering fire, and I watch the graceful shape his hand makes in the air. I swallow roughly, feeling the spit grate against my raw throat, feeling air bubbling through the fluid in my lungs.

"Thanks," I manage after a moment. "Close one, huh?"

Vance lets out a thoughtful hum. "I've seen closer, but I'm glad I got up when I did," he replies. I wonder if the snake got any of my herd, if that's why they've been so still tonight.

"Why'd you get up?" I ask. "You're the boss. It's me and Jake's job to take watches; you ain't getting paid to be awake at the ass-crack of midnight."

"I like the desert at night." He gives me a clap on the back that lasts just a second too long. "There's so much life, both sleeping and waking."

I nod wordlessly, feeling the warm imprint of where his hand pressed into my skin. "Sure," I say. "Lucky for me, I guess."

"You should go sleep, if you want," he adds softly. "I can take your watch; it's really not a big deal."

I shouldn't say yes to his offer, it's both unprofessional and dangerous, but my eyes feel like they're full of sand, and I'm already tired out by the knowledge that I'll wake up choking on mucus and gasping for breath. I'm not worried about him taking off by himself while me and Jake aren't watching, either. The idea of him being able to round up the whole herd is laughable. Part of me is convinced that Vance knew this, but he's already paid. It doesn't matter.

"All right, wake up Jake once the fire burns out all the way," I hear myself saying, and I'm not surprised at it. He gives me a satisfied smile, looking like this is what he wanted all along, but I'm too tired to care about why that might be the case. I stumble into my bedroll without another word.

I sleep from hour to hour, tormented by confused dreams of mushrooms growing in flesh and solar systems consumed by clouds of stellar spores. Sometime before dawn, I wander out blearily to take a piss. The silhouette of a man is visible wandering through the rows of sleeping cattle, flickering in and out of my vision in the blue haze of lightning and dust, but he disappears when I blink, leaving no trace.

I fall asleep again before I can figure out whether he was part of my dream or not.

Something is wrong with the herd.

I noticed their eyes first. They didn't open right when me and Jake went to go feed and water them. The pupils were swallowed under a coating of milky white, shot through with threads of blue like a fancy cheese. They smell just as bad, too. It rises from them in an overpowering fog that keeps all three of us riding as far away from them as possible.

They're walking differently now. Slow and shambling on shaking legs. I ask Jake what he fed them last night, but he promises all he did was let them loose on the desert scrub like usual. I believe him, if only because I know how badly he needs to keep this job.

It's Vance that I can't figure out. He's paid for the herd already, so I guess that means he can do whatever he wants with them, but he also paid for our time to drive them somewhere, and there's no reason for him to do that if he was going to poison them. I ride by him again today, to watch him, and he looks the same as always—unhurried and mild. This reaction makes me more suspicious than any other one would, but I could also assume that he doesn't know enough about cattle to notice anything off about them. He might just think cattle stink.

One of the cattle collapses an hour after sunrise, yellow froth bubbling from its mouth and falling off in crusts out of its nostrils. Vance has been guiding us towards his mystery destination with no comments, but even though me and Jake agreed with each other to drive them for a little while, this forces our hand.

"The herd needs a rest," I tell Vance. "Something's wrong with them, and we gotta figure out what before we go farther." My lungs feel tight and stiff.

The smell is making it even harder to breathe than usual, and my head is spinning in the heat.

His eyes go distant, and he looks around for a moment. The three of us are in a small valley, but he focuses on the horizons both behind and ahead of us instead. I'm overcome with the sudden powerful feeling that he is somehow somewhere very far away, and then he blinks, and he returns to the space behind his eyes.

"No, we continue," he says firmly, like he's decided something. "I can't work here."

Jake rides up to us before I have a chance to respond. He's nervously twisting his gloves, and I'm tempted to slap the hesitant look off his face as he glances between the two of us.

"I dunno what's happening," he mutters. "I don't get it; they were fine yesterday. I just don't get it."

"They were moving slow, idiot, why didn't you say anything?" I snap, aware that my anger is aimed more at myself than him. My lungs ache, my whole body is in pain from too much riding, my head pounds, and he's an easy target.

"If you noticed that, you should've said somethin' yourself," he mumbles. "I thought they were normal."

"Enough." Vance's rough voice crackles through our conversation, no longer anything close to mild. Jake flinches and I turn my head just in time to see Vance cocking a pistol he's produced out of nowhere. "Just to make sure we all understand each other properly," he adds.

There's a moment when both Jake and me consider lunging at him—I can see it in the way Jake's muscles tense—but neither of us carry weapons, and the instant Jake raises his hands in the air, I have to raise mine too. I'm not attacking a man with a gun by myself.

"I see that we do understand," Vance says flatly. I glare at Jake out of the corner of my eye for giving up so easily, but he's already looking at the ground in shame. I shouldn't blame him, I should be frightened by the threat of violence, but any fear is swallowed up by anger.

I wanted so badly to like him. I wanted so badly for him to like me. More than anything, I'm furious at myself for letting that cloud my judgement, because I should've seen something like this coming. It's not stranger than anything else about this job.

"I dunno what's wrong with the herd," I say out loud, "but they're gonna start dropping like flies if we keep forcing them onwards." I'm trying my best to keep my voice calm and level, but Vance just looks at me unsympathetically.

"I'll have enough of them, even with some missing," he replies. "We'll leave the ones that can't continue where they drop." He gestures towards the horizon with his gun. "Move along, now."

Jake immediately wheels around and starts rounding up the herd, hunching his shoulders like he's expecting a bullet in his back. I stare at Vance for a few more seconds before turning aside to cough. He just shrugs.

"I can promise it's not personal, at least. I like you boys," he tells me.

"Why pay for our time at all if you were gonna pull this?" I ask, and he lets out a small laugh.

"Do I look like someone who can round up a whole herd of cattle by myself?" He shakes his head, still grinning a bit, and I have to agree. He rides well, but even in his borrowed chaps and hat, he's obviously a big-city man from the East. It's something they all have in their eyes, some visible wish for life with a smaller sky. He has that, along with something else that I can't quite place.

"Fair enough," I say. "I'll keep drivin' your herd, but I'll make sure everybody knows what your style of business is when we get back to the ranch."

"Fair enough," he echoes me. "Just get them where I need them to go."

The three of us ride the day away in sullen silence. We lose three more cattle before noon, but Vance doesn't spare them a glance. His eyes stay fixed on the horizon, and Jake and I dutifully drive the remaining herd where he guides us.

Jake asks if I have any idea where we're going after our cold horseback lunch, but I have nothing to tell him, and he has no poorly thought-out theories to suggest for once. It's only gotten harder to breathe in the wake of the stinking herd, and neither of us feels like doing anything except pulling our bandanas over our faces and soldiering on. The cattle smell rotten and overripe. I can't shake the image of them exploding in the heat like smashed fruit, and my breath rattles in my throat as I fight waves of nausea.

Vance forces us along until evening. He hasn't let us take a break since dawn, and all my muscles are burning by the time he comes to a sudden stop.

"This is it," he says, with a visible fierce joy on his face. "This is where we prepare."

Jake and I look at each other, confused. This patch of scrubland looks no different from any other that we've ridden through. The oat grasses and bitterbrush and little yellow flowers poking out of the sandy dirt aren't special, and neither is the flat landscape, but there's no doubt in Vance's voice as he dismounts and tells us to arrange the herd in a circle.

"We ain't circus ringmasters," Jake complains to me under his breath, but the sick cattle follow our guidance easily enough.

Vance seems pleased. The pistol remains on his belt, but after the cattle settle down, he calls us over with a smile. "You've done a good job, boys," he tells us. "I just have one more request, and then you're free to go back to your lives, if that's what you want. Stay with me until the moon rises, that's all."

"If that's it, how come we shouldn't leave now?" I ask. The sun is already setting in swollen reds and sick yellows, but I don't want to spend any more time with this madman than I have to. Jake nods his head in timid agreement.

Vance's handsome face smiles up at me as he settles on the ground. "I won't shoot you, if that's what you're worried about, but I think you'd enjoy waiting."

Behind me, I hear a guttural groan unlike any other sound I've heard a cow make before. The hair on the back of my neck stands up. Next to me, Jake lets out a choked gasp, and I slowly turn around. I don't want to see whatever it is that Vance has done to our poor cattle, but the idea of coming all this way with so many questions and having to wonder at the answers for the rest of my life is deeply painful.

I don't know if it would be as painful as what I see now.

The herd writhes. Shapes move under their skins and push up through them with an awful tearing sound. Corpse-pale fingers of fungus probe the soft jelly of their eyes from the inside, waving in the air with inhuman agility.

Blue and brown fruiting bodies tear through muscle. They glow eerily even under the blood that drips off them. I see mouths forced open by gushes of spore pods, see the delicate tendrils threading through the ground around piles of intestines.

"I have a whole new world to show you," Vance says behind me. I feel his hot breath on my ear and hear Jake retching.

Stinking fluids ooze from the cattle's bodies as they start to break down. Their skeletons are peeking through now, but the bone is yellow and corrupted. It's hard to tell which bones belong to which cow. The entire mass of flesh is sliding together into a horrifying tapestry of decay and mushrooms. The stench lodges in the back of my throat, and I start hacking out coughs so violent that they drive me to my knees.

"I can offer you a life better than this, better than endlessly hoping that what you need is just over the horizon," Vance whispers into my ear. "Better than spending all your time with men that you're too afraid to touch because it's better than nothing."

He places his hands on my shoulders, and my entire body goes rigid, but his fingers are as warm and soothing as ever. I taste blood on my lips and realize that it came from the inside of my lungs. I'm not surprised he knows what I want. It seems like such a tiny secret compared to his.

In front of me, what's left of the cattle sinks into a cradle of soft fungus, soft as rot.

Vance pulls me to my feet. I turn to face him, and in the last gasps of sunlight, I see that he has the same growths breaking through his skin where his scars used to be. He clasps my face in his hands and gently brings his lips to mine, and I don't fight it. I don't know why I don't fight it.

It's nothing like my first kiss was with a schoolgirl back in South Dakota. Vance's lips are rough against mine, and I can taste my own blood as my tongue hungrily pushes into his mouth. He tastes like salt and dust. There's nothing soft about this kiss, and it's everything I ever dreamed of. His chapped hands slide into my hair. They knock my hat off, and I groan into his mouth. I *know* why I didn't fight it.

His tongue slides against mine, wet with spit, but it suddenly feels wrong. It's too soft, too mobile. I feel those fungal tendrils reaching down my throat and push him away with a cry. My body goes cold, even though I'm sweating through my clothes, and I gasp for breath.

It's a deep breath; full and reaching to the bottom of my lungs in a way I haven't felt for years. Vance smiles at me. The crawling tendrils dart out to lick a speck of my blood off the corner of his lips, and I wonder how deep they got inside me. I think of spores in my lungs, widening my air passages and clearing away the fluid.

"You see what I have to offer you," Vance says hungrily. "A life free from pain, an accepting home… Everything you think you could never have."

I stand there, frozen, trying to somehow understand the events of the last few minutes. I knew I was a fag, but I never expected to have a kiss so perfect and so horrifying in my entire life. Blood rushes in my ears like I'm falling from a very high height, but Vance just smiles. He turns to Jake, who's staring numbly at the ring of flesh that used to be our herd.

"I know how lonely you are," Vance tells him. "I know you think no one will ever love you, and I know why, but I promise that none of those things will matter in the place I'm going to."

"Where's that?" Jake asks quietly after a second. "That sounds nice."

"Jake!" I hiss at him. My mind might be a muddle right now, but at least I know to not trust Vance with anything.

Vance points at the dark horizon and the sliver of moon poking above it. "The mycelium realm of the Sporestorm Lord," he intones. The moon creeps higher, and I feel something deep inside the world begin to shift. "The Dominion of Life that Devours the Void, Oldest of the Outside," Vance continues, throwing both hands into the air like a plea. "Bless the King of Perfect Quiet, for He has blessed a million planets and hungers to share His gift of endless peace with a million more."

He turns to me and Jake, eyes burning with the same fleshy glow of the erupting bodies behind us. "You will never have to feel lonely again in His embrace," he promises, and I believe him. I believe him down to my boots, and it terrifies me.

The moon rises above us, and as its light hits the ring of moaning cattle, everything changes.

It's cosmic, planetary. Great gears click into place under the surface of the universe, and a silver-blue haze erupts across the ground inside the ring. It all melts together; flesh, bone, and fungus. The shaft of moonlight, focused through the ring Vance constructed, becomes a tunnel that shines through a gap in the machinery of the world to some other place. I don't know how I know, but I can feel it in my soul. For a moment, the universe itself has been altered.

I look over at Jake, and the awe on his face is so pure that it almost makes me cry.

"Join me in Him," Vance says, walking towards the ring with his arms outstretched. Jake takes a step after him, and I cry out instinctively.

"No, don't go with him!" The same part of me that feels the vast scale of this knows how little we humans are in comparison. The forces at play can barely see us, and I don't want Jake at their mercy. He's barely a friend to me, but he deserves better than this.

"Vance is right, you know," Jake says over his shoulder. "No one here's gonna love me." I open my mouth to tell him it's not true, but I've known him for four years now, and I don't even know what he likes doing for fun. "Hey, maybe the girls on the other side like chinks enough to go to bed with one for free," he adds with a small smile, and I finally realize just how lonely he's always been.

I realize just how lonely I've always been.

"Don't go," I whisper. I want to tell him I could learn to love him, but he's already stepping into the shimmering circle before Vance, who turns around to look at me one last time.

"Every time you take a deep breath, think of this moment and thank the mycelium," he calls, "and when the dreams start, and you hear His voice calling you, know that we will be here to welcome you."

"Go to hell," I snap.

He only smirks in response, and then the two of them are gone in a flash of light, leaving nothing behind but a stinking ring of flesh and moonlight shining on the desert hills.

I sink to the ground, alone with the remains of my herd and an uncaring horizon.

WOULD YOU LIKE TO HEAR ABOUT OUR TRAVEL PACKAGE DEALS

CLAY MCLEOD CHAPMAN

ALWAYS UPSELL. OFFER the client any one of our exclusive package deals, the once-in-a-lifetime opportunity to see these calamities up close and personal! Wander through the rubble. Tally the human toll. Our clientele have, shall we say, *discerning* tastes when it comes to the particular tours we offer. They're hungry for tragedy. Absolutely famished for disaster—and they can afford it—so sell the devastation. The ash coating their throat.

Vista Destinations has always been on the frontlines of disaster. We pride ourselves on offering our clientele a waltz through the war zone. Wade into the floodwaters. Step into the blast radius. There's no police tape barricading onlookers yet, no barrier between you and the tragedy—whatever it may be—because we're there before anyone else. The military. Recovery efforts. Humanitarian aid. The first responders just so happen to be our clients.

We prefer not to use the term *tourist*. No, our customers are on a sojourn. A pilgrimage of tribulation. The world is constantly on the brink of calamity.

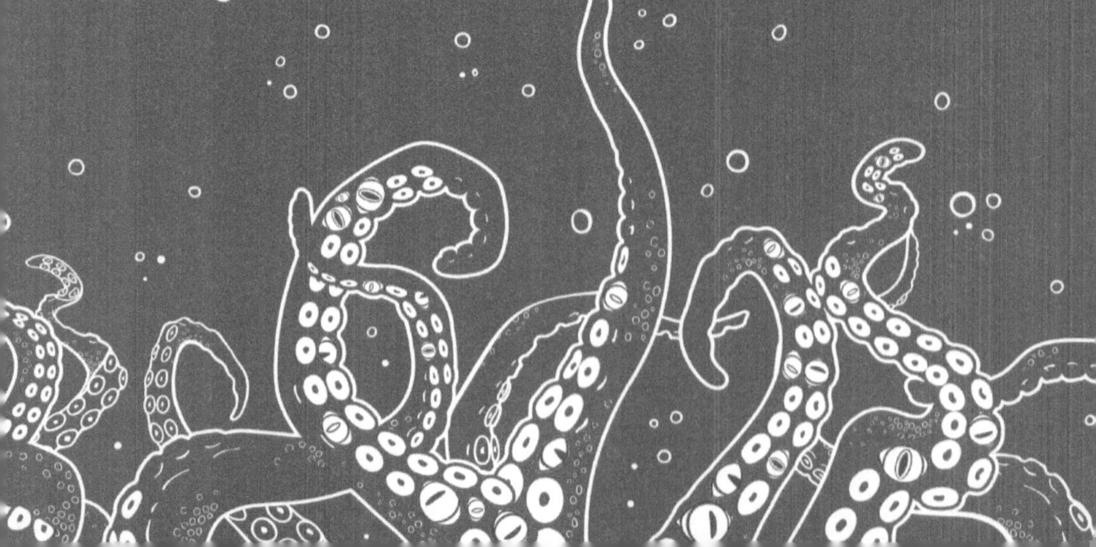

When tragedy strikes, whether by way of forest fire or firearm, there's a need to see. To bear witness. Experience.

We shepherd you there.

Just don't call us travel agents. That's crass, if you ask me. I've always considered myself more of a sherpa for the apocalypse; I'll take you right up to the lip of the volcano.

Catastrophe cache. That's what I peddle. And it sells. It *always* sells.

I might have something for you, I start my sales pitch. Today's no different. I have about ten clients on speed dial that I call whenever there's a new emergency brewing. Volcano. Tsunami. School shooting. My preferred customers want first dibs, while things are still developing. Unfolding. *We're not entirely sure what we're dealing with yet…but it's big.*

No idea? I hear the anticipation in my client's voice, the hitch in his breath. He's in his penthouse apartment, his hermetically-sealed office space overlooking the world.

He wants to be down there. In the thick of it. The lava flow.

Could be natural…or not. We just don't know. I wanted to reach out to you first and let you know we may have a new destination set for you soon…say, in twenty-four hours?

I have no idea what I'm even selling yet. There's a media blackout in the middle of America, which could only mean a few things. I offer up a breakdown of what we know thus far: Small town on lockdown. Everyone within has slipped into complete silence, while nobody on the outside can peek in. Phone lines are down. Zero social media posts. Nothing. Completely quiet. No cries for help. No beseeching the heavens. Just…silence.

That never happens. *Ever.*

My bet is it's a manmade disaster. I'm banking on a domestic terrorist bombing. Or a nuclear core meltdown. Maybe it's a disgruntled employee with a machine gun. The FBI raiding the compound of some militia of patriots. Perhaps a needy teen desperate for attention. Who knows. But it's got to be by hand, not a natural disaster.

I've got just enough info to start putting together a new package—the general location of the event, the nearest airport, the level of radio silence.

I have to peddle the urgency. The ticking clock. You want things fresh, untampered. *With the way this is shaping up,* I say, *we may be looking at a death toll in the dozens…*

I'll take it, my client finally says. Always says. Goddamn venture capitalist. *Book it.*

Wonderful, sir. I'll have more information for you soon. Start packing.

So what's our new tour package, exactly?

Good question. Your guess is as good as mine. Still too early to tell. The news usually picks up on these events in minutes, but this one's a total ghost. It may sound counterintuitive, but it's the very negative space surrounding the cataclysm—the lack of coverage, the absence of social media—that's leading me to believe we've got a live one on our hands. You can't cover up an earthquake. People would talk about it. Post about it online.

Nobody's talking about this.

I have a team whose sole job is to sit on their asses and comb through the internet for the next cataclysm. I call them my *soothsayers.* Look long enough online and you can start to see the signs for the next big event. All it takes is scoring weather reports, police band radios, government intel, simply tracking the atmosphere of the world at large.

Think of the web as a crystal ball. If you know how to read it, look in deep, you can nearly see the calamity coming before it even happens. We need to be three steps ahead of disaster for our travel packages. I want our planes gassed and ready for liftoff before the floodwaters recede. That means anticipating the disaster. Pitching them in their infancy.

Got one brewing, my top soothsayer told me this morning, just three hours ago.

Oh? Do tell.

That's just it, he said. *There's not much to tell. I don't even know what I'm looking at.*

And you're waking me up for this because…?

Because it's the weirdest fucking thing I've ever seen. There's like a, I don't know, a black hole in the middle of a cornfield and nobody's talking about it, like… at all.

A black hole? In a cornfield?

That's what it looks like. Bunch of folks clocked in to work at some factory and suddenly their phones all blitzed out at the same time. And it looks like it's expanding.

Could be a cell phone tower going down.

Yeah, but not like this. This doesn't feel right. Something fishy is happening...

You sure?

Not really, my soothsayer said. *But it's definitely got me spooked.*

That's all I needed.

Once the news reports on a catastrophe, whatever it is, that clock starts ticking. There's little time. We need to hurry and put together a package if we want our customers to be on the frontlines. Nobody wants to get there second, trapped behind the barricade.

That usually means I go first. To test the floodwaters, as it were. See what we're dealing with. Our clientele prefer not to go through the crass disaster tourism companies. No charter buses, no guided tours, no t-shirts. For those discriminating travelers who prefer to explore alone, in private, we offer a much lower profile. Vista Destinations provides paths not tread by the rest. You'll see it first, you'll see it fresh. The closer to the cataclysm you are, the more you feel it. The cinders. The friction. The deafening silence of tragedy. That's ultimately what our clients desire. That sense of being there. Feeling it first-hand.

The *resonance.* That's what I call it. The electricity in the air. A friction lingering in the atmosphere. Can you feel it? A beachside attraction won't have that. But after a tsunami? Amongst the debris? The aura itself changes. The very area sanctifies itself. Becomes holy.

New Orleans felt fresh. At first. Everybody pounced on that one. Fucking vultures. The water levels in the lower ninth had barely receded by the time there were guided tours. The charter buses jammed traffic so much, recovery efforts could barely use the highways.

Vista, on the other hand—we were a bit more covert about our journey. We took our clients through St. Bernard's Parish by boat, courtesy of the Coast Guard.

The houses caked in mud. A child's shoe, just one, left in the street. Pieces of living history littered the floodwaters. That was our highest selling package. Still our top seller today.

Tourism is a part of our very nature. Travel to any destination around the world. Where do you go? What do you see? You visit the ruins. The churches. The monuments.

Why?

Don't lie. What are you really after? You want to capture that sense of disaster. Smell death in the air. So go ahead—travel to the cataclysms. Visit the sites of tragedy. The battlefields. The temples. The ruins of civilizations. There's real history in these moments.

But don't lie about why. Be honest with your predilections.

You want to see death.

We offer the freshest history. Why wait two hundred years? Our clientele puts their faith in Vista Destinations to offer tomorrow's history today. We have never led them astray.

We take you there.

We have our own personal fleet of private planes, from Cessnas to Gulfstream jets. We can deliver our customers just about anywhere in the world that we need to go.

Such as Pickerling, Iowa.

I didn't find out where I was flying to until after we had wheels in the air. Pickerling. Never heard of it. It didn't pop up on my phone when I typed the coordinates in. It simply wasn't there. That's nothing new. These towns—Littleton, Sandy Hook, Chernobyl—they're nothing. Names no one knew. Fly specks on the map. They meant nothing to the world…

Until. Always until. Until a man with a gun opens fire. Until there's an explosion.

Now everyone knows their name. These small towns enter the lexicon, steeped in their own tragedy, synonymous with tsunamis. Infamous with insurrection. With chaos.

This time tomorrow, the world will know the name Pickerling. It'll be whispered with the same breathless adulation as September 11th. As Waco, Texas.

Why still remains the million dollar question. Which is why I have to get there first.

To see for myself.

Pickerling has a population of 600 people. The town itself seems to be built almost entirely around its chicken processing plant, employing most of its citizens. There wasn't much online about it beyond a few health code violations. A meat recall not too long ago.

What are we dealing with here? What's going on in Pickerling? The news would've reported on a school shooting by now. Somebody would've tweeted about an explosion.

What the hell is this?

A tsunami without water. A flood without rain.

A black hole.

I'll get the lay of the land, assess the disaster itself, and then I'll be booking trips before the end of the day. Our clients will be making their sojourn by tomorrow morning.

Chernobyl was cheap. Easy. The distance of decades dulled the resonance. I could never pick it up, personally. The longer time has elapsed since the initial cataclysm, the impact lessons for me. Deadens it. It simply becomes another location. Tragedy becomes history becomes past tense becomes boring. Anyone can go there. Take their selfies. Happens everywhere. Anyone can visit the World Trade Center. Auschwitz. You can book a night in a concentration camp like it's nothing but an Air B&B. There are bus tours to Columbine. Cruises through Prince William Sound to see the lingering sheen of the Exxon Valdez. You can visit the ruins at Pompei and pose next to the negative space of the petrified remains of those wiped out by Mount Vesuvius. Anyone can do this. Anyone.

What disaster is happening *now*? What tragedy is unfolding *now*?

Call it grim. Call it morbid. *Profiting off the macabre.* At least it's honest, unflinching. Tragedies map the world. Rather than look away from these events, you can see with your own eyes. Bear witness to history. Capture that moment. Taste it, at times.

Trust me on this, I say to another customer. I'm trying to tee up a couple more clients before landing. *Our window of exclusivity is extremely narrow. It'll tighten by lunchtime.*

I'm afraid I need more details, my client says. I can hear the uncertainty in her voice. The timidity. Some customers just need a push. A simple shove into the volcano's mouth.

Think of what's waiting for you on the other side of tomorrow. The world doesn't know what's coming, but you do. You're one of a small handful of people that even know this is unfolding. I'm offering you this opportunity to see it for yourself before anyone else.

I've given a version of this spiel I don't know how many times. Hundreds. Thousands. *I'm placing you at the forefront of history,* I say into the phone, growing impatient. I've got three more calls to make before landing. *This is your chance. It won't last for much longer. The window is already closing. Which side of history will you be on?*

I glance out the plane's window and take in the vast expanse of land 30,000 feet below. Look. Just look at it all. Look at all the tornadoes brewing. The forest fires sparking. The floods beginning to rise. Tragedies just waiting to happen. They're everywhere.

Let me think about it, she says.

Thank you, I say, already mentally striking her from my preferred customer list.

Mount Merapi might have been one of my personal favorites of our tour packages. Sending our clients to Indonesia wasn't easy, but the area had already been a tourist destination, so the infrastructure was already in place to charter our flights to and from. Air travel reopened two days after the eruption for evac, so I made sure our fleet had a spot on the tarmac. Nearly four hundred people were swallowed up by pyroclastic lava flows. Our clients walked amongst the bodies before they were even gathered up. Villagers were still picking through the debris of their homes when we arrived, believing we were Red Cross.

By the time I land in Iowa, I have three confirmed reservations, two tentative bookings, and one pass. I can book seven more tours before the sun sets on these cornfields.

Can you get anybody on the line? I ask my top soothsayer over the phone. *Find out what the fuck we've got on our hands down here? I'm getting jack shit.*

Maybe I was wrong, I dunno… False alarm.

Does this feel like a false alarm to you?

I don't know what this feels like. If I were you, I might think about cutting your losses.

Too late for that. I'm here now.

I'll put in a few phone calls to the local law enforcement when I reach my rental car. See who's running things down here. Vista Destinations is proud of its financial contributions to help with local recovery; we offer a portion of our funds to the people in charge, who in turn offer our clients exclusive opportunities to see the devastation up front.

I find it's better to make donations directly to the sheriff than any of the nonprofit agencies that swoop in at the last minute like flies on a corpse. Our money is better spent in the hands of the people directly affected by these particular tragedies. We want to help the local economy grow back, even stronger than it was before.

But there's nothing out here. Nothing at all. Cornfields on either side of the highway. I still don't have a fucking clue what I'm dealing with yet. I'm beginning to feel a little squeamish about getting our clients to agree to this. I don't know how to spin this one.

But there's an electricity in the air. A current.

The resonance. I feel it.

It's here.

So…where are the police barricades? The wail of sirens? The fire trucks and ambulances? Is anything actually happening out here?

This smell slowly takes over. I have the window of my rental car rolled down. This scent, cloying at first, gradually fills my nostrils. Sweet decay. Death in the air. Miles of it.

All kids luv lickin' their Pickerlin' chickin'!

The ancient billboard just outside the Pickerling Chicken processing plant is nothing but a chipped mural of a little gap-toothed girl holding up a drumstick as if it were a lollipop. She is, in fact, licking its breaded skin. Her freckles have flaked off from the wood.

The rhyme scheme seems off to me, mainly because of the usage of the town's name. I had assumed Pickerling emphasized its *-ing*, but reading this company's motto, how they dropped the 'g' altogether, makes me think I might've been mistaken.

A listeria outbreak. *Fuck.* Is that all this is? I came all this way for contaminated meat? How the hell am I supposed to sell a tour package for fucking food poisoning?

Pickerling Chicken supplies most schools with their chicken tenders. They're the kind of company you won't find in the freezer of your local grocery store, but it's safe to say the majority of students throughout the US have eaten hundreds of their nuggets.

This particular processing plant here in Pickerling is the major hub of their business, the pumping heart of their food provisions. Miles of chicken coops. The outright sprawl of poultry reaches well into the horizon. These chickens are fed and raised right here, then processed into nuggets, then sent along the arteries of interstates branching out into the rest of the country via refrigerated semis, where they are delivered to your local public school and served for lunch. The cycle of life for a chicken nugget, farm to cafeteria table.

I hear them the second I climb out of the car. All of them. The chickens. I've never heard anything like it. Choking. As if the air itself is gagging. The very atmosphere has something caught in its throat—a feather—and can't hack it out.

The smell is stronger here. The air is dense with iron. With blood.

I have never been to a chicken processing plant. I have never *wanted* to visit a chicken processing plant. I can't imagine any of our clients—not a single fucking customer—is going to want to set foot in this foul smelling factory.

Black hole, my ass. This is bacteria at best. Noncompliance for food regulation. I can't believe I've come all this way, to the middle of nowhere, just for an outbreak.

Hello? I call out, just for the hell of it.

Only the chickens respond.

I haven't seen one single human being. It shouldn't be this easy. Usually there's a police officer telling me to stay back, or a barricade of saw horses, or news crews clustering around the event itself. There's nothing here.

Just chickens. Thousands of them, clucking their fucking heads off. I can barely hear myself think anymore, it's so loud.

Nobody's picking up their phone. Cell service is shit out here. I can't get anyone to answer my calls.

I'm all alone.

What other choice is there but to go inside? This is why I'm here, isn't it? I'm a first responder. The first tourist. I've come here to bear witness, so that others may see.

Might as well, right? I've come this far…

In we go.

From outside, the factory looks like an airport hangar with a corrugated metal roof. The only flash of personality comes from the old billboard, the smiling freckle-faced girl licking her lollipop of boneless chicken leg, but that's about it. The inside should be metal as well, shouldn't it? Easy to hose down concrete flooring? I'm expecting bland beige cinderblocks.

But it's all pink. The walls. The ceiling. There's a mottled bubblegum complexion to everything. I don't know what I'm looking at yet, but it's everywhere. On everything.

I feel like I've entered a stomach. Something intestinal.

The air is sweltering. Humid. There's no ventilation. It was thick outside in the open, but in here, the atmosphere has coagulated. The air is completely weighed down with the tonnage of blood, so thick it coats my throat. It's greasy to breathe.

I'm on the factory floor. The first thing I notice is a conveyor belt. A river of pink chicken cutlets purls on by, heading downstream to the deep-fat frier. They'll be breaded and fried and then sent on their merry way to whatever school is feeding their kids these yummy nuggets. But there's no one here. Nobody's manning the factory floor. There's a bedding of feathers at my feet, swallowing my shoes. It covers the entire work floor. It has to be an inch or two thick. Everything's eclipsed in chicken feathers.

I hear choking. Someone's gasping for air. It's coming from the walls.

It's the cutlets. That pink paste has adhered to the surface of…of *everything*. The meat—still raw—has bonded, congealed somehow, in a gelatinous layer. It's on the walls. The machinery. A webbing of pink tissue dangles off the light fixtures just over my head.

I'm aware—tangentially, at least—of how this chicken must be processed. They take the fowl and pulverize it into a paste, squirt the meat porridge into a mold and bake it back into the boneless shape of a nugget. You want to believe it's a prime cut of chicken breast, but in reality, it's more like meatloaf. What I'm looking at here must be the precooked paste coating every inch of the factory. It has to be that, right? There must have been an explosion of some sort that sent this chicken pulp spreading everywhere.

So why is it moving? Why is it *breathing*?

Trying to, at least. Every labored inhale has a wet rasp at the back end of it, a gravel bed of air. The exhales are even worse. They're screaming. Shrieking. Raw chicken cutlets.

All the health code violations flicker in my mind. A factory like this, in the middle of nowhere, miles away from prying eyes, could go about its business with the Department of U.S. Agriculture being none the wiser. Sure, there would be red flags. Even recalls. But it would take months, maybe even years, for a business like this to shutter if they wanted to keep going. Happens all the time. How long have kids been lickin' their Pickerlin' Chicken?

Something nimble shifts within the pink tincture. It looks like a limb. A human arm. It's breaks through the surface of the wall, then dips back under, there and gone in a blink.

Someone is swimming through the wall.

A factory worker.

I spot their head bob above the surface, just for a quick second, smiling as she spirals below all over again. She's wearing a hairnet. I can tell because the pink ooze sluices through the tiny diamond-shaped webbing along her head, creating these long dangling strands of pink meat spaghetti.

There's another. Three Pickerling employees. A man, two women. They're in a cluster, gliding along the wall. The ceiling. Defying gravity. They are swimming in it. Through it. On their backs. I spot them all, more now, dozens of hair-netted workers gliding through the pink poultry waters like synchronized swimmers doing a water ballet on the walls. They may as well be on vacation, basking on the beach. Smiling. Having the time of their lives.

This isn't a black hole. It's a pink one.

One woman reaches out to me. She's in her forties, from what I can tell. Curly auburn locks spill out from her hairnet. I think maybe she needs help. Wants to escape. But the second I take her hand and pull, she tugs back, harder, stronger—and I realize, too late, she doesn't want my help. She wants me to join her. *Come on in*, she sighs, *the water's fine.*

Do I want to dive in?

My first instinct, my gut, God help me, is to think—*Maybe I can package this after all.*

I poke my finger in. It's warm. Sticky. I bring my finger up to my nose. Take a sniff.

I dab my fingertip against my tongue.

Taste it.

The wall opens. Respires. Ripples with resonance. The water is calling for me. Beckoning. I feel the warmth against my skin. Like the sun. I just want to go for a swim.

Take a dip.

Think of all the children who'll be eating these chicken nuggets tomorrow. What if this spreads? What if whatever begins here crops up in cafeterias across the country?

I can already see it. Sense it. Tomorrow there will be a report of an outbreak in Minneapolis. Another in North Carolina. Before long, they'll be everywhere. Pink tide pools. Soon, they'll expand. Across the walls. The ceilings. Students will be swimming through. Their water ballet. Twirling like starfish, limbs spiraling through the tide. Pink and luscious.

I want to swim, too. To bask in its warmth.

I take my shoes off first, left then right. Then my socks. My pants. I'm down to my skivvies in seconds. The waters are thick but warm. It takes some force, but I'm able to press my foot into the wall. The waters pry apart, rippling around my ankle. It almost feels like a set of lips wriggling over my skin, getting a taste for me. It tickles at first, then it's soothing. So warm. God, I've never felt anything like it in my life. I want to swim. Swim.

I'm on vacation. I'm at the beach. The waters are so warm. This place is beautiful.

I never want to leave.

Already I'm picturing the pitch. *Oh, do I have a travel package for you... You'll never want to go home again.*

IT FEASTS

HAROLD HOSS

After parking in the driveway, Chris lingered in the alleyway between his tiny black sedan and his wife's minivan to look up at the moon. He chewed mindlessly on a flavorless piece of gum and wondered how many people out there noticed the moon looked unusually big tonight—and how those people would feel if they found out it was *true*. Over the last three weeks, the moon had expanded over ten percent and not a single person at NASA knew why. They had plenty of theories and plenty of degrees, but not a single believable reason, after all these years, the moon would begin to grow.

Sighing, Chris forced his gaze away from the great white orb and down to his house. The house Chris lived in with his wife and daughter was shaped like a golf club, with the living room, kitchen, dining room and office forming a square next to the garage before tapering off into a hallway leading to their bedrooms. Giant bay windows curved around the kitchen so he could see Jean, his wife, moving around the kitchen island while talking on the phone.

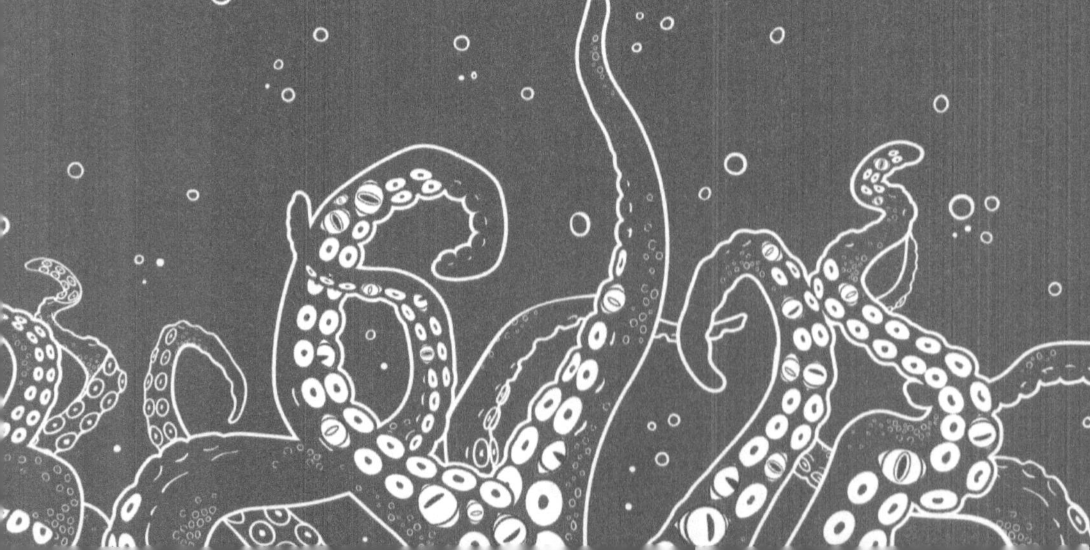

She looked happy, bathed in the warm lights, and he didn't want to ruin that by bringing in his negative energy from work.

He tried to take a calming breath but found his head unconsciously tilting back up towards the moon. Seeing it so big, like a balloon ready to pop, made him uneasy. He couldn't shake the feeling that he was on the verge of piecing things together, like the lingering déjà vu hangover from a bad dream. Looking at it again, he heard the thumping in his ears even without the cumbersome company headphones. The steady "one-two" bum-bum beat made up the second part of the moon mystery.

Chris grunted, shaking his head to clear it, then squeezed the bridge of his nose. He wasn't much of a drinker, but he wanted a beer. Something to make him relax.

Still feeling tense around the neck and shoulders, he walked through the gate and up to the back door. Pushing inside, he let the warmth and familiar smell of Jean's cooking wash over him as he kicked his shoes off. He could hear his wife speaking in Korean in the other room. He could never remember the time difference between here and Seoul, but knew an evening call meant Jean was talking to her sister.

Chris stepped into the kitchen. A boiling pot with red soup sat on the stove while Jean leaned against the sink, laughing into her phone. She held up a finger and Chris shook his head, indicating she shouldn't hurry.

Instead, he walked around to the trash can and popped the lid. It always sprang open quickly, but took its time closing, giving Chris plenty of time to toss his gum and catch sight of an empty packet of silken tofu. His stomach growled in anticipation. He had a pretty good feeling he knew exactly what boiled in the pot and, hearing Jean's conversation wind to a close, he looked up.

"That was my sister. It's the lunar new year, so they're on holiday," Jean said. Chris visibly winced at the mention of the lunar new year, and Jean made a sympathetic face. "Sorry. Any good news from work?"

Chris shook his head. By *any good news,* he knew Jean meant *any idea what's happening to the moon,* but the truth was everyone at NASA was stumped.

"Any more questions from Hana?" Chris asked.

Last night before bed, their daughter, Hana, had burst into their room to announce her dad was on the news. Irritated, if not surprised, Chris could only thumb through the news article until he found his name among many "high level scientists stumped by the moon's strange behavior" according to an anonymous source. Later that night, thanks to another anonymous source, the news sources began speculating the moon had entered a rare harvest orbit that made it *look* bigger.

Chris suspected the second source to be one of his coworkers. While NASA's official policy might be to ignore the plebeian media, most of the team members bristled at the idea of watching their names and reputations take a savage beating online, kicked like a can first between the newspapers and then down into the writhing pit of anger and frustration that were online message boards.

Chris considered telling Jean about the sound they detected today, the steady one-two rhythm, almost like a heartbeat, but decided against it. Listening to the sound made him break out in gooseflesh, while several coworkers became nauseous and more than one had a nervous breakdown. No need to scare his family unnecessarily.

And besides, Chris thought, the moon was over four and a half billion years old. Who's to say it wasn't going through a new phase of some kind?

Chris realized Jean had said something and looked up. "What?"

"I said Hana has some good news," Jean said. Turning away, she opened the fridge and took out a carton of brown eggs. "Where is she? Hana!"

"I'm right here. Why are you yelling?" Hana said, moving out of the living room and into the kitchen.

Chris was pretty sure Hana hadn't been standing there a moment before, but he had noticed his daughter liked to come out swinging in conversations with her mom.

Seeing Jean turn, eyes narrowing, Chris made a move to cut her off. "What's the good news?"

Hana might have her mother's temper, but she had Chris's smile. A wide, toothy grin that seemed to wrap around her entire face.

"I got an A on my science report," Hana said.

"An A+," Jean added.

For once Hana didn't argue as she strutted through the kitchen, dropping the bound science report in front of him. Sure enough, a big red A+ marked the front. "Ask me about reaper eels. Ask me anything."

Chris didn't know the slightest thing about reaper eels so he started with something basic. "Why do they call them reaper eels?"

Flipping open the report, Chris saw this was the first question answered on the inside of the first page. Allowing him to read along as his daughter spoke, moving her arms wide and low like a roman orator.

"Many people think it's because of their distinctive coloring—black and gray with yellow eyes. Or the distinct scythe-like marks on their skin. But this is not the case!" Hana said.

Out of the corner of his eye, Chris saw Jean nodding with approval and he smiled. He knew his wife took Hana's grades personally and would be secretly just as proud.

"The reaper eel gets its name because the reaper eel *reaps what it sows*," Hana said.

Chris turned the page, happy for the distraction.

"Reaps what it sows? What does that mean?" Chris said. "I mean, I've heard of fish farms but I've never heard of a fish that farms." Chris couldn't help laughing before he got the dad joke out.

"Horrible," Jean said. She took out an egg, then stepped up to the pot, tapped it twice against the rim, and broke it in one solid strike, splitting it apart and dumping the contents inside. She tossed the two halves of the shell into the trash can.

Seeing the egg crack, Chris shivered. His mouth suddenly felt hot and sticky, and he thought of his coworkers that morning listening to the moon's heartbeat. The ones who broke down with complete panic attacks and required medical attention. He could feel the waves of panic lapping at the back of his brain, threatening to wash over him, but he didn't know why.

Chris forced himself to look back up and focus on Hana, just in time to see her roll her eyes at his joke before continuing. "The pregnant reaper eel will find a cave and lay her eggs around the outer rim of the only exit. Then she will protect that cave from predators, letting it fill up with tiny fish, mussels, and sea urchins."

Chris saw Jean approach the bowl, holding another egg. Again she tapped the egg twice against the rim before splitting it with one deft strike.

Now the shiver spread down his arms, through his lungs, and into his stomach, twisting it into an icy knot. The waves of panic grew stronger, bringing with them an undertow that threatened to pull him under. Chris tried to keep his face impassive, but beads of sweat broke out on his face and palms. He leaned in, trying to hear his daughter over the rising sound of rushing water in his ears, so loud it threatened to wipe every sense from his brain if he didn't mentally hold the line.

"Then the eggs hatch—and suddenly the safe cave becomes a trap. The young reaper eels begin to feast," Hana continued.

Chris didn't dare take a breath, afraid it would come in a ragged gasp. Instead, he looked down at the book, flipping through the glossy pictures. The tiny part of his brain that tried its best to make light of everything wondered how much this cost him. When he was ready, he eased a slow breath in through his nose. Then he exhaled just as slowly before taking another small breath.

Chris turned another page in the report. He was fine. He just needed a glass of water, or maybe a beer, after a stressful day.

"Very scientific. Just like your old man," Chris said, relieved to hear his voice sounded normal.

"Please," Hana said.

Chris had his breathing under control. He felt the waves of panic receding, as if the tide had changed.

The tide, Chris thought, stumbling over the word. The moon controlled the tides. Everything came back to the moon. He felt like he was on the verge of solving a puzzle. He could see all the pieces and a part of his brain, somewhere deep in the back, knew how they fit together. If he could just tap into it, everything would snap into focus.

Looking back up, Chris thought Hana was ready to say something else when Jean approached the pot with another egg out of the corner of his eye. She reached out and tapped the egg twice against the pot, and Chris screamed.

"Please—Babe! Stop!" Chris rarely raised his voice above his soft, scientific mumble and the sound of him screaming hit the kitchen like a bomb, freezing everyone in place.

Jean recoiled in shock, dropping the egg so that it shattered on the ground. On the opposite side of the room, Hana gasped, then pointed at Chris and shrieked.

"My report!" Hana cried, then sobbed.

Chris looked down and found his fist had crumpled around one of the glossy photos, mangling the page beyond repair. He heard footsteps vanishing down the hallway and looked up to find Hana gone and Jean glaring at him.

"Shit," Chris said.

Jean muttered something in Korean, ripped a paper towel off the roll, and dropped effortlessly into a low squat. Despite being the smallest in the family, angry Jean could easily fill any room in the house.

"I'll go talk to her," Chris said. He watched Jean's back for a response, but she simply wiped away at the spilled yoke.

Pushing his stool back into the island, Chris felt his phone vibrate and reached for it. Seeing it was the office, his heart sank.

"This is Chris," he said into the phone.

He never heard what came next. A deafening roar like a thunderclap just inches above his head knocked him to the ground, his head bouncing like a pinball off the island counter and then the floor. The one, two punches knocked out his vision and then his hearing, leaving him alone with a blinding white light and high-pitched ringing before his senses snapped back into place.

"Jesus," Chris said, slowly looking around.

All the lights and all the windows Chris could see had shattered, covering the ground in broken glass that glinted like a fresh layer of snow. Outside, he could hear car alarms going off up and down the street and distant sirens.

"Jean? Babe?" Chris pushed to his feet, peering up over the island.

Looking over the island, he saw Jean sitting with her back to the kitchen sink. She clutched her left arm to her chest, one laced with upraised lines of freshly cooked skin. Chris saw the overturned pot nearby, its steaming contents dripping down the cabinet and onto the floor.

"Babe, don't move," Chris said, looking at her bare feet and then the broken glass. "I'm coming to you."

Chris looked around. Glass covered the floor, so instead he hopped up on the kitchen island, crawling across to drop next to his wife.

"I'm okay, just. What happened?" Jean said.

His first thought was a bomb of some kind, but instead of saying this, he reached for his wife, wrapping an arm around her. Despite her feigned strength, Jean sank into him, a violent sob wracking her body.

Chris tightened his grip, fighting the urge to cry himself. Looking through the broken windows at the street, he saw a few cars had turned on their sides, their lights flashing while their horns blared.

"Mom? Dad?" Hana screamed. Chris's head jerked up, as if yanked by some primordial string.

"Hana? Hana!" Jean screamed back, her nails digging into Chris's arm. "Go to her!"

Chris didn't hesitate. Driven by the instinctive urge to protect his offspring, an urge kicked into overdrive when he heard Hana scream again.

He stumbled through the kitchen, ignoring the way the glass frayed and then cut through his socks before grinding its way into the flesh underneath. By the time he reached the wood paneling of the hallway, his feet smacked wetly with each step. He paused only once to toss aside a piece of furniture, then ran down the hallway to where Hana sat staring up out the window. She held her hands on either side of her face, her lips twitching through every emotion, before her jaw fell slack and her eyes rolled back.

"Hana," Chris screamed, running to catch her before she fell.

After a few shakes, Hana's eyes snapped open. None of the feisty anger she always directed at her mom, nor the overdramatic annoyance with which she treated his jokes, remained. Her eyes were blank. She could only turn her head away, whimpering as she looked past him out the window.

Following her gaze, Chris looked up and out at the moon. Only he couldn't see it. Or, to be more precise, his brain wouldn't let him see it at first. It was like staring at one of those old two-dimensional visual illusions where, if you found the right angle, a three-dimensional shape would appear. Yet he couldn't find the right angle. His eyes kept tracing around the moon's circumference, until with effort, he forced his eyes to look towards the center, focusing on the large black crack now running down the middle, dividing the moon into two halves until it widened, unraveling like a zipper and revealing a single giant, unblinking eye.

The moon now filled the sky, and as Chris watched, it broke apart in chunks, held together by strings of red yolk that stretched to thin fibers before snapping. The scene played out in complete silence, as if the night sky were just a giant screen and the sound had been cut. Only Chris knew, as any young scientist knew, that whatever sound the moon might make was too far away. Thirteen days away, to be exact.

Something in the air shifted. Unable to turn off the analytical part of his brain, or perhaps retreating into it, Chris realized that the thunderclap he heard earlier was some sort of gravity storm, the earth's axial tilt going haywire without its stabilizing force.

The moon blossomed outwards, temporarily held together by the red yolk inside and reminding Chris of the molecular models they used to make in college, before the chunks of the moon hurled off in different directions, some spinning off into space and others crashing down towards earth like shooting stars. Two long crescents unfolded like giant rabbit's ears above the eye, holding onto their shape as they straightened up and out. A matching pair of crescents emerged from the bottom; for a moment, it resembled a giant propeller, with the blades slowly turning around the unblinking eye. Then all at once, the blades broke apart into a mass of writhing tentacles, as if the moon were replaced with a giant red sea anemone.

He heard Jean's footsteps behind him, and looking back, he saw her make it halfway through the living room before she caught sight of the thing in the sky and stopped. Her eyes widened as her mouth bobbed open twice, then hung slack. She fell slowly to her knees, ignoring the shards of glass that cut into her smooth tan legs.

Turning back, Chris saw the tentacles arc up and out, diving towards the earth. He couldn't be sure how long he watched. It might have been a minute, or it could have been an hour. Two of the tentacles streamed through the atmosphere like shooting stars before swirling through the clouds and crashing down towards the earth. As the three nearest to him drew closer, the area tips, charred black by their entry through the atmosphere, broke apart.

The tip of each tentacle blossomed a halo of blood red pedals, blooming out like a giant sunflower around an obsidian colored center.

Seeing it happen, a strange thought came to Chris.

"It brought flowers," he said out loud, still holding his daughter and watching the obsidian center of the flower grow larger as it drew closer. "Maybe it came in peace."

Then, Chris saw the first of the tentacles touch down on the ground and it began to feast.

FROM BLACK CLOUDS

AMANDA M. BLAKE

THE SUNRISE OF a clear sky is not a spectacular one, but Daria and I enjoy the quiet together, holding hands on the porch while we drink our morning tea. Her silicone wedding ring she wears for work warms in my palm. By the time I pull on the diner uniform, my wedding ring on the nightstand, Daria's moved on from feeding the chickens to work in the barn, and clouds have formed a hazy edge on the horizon.

At the diner, I block out the drone of "news" on the television and the conversations of patrons between orders and refills, and zone out until I come back to myself after an indeterminate stretch of time; all the booths are empty.

I set down my coffee pot, breaking several diner regulations in the process. Breaking a few more, I step out into dense, humid, oppressively anticipatory air. Sweat blooms low on my back against the gingham skirt.

Everyone stands on the sidewalk of the town square, in the street, on the grass, and stares in every direction. The clouds have piled up like laundry to

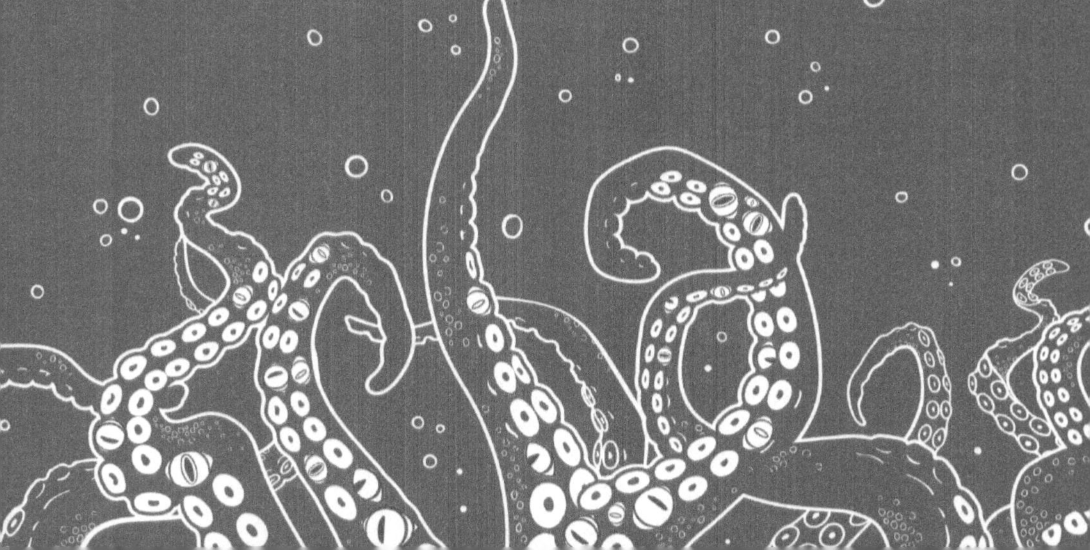

the stratospheric ceiling. On all sides, they're closer, closing, and their heavy, boiling bellies are pitch black.

Daria and I have ridden out systems in our storm cellar, repaired hail holes in the barn roof, huddled in our small cabin's bedroom while a storm sinks us into night and disorients us on the other side, and we always point out a rainbow.

But I've never seen such clouds—darker than ash, darker than smoke, without even a strobe flash of illumination. No lightning. No thunder. Just baleful clouds, black as tar.

"Do the weather reports say anything?"

"They're still saying no rain in the forecast for the next five days. I can't get it to refresh."

"None of the apps are working. We can't connect."

"That's impossible."

"Did someone shoot down a satellite?"

"It can't be one of those freak storms. Surely, not here."

"What storms?" I join Norm Peterson's small group of weather-watchers, which seems to be happening all around the square—consolidation like raindrops into puddles of whispers.

Norm lowers his hand shielding squinting eyes. "Haven't you been paying attention to what's going on in the rest of the world?"

Daria and I don't own a TV or radio, barely any internet, and that's only if we have electricity. We don't want to know, as long as it's not here. "Daria installed our telegraph last week, but it hasn't quite caught on yet. Just someone Morse-coding us about our car's extended warranty."

I'm granted a rare smirk from the common curmudgeon. "There've been storms popping up all over the country for the last few days."

"All over the world," his wife, Jill, corrects him, her arm crooked tightly around his elbow.

Norm continues with a well-worn frown, as though annoyed there's a rest of the world to consider. "When they pop up, unpredicted, a whole town might as well disappear on the weather radar screen, and they can't tell you what's going on underneath. If there are survivors, what they say makes no sense."

Jill grasps her cross necklace with the same talismanic fervor as she holds her husband. It's not Sunday, but she's wearing a nice floral dress that tells me First Baptist was having some kind of gathering, which explains why there are so many people in town along with the backwater tourists to our quaint, paint-peeling storefronts.

"It's like the end of the world," Miriam Monaghan says, in a different floral.

"It's not the end of the world if there are survivors," Norm replies.

"Might as well be." Daria finds me in the crowd, a bag from the general store swinging from her fist. On just the respectable side of Dorothy Gale, I'm not difficult to spot, even among the panic steadily rising as the barometric pressure drops.

Her cello neck flexes with tension. The prominent veins at her temple quicken their pulse. Everyone else doesn't stop looking at the clouds, except when trying their phones, but Daria stares across the sea of florals, flannel, denim, and carnations in collars, her thick-rimmed and thick-lensed glasses unable to conceal her worry.

"I can't reach my girlfriend." Sheriff Wilson walks between us. We quickly break away from each other, but he's not paying attention to us. He gazes into his phone as though he can make it tell him what he wants to know by force of will. "She was on her way back from Amarillo this morning. She should've been here by now."

"I can't reach my husband," Miriam says. She lives in the boonies, like us, but in a flatter direction.

Norm glances from American flag to American flag across the square. They don't so much as twitch. "How fast is it coming in, do you think?"

"I don't know, Norm. Let me get my tape measure and stopwatch," Daria snaps.

Jill glares at her for the sarcasm, but Norm harrumphs before turning back to the skies. He can hardly harp on her barbs when he can't get it through his skull, either through confusion or sheer blockheadedness, that she's not 'sir' or 'young man'. If he or anyone else had a name to throw in her face, they'd do that, too.

Daria doesn't even correct them anymore. Just like me wearing a dress at the diner, we both break promises to ourselves all the time. The ranch was our sanctuary to escape from the world. We didn't anticipate inevitable failure. For our dream to survive, it required a more realistic edit.

A warning siren breaks everyone's stupor. Some people immediately flee to their respective churches. Most of them came from there to begin with, in their lovely patterned dresses and lapel carnations. The church basements double as shelters.

"Thunderstorm warning," intones the voice after the siren finally stops. "Thunderstorm warning."

No additional information. As though the question on everyone's mind was whether the clouds closing in were thunderstorms or not.

Some people—tourists, business owners and their families, administrative employees from the courthouse and nearby offices—return to what they were doing. The siren declared the clouds mere thunderstorms. That's a monster they know. In Texas, if you hear a tornado warning, you step outside to watch it rope by. Right now, under blue skies, nothing can hurt them.

The rest of us—panhandle ranchers, rednecks, and retirees—keep an eye on the clouds as we inch to our trucks, because the square is in the center of the eye, but our lives are on the edges, the first place these strange storms will hit.

As we head a cavalcade of our neighbors into the hills, we don't talk or turn on the radio. We never fill our world with a lot of noise. The animals, working or rescued, do most of that for us. We stare instead at the hills that have made our horizon for going on two years. The clouds looming above them span the panorama of the windshield. They're closer than they appear; our cantaloupes can't comprehend the size of titans.

I rest my hand on Daria's leg. She drives one-handed to grasp it until I lose feeling in my fingers, but I don't let go.

The procession stops at our sanctuary, because we're the edge of the map. Too many cars clog our long patch of driveway.

My heels aren't conducive to the dirt road, nor the climb uphill on rough asphalt. Miriam struggles in slenderer heels than mine. Daisy, one of our Pyrenees, leaps joyously from grim face to grim face. Storms never bothered her. All she knows is that dozens of people are joining her for a jaunt.

Well before we reach it, the storm rattles our bones like the hum of a million power lines, disturbs loose gravel—not thunder but pounding rain that we can't see through the black. Until, staring up where the cloud slowly crests the hill, we realize that the black *is* the rain.

The clouds move forward—inward—without wind. The rain falls like straight wet hair from the rolling underbelly, but it doesn't flow down the ditches on either side of the road or down the asphalt to us as rain should. It stops where it hits, pouring *in* the black and *of* the black.

Some of our cows stand in the field to the left, placid under their patch of clear sky. If the storms baffle us, how much more must they bewilder the bovine? They don't understand what comes toward them except that it's rain, in which they graze without trouble, so why should they fear?

I clutch Daria's shoulder.

As the wall of rain approaches, the cows raise their heads, mildly intrigued by the shadow shift from sunlight. The first patters of black strike their backs.

Anything with a voice can scream under the wrong circumstances, and it's always awful—not just sound but state.

I yank Daria back from trying to help them as thick, viscous black dribbles down their sides, peeling hide away with it, brushstrokes of flayed muscle. Their eyes roll in collapsing heads until they burst and pour from the sockets. They scream until what they scream from melts away, and they fold into a mass of liquifying meat, gradually curtained by thickening rainfall.

Everything disintegrates—brush, grass, weeds, trees. The soil itself hisses with chemical evolution.

Even after the cows stop screaming, the rest of us don't, if we can make a sound at all. Daria and I remain silent, nearly frozen, but unlike the cows, we know the danger in the rain, so we finally turn tail toward the chaos accumulating in our driveway—honking horns, the crush of metal, gunshots as everyone retrieves their weapons from glove compartments and threatens everyone else to get out of their way.

Daria and I almost keep walking, but Daisy barks at the scared rancher, Hector, who fired the first shot, and at Sheriff Wilson and Deputy Rainier, who both point their guns at the man and at Daisy. Daria darts in front of her.

"Everyone needs to calm down," Daria says, deepening her voice to cut through the shrillness of everyone's panic.

"The storm is raining acid," Rainier shouts back at her, "and you want us to *calm down?*"

Daria keeps her hands up while I crouch next to Daisy to soothe her, her fluffy white fur hot on my legs. "Right now, y'all are on *our* property," she says. "We don't allow guns here."

Sheriff Wilson laughs without a shred of humor. He doesn't lower his shotgun. "We're trying to stop him from shooting up *your* driveway."

"They *all* scare the animals," Daria snaps. "Hector, put down your goddamn gun."

Hector reluctantly tucks his firearm into his pants. The sheriff raises his shotgun, bore to the sky; the deputy lowers his.

"Now, back out, one at a time, same as you came in," Daria says to everyone. "We can discuss insurance or lack thereof later. We need to let the people in town know what's happening."

"Why?" Sheriff Wilson slings the shotgun behind his shoulder. "The storms have us surrounded. Leave the poor assholes in peace for a while longer."

"Someone has to warn them," Miriam wails, high and broken. "They need to find shelter. *We* need to find shelter. Daria, Taryn, you have a storm cellar, don't you?"

"Shelter?" the sheriff scoffs. "That rain melted those cows in a matter of seconds. It's burning through the *ground*. You think a shelter is going to save you?"

Mr. Larkin, the science teacher at the junior and high school, polishes his glasses, then blots his sweaty forehead. "It depends on the acid."

"You can't science your way out of this, Teach. This isn't your normal pollution-filled acid rain here. I bet it's nothing anyone's ever seen. I've heard enough preachers to recognize the End Times when I see them."

Mr. Larkin replaces his glasses on the bridge of his nose. "There's no need to be superstitious just because you don't understand—"

"Don't sit there with your fancy college education and pretend it can help you begin to comprehend what this is before the rain dissolves you like a drain clog. This is bigger than a little man like you."

"But *why* is this happening?" Joel Robertson—accompanied by his son, younger daughter, and nervous wife—gathers with us. I gesture their daughter over to take comfort in Daisy's fluff. With her short hair, overalls, and muddy shoes, the girl reminds me of myself at her age.

"They don't know why these freak storms hit." Norm wraps his arm around his wife, capillaries dark purple under their eyes. "There's no rhyme or reason to it."

"Of course there is." The sheriff leans against his car, a terrible grin on his face; like his laugh, it holds no joy. "They didn't know what a warning siren was back then, but they'd probably call it a trumpet, don't you think?"

"Enough of that nonsense." Miss Connie, the part-time librarian, stamps her cane in the dirt. She outlived both her husbands into some measure of comfort, and at eighty-six, she's still living more or less independently on her own little farm, which usually inspires a certain veneration. "All that matters is what we can do, if we can do anything. Where's this shelter of yours, child?"

Daria points to a metal door embedded in sloped-top concrete in the front yard. "It can't hold everyone. It's advertised to hold seven, but it barely holds two."

"So, even if it works, we have to decide who gets to live?" Mr. Robertson clenches his wife and son with such white-knuckled fervor it would take broken bones to wrench them away. "I have children."

The sheriff laughs again, acerbic as the rain. "That's not the question before the court. We all have families—children, parents. We all have lives. Yet here we all are, presenting our collective buttocks to the great clouds and spreading our cheeks for their cosmic dicks."

Mrs. Robertson covers her son's ears, as though he hasn't heard worse, but her daughter's mouth drops open with a grin, as though she's getting away with something by hearing it.

"Then what's the question?" Mr. Larkin asks angrily.

"It's not about who lives. God decides that." The sheriff crosses his arms. The short sleeves show off his arm tattoos, one a series of Roman numeral dates wreathed in red roses and bluebonnets, the other an elaborate Celtic cross. "The question is who dies."

"What do you mean?" Jill's wide eyes suggest she understands perfectly, but like others who've joined us, shellshocked terror wars with terrible, unprecedented belief. Jill worries her cross again—gold instead of ink. Daria and I have our own ways to worship that sometimes slip into something similar to how we were raised and reviled, but this ersatz cemetery is marked with an overabundance of crosses, dimming light casting baleful shadows.

"We've heard of toads, fish, blood, stones raining down," the sheriff says. "When the fuck have you ever heard of black acid? Also, I'm no meteorologist, but even I know that storms don't form like a goddamned bullseye. It's the finger of God pointing at us, saying 'this place deserves to be smote.' But does the *whole* town deserve to die?"

"Oh shit," Daria whispers.

The sheriff paces in the loose, weeping circle that's made him the center. Deputy Rainier mutters agreement and encouragement, a congregant response to the sheriff's call. His other deputy, Sean, nods, slack-jawed, tears gleaming on the whiteheads that cluster between the bristle attempting to grow above his lip.

"They put criminals and perverts in our midst and told us we must *tolerate*. We can't lift a finger, can't say a word against them, even though we *know* it's an abomination. It makes us sick, but there's nothing we can do, right? Until God gets to have His say, and all our false idols fall."

"I taught you, Sheriff. I wouldn't trust you with a pig dissection, much less theological interpretation," Mr. Larkin says, flushed in patches under the gold rims of his glasses. "You really think God decided a small town with more churches than banks needed to be punished because He doesn't like the way a few people live their lives?"

"Paul tells us none of us are righteous, not one," Jill recites like a child. But she's not looking at us. No one's looking at us.

"We're all sinners, but God forgives," the sheriff replies. "He forgives the repentant sinner. And I think we all know who really doesn't fit into our otherwise God-fearing town."

He flips his shotgun from his shoulder and points it at Daria, because he doesn't expect me to come up with rocks in my fists. Gravel flies in his face as I swing, but Rainier grabs me before I can knock his cheek with the stone.

This man, who drops my tips on the floor to watch me bend over, who once got sloppy drunk on weak beer and tried to stick his tongue down my throat at the end of a night shift, who carries pictures of his ex-wife and kids in his wallet while complaining every week about child support and alimony. This man is forgiven, and I am judged.

"You really think sacrificing us will make the storms go away?"

"I don't have a problem with you, hon." The sheriff surveys my attempts to break free of Rainier's grip on my arms with lazy amusement, but he keeps the shotgun trained on Daria. "You married a man, as God intended. He's the one who thought he knew better than God what he should be."

I shower his sheriff browns with spots of foamy saliva. Snarling, he swings the shotgun stock, striking stars across my cheek.

Daria falls to the ground, one hand up in surrender and the other on my back to tug me upright. The sheriff lets her, maybe because my skirt rides up my legs, or maybe because she's the only one who reacts to save me. The rest stare down into our amphitheater, anxiously anticipating the lion.

With the apron of my pinafore, I brush my face clean of red dirt and nose blood. Daria helps me stand, trying to get between me and the bore, but I force myself in front of her. "I married a woman. I like women. I *fuck* women. You condemn her, you condemn me. You think wiping the sins out of this town before the storm wipes them out for you will help? What happens when that doesn't work?"

"Well, you're a start."

"You can't possibly be serious…" Mr. Larkin blusters, stepping forward then back, wanting to interfere but afraid.

"Ignorance. Blasphemy. Execution. We didn't elect you to be hangman." Miss Connie doesn't move from where she stands at the edge of the circle. Her cane quivers.

"Who do you think goes after them if they don't appease the storms?" The sheriff nods for his deputies to train their pistols on the two elderly agitators. "We all heard the rumors about you, Mr. Larkin, but we saw enough to know why you never married. The kind of kids that go into your office…"

"No, that's not… They just needed someone to talk to, someone who understood. I never—"

Rainier punches Mr. Larkin in the throat. He grabs his neck and doubles over, gagging.

"And you, Miss Connie," the sheriff continues. "No one could prove anything, but we all knew. An ancient black widow is still a black widow."

"Fuck you sideways with your own shotgun," Miss Connie says, surprising everyone with her vehemence. "If this is God's judgment, you're the kind of smutty snot He's trying to clean off the nose of the world. Who's after us? The tomboy?" She nods to the little girl hugging Daisy for dear life. Jill grabs her away from the confused dog, as though our corruption is contagious through everything we've touched. "Perhaps the teen mothers, the cuckolds, the divorcees… Everyone but those bearing arms, I'll bet, even though you're included in that number, Sheriff—twice."

Sean kicks Miss Connie's cane into the ditch, leaving her at the mercy of her own trembling, bloodless balance. Then he trains his pistol back at her head, like Rainier upon Mr. Larkin and the sheriff on Daria through me.

"I'll bet you're wishing you had some God-given guns now." The sheriff prods me with the bore. "Get moving."

I spin around, surrounded not by black clouds but by the empty faces of neighbors who make strangers of us. Tears distort them—or maybe reveal. "Oh, you motherfuckers. You didn't mind when we were saving the animals you wanted to kill, fixing the appliances you couldn't afford to replace, refinishing your furniture. But now we're an acceptable loss to save your skin because you think you're *better* than us?"

"Taryn." Daria presses her forehead to my hair, her breath hot on my sweaty neck. "Taryn, sweetheart."

"No, this is not okay. It's murder. It's human fucking sacrifice."

She wraps her arms around me; there's no point in plausible deniability anymore. When she kisses the corner of my mouth, I taste her tears. "We're all going to die, anyway."

Mrs. Robertson holds Daisy's collar and keeps her children close, including her son, who desperately wants to follow with the rest, to watch the legs swinging, viscera pooling at our feet. He's not even seventeen.

I've never been able to stay mad, but I stay mad longer than Daria, lasting until we can't see the driveway of our sanctuary when we look back.

The billowing clouds anvil inward now, like the constricting of a gigantic blue pupil to a narrow point above the town square. They cast jaundiced shade, gentler in the still, stale, sour air of this hollow corpse.

We walk on either side of the yellow line, hand in hand. The sheriff's car trundles behind us like a stalking beast, with Miss Connie and Mr. Larkin caged in the back seat, until the sheriff raises his hand to stop the uneven shuffling of our audience behind him.

Before us, the blackness creeps, inch by sizzling inch, obliterating everything in its wake. Maybe it's all gone beyond that, a poisoned sinkhole to the other side of the world, and we're the last island.

"I'm sorry. I'm the one who brought us here." I grip Daria's hand so tightly that something crunches underneath, but she shakes her head and doesn't let go.

"There was never anywhere to run. We already learned that. They'll learn it, too." She pulls me across the dividing line and kisses me like the sunset and sunrise we'll never see.

"Go on." The sheriff lowers his gun to point—not at Daria's head but her spine. "Or else you'll be dragging her in."

The sheriff and his deputies aren't the only ones with trembling guns, and they aren't the only ones scared out of their minds. We walk, holding each other but not crying, not talking, not begging, to the edge of the black rain.

We're not going to be enough. Obvious understudies wait in the wings, but the rest are fools if they think they won't also be measured by the range of bullets, at least until there's nothing left to shoot at. The storm doesn't care about ammunition. It bleeds its own.

With the black edge inches from the smooth toes of my shoes, we don't say it, but we think it more loudly than the deafening downpour. In case we get lost, we've always held hands to dance in the rain.

DARK WATERS TO NOWHERE

REKHA VALLIAPPAN

"'Twas night, said they, such birds to slay,
That brings the fog and mist."
— S.T. Coleridge

IT WAS THE farthest north they had ever been. That ill-fated *Mystic*. Additional ripple effects placed the misguided steamship further along cross-flowing ocean currents. Darkness and pale seagulls floating lifeless like stationary ice floes in the swirling mist.

On the night of March 19th, 1882, *The Mystic* was reported missing. A luxury vessel of the times by any standard, it had set sail in fair weather on its maiden voyage from New York to Liverpool, with a crew of the hardiest sailors on board.

There is a strange legend, grown since out of the archipelago of Chiloe that a ghost ship resembling *The Mystic* comes into being every night of the full moon, when there is heavy fog. The outline of this mysterious ship of the

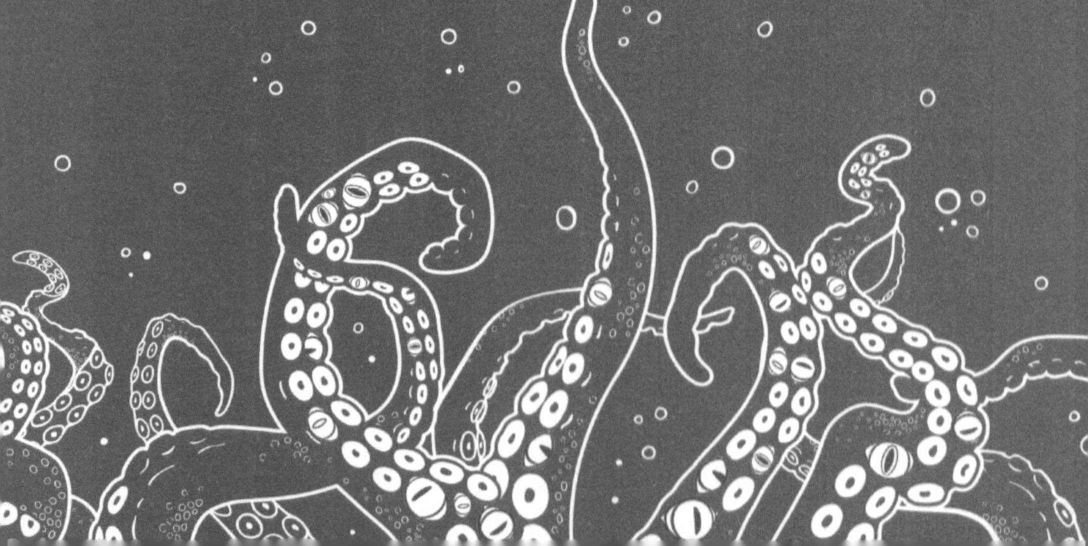

mist—like a skimming albatross—is visible for over an hour, say those who have heard some ghostly tales. And then disaster strikes in the retelling—human cries, dead souls howling in anguish.

The Mystic was found marooned in the South Pacific. When towed back by a salvage vessel, it was discovered that not only were its trim, body, and bulkhead intact, but the ship was in perfect running condition. There was plenty of food and water aboard. The cargo was untouched, even the alcohol. Moreover, the hull was watertight and undamaged. However, everyone on board was missing, not a body part in sight. In the ensuing days, no one washed up on beaches or was ever found. To make matters worse, the logbook was missing.

Between the sea and sky lie the greatest of mysteries, opined the majority, exchanging doom and gloom. There was no other reasonable cause to explain why a ship bound for Europe would end up in South America. *The Daily Gazette* would report—among other unnecessary details—that neither the owners of the vessel nor the authorities could determine why a seaworthy ship had strayed several thousand miles off course despite being fitted out by the most up-to-date technology in chronometers and compasses.

Jenny Scolari could not tell what was happening. At nineteen years, she was the youngest and greenest passenger on *The Lunartic*. All around her cabin blinked a pale light, streaming through the porthole, growing brighter. She could hear muffled voices raised in different tongues, punctuated by vile-sounding curses. A scuffle was breaking out. Blows, thumps, punctuated screams. She did not understand. There was no mistaking the tone of fear, even through her grogginess.

It was the 14th of July, a little past 8:32 p.m., ten days into the voyage—although the date and time meant nothing to her on the ship except it was a full moon. She had stubbornly wanted to be on deck, feeding off the salt and sea air, to catch glimpses of eternity in the gray visions of the full water moon. But a sudden feeling of seasickness had seen her retire to her cabin. She had drifted off to sleep. They were making good time. This much she knew from snatches of conversation among the passengers. Weather was fair. She was resigned, her thoughts drifting to the family reunion at voyage end.

Whump! Thuuump!

A series of loud noises. A fight had broken out above deck. *It was a fight!* Jenny Scolari was in a panic. The crew had resumed their noisy jabber when she was startled by the loud blare of the ship's claxon. She clutched at her chest. A fit of uncontrollable coughing seized her.

Thousands of miles away, the coastguard was furious. The station had lost all contact with *The Lunartic.* The last lingering sound the monitoring station could detect was that of chaos on the bridge. The ship was entrapped in a brilliant field of treacherous white. This seemed unreal. *Was it a beam of light?* The white stretched all the way to the horizon. *Couldn't tell!* The voice of the Captain was heard ordering the ship into an ice field. *Ice?* But it could not be. The ship's claxon blaring a mournful distress drowned the rest.

"Steady does it! Ice or fog?" roared the coastguard. "Someone, give me the compass readings. Where *are* they? The coordinates, anyone? Fuck technology!"

Simple to assume a cold gray fog swirled around the ship. The sudden question on everyone's mind was whether *The Lunartic*—a whole century later—was about to go the way of *The Mystic.* A ghost ship? *Impossible!*

On the bridge, there was an uneasy silence. Jenny needed help. Desperately. She thought she heard the captain reassuring the other passengers and crew. More thuds, screeches, and splashes followed, as if big crates were being dragged on deck and thrown over the side. Someone had glanced at the ship's compass to note the bearings. Another round of exclamations and disbelief followed. She could discern the faint voice of the third officer, all choked up. The needle of the useless compass was spinning around and around.

Her distress mounted. The abrasive noises were distant. *What a savage light piercing the porthole*, she thought, confused. Whatever would induce a captain to sail a ship without instruments? Turn on piercing strobe lights? *Turn off the claxon! Please!*

Jenny staggered weakly to the porthole. In the foggy exterior outside, a strange sight greeted her. A vast sea of white, a ship's outline, floating in bursts. *The Lunartic* hovered like a great ghost ship, sheathed in gray. *It couldn't be!* The full moon broke through snatches of swirling mist while the ship creaked and swayed. The cold wind rose and fell, keening and moaning, rising to a human scream, an albatross' high-pitched whine, louder than the ship's claxon.

Jenny scrambled in vain out of her stupor. What ship was that? Whose voices were those? What twisted voyage was this? What strange sea? Terrified, she screamed and screamed in anguish, then fell in a dead faint.

Meanwhile, in Liverpool, Jenny Scolari's anxious parents were awaiting news of *The Lunartic*. With them were scores of concerned family and friends. They demanded answers. Together they had flooded the offices of The Daily Gazette, making their case loud and clear to the world. This was unacceptable in modern day—a sudden disappearance of a well-equipped ship in perfect weather.

The Scolaris were livid. They blamed the cruise line. They should never have listened to Jenny's old physician in New York, a family friend they were well acquainted with from the old days in Christchurch. They should never have listened to Jenny, either, unwell yet obdurate, with a mystery illness that had almost killed her. They should never have listened to Jenny's boyfriend, Jay, who was to have been onboard with her, but canceled. They should never have let their only daughter undertake the voyage alone. They had been misguided, swept off their feet by undue persuasion.

As it turned out, Jay had taken the flight—a last-minute family emergency, which required his immediate presence in Penang, his hometown. Her doctor's persuasion had worked like a charm, the strongest inducement for clearing clogged lungs—sea breezes. Jenny had made up the rest, time with Jay, her love of the sea.

They were not to know the ship was an old re-built relic of the previous century, pulled out of the shipyards. They were not to know that despite its dubious past as scrap iron, and having changed names and owners five times, she was repaired and re-fitted in New York's dockyard. Made to be seaworthy to sail the cruise lanes once more, but only along the coast. New York to Liverpool was never a lot for ships under optimal conditions. But never *The Lunartic.*

They were not to know the current owners exercising their close friendship and connections with the license agency in charge of private vessels had decided to sail the ship across the ocean instead, rather than stay within the limits of the coastal permit. Furthermore, they were not to know the vessel was exempted from inspections. This had allowed the bypassing of several sailing imperatives—one of those the hiring of experienced ocean worthy crew, not a bunch of foreign sailors at low pay.

As a result, *The Lunartic* sailed with a motley crew and a forty-three-year-old Captain, with names like Jorge, Nizal, Yamaguchi, Baird, and Moder, to suggest they were all locally outfitted. In reality, they were of the distant four corners of the earth, all international. Big difference.

When on the day of embarkation more than half the original crew failed to show, newcomers were hired. Their level of experience varied widely. Thirty of the fifty knew nothing about big ships, the rest knew nothing about small vessels, never having sailed one. Some concocted weird tales of fishing boats and shrimp and crab boats, desperate as they were to be hired and to get away. None of them had the required expertise for compass readings, except the senior officers.

The Lunartic, when it sailed out of New York Harbor, had a captain, ten officers, five cooks, and a crew of seamen, whose job as deckhands was to swab and clean and undertake rigging and repairs. The pay was beyond expectation.

Jenny Scolari knew nothing about ships. She dutifully maintained a daily diary which, as the days wore on despite fair weather, was worrisome with complaints. First, it was the swell of the sea and ten-foot waves. Then it was the flying fish that quickly changed to grunting sky things, to scudding sea aliens. Only she knew what she was experiencing amidst a shipload of passengers enjoying an Atlantic cruise. She missed Jay. Her cough worsened. She grew suspicious. She regarded the crew as no better than self-important pompous fools. She thought everyone unfriendly.

She struggled awake. She knew the whole ship had been keen to view the full moon over the water. It was the talk for three whole days. If not for her coughing bouts and seasickness, she would have been on the viewing decks, taking in the shimmering moonlight with the rest. None had noticed her quietly slip away to the cabins.

With her bearings askew, the light percolating through the porthole was hellishly bright and blinding. The claxon had stopped blaring. She strained to see. The voices raised in anger and fear had suddenly ceased. No growls. No more thuds.

She half-stumbled to the decks. Not a soul in sight, neither passengers nor crew. She called out. No answering shout returned her call. She staggered the length of the deck, grabbing the sides. With the dense fog still swirling in shapes, she could not tell if she was seeing a ghost ship or a mountain crag or a monster of the sea or an alien life form.

She shrieked over and over. Louder. All through the night. In the haggard shaft of daylight, the transformation on deck was hard to believe. Gone were the stacks of crates and barrels fastened to the foredeck and aft. She rushed to the bridge.

There was no one, none at the helm, only the steering wheel spinning in frantic circles. Her voice hoarse, she called for the captain, the officers. *Anybody*. The winds bore her cries away. She studied the instruments. The elaborate compass, which she could not read, spun crazily round and round, just like the wheel.

She rushed to the cabins below, knocking frantically at each door. The pain in her sides was unbearable. She could not fathom spending another night aboard this empty vessel, encircled in a strange wreath of fog. The sound of the sea played havoc in her ears. *Where was everyone?*

The Daily Gazette would report finding *The Lunartic* floating lifeless, after an extensive sea and air search conducted by many maritime stalwarts, in which several countries participated. On the 27th, October, more than three months after it set sail from New York in clear weather on a voyage bound for Liverpool, *The Lunartic* was found. Authorities had good reason to believe the ship had run aground in the Sea of Chiloe. Of the crew and passengers, there was not a trace. There was no logbook, no lifeboats onboard—just a madly spinning compass and wheel. The disquieting connectivity was that it was found on the same day, in the same angle of the shore where, in 1872, *The Mystic* had also been found marooned.

Both ships had traveled far off course from their original destinations, despite the absence of hurricanes or storms to force them adrift. More astounding was the fact that both ships were one and the same. This shocked the maritime industry to the core. How could one ghost ship under a different name ever have been allowed to sail? How could two ghost ships be forever bound in a dark pact down the ages? It was inconceivable and called for a national review.

Warming to the debate were the grieving families and friends of those aboard *The Lunartic*. None could make head nor tail of the cargo of barrels and crates onboard. Many speculated they were filled with dangerous chemicals. They drew the conclusion they contained rare goat's hair mixed with a dangerous species of rats that released chemical compounds into the ship, spreading a contagious madness disease, resulting in many on board taking their own lives as a way out. Most stayed steadfast to the original *Ghost Ship* of Chiloe from which legend was born as the culprit. Considered inconceivable, both stories and facts, the rolling mosaic of forests and hills on Chiloe Island were extensively searched. All to no avail.

Jenny Scolari, the only living being found barely alive, was under close medical observation. Sailing to nowhere, she had taken to the dark waters of the roaring sea. She had been found adrift, battered and wrecked, in an advanced state of madness. To hear her was to see giant icebergs, abandoned ships, unmanned structures, blinding moons, vanishing into the stabbing white mists. She never spoke of the sea. Or the crosswinds. The search and salvage crew sailing out of Sydney had been the first to reach her. Starved beyond recognition, drifting in and out of consciousness, mumbling incoherently of a white albatross to her last conscious breath, she was found on the last remaining lifeboat from *The Lunartic*.

FINDER'S FEE

EDWARD AHERN

THE HOUSE SMELLED of cat piss. The man had died two years ago, the cat farmed out to a neighbor right afterward, but the place still reeked. It was owned by an obscure foundation that paid the taxes and utilities—which made it relatively easy for Robbie to get into.

Robbie was a finder, a half-low tech, half-mediumistic dowser. If there was something valuable thought to be hidden in a house or on a property, he was paid to try to find it. He took a small initial fee to cover expenses and a pre-agreed payoff if the item was unearthed. About a third of the time, he was able to locate whatever it was, an astoundingly high success rate. Robbie credited his intuition, but competitors said it was something darker.

This house was late nineteenth century large, five bedrooms, three baths. The item desired was reportedly only about the size of a brick. Robbie allowed himself five days to either find it or admit failure.

As he got out of his panel truck, Janet called.

"You get that wild party going?"

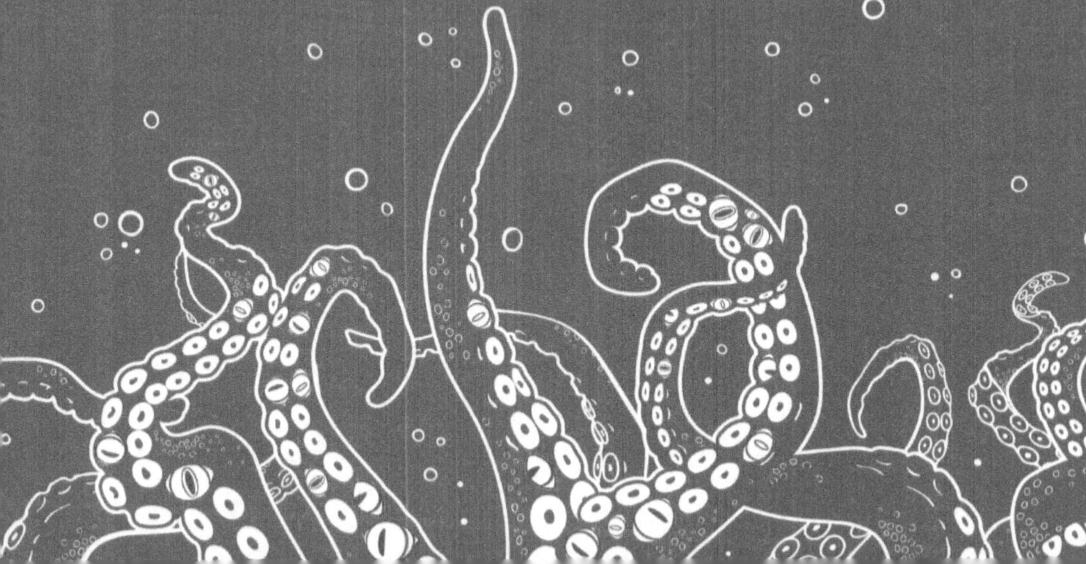

He laughed. "I love you too. I wish there was something salacious here instead of just scummy. Going back in now. I found the sandwiches, thanks."

Janet was his wife, business partner, accountant, and gentle nag. They were both relatively short and relatively round, congenially matched. He already wished he could spend the night next to her, listening to her gentle snore.

"The neighbors get nosy yet?"

"Didn't have to. I knocked at the two next door houses, introduced myself, and told them there'd be no remodeling noise after 9:00 p.m." He glanced at the painted advertisement on the side of his panel truck, *Sullivan's Remodeling and Landscaping*. His presence in the house was almost legal.

"Okay, but watch your middle-aged tush. There's something peculiar about this guy's answers to our interview."

She was right. One of their first questions was: "Is the object alive, dead, inert or other?" Malachi Falcone had said *other*. Other was okay, there were a fair number of occultists looking for missing amulets and talismans. But Malachi offered no other explanation, just a description of its container: a dark mahogany box with gold fittings and trim and gold cuneiform characters. The payment for its recovery was fifteen thousand dollars.

"He's also morbidly suspicious. He had cameras installed inside the house to monitor my activity and make sure I didn't steal the box."

Janet had wanted to turn him down.

"Listen, I've run some checks on this Malachi and come up empty. *Thorough* checks, and he doesn't exist in either human or supernatural records. His phone, internet, and bank account trace back to a shell company that almost doesn't exist. All of which suggests he's violating a human law or spirit code, maybe both. Could we just give him back his money and move on?"

"Too late, I think we've spent it."

When he met Malachi, Robbie had thought of Boris Karloff as painted by Picasso in his blue period. Business was slow, however, and Malachi's retainer had cleared promptly, so Robbie took the assignment.

And here he was, alone in urine central with a blueprint of the house, a ground-penetrating radar to locate cavities in the walls and floors, and— most reliable—Hector the sledgehammer. *Furniture first,* he thought, and took out his assortment of surgical steel probes. These looked like extra-long hat pins, but with wood handles to enable more forceful insertion.

Malachi had told him he hadn't conducted a search of his own, but Robbie noticed several small puncture marks on the chairs' upholstery. *Lie one*, he thought, and guessed there would be several more before the session was over. It took Robbie only two hours to impale every chair, sofa, and bed. No box.

He put the probes away and set up the portable radar. The high-voltage batteries were in a backpack that Robbie strapped on. He started as usual in the kitchen, where self-help hiders often thought others wouldn't look for a hiding place. But walls, floor, and ceiling yielded nothing of interest beyond a dead space cubby sealed off in a remodeling. Hector made short work of the drywall, but Robbie only discovered a bulge-lidded mason jar of fruit preserve that screamed botulism at him.

Robbie was able to check out all the drawers in the house before it got to be 8:00 p.m., time to quit for the day. Once back in his two-star motel, he flushed off the dust and sweat, ate a sandwich, and called Janet.

"Hi. Nothing so far, but there usually isn't this early."

"Be careful when you tune into that out-of-body stuff of yours."

They exchanged bonded nothings for another few minutes and ended the call.

Early the next morning, Robbie returned to the house. The smell of cat urine was still overpowering. He stopped himself from waving at the cameras and started in the attic before the heat got suffocating. Access was a rickety pull-down ladder. The attic itself had a few haphazard boards laid across the joists for hopscotch navigation. The radar found nothing, which was pretty much all there was in the attic.

He clambered downstairs and was working on the second bedroom when he caught sight of movement in the corridor. He took off the battery pack, unzipped a pocket on it, and took out a .38 Special. The motion had been right to left, and Robbie slowly paced down the corridor toward the bedroom at the end.

The door was open and he went in, looking for something large. Nothing. As he turned to go back out, he caught sight of a dull black cat lying on a dusty bed as if it owned it.

How the hell did you get in? he thought. The cat didn't hiss, but also didn't purr. Robbie wasn't about to chase a possibly infected cat through the house, so just nodded at it. "Stay the hell out of my way," he said, and left the room, shutting the door. *That*, he thought, *explains the odeur de pisse.*

Except for a short drive to get coffee, Robbie spent the morning radar-sounding. The backpack was heavy and impossible to adjust properly, so his own spine ached. He stopped to eat lunch, gingerly sitting down in an easy chair that puffed up swirls of dust.

The cat padded silently into the room, sat across from him, and stared. "How the hell did you get out?" But Robbie thought he knew. The house was full of warped and dry rotted baseboards and paneling that would let a cat squeeze through. It seemed utterly unafraid. Robbie broke off a chunk of liverwurst and tossed it to the cat, which disdained it. *Maybe*, Robbie thought, it's true what they say about preservatives and cured organ meats. They proceeded to ignore each other.

Robbie braced himself for the next necessary phase. The easy parts of a finding were mechanical and technical. Getting into himself deeply enough to activate his sense of presence was straining. As he began to do so, the cat got up, paced over to him and stared up into his eyes, as if trying to learn the process. Robbie ignored it and went down inside.

In here there was no precision, just pulsating coronas of impressions. He shifted his thoughts to the grounds surrounding the house. Something large and long dead was buried next to the swamp oak in the rear garden, the bones of man or maybe horse for someone else to discover, but Robbie passed on. After two hours, he resurfaced, sweating so badly his toes felt squishy. The cat was gone but its fetor abided.

He'd sensed nothing else in the grounds outside the house, and he'd run out of energy to search further today. Robbie stood up. The cat rejoined him as he walked toward the front door.

"Buddy," he said aloud, "no offense, but you stink and are undoubtedly infested with fleas and ticks. No way you're coming with me. Should give you a name, though."

They studied each other. An obscurity oozed up.

"Mastema. I'll call you Mastema."

The cat stared at him for another second, then turned and padded back into the house.

Robbie drove off. He avoided most of the greasy food on the diner menu, got back into his motel room, and called Janet. After some long-married shorthand, he said. "Sweetie…"

"You only use endearments when you're going to ask me to do something crappy. What is it?"

"The house is around a hundred and forty years old. Could you use your internet magic and find out who built it and who's owned it since then? Oh, and what was on the land before?"

"Next you'll want me to sacrifice my virginity." She sighed. "Okay, I was going to misspend some free time, but I'll do it. Providing once you're back, you do the cooking and laundry for two weeks."

"That's harsh, but okay."

After his usual pre-sleep shower, Robbie pulled out the architects' plans and yet again scrutinized them. There was something peculiar about the layout of the ground-floor rooms. His aching muscles held him awake long enough to realize what it was. The center, the core of the house, had three little rooms that looked like they belonged in a much smaller cabin or farmhouse. They'd carefully kept the configuration of an earlier structure. But why?

He was back at the house shortly after 7:00 a.m. and went immediately to the three rooms. The radar revealed that the interior walls were both thick and dense, probably stone-on-stone under the plaster and lath, so thick that something small could be concealed in them without being detected by radar.

Breaking into those walls would take much more time and effort than he and Hector could devote to it. *Shit*, he thought, walked over to yesterday's chair, and sat down. He segued inside himself and moved back to the three rooms. There was a tactile unpleasantness on the stones inside the finished walls, a sense of aged, repugnant history, but nothing within them that could have been a mahogany box.

After he came back out of himself, he called Janet. "Me. Find out anything?"

"I did. The place has considerable history, all bad."

As Janet was speaking, the black cat came back into the room and settled in front of Robbie's feet. Robbie had the uneasy feeling that Mastema could hear both sides of his conversation.

"Robbie?"

"Still here."

"Anyway, there were only four owners of the house since it was built, two couples and two single men. They all lived to advanced old age and died unspectacularly. What's interesting isn't what happened in the house, but near it. Way more divorces, thefts, arsons than usual for a quiet town, even several murders. It's like the house is the vortex of really bad stuff happening around it. What kind of vibe are you getting?"

"Just got a hint of that this morning, but if it's here, it's well concealed."

"And you were right, there was a little croft on the site before this one, with a stone and mortar cottage. Somebody, rumor said the neighbors, burned the place, leaving just stone walls. They also reportedly burned the owner."

"That's extreme. Good on you for finding that out so quickly. Just for that, I won't put garlic in the food I'll be cooking."

Janet's tone got serious. "Walk away, Robbie. Just tell Malachi you couldn't find it. You could even tell him what I've found out, though he probably already knows."

"A deal's a deal, hon, I gave my word to make a sincere effort." He segued before she could further protest, "But I'll chew on what you said."

An hour after they'd hung up, Malachi called. "What progress?"

"Hello Malachi. None, I'm afraid. There's a dead something-or-other in the back garden I'm not going to dig up, and it looks like the house was built around the bones of an older cottage, but no indication at all of a mahogany box."

Malachi asked no questions, and Robbie guessed that he already knew the house's history.

"It would help me locate it if I knew what was in the box."

"I can't tell you that." Malachi's tone was brusque, as if he either didn't know himself what the contents were, or was deathly afraid of the knowledge getting out.

"Then I'll give it three more days of all-out searching, but I have to advise you it's not looking promising."

"That could be most unfortunate for you. Most unfortunate."

Once they'd hung up, Robbie paused. Malachi had just threatened him, a sign of his desperation or malevolence. Either way, it sounded like a bad deal for Robbie. *Get back on problem*, he thought. Too close of a focus, maybe? He went back to the dust chair and sat. Once back inside himself, he put himself a hundred feet above the house and instead of trying for close-up images, he tried for vague overall impressions, for tinged hints. *There*, maybe, just maybe.

He roused, went back into the three original rooms and stared at the stone fireplace. "I wonder," he said aloud. He knelt, grabbed a bent, brass-gone-green poker, and stirred the ashes. Under the ashes was a cast iron plate that, once removed, would let the ashes be swept down a chute to some kind of storage kiln. "I wonder."

He retrieved a flashlight, went back to the kitchen, opened a solid oak door, and went down the cellar stairs. The only lighting was a low-watt naked bulb that did a better job defining deep shadows than it did illuminating the space. Robbie had expected to see piled up moldy bric-à-brac, but it was empty, as if waiting for its next event.

Mastema was also waiting for him.

"How the hell did you get in? Solid oak door and stone walls, what rat hole did you find?"

Robbie pointed the flashlight at the footing for the fireplace, massive rocks mortared together. Mastema made his first sound, a harsh chirring.

"Am I getting too close for comfort?"

Robbie found the hatch door for the ash scuttle and, using a large screwdriver, pried it open. The dusting of ashes on the stone floor swirled as he looked at it. *Nothing to see here.* He turned around and swung the flashlight around the cellar. No other doors or lids. Not even any spiderwebs, as if they'd been warned off.

There was nothing to sit on, so he knelt down on the concrete. He didn't want to, but knew he had to, and went under.

In a tainted color way, the cellar was brighter now than it had been with bulb and flashlight. Mastema gave off an infernal glow—*suspicions confirmed,* Robbie thought. He focused on the foundation of the fireplace, moving down forty feet, almost to bedrock when he sensed it. It felt both animate and inanimate, and immensely powerful. It was—indifferent, abiding, ruthless, waiting. It both sensed and dismissed him. Robbie, as fearful as he was, felt like a bird picking bugs off a rhinoceros, too inconsequential to be menaced. He had a hazy image of the box containing it, but the box was merely a buried manger for something transcendent.

Mastema scratched him, and Robbie was pulled roughly back up into himself. The cat stared at him as he refocused. Thoughts swirled in dust devils. Who had buried the box under tons of rock and house? How could they ever get at it without major excavation? What was the purpose of all that foreboding power?

He needed to sit. Mastema cat-footed up the cellar stairs alongside a shambling Robbie, who flopped down in the living room chair. He realized he had to tell Malachi that he'd found something, but had no way of getting at it. He also realized that since the box was inaccessible, Malachi was going to be dangerously displeased.

An hour later, the unlocked front door opened and Malachi walked in.

"Hello, Robbie. Sorry to interrupt you, but I watched you in the cellar. What have you got?" Malachi's tone was brusque, his expression both worried and foreboding. Whatever he was attempting, he looked fearful about being caught.

Nothing was the easy lie, but Robbie was a bad liar and Malachi was suspicious.

Robbie cleared his throat, trying to find the words that would keep him alive and solvent. As he opened his mouth with no idea what he was going to say, Mastema padded into the room.

Malachi put his hands up in front of his face. Words jumbled out of him. "I didn't mean… Please, lord, do not…"

The motionless cat seemed to silence him with its stare, then held his eyes. For a few seconds, the only sound was Malachi's ragged breathing. His mouth opened round like an Edvard Munch silent scream. His body began to sag and shrivel, acrid smoke wafting out from under his collar and pant legs. The body crumpled into itself like fireplace embers; the clothing was the last to char and burn.

Robbie stood as gaping as Malachi had been. Mastema's stare shifted to Robbie, and without willing it, he was back under.

Mastema, still wordless, wrapped the avatar of Robbie in its arms and carried him down to the bedrock, down into the mahogany box. The radiant heat was intense, painful. The light was—*other*—somewhere on the spectrum that Robbie normally couldn't see.

The being was equally wordless, but probed Robbie's Geist harshly, as if buying a cart horse. It took over his consciousness and rummaged through his capabilities like a petulant child with a toybox.

Robbie stopped struggling and noticed that the thing—the being—was of no sex and yet all. It took no notice of limited human intelligence, its awareness so all pervasive that questioning was unnecessary.

It began to display visions to him, long potential life segments where Robbie would do wondrous, terrible things, responsible for wrenching changes and deaths, and ecstatic frenzies, and gratifications of senses he was as yet unaware of. All this Robbie could have, could be, could do, in service to the thing laired below the house.

Mastema, bone-breaking protective of this nameless being, could not act as Robbie could, as the interface of a being that would eventually rise and shatter existence. And Robbie knew, expecting death, that he had to decline the offer. He was capable but not suitable, not willing to do the horrendous things required.

The being knew his decision as soon as Robbie thought it. And didn't kill or enslave him. Not, Robbie realized, from any sense of morality or fairness, but from some unknowable cosmic sense of equity. Instead, it compensated him.

Robbie resurfaced two hours later, surprised to still be alive. Mastema was absent. His whole body was sunburned so badly that he teared up, moaning. Then he quakingly got up, went out to his car, and called Janet.

"It's done, hon."

She heard the quavers in his voice. "Are you all right?"

"It hurts like hell, but once the old skin sloughs off, I should be okay."

"What was that thing you were looking for?"

"We have no words. And I'm bound to secrecy. But I was told where to find enough gold to buy a couple of expensive cars. And you needn't worry about Malachi."

"You sound shaky. Can you drive?"

"I think so."

"Come home, drive slowly. I'll cook dinner."

IN EXTREMIS

J.J. SMITH

THE ROAD TO the couples' retreat where Rachel Goddard, RN, volunteered every other weekend took her along the Miskatonic River, a channel with a jet-stream like current produced by a waterfall that is powerful enough to turn a waterwheel that generates electricity for the Village of Dunwich, Rachel's hometown.

The river also killed Rachel when she was a teenager, more than twenty years before.

Most visitors to Falls Mill on the Miskatonic were usually both awed and frightened by the power of the water that careens wildly over the cataract. Such visitors probably wouldn't be surprised to hear that, far upstream, the river could be deadly and had claimed many lives. However, the same visitors *would* probably be surprised to hear there were scores of teens and young adults who lived along the river and regularly risked their lives by swimming in it. Those reckless youths jumped into the Miskatonic and rode the current

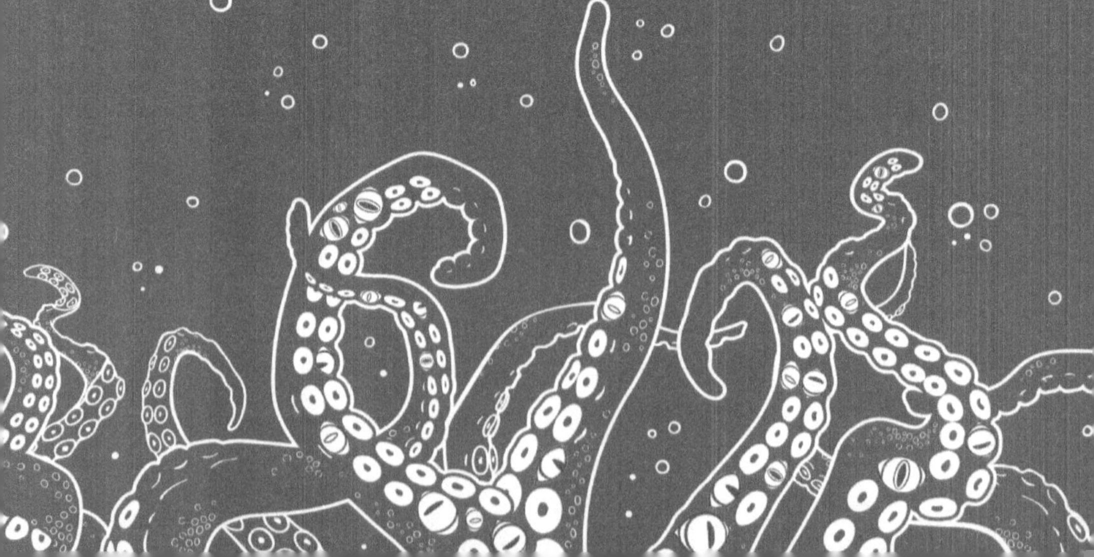

pulled by the waterfall until they reached one of the many ladders embedded into the cement banks that flanked the waterway in the area of Falls Mill.

Rachel had studied art in high school, where she'd been a pretty, popular, and thrill-seeking teenager who loved having fun, especially with her best friend, Mary. On the day she died, Rachel had told her mother she was going to the Dunwich public pool while in reality planned to join about a dozen youths to swim in the river. To do that, she followed Mary out to a section of the riverbank upstream from Falls Mill.

Mary was also popular, but she'd been known for engaging in risky behavior—not unlike swimming in the Miskatonic—and she coaxed Rachel into joining in the fun. Coupled with the fact she would be swimming with a bunch of friends, it was enough for Rachel to put on a false front of courage.

Rachel had followed Mary about a mile down the shore to where the river was mostly whitewater rapids rushing by with a roar. There was no pier there, but there were several boulders jutting out from the bank that the teens would use as platforms from which to jump into the river.

While certainly reckless, the youths weren't stupid. They dressed appropriately in shorts, or swimsuits, t-shirts, and deck sneakers or thong sandals—which they tied to a belt around their waists, so they'd have something to wear on their feet after climbing out, about a mile downriver. That none of the swimmers jumped into the Miskatonic alone was an unwritten rule practiced by the many groups of teens to ensure safety, but even that could fail.

What came as a surprise to many swimmers—including Rachel—was how the river could induce a hypnotic-like state on those looking at the swiftly moving current, which is what Rachel was experiencing until the sound of Mary's voice pulled her back from her near trance.

"Are you ready?" Mary asked.

Rachel nodded in the affirmative and said, "Yeah," with a false confidence that she hoped would engender real courage.

Mary must have sensed Rachel's fears, for she said, "Why don't we go in holding hands and ride the current together?"

Rachel smiled and again nodded. The pair then crept out over several boulders, and once they reached the jump-off rock, Rachel stood behind

Mary, who seemed to sense her friend's trepidation and said, "Don't worry. This'll be fun."

Mary then leapt off the rock, pulling Rachel along who yelled, "No!" Fear filled her every being, but it was too late.

Despite being July, the water was cold and hit Rachel with a shock she wasn't prepared for, but she wasn't thinking of the water's temperature when she grabbed hold of Mary and wrapped her arms around her friend's neck. Mary fought to break free from her grip, but the panic-stricken girl was holding on so tight Mary couldn't pry her off. As a result, the two didn't surface.

Neither girl realized they were now being held under by the river itself. Rachel continued to hold on tightly to Mary, preventing her from placing an arm around Rachel and swimming in such a way that the current would push them to the surface. Rather, they were like a sack of wet sand moving along so close to the bottom they could feel the weeds that grew there. Which was a first for Mary, who, along with Rachel, was now drowning.

In what seemed to be seconds, the water ran through Rachel's nose and mouth and filled her stomach and lungs, causing her to lose consciousness, but even as unconsciousness enveloped her, she saw something…something weird.

As she stared at it, it formed into a tunnel composed of strobe lights with colors as dazzling as a rainbow. All those colored lights spiraled into a funnel that led to a single white light at the end. As Rachel drew closer to the white light, she realized she wasn't alone. Mary was alongside her. Rachel then returned her gaze towards the light as black lines appeared across the white background. She stared at the lines and quickly became aware that it was a message that wasn't in any language she'd ever heard of, but it was a message, nonetheless.

She complied, and then she blacked out.

A few hours later, Rachel found herself in a hospital bed where she regained consciousness, but had yet to speak. Her doctor said it was likely because her brain had been deprived of oxygen for ten minutes, possibly longer.

"All we can do is monitor her. She may not be able to speak again." The good news was she could hear just fine, so she understood when they told her how a young man who had undergone lifeguard training was fishing along the river when Rachel had surfaced. Without hesitating, he dove into the water and pulled her to shore, where others helped drag her out. He performed both mouth-to-mouth and cardiopulmonary resuscitation on her until emergency medical technicians arrived and used a defibrillator to restart her heart.

Despite being unable to speak, Rachel needed to communicate, so she used her hands to pantomime writing, and a pad of paper and pen were given to her. On it she drew the image she recalled—mostly black lines in a circle—which puzzled her parents. Eventually, her mother asked, "Don't you want to know about Mary?"

Rachel didn't want to be interrupted as she drew, so she held up her hand in a such a way as to silently say, *In a minute, Mom, I need to do this first.*

Her action caused her parents, the doctor, and the nurse in the room to exchange uncomfortable looks. That prompted her father to say, "Mary hasn't been found. She…may have drowned."

The teen looked at her father, and then away, as if in deep contemplation for about twenty long seconds, before she surprised everyone by saying, "I wonder if she saw it, too? Either way, I'm the one."

That she spoke at all was reason to feel joy, but what she said and how she said it increased the discomfort of all those around her.

After a short pause, her mother asked, "Saw what?"

Rachel looked at the confused faces surrounding her before holding up the drawing. "I want to get this as a tattoo."

More than twenty years later, Rachel had settled down, studied nursing, and was eventually appointed charge nurse of the newborn nursery at Arkham General Hospital. When she'd been offered the position of charge nurse, she'd accepted with the caveat that her schedule included at least two weekends per month in which she was free, so she could volunteer at the couples retreat offered by the church at which she was an ardent member. The hospital administration agreed, and Rachel surprised the administrators when she asked they put their agreement in writing.

"Do you really need that?" the director of the hospital's human resources department asked.

"Yes. The couples retreat is very important to my church and the congregation. They need volunteers to staff it. I can't promise to volunteer there every other weekend and then call the church on a Thursday to say I couldn't make it because I'm scheduled to work at the hospital. You'll have me every other weekend, but if you don't put it in writing, I can't accept the position."

The H.R. director smiled and said, "If you show as much dedication to the nursery as you're showing to your church, granting that stipulation would be a smart move on our part."

Both the hospital and Rachel honored the agreement, and it was one such weekend that the charge nurse was preparing for before departing for the couples retreat. As was her routine, she made a final inspection of the nursery's patients, focusing on three sets of twins, ensuring they had everything they needed. Rachel knew her dedication to the nursery was noticed by both hospital staff and administration, and when asked why she was so devoted, her answer was always the same.

"The next generation is the future."

The quickest route to the retreat was Aylesbury Pike, which crossed over the Miskatonic River, downstream from Falls Mill. Once on the north side of the river, Rachel turned the car west, driving through Dunwich where the road made a long southwest curve until it ran parallel with the water. As she followed the pike, she couldn't help but look to the river and recall that was where her old, carefree existence had died and her current life began. Some people might've been squeamish, even fearful, to pass by the river where they had drowned, but not Rachel, who steered the auto with no hesitation.

She followed the pike west for twenty miles until she saw the sign. It was a large version of the drawing she'd made in the hospital those many years ago. Although she'd switched her studies from the arts to nursing, Rachel had never stopped painting, and she'd painted that sign indicating motorists they had arrived at the retreat.

She turned off the highway and followed the dirt road for nearly a mile before reaching the main lodge. Surrounding the lodge were six small cabins where the couples stayed. As she parked, Rachel recognized three of the four other cars as those belonging to the volunteers who staffed the retreat, but she didn't recognize the fourth automobile. She reasoned the car likely belonged to some pain-in-ass early birds, and she would have to deal with them.

Lucinda and Ike Ashman sat in the lodge when she entered. Concealing her displeasure, Rachel said, "You're early. The facilities aren't ready and won't be for another couple of hours."

"We… It's my fault. I made Ike leave early because I'm anxious to, you know, get our family off the ground," Lucinda said.

"I see, well since you're here, I might as well ask if you have any questions. Do you?"

"What are the chances something could go wrong?" Lucinda asked.

Having fielded this question before, Rachel didn't hesitate, however she started by explaining the difference between clinical death and biological death before continuing, "It was the advances in medical technology that made this procedure possible. I practiced it for ten years at medical facilities in Boston, where I honed it to perfection before implementing it among our people. Nonetheless, there are risks with every procedure, but with this technique, I've minimized such risks to nearly one percent. You should feel honored to be chosen to undergo it."

"We do. It's just…well, I'm a little scared."

"There's no reason to be scared. I've personally calculated every variable and developed responses so you can take that big step and add to our church's family." She paused, then added, "I hope that puts you at ease."

"It does, thank you."

"Good. Now, please do me a favor and if you have any more concerns, wait to ask them until we're in your cabin, and not in front of the other couples. There is an official greeting for all the couples later, at which point I'll go over the same material that I discussed with you two. The couples won't be getting any special treatment like you two are." Rachel let that sink in, then said, "So, please respect the time the other couples will have with me."

"I'm sorry we got here early," Ike said. "It wasn't just Lucinda. I wasn't sure about the directions and we didn't want to be late."

"I understand, but like I said, respect the time I'll have with the other couples. Besides, tonight is all about all of you, reaching the point in all your lives where service to His magnificence surpasses mere talk, and becomes action."

In unison, the couple said, "Praise His name."

"Good. Now, I'll have one of the staff take you to your cabin. See you at dinner." And Rachel left for her office.

The other couples attending the retreat arrived at the appointed time, and Rachel was waiting to greet them. She directed them to the lounge where introductions were made, and then Rachel took questions from Gary and Tracee Spidell, Darryl and Andrea Tibbitts, and Kenneth and Emily Jones. The Ashmans joined the group, and Rachel led them to dinner. There were more questions during the meal, but nothing Rachel hadn't been asked before. When the couples finished eating, volunteers entered the dining room to lead them to their cabins. Rachel called after them, "Rest up, for tomorrow, you conceive."

The next morning, the husbands were the only guests allowed to eat breakfast because the wives would need their stomachs empty to avoid complications during the procedure. Rachel instituted a simple process for deciding which couple went first. She went from cabin one to four, with the first couple to sign up for a specific weekend being assigned cabin one, and the second couple cabin two, and so on. For this weekend, the Spidells occupied cabin one. Gary wore a fluffy white spa robe that was provided to all the couples. It was nearly noon when he answered the door, but he said, "Good morning," nonetheless.

Rachel responded in kind as she entered the cabin, leading two staff members who were there to assist. They were all dressed in scrubs.

"Tracee is in the bedroom. She's a little nervous."

"I understand. Being nervous is not unusual, but would you please get her, so we can get started?"

"Sure," he said as he headed to the bedroom on the right side of the living room. All the cabins had the same design. The main entrance to the cabin provided access to a small kitchen with a bathroom to the left. On the right side was the living room, featuring sliding glass doors that led to a deck. On the far side of the living room were the bedrooms, one reserved for each couple, while the other was clinical and contained medical cabinets, a hospital bed, and state-of-the-art medical monitoring equipment.

Rachel beckoned to the staff to enter the medical room while she waited for Tracee, who emerged first from the bedroom, a frightened look on her face. Rachel smiled.

"I understand you're nervous, of course you are. This will be your first baby, and you're to be commended for taking such a risk. But the procedure is as safe as can be. With guidance from His magnificence, I developed the procedure myself. I started in a hospice, and once I determined the correct dosage of potassium needed, I moved to a hospital where I developed the second part of the procedure. Since those days, the technology has only improved."

Tracee gave a wan smile and said, "I'm ready."

"Good, then let's get started." Rachel gestured toward the second bedroom.

Once in the second room, Tracee sat on the bed, and Rachel conducted a cursory examination, checking the young woman's heart, lungs, pulse, and other vitals. Satisfied, Rachel stepped back, and another staff member approached Tracee. He pushed back her hair, exposing her forehead. Using a grease pencil, he drew the same sigil that indicated where to turn off the highway to the retreat, and that was also present all over the grounds. When he finished, Rachel directed Tracee to lie on the bed and open her robe. Tracee complied, and the fullness of her stunning beauty filled the room. But Gary was the only one moved by her lusciousness.

The size and firmness of his erection satisfied Rachel that he'd ingested enough erectile dysfunction medication with breakfast to perform. A staffer provided Gary with a tube of lubrication, and he turned toward the wall as he applied it. All that was left was to administer to Tracee, so Rachel lifted the cover off a tray to reveal a pre-prepared syringe. Earlier, Rachel filled the syringe with potassium chloride and had the staff place it on the tray, just as they had done hundreds of times before. Rachel took an alcohol swab and sterilized a section of Tracee's upper arm and then injected the potassium into the woman.

As she did so, she couldn't help but ruminate over how she had researched other drugs such as morphine, epinephrine, even insulin, to induce heart attacks, and had rejected them all. The reason being that potassium not only induced a heart attack, it helped cover up the heart attack that it induced. How? Should cardiopulmonary resuscitation be performed on such a victim who'd died from a potassium-induced heart attack, and an autopsy was conducted that revealed increased levels of potassium within the deceased, those levels would be attributed to CPR, because—as every nurse knows— CPR actually caused the body to produce potassium, making it very unlikely any hospital death would lead back to Rachel.

Once she depressed the plunger, Rachel and the staff chanted, "Ph'nglui mglw'nafh Cthulhu R'lyeh wgah'nagl fhtagn," and Gary joined in. However, while Rachel really enjoyed causing someone's death, it was the second part of the procedure that made her feel god-like.

The potassium performed exactly as expected; Tracee bent and clutched at her chest, her face turning bright red, and then she flatlined onto the bed. Rachel placed her stethoscope on the woman's chest and listened. After about five seconds, she announced, "She's dead." The two staff then took hold of Tracee's legs and spread them wide while Gray crawled between his wife's thighs, his erection aimed toward her now cadaverous vagina. "You have four minutes," Rachel instructed. "Go!"

Gary then got to work in earnest. With her attention on a stopwatch, Rachel chanted, "Ph'nglui mglw'nafh Cthulhu R'lyeh wgah'nagl fhtagn." The two volunteers joined in.

As the chanting echoed around the room, and Gary took his first thrust, Rachel couldn't help but recall her near-death experience in the river, an NDE that changed her…life? *Is it still "my" life?* she wondered. Or had she become part of a bigger existence the moment she'd shoved Mary to the bottom in exchange for not only more time, but for a clear purpose? As she'd been drowning, something had wrapped around her, something muscular and strong but as bendable as hard rubber, and, most incredible of all, something she couldn't see. Whatever the invisible restraint had been, it enveloped her completely and once she was fully encased by the invisible…tentacle, a voice said, *"This is no hallucination, or dream."*

It had boomed around and through Rachel. A voice as unnatural as it was patrician.

"But it might be your nightmare, or salvation," it said. That was when Rachel realized it was coming from the roar of the river.

"Do you want to live?" it asked.

Yes! Rachel had screamed in her mind. *YES!*

"Then ask me to take the other."

What?

"Prove to me your desire to live is great by serving me… Ask me to take the other."

A desperate Rachel silently screamed, *Take Mary!*

The invisible tentacle had then released its grip, and as it did so, an intense light appeared. It surrounded and highlighted black lines that formed the sigil that Rachel only saw for a few seconds before the black lines grew and expanded to become darkness. But it had been forever seared into her consciousness.

Rachel interrupted her chanting to announce, "Thirty seconds left." That seemed to motivate Gary, who increased his tempo, and a few seconds later he arched his back and vibrated before collapsing onto his dead wife. "That's it, pull him off," Rachel commanded.

The volunteers did as instructed, and as Gary was helped to a nearby chair, he said, "I didn't know it would be… I never felt that much pleasure."

Rachel ignored him as she placed the defibrillator pads on Tracee's chest. They had to be positioned in such a way as to provide the greatest possible jolt to her heart. Once in place, Rachel again chanted "Ph'nglui mglw'nafh Cthulhu R'lyeh wgah'nagl fhtagn," as she hit the *shock* button, sending the electric charge into Tracee's chest. At the same time, the power of life over death ran through Rachel like an orgasm. Immediately after the jolt, the monitors indicated Tracee had a heartbeat. She was back, and Rachel had brought her back, the way Lazarus was alleged to have been brought back. In Lazarus' case, he'd been brought back from biological death, while Tracee was brought back from clinical death, a distinction that didn't matter to Rachel because it was still death. Not that long ago, Tracee would be have been gone forever. *He said our expertise and technology had reached the point where resurrection was possible,* Rachel thought. *So it was time for Him to use that to add to His following. Once He has the right amount of adherents, it will be his turn to be resurrected.*

Rachel went to cabin two, which held Darryl and Andrea Tibbitts, and repeated the procedure nearly verbatim, with the same results. It was in the third cabin—which housed Lucinda and Ike Ashman—where problems arose.

Most of the procedure involving the Ashmans went as with the first two couples, but like with Tracee Spidell in the first cabin, Lucinda Ashman expressed fear. So, like with Mrs. Spidell, Rachel gave Lucinda her reassurances, which calmed her down. Rachel then proceeded with the procedure, but Lucinda said something that changed everything.

As Lucinda lay on the hospital bed, just before Rachel administered the potassium chloride, the woman who was about to die looked at her husband and said, "I love you." With that, Rachel injected the potassium, and Lucinda suffered a fatal heart attack.

When Lucinda fully collapsed on the bed, Ike Ashman stood ready to copulate with his dead wife, but Rachel said nothing. After several long seconds, Ike said, "Shouldn't I do it?"

Rachel then held her hand up in a gesture to stop him from proceeding. "Love… There is no love here. Only fear and blind obedience."

"What, but…but?"

"You'll be transferred to another church, another life, another woman to impregnate. Now get dressed, and wait in the other room. No more mixing with the other couples. Your meals will be brought out here until late tonight, when you'll leave for your new church. Full directions and instructions will be provided." As she spoke, the volunteers covered Lucinda's body with a sheet. "Her remains will be disposed of."

"I don't know what to say," Ike stammered.

Rachel had moved to the door, and just before exiting the room, turned and said, "Again: there's only fear and blind obedience."

The procedure in the final cabin went as the first two, enabling Rachel to relax for the rest of the weekend. But come Monday, she was up early and on the road before five a.m. She drove straight to Arkham Hospital and soon she was in the nursery, inspecting all her tiny charges, including the last set of twins who were born the week before.

Jacob and Heather Jones had been in the nursery with two other sets of twins who were born the preceding Wednesday and went home on Saturday. Rachel pushed together the clear plastic bassinets that held the twins and hovered over the infants, eventually holding up a card containing the sigil. She moved it back and forth so each baby could get a good look at the drawing, and after a few seconds, Rachel addressed this set of twins with the same question she'd put to the twins born earlier, saying, "Tell me, do you hear the call?"

The only reply was blank stares, which wasn't unexpected. Rachel then pulled back the long sleeves of the tee shirt she wore under her scrubs and held her bare forearms up so the babies could see the tattoos on each. That changed the look in the newborns' eyes, for they fixated on the sigils. Rachel then said, "Conceived in a dead womb, touched by him, tell me you hear His call."

In unison, both infants said, "Ph'nglui mglw'nafh Cthulhu R'lyeh wgah'nagl fhtagn."

Then, in a voice that wasn't Rachel's, she said, "*Now ask me to take the other.*"

The infants looked confused by the request, and they remained silent, so Rachel held up a syringe. "*Prove to me your desire to live and serve His plans for humanity by growing to adulthood and becoming a police officer, or lawyer, or politician, or concentration camp guard, or nurse, by asking me to take the other.*"

No longer confused, both babies asked for Rachel to take the other. The nurse then turned and walked away, which caused the babies to resume acting like babies. Rachel bore a smirk on her face, for one twin had spoken up a fraction of a second before the other, and she knew which of those it was. Rachel was an adherent of the doctrine that only the strongest should have the privilege of serving Him, so the slower infant would receive a visit from Rachel within a few weeks, long before the parents had formed any real attachment to the child.

Because, Rachel knew, in this world, you either sank or you swam.

PIEXE VAMPIRO

TERRY CAMPBELL

I HAVE SEEN THE *Piexe vampiro*—the so-called vampire fish, as the aborigines of the lower Amazon basin called it—three times in my life. Time has a peculiar way of distorting itself, of making vast expanses meld inward upon one another, like an ethereal accordion ignorant of and unbound by the laws of man, until events that occurred years ago seem no more distant than a few days. Several meager months passed between my first and second encounter with the fish, but fifty-five years, seeming at times no more than fifty-five minutes, have somehow elapsed between the second and third.

The first time I saw the fish, I was shocked but highly intrigued, for it was a beautiful and remarkable animal. The second time changed my very existence and sent me spiraling into a life of depression and paranoia. After beholding that haunting vision from my past for a third time, I now fear that my life, and possibly the entire existence of humanity, will soon be at an end.

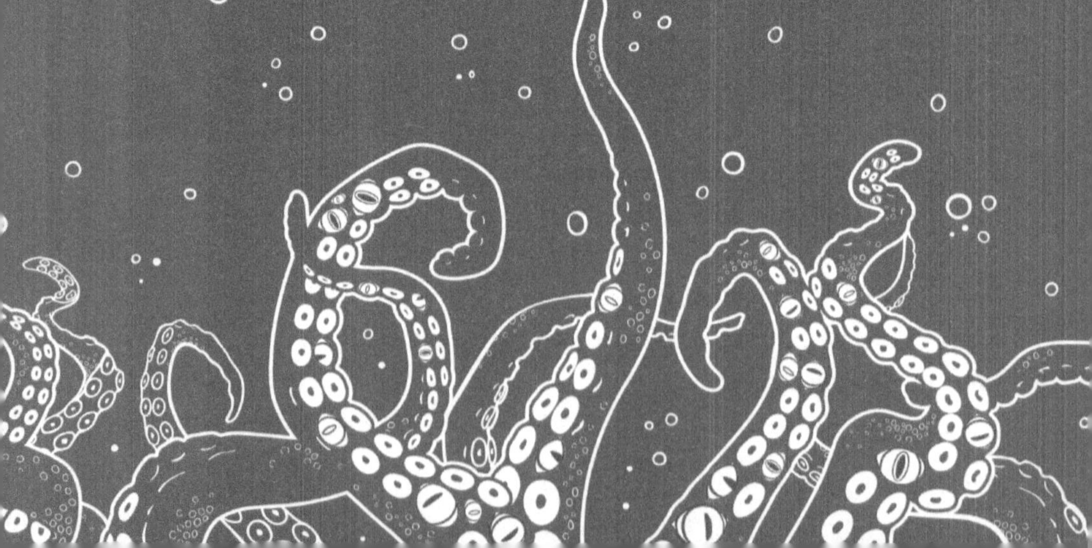

I was a student at Justus Liebig University in Giessen, Germany, in 1937, majoring in zoology. I suppose you could say I was the star pupil of Dr. Albert Ruediger, but I was quite taken aback when he invited me along on his next trip to the Amazon. His objective, he told others, was to replenish his collection of tropical fish he had brought back from his previous trip. But in secret, he told me that he wished to collect a breeding pair of *Piexe vampiro*. You see, my teacher had returned from that same adventure with a single specimen of the vampire fish. He had placed all his collected fish into one tank upon his return that first night. In the morning, the *Piexe vampiro* had turned every other fish in the aquarium into shriveled husks.

I'll never forget my first look at this strange new fish. It was very small, no more than twenty millimeters. It had an equally small mouth and abnormally large red eyes atop its head. The simple rays of its dorsal fins, as well as the rays of the pectoral and pelvic fins, were extremely elongated, looking somewhat like miniature tentacles. Its vital organs could be seen in its chest cavity, but the rest of the body was as transparent as glass. It reminded me of *Pterois volitans,* the saltwater lionfish.

I slept most of the nearly thirteen-hour flight from Frankfurt to Manaus, Brazil, but I don't believe Dr. Ruediger slept much at all. During the first few hours of the flight, Dr. Ruediger informed me of what to expect once we began our trek into the jungle. It seemed that the local tribes were quite superstitious regarding the *Piexe vampiro.* The elders claimed that there were only approximately one-hundred of the fish in existence—which I found difficult to believe—and that their proliferation would signal the return of an ancient race of otherworldly beings into our world, beginning the end of life as on Earth as we knew it. Ridiculous, of course, but it would make extraction of the fish difficult. Dr. Ruediger had made a connection with a young guide who had assisted him in bringing the previous specimen home. We were to meet Aquito at the airport in Brazil. It all sounded extremely exciting to a young man who had never been out of his hometown.

Aquito and a few of his friends greeted us at the airport. A short bus ride followed by a two-hour excursion down the Amazon and, finally, a three-hour hike through the sweltering jungle culminated in our arrival at the village in the early evening. The tribe was most hospitable, with a splendid dinner consisting of fruits and vegetables with a main course of grilled arowana.

Aquito had pointed out the village elder, an aged white-haired man named Esquatir, earlier at dinner. During the course of the evening, I would momentarily study the old man's face. There seemed to be such an air of wisdom and knowledge about him, as if he knew of things no mere mortal could fathom. He didn't say a word throughout dinner or afterwards, which was why it was so unexpected when he stood and approached us, offering cigars. He said something to us which Dr. Ruediger nor I could understand.

"He is speaking in our native tongue," Aquito explained. "But he wishes to speak to you through the Tambaki leaves."

"What is this Tambaki leaf?" I asked, rolling the dry leaves in my fingers. "Is it a stimulant?"

"Somewhat," Aquito said with a shy grin. "The Tambaki will clear your mind and allow you to communicate with Esquatir."

We all sat at the base of the campfire. Short tongues of flame leapt sporadically from the dying embers and thin wisps of smoke rose from the coals like dancing ghostly specters. We reached for the hot coals and lit our primitive cigars. I dragged on my smoke, watching the tip grow bright red in the dark night, and coughed. After a few more draws, my lungs grew accustomed to the alien smoke, and I realized that the leaf had quite a pleasant taste.

Suddenly, I became aware of voices. They seemed slow and distant, like a recording played at a slow speed. I noticed through the smoke that the elder's mouth was moving, and I was hearing him speak, but not with my ears. I heard him in my mind. My senses were foggy, yet I understood every word he said perfectly. I glanced over at the doctor, but he seemed to be mesmerized by the events.

"I know why you are here," the elder said. "You wish to take the *Piexe vampiro* from the river. You wish to take it back to your homeland."

Dr. Ruediger made a comment in return to the elder. I did not know what language he was speaking, yet I understood his words.

"There is a great race of beings that watches over this land. They are called the *Nahui-Quiahuitl*, "The Four Rains". *Tecpatl*, the Earth Lord;

Moumbogalt, the Keeper of the River; *Xabical*, He Who Grows From the Soil; and *Quetzalcoatl*, the Watcher from the Skies."

"I fail to see what the gods you choose to worship have to do with my fish," the doctor said.

"Please," the elder responded. "Allow me the opportunity to finish. Thousands of years ago, the *Nahui-Quiahuitl* punished many of our ancestors. The ancient tribesmen wanted more than the *Nahui-Quiahuitl* would allow them to have. They wanted power, they wanted knowledge. The *Nahui-Quiahuitl* destroyed the world by releasing their wrath—the coming of "The Four Rains"—which resulted in a great flood. Many survived the flood by seeking higher ground. The *Nahui-Quiahuitl* chose to place a curse on those who escaped punishment, a curse of transformation and longevity, and to extend that curse to the entire ancestral lineage of the offenders. This land is filled with many strange and amazing creatures. Not all are of what your kind would consider a natural creation, doctor.

"In the future, the *Nahui-Quiahuitl* will face a new threat, and one more substantial than a few rogue individuals seeking forbidden fruit," the elder continued. "When this new threat arrives, the *Nahui-Quiahuitl* will awake from their slumber inside *Tiahuanacu*, the City of the Dead, and return to our world once again to wreak their havoc."

"What will initiate their return?" Dr. Ruediger asked.

"The rape of the land," the elder answered, staring into the smokey remains of the fire. "The infringement of civilization into these sacred lands. The rivers will dry up, the forests will burn, the animals will disappear from this land, and the mountains will crumble. When this happens, the *Nahui-Quiahuitl* shall come forth from *Tiahuanacu*, the great City of the Dead, and into our world to reclaim what is theirs. Leaving great destruction in their path. Much as the offenders from so long ago were punished, so shall the *Nahui-Quiahuitl* deal with future transgressions.

"The *Piexe vampiro* is the offspring of *Moumbogalt*, the Keeper of the River, for he is the one that transformed some of the survivors into savage fish, as a reminder to all who would disobey the teachings of the *Nahui-Quiahuitl*. This fish is a part of this land, as are the waters, the trees, the mountains, but more importantly, it is a part of the *Nahui-Quiahuitl*. It is the only tangible link my people have to the Great Lords of Antiquity; it is through the *Piexe vampiro* that we worship the *Nahui-Quiahuitl*. After all, they are our ancestors. As the *Nahui-Quiahuitl* watch over us, so do we watch over the *Piexe vampiro. Moumbogalt* does not want his children taken from him, and it is the responsibility of our tribe as guardian of the fish to make certain this does not occur. Only when the return of the *Nahui-Quiahuitl* becomes imminent will he allow the fish to go forth and multiply.

"You already have the fish, doctor, yet you return for more. Will you return again? And again? Will mankind in general return for more and more? Where will it end? This fish must not proliferate; it must remain indigenous to the river. It has been so for millions of years, and it shall remain so, until the *Nahui-Quiahuitl* choose otherwise. Until that day, the *Piexe vampiro* is ours, not yours. Not only must I forbid your wishes for us, but I fear for your safety, as well. I foresee tragedy for you if you continue your expedition. I must forbid your wish, doctor. I am sorry."

As I groggily listened to Dr. Ruediger stating his case to the elder, I watched the dying flames lick at the dark shadows. As the smoke curled and danced skyward, shapes flickered in the flames. Crude, misshapen forms seemed to be dancing, and I could hear something—something remote and distant, like a lost, lonely child crying for its mother. I assumed the visions were induced by the Tambaki leaf, but to this day I am not sure.

When I looked up from the fire and the strange visions in my head, I noticed that Esquatir had left our company.

"Do you think what we are doing is wise, Dr. Ruediger?" I asked.

"Adrian, don't tell me the elder's ridiculous superstitions have lent you to feelings of paranoia. Surely you do not believe such nonsense. What he told us is merely an ancient culture's explanation of the Biblical Flood, and nothing more. Tales of monsters metamorphosing humans into fish. Really, Adrian. I thought you wiser than that."

"But it all sounded so real, and we were able to understand his ancient language," I contested.

"I came here for this fish, Adrian," he said, lighting a cigarette. "I don't intend to leave without it." His voice had a tone of finality to it.

I nodded apprehensively, beginning to wish I had never left the safety of Geissen. Aquito and his brother, Gambeel, loaded our equipment onto the small canoe. I could not shake the uneasy feeling that lingered over me, could not drive the visions of the flames from my mind.

"Aquito, is it wise to go against your elder's wishes?" I asked.

"Give me a hand, please?" he asked, struggling with a large, rolled net. I grabbed one end of the net, and we hoisted it into the canoe. "I do not believe in the *Nahui-Quiahuitl*, Adrian. It is merely old native superstition."

"But shouldn't you respect their decision?"

"The elders are wise, indeed. Truly, it may be wrong to go against their decisions, but it is also wrong to not do what it best for my people. Our leaders are uncivilized; they do not know what is important. My people cannot live off the land forever. Dr. Ruediger is paying us good money for our help. We need the money. I need the money for my schooling if I'm ever to escape this cursed jungle."

"Do you think our expedition is dangerous?" I asked.

Aquito looked out across the river, his eyes squinting in the early morning sun. "Anytime you confront the mighty Amazon, it is dangerous."

The sun was high above us, beaming mercilessly on our heads when we at last began moving towards Rio Sangue. Aquito and Gambeel rowed the canoe while Dr. Ruediger and I labored at untangling some snags in one of our nets. The air was very still and humid, and I was forced to wipe my sweaty brow repeatedly. Dark storm clouds were gradually forming overhead, intermittently casting cooling shadows over us.

We made a turn at one junction, though the river was so wide I couldn't be sure if we were still on the Amazon or one of its tributaries. Dr. Ruediger stared ahead in grim determination. The previous night's incident with the tribe elder, along with all the legends and warnings, only seemed to stir his desire that much more. I, myself, could not stop thinking of the words the elder had spoken, words that I should not have been able to comprehend. I had been made aware of things I should not know, in a language I should not have been able to understand, and I could not shake the portentous feeling of doom that darkened my soul, just as the gathering clouds darkened the sky.

Gradually, the river began to taper, until it was no more than ten meters wide. The long, grasping branches of the trees stretched across the water, hanging so low that I began to duck the leafy appendages. The foliage was very dense and, coupled with the darkening skies, limited our visibility.

I looked down into the river and discovered I could see the bottom. It could be no more than three meters deep at that point. The water was taking on a brownish tint, typical of the "black water" Amazonian streams of which I had read so much.

Aquito said something to his brother. He and Gambeel slowed their oar strokes, and for the first time, I became aware of how still and silent the surrounding area was. There were no birds, no monkeys, not even the sound of leaves rustling in the wind. The stillness only added to the apprehension that was overcoming me.

Aquito put down his oar and turned to face Dr. Ruediger. "We are here. *Rio Sangue*. Blood River."

I could not help but chuckle slightly. "*This* is Blood River?" I asked skeptically. Somehow, I had pictured a wider, much more intimidating body of water. This was no more awe-inspiring than the streams in which I used to net for sticklebacks. True, the decaying vegetation did give the stream a reddish color, and I could no longer see the bottom, but the entire scene was not very imposing.

Aquito seemed to ignore my remark. "This is where you will find the *Piexe vampiro*," he said to the doctor.

Dr. Ruediger did not answer, but instead began rolling up the legs of his trousers, questioning not for one moment Aquito's words. Aquito and Gambeel hopped over the side of the canoe, beater sticks in hand. Dr. Ruediger hoisted one leg over the side of the boat, and I began rolling up my pants. I looked to the high branches and could see no hint of the sun. A crack of thunder erupted from somewhere not too distant. I prayed it would not rain, for the river could swell rapidly during a severe rain. How odd that it should storm during this time of year, I thought, for I had read that it never rains during the dry season.

Aquito and Gambeel moved to the edge of the stream; then I joined Dr. Ruediger in the river. The dark water came up to the middle of my chest. I grabbed one end of the net and carefully stepped backwards while unrolling it. We stretched it across the width of the stream, holding it down and letting the weights drop to the bottom. We stood behind the net, and Dr. Ruediger motioned to Aquito and Gambeel.

"Ready?" Aquito called out.

We nodded, and the two young men moved towards us, slapping their sticks on the water's surface to drive the fish into the net. When they reached us, we quickly pulled the net out of the water.

We found only one thing in the net, but I'll never forget it. It was the shriveled, prune-like carcass of a large shovelnose catfish. I estimated the fish to have been at least a meter long when alive.

"They are in here," Dr. Ruediger said, tiny droplets of anxious perspiration beading on his forehead.

"Do they know we're here?" I asked. "Did we make too much noise?" I was frightened beyond belief.

Aquito looked at me, saying nothing, but I could see in his eyes the doubt, the uncertainty. How much experience did he really have at sailing the rivers and, more importantly, how much did he really know about the vampire fish?

"They're smart little buggers," the doctor said, "but we'll get them."

Aquito and Gambeel moved to the other side of the stream and stepped out of the water. They walked back along the bank and reentered the water to minimize the inhabitants' awareness of our actions. They made another pass towards us. Again, the net yielded nothing. Several more attempts brought the same results.

"Let's move further upriver," Dr. Ruediger said.

He and I crawled back into the canoe and rowed slowly upstream while Aquito and Gambeel walked the banks. A loud crack of thunder, closer than the earlier rumbling, roared down from the skies. The vegetation grew even more dense, and Dr. Ruediger at last had to light a gas lantern.

He set the lantern on the seat and we reentered the water. We positioned the net again, and the brothers advanced towards us once more. When they were only a few meters from us, something brushed the back of my calf. I froze momentarily; I had no idea what it was. The vampire fish was the least of my worries, for I suddenly envisioned huge anacondas, schools of famished piranhas, an aquatic fer-de-lance. I shut my eyes in fear until Dr. Ruediger shouted at me.

"For God's sake, Adrian! Lift your end!"

I quickly snapped out of my paranoia and deftly hoisted the net up and out of the water. There were small flashes of movement at the center as the doctor and I swiftly moved the net over to the boat, lifting it up and over until it was safely within the confines of the craft. Only then did I see the long rays, the huge red eyes of the flopping fish trapped in the net. It was a pair of *Piexe vampiro*, the vampire fish.

Dr. Ruediger laughed aloud almost hysterically. I laughed too, but it was more nervous laughter than anything. I was happy for Dr. Ruediger, for he was succeeding at his task, but my insides were screaming to leave this frightening world. Thunder roared overhead again, and torrential rain began to pelt the treetops high overhead.

Dr. Ruediger dipped a large jar into the stream, filling it with water. I was astonished to see the coloring of the water in the glass for, when held up to the light, the water did seem bright red. The doctor handed the jar to me as he reached for a smaller scooping net. He lifted one of the fish out of the larger net and skillfully placed it into the jar. We placed the other vampire fish in a separate container, for we were uncertain of their behavior towards their own species, especially in cramped quarters.

Dr. Ruediger held one jar to the lantern, inspecting his prize catch. The distorted view that the glass container offered made the fish look even more unearthly than usual. "Oh, you exquisite creature," he whispered. "Are you really the remains of a being that once walked on two legs? Are you truly the offspring of some ancient, unearthly demon?"

There came a crashing noise in the trees to our right, and I then realized that the wind had increased considerably. Precipitation from the storm trickled through the foliage and into the stream. Aquito looked uneasy.

"*Parab*, doctor! You have a pair of *Piexe vampiro*!" he said. "I think we should go now."

"What?" Dr. Ruediger sounded insulted. "We can't leave now. How can we be sure that I have representatives of both genders? And even if I do, how do I know I have a compatible pair? These may be a cichlid sub-species, and cichlids can be very selective."

"But, doctor," Aquito warned, "the storm is getting worse. You don't know this river like I do. It can rise very quickly during a rain. We are in danger!"

The doctor proceeded to roll the net out again as the skies roared menacingly, high above the jungle. "*Unsinn!* Now listen, Aquito! I'm paying you damn good money to guide me, and we're not leaving until I have a satisfactory number of these fish! Do I make myself clear?"

At that moment, Gambeel released a blood-curdling cry that has haunted my existence for over half a century. I wheeled about to see what was the matter. Aquito was already moving to his brother's aid. The water around Gambeel churned in a frothy frenzy as he beat madly at it, his body jerking and quivering violently. Large drops of red liquid splattered onto his bare chest, and I couldn't tell if it was the water or, God help us, his blood. Aquito reached his brother and, throwing his arms around Gambeel, pulled with all his might. That is when Gambeel's right leg broke through the water's surface...

And I saw *them*.

With the amazing speed of a modern computer, I counted them; twenty, thirty, forty of the *Piexe vampiro* latched onto Gambeel's leg, their tentacle-like rays looking like a mass of tangled fishing twine. Their tiny teeth attached to his skin; I could actually hear the gnashing of the bites, hear the *thump-thump* of the tentacles penetrating his flesh as the tiny fish grew deep crimson and swelled to three times their size. I watched in horror, unable to tear myself from my frozen stance, as Gambeel's eyes rolled up into his head until only the whites were visible. Then they began to shrivel, as did the remainder of his body.

I broke from my trance and threw myself into the safety of the canoe. Aquito screamed, and I could only assume the vampire fish had attacked him as well. I was vaguely aware of the rain cascading down over my back, of the wind howling through the trees. Dr. Ruediger's hands came up over the sides of the boat, and I knew he was in trouble when I saw his face twist into a gut-wrenching scream. I reached for him, clutching him by his forearms. Glancing over at Aquito, he was nothing more than a dried corpse floating and bobbing on the water's surface; Gambeel had completely vanished from sight. I pulled hard on the doctor's arms, attempting to hoist him to safety, and my heart leapt into my throat. Something was pulling on him from below! I called on God to grant me every ounce of strength in my body as I pulled and pulled. Dr. Ruediger cried out in terrible pain. The canoe rocked savagely in the torrential water, but I wouldn't let go.

Suddenly, there was a crash to my right. Glancing back over my shoulder, there was what I could only describe as a tentacle, like that of an unearthly octopus. It whipped back into the air and smashed into the tiny canoe. Reacting out of sheer terror, I looked up and saw about six more tentacles dancing about over my head. My gaze followed their length back into the water. They were coming from directly beneath Dr. Ruediger. The tentacles whipped and wavered and slapped at the water, one of them striking Aquito's withered body, crumbling it to dust. I tore my eyes away from the gruesome sight back to the struggling doctor, and the shock of what I saw—and I am pained to say this—made me release my grip on my good friend.

I will never forget the visage I observed in that brief moment, and believe me, I have tried. I will venture to say that I'm the only mortal man that has ever glimpsed the likes of which I saw at that precise instance.

I noticed—subconsciously, I think—that the area immediately around me had become much brighter, yet my surroundings were still dark as pitch. As the doctor went under, I saw, to my overwhelming shock, that the light came from below the surface. The water seemed crystal clear, for I could see into its depths, but just as blood red as it had been. Dr. Ruediger was being pulled further and further from my reach, and only then did I see what I had been pulling against.

My mind wants to shun what I saw, to use insanity as an excuse, to deny that such things can exist, but it cannot. The long tentacles that slapped at the boat and grabbed Dr. Ruediger were attached to a being of disproportionate size, an entity of such a scale my mortal mind could not comprehend. Shaped more like a crustacean than a fish, its body was fishlike from its head to midway down its length, but it had the tail of a crustacean. Thousands of tiny legs protruded from its underside like a centipede, yet it had fins, and it must've been several hundred kilometers in total length. It was deep blue and black and had the same huge eyes as the vampire fish.

As terrifying, as inexplicable as the monstrous creature was, its existence was not the most difficult part of the vision with which my mind had to cope. The stream was only ten meters wide, but staring into the brightly lit water was like bearing witness to an entirely different world. The dimension, the physics, just *didn't work*. I could look down at this terrible creature that was larger than my mind could conceive, yet when I lifted my head, I was still in a shallow Amazonian stream. Not only did I see the creature, but I could see a city as well. Ornate bridges, tall slim buildings, all of a deep emerald color and an architectural style I could not comprehend. I was perceiving a whole new dimension, yet I was still in a small canoe on a tiny South American tributary.

There were no more signs of Dr. Ruediger, but the hideous creature was still thrashing its tentacles about my head. Several of them had wrapped around the ends of the canoe, and I feared the tiny boat would be torn to pieces. It was at that moment that I remembered the words of the elder: *Moumbogalt does not want his children taken from him.* The vampire fish! I quickly reached into the chest and retrieved the two jars holding the fish. My hands shook so feverishly that I feared I would be unable to remove the lids. I leaned over the boat, once again greeting the red-and-emerald world of gods, and hastily opened the jars. The two fish dropped from the containers into the seething water, and just as swiftly as they had appeared, the massive tentacles withdrew, the red light dissipated, and the waves began to subside.

I continued to stare at the city for, despite being in a state of terror beyond human conception, I could not deny the gnawing feeling that, somehow, I wanted to be there. The bright flashes of light bouncing off the rippling red water produced a queer, hypnotic effect and I watched, mesmerized, the underwater world tortured even further by the rolling of the slowly calming waters. Finally, the water smoothed over, I closed my eyes, and the glimpse into another world was no more. I collapsed into the bottom of the boat and wept. My dearest friend and colleague was dead. He had insisted on tampering with something that was never meant to be a part of our world, and he paid dearly for it.

I lost consciousness and awoke several days later, drifting in the canoe down the main body of the Amazon. I had no idea how I had got there; my mind was a blank. Blood River was far behind me now. I had no idea where it might be and had no desire to know.

I have carried the memories of that terrifying experience, along with my vision of a world of ancient and evil immortals, for fifty-five years now. I explained the disappearance of Dr. Albert Ruediger as a tragic, yet unarguably routine—a drowning accident on the river. I've never told anyone my story, for who would believe it?

I'm seventy-five years old now, and I still live in my hometown of Kassel, Germany. At my age, I have frequent memory lapses of everyday normal experiences, but I've never forgotten a single event, a single action, not even a single word spoken during that fateful expedition so long ago. I remember every word of the elder's warnings to us through the Tambaki leaves, and how it was all true.

Every day I pick up a newspaper and read about global warming, or the blasting of mountains in the name of man's greedy search for gold, or the destruction of the Brazilian rainforests, and I remember what the old man said: *the rape of the land.* I can't help but wonder, with every square kilometer of forest cleared, does another drop of precipitation from "The Four Rains", the Ancient *Nahui-Quiahuitl*, fall to our unsuspecting earth? Does the length of time between each vile drop decrease with every passing day until soon a torrent of evil will lash out into our world? How near is the return of these loathsome, evil beings? Will I soon come face-to-face once again with that hideous creature? Will I peer once again into that incomprehensible, yet inexplicably beautiful, emerald world?

Time has healed some of the scars, but I still relive those last moments in my dreams every night. I went to war several years after that, and the horrors I experienced during that awful time pale in comparison to the thought of The Four Rains. I haven't kept aquarium fish since returning from that trip. I quit college; I've worked in a local bakery my entire life.

Yesterday, I made a trip up to Frankfurt with a good friend of mine. As we were strolling down the sidewalks of the city, we came across a pet store. Gerard wanted to go in and look at the dogs, but I couldn't bear to look in and possibly see the aquaria. I do not wish to view aquaria anymore. Gerard couldn't understand my reluctance to enter, but he respected my wishes and went in without me.

I wish we had never seen the pet store.

I peered into the pet shop window a few moments later to see if I could spot Gerard, and my eyes came across a large aquarium situated along the back wall. I wanted to immediately tear my gaze from the tank, but they were fixed firmly in place. Red gravel lined the bottom, giving the water an eerie reddish glow. Green plastic castles and bridges, and an algae-laden plastic skeleton, sat at varying angles atop the gravel, looking disturbingly like a horrid scene from my distant past.

And floating effortlessly at mid-tank, alone, their long simple rays drifting softly in the flow from the power filter, their large, blood-red eyes eagerly scanning the top of the water, were eight *Piexe vampiro*.

DESCENDENT

BRYSON RICHARD

Carl Rooth saw it on a pleasant Sunday afternoon in May, after relocating a spindly black and yellow garden spider from his tomatoes to the lavender between his yard and the cotton field.

He removed his favorite hemp sun hat, bent backwards at the waist until his old spine popped audibly, and caught something small and still out of the corner of his eye. Glancing up, expecting an airplane, he saw instead a single dark form hovering in the sky.

It was a person. The distance was far enough that gender and facial features were ambiguous, yet near enough that he could plainly see the dimensions of arms, torso, and legs.

Carl couldn't tell for sure, but the person seemed to be looking down at him. Not falling, though not exactly flying either; just standing in the sky, watching.

So he did the only sensible thing—he waved.

The figure waved back.

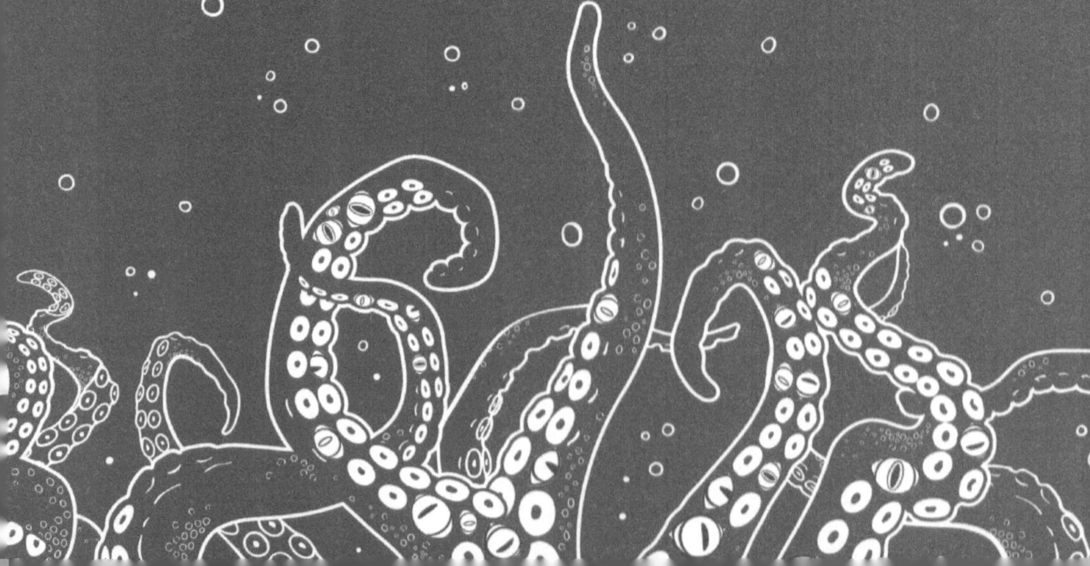

Confounded, Carl took the next logical step, cupped his hands around his mouth and shouted, "Hey!" His deep baritone that had once regaled those in attendance at *Our Brethren in Christ*, carried across the sky.

He caught the strained echo of a feminine voice in response, though he couldn't understand what was said.

Shaking his head in disbelief, Carl decided somebody needed to come handle this.

He'd left the television on in the brick ranch-style house and was distracted from picking up the landline by a special announcement. According to the talking head, people were appearing in the sky all over the world. No one had any idea why or how. The best the news could offer, absent any clear explanation, were various clips and footage of these mysterious floating people obtained from across the globe. Some of it was professionally captured by news stations, some of it was CCTV footage, grainy and strangely distant. The most unsettling for Carl, though, was the stuff captured by cellphones at higher elevations—sporadic figures floating in the valleys between mountain peaks, denser crowds hovering outside the upper floors of skyscrapers, and short snippets of video from out of the windows of passenger jets of people seemingly standing on air—as if waiting for one of the jets to pull up and offer a lift like a taxi.

The images of all those figures in the sky bothered him. He understood it was because they weren't falling. People weren't supposed to stand around in the air, way up in the clouds. People were supposed to *fall*.

He saw much in the flicker of the TV, watched longer than he'd meant to. Footage of the Eiffel Tower with a halo of people surrounding its peak like a cloud of gnats hovering near a sweaty head. Large concentrations of people floated over cities like entire battalions preparing for annexation. Their numbers dwindled in rural areas, sometimes a trio, sometimes just a pair.

Carl had just the one.

The news went on to say that communication with the people was top priority, however, there was difficulty in reaching them while they remained in middle space. Couldn't just pile into a whirly bird and fly up and ask them what the hell they were doing and expect to be heard and understood and to not accidentally dismember one or two of them in the chopper blades. No, in fact, all flights and aircraft were grounded until some understanding could be gained.

When the TV switched to footage of chaotic airports, Carl stood from his chair, stretched, and journeyed again into his backyard, having forgotten all about why he originally went inside.

He could immediately tell the person was lower.

A massive two-hundred-year-old maple shaded his house from the backyard. It had been there longer than the house, longer than the road he lived on, even. The woman in the sky was near enough that the tree worked as a means of measurement, and she was about level with the top, a stunning 115 feet off the ground.

He made out white tennis shoes, a green and black striped shirt, and the evident poise of a feminine form. She was, he verified, the only thing in the entire sky as far as he could see. No clouds, no jet streams, no birds, just blue sky and her, standing on air.

He studied her, craning his neck back, moving so that he was directly beneath her. Then, hoe in hand, he scratched an 'X' in the turf to mark where he presumed she would land.

His mind swam with questions, new ones forming with each breath. It was dizzying. Or it could be all the looking up he was doing. It was killing his neck. He bent his head from side-to-side and gritted his teeth at the crunchy, gravelly sound of his spine. At seventy-four, he was too old to be gawking up at the sky like some half-wit star-gazer.

Carl sat on the grass, feeling its cool prickles in the palm of his hands, then slowly stretched his legs out on the spongy sod. It was soft, clean sod, and he'd worked hard over forty years to make it so. It was delightfully comfortable. He reclined, laying all the way back with his arms behind his head like he had in childhood, and stared up at the floating woman. He felt certain she was looking directly at him.

He waved, and she waved back.

He cupped his hands around his mouth. "Hello!" his baritone voice boomed.

"Hello!" she shouted back.

"Are you okay?"

"I'm not sure! I think so!"

"How did you get up there?"

"What?"

"How did you get up there?" he strained. He could already tell this means of communication was going to be short-lived. They had to shout at each other, and it was hard to maintain that volume, hard on the throat.

"I honestly don't know!" She shrugged animatedly.

He detected an accent but couldn't place it. Perhaps if they were simply talking in their ordinary voices he could have, but shouting made it difficult.

"There's more like you!"

"What?"

"There's more…" He stopped. If he was going to shout up into the sky like a madman, then he should at least make it worthwhile. "What's your name?"

"I don't know!" she called down and he could hear confusion in her voice. "I…I can't remember!"

He nodded exaggeratedly to ensure she could see and shouted his own name up at her. His voice broke and something grated in his throat. He massaged the front of his neck, swallowed repeatedly, hoping to ease the strain on his vocal cords before shouting again, "I've got to call someone! I'll be back!"

He made his way into the house. The TV still flickered. He paused to catch up on new developments.

Someone had the idea of using hot air balloons, which were both quieter and slower than any other kind of aerial vehicle. Now balloons were going up across the world, hovering near the people in the sky. Police, emergency responders, military personnel and scientists, cameramen and reporters for every station, were up in balloons, trying to interview these apparitions, trying to help. Trying to understand.

But the people in the sky were just as bewildered as those on the ground. They seemed like average, everyday people. It couldn't even be said that whatever was happening to them was regional, because they appeared to be from all over the world, from all walks of life. None could give a reason for what was happening to them, or why.

After finding communication successful to a degree, the next step was to get them out of the sky. A series of mishaps followed, in which would-be rescuers fell out of balloons, or entire balloon apparatuses plummeted to the earth. More concerning were the heavy black clouds, alive with a strange green lightning. These sooty clouds rolled across the sky, enveloping all and severing communication between those in the air and those below.

Authorities knew nothing, of course, and the media spewed speculation. The only thing that could be said for sure was that the people were descending slightly, little by little. Carl knew as much and now the news said as much.

He kept watching but picked up the phone and made his call. He expected the old *"911, what's your emergency?"* but instead got a prerecorded message that said if the call was about the people in the sky, to hang up and call another number, which was then provided. If it was an otherwise unrelated emergency to press the 1 button, now.

Carl hung up.

Most of what was on the TV was worth skipping, at least for now, but he wanted to stay in the loop, to be on hand when the breaking news finally arrived. He had an old radio and might have some batteries lying around, but it all had to be found, dug out, and he already felt a pang of guilt over having left the young lady out there for so long alone.

He decided to check on her, fill her in on what he was doing.

Going outside was like stepping into another world. The blue sky had turned a wispy gray, and the warm sunlight he'd been enjoying was buried. Billowing clouds moved fast. He glanced around, unsettled. The tops of the trees in the fencerow rocked gently but clearly. Behind him, over the top of his house, darker clouds like fresh purple bruises rolled towards them from the north. They were the lowest clouds he'd ever seen, and the darkest. He thought perhaps it was smoke, but he could smell nothing burning.

It wasn't natural, whatever it was.

Thunder rumbled, and frightening green lightning strobed within the marching darkness.

"Good Lord, no," Carl muttered.

He looked up at the woman, who looked down at him.

"That front's coming hard!" He gestured at the darkness.

The woman gazed at it, nodded. It was all she could do.

And all Carl Rooth could do was watch and listen to the rumble of approaching thunder. He remained as long as he could, the wind lashing him, the darkness spreading above like black ink spilled in a basin of water. The clouds were so low he could nearly reach up and dip a hand into them, like an inverted river. It wasn't until tendrils of low, frothy black fog had enfolded the woman and he couldn't see her anymore that he retreated into the house.

He sat in a kitchen chair at the sliding glass doors and watched the storm in the backyard, gnawing at his knuckles and lower lip. No rain fell, only strong beating wind gusts and more green lighting strobing the sky every few seconds. Each time it made him jump; he couldn't imagine what the woman was going through up there.

The storm didn't let up either. It raged for a solid hour, and then, even when the wind and lightning were gone, the heavy clouds remained, flowing low and swollen, keeping the woman obscured. He began to wonder if she was still there, or if—like in the famous story—the storm had carried her off some place else.

Shortly before dusk, the tail end of the ominous clouds appeared in the north. It moved overhead—like a window blind rolling up—leaving a murky sky tinged a yellow sepia. Thunder still rumbled in the charged atmosphere.

Carl brought a lawn chair out to the X he'd carved in the sod and waited for the clouds to pass. Time crawled. The humidity was already considerable and only getting worse. He wiped sweat from his brow and gulped from a glass of iced tea. He looked up and there she was.

Startled, he stood so fast his chair and tea tipped into the grass. She was lower, gauging by the silver maple, perhaps sixty feet off the ground.

"Hey!" He waved both hands at her. "Hey, by God, are you alright?"

She nodded enthusiastically, using both of her own hands to wave back. "I'm okay! It was amazing! Incredible!"

Relieved laughter burst from Carl's lips. He'd never in his life experienced anything startling, unexplained, or even enlightening, but he'd always, *always* wished to. He'd suspected, even as a child, that he just wasn't special enough. So, to be thrust into this remarkable situation, it both thrilled and unnerved him. He felt an overwhelming sense of responsibility to aid her however he could, and yet, there was absolutely nothing he could do. And to see she had made it through the storm unscathed was a triumph that made him grin like he hadn't in ages.

He couldn't put words to his excitement and so, just to say something rather than stand there and laugh up at the sky, he shouted, "This is impossible!"

She shrugged, shook her head again.

A stretch of silence spread between them. They still had to shout, so communicating was a chore. Carl moved around the yard and picked up the sticks and branches knocked loose by the storm. He had a nice sized burn pit near the property line in the back, next to the raspberry bushes, but he piled all the sticks and branches about ten yards from the X. This was typically a big no-no, to scorch his well-manicured sod, but he forgave himself under the circumstances.

With nothing else to do, the woman watched as he toiled. Occasionally he looked up, waved, and she returned the gesture in kind.

By the time he was done cleaning up the yard, the western horizon was a light blue, all that remained of the daylight. He could hardly make her out in the gloom.

He surveyed the coming darkness reluctantly. "I guess I'll be going in now!"

"Okay!" Her voice rang down from above. "Goodnight!"

He lingered for a moment, not wanting to leave her alone outside in the dark, but then admitted he was still helpless. She was, he reminded himself, getting lower though.

"Goodnight!" he called up.

Restlessness hammered his nerves, and he realized he hadn't eaten since lunch. He made a toasted ham sandwich, ate it while watching television and shaking his head in contempt.

Each network spun the situation into a shape that fit their narrative.

"Panic as mysterious figures appear in the sky, seemingly overnight. Authorities are at a loss to explain what exactly is happening, or how such a phenomenon is possible. The Pentagon has instructed—"

Click.

"Perhaps we've passed through some kind of quantum field, a sort of rupturing of the membrane between universes. NASA has declared—"

Click.

"Clearly, these entities from the sky are the angels of heaven, sent to collect the faithful, as we have—thankfully—entered the end times—"

He flipped to another channel and watched a report on the strange weather activity that seemed to arrive with the people. Pitch black storm fronts sparking with green lightning across the globe like disturbed sediments in a dirty fishbowl, obscuring observation and communication.

The last thing he watched was astonishing footage from the International Space Station of scores of people floating outside the atmosphere. Still, stoic, hovering around the planet like satellites, trails of people strung away from Earth's orbit into the void of outer space.

It was clear, though; they weren't leaving, they were *arriving*.

Carl drowsed in his chair, dreamed of falling in the night sky, falling through a violent thunderstorm, and as the perfect sod of his backyard reared up out of the dark, he woke suddenly and tearfully.

He took a piss, then rummaged around in drawers and closets until he found a large, industrial flashlight and went into the backyard. Scanning it through the night sky, he illuminated the woman in a round, misty halo.

She was lower and awake.

"I can't sleep." He spoke at a regular volume. The night was still, quiet, and it carried his voice easily.

"Neither can I," she said.

He remained with her the rest of the night, though they did little talking. Occasionally, he wondered if she was sleeping, but felt it rude to simply shout the question or shine the light at her.

Dawn came. The sunlight warmed the lavender and raspberries on the edge of his property, illuminated the tall maple and the floating woman. She had lowered more in the night. If Carl had to guess, he would say she was only about thirty feet up now.

He called to her, "You must be starving?"

She nodded slowly. "Famished." Her accent was clearer now, heavy, but still undiscernible.

He took advantage of the cool early morning air and hoed weeds wet with dew from his garden. He enjoyed the physicality of it. Done right, weeding was a hell of a workout, let alone for a senior citizen. The spindly black and yellow spider had found its way back into the garden and again he relocated it to the fencerow. A twinge of sympathy tickled his belly after destroying its web in the process, but it could always rebuild, he assured himself. He raked up the dead weeds and added them to the pile of limbs he'd gathered after the storm. All the while, the woman watched from above, looking down in quiet observation.

By the time he started the fire a little before noon, she was roughly twenty feet off the ground.

She's falling faster, he thought.

They watched as the fire grew and consumed the fallen limbs. The flames danced and Carl looked up at the woman. "Can you feel it? The warmth?"

She smiled, but it was a sad smile. "No, I'm afraid not. I'm afraid I don't feel much of anything."

Carl nodded and wondered if that's what it was like to be dead. He tried to place her accent again, but he kept coming back to the strange cadence of GPS navigation, the robotic nuance of a computer speech, but he knew that couldn't be right. He wondered if she was German.

"In fact," she continued, her voice rising a little, "I'm very concerned. Have you any idea what happens when I land?"

Carl used a crooked branch to poke at the fire. "They're not saying much about that. No one knows."

"My friend, any information you have would comfort me greatly. I'm reliant on you. You're the only thing I've got."

Carl smiled. "I wouldn't do you the disservice of lying, especially while you're so hampered." He hoped he sounded reassuring.

"What about the media? What are they saying?"

"They say you're out in space, too. Or ones like you. They showed it on TV. People floating in outer space. Were you in outer space?"

"I…don't know."

"Doesn't seem like anybody knows anything." He poked the fire again.

"I'm sorry I'm not more help. I truly don't know why this is happening, or what it means."

He nodded, sat quietly for a moment before rising to his feet. "I suppose we'll find out together. I'll do everything I can to see that you land safely." He offered a genuine smile, stretched. "I've worked up a hell of an appetite, and it seems a shame to let this fire go to waste. You like hotdogs?"

"What?"

"Hotdogs? Wieners? Franks? I figure you'll be making contact here in the next hour or so. I'd like to have something on hand for you."

"Is it food?"

"It is." He gestured towards the house. "Got some hotdogs in the fridge. Be right back."

The whole way inside, Carl tried to imagine what could possibly happen once she reached the ground.

Halfway back across the yard, pack of hotdogs in hand, he found out.

She fell abruptly, dropping twenty feet and landing hard on the Xin the sod. Whatever had tethered her to the atmosphere had been released, snapped, perhaps even cut. She lay face down on the lawn.

Carl hobbled towards her, tossing the package of hotdogs, his heart thudding in his chest much too hard for his liking.

"God," he mumbled between gasps. "Oh God, please, please let her be alright."

Her body twitched, her legs kicked, her arms drummed on the soft sod.

"Lady?" He limped along as fast as he could. "Lady, what's happening?"

He didn't expect an answer, but when she lifted her head, he stopped mid-step and gasped in sudden revulsion. Her face, like paper in a furnace, curled into soot and dissipated. She tore open the skin of her breast like a certain reporter ripping open his clothes to reveal the colorful costume beneath. And she *was* colorful, Carl saw, a weird pulsing blob of colors. Untethered, her form dissolved into ethereal wisps like multicolored cobwebs. She came apart, and what was left was a sickly, shimmering mass, proportionate to a human being but already expanding, unfurling, taking on a shape that seemed much more natural to it. A cross between a stingray and the greasy rainbow of an oil slick or the noxious colors of spilled gasoline on cement.

"My friend." Her voice had become even more robotic, like the metallic crackle of an electrolarynx. He wasn't sure, but the next sound, a static-y, buzzing noise, might have been laughter.

"Wha—what happened? What is this?" he stammered.

"An invasion," Came the electric voice. It hung wide, spread like a sheet out to dry in a steady breeze. Ghostly, flowing on unseen currents, glistening, the sickly rainbow of colors both intoxicating and nauseating.

"What do you want?" Carl balked.

"Did I not tell you how famished I am?" Moving faster than he could comprehend, it enveloped Carl bodily in its viscous, colorful folds. It swathed him, contorting to his every bend and angle like a wet sheet. Each frantic inhale sucked a piece of it further into his mouth, suffocating him. His eyes were plastered shut. All sounds and sensations were severed.

An electric whisper filled his head. *"If we let gravity drag us down, we'd burn up like most things, but the gradual descent gives us a chance to acclimate ourselves. It takes time, but we've perfected it. We use preliminary data, snatched out of the airwaves, to determine the shape we need to cause as little disturbance as possible. Your planet saw a bunch of 'humans' descending from the sky and acted compassionately. Had we been in our true forms, we would have been annihilated."*

Let me go! Carl did not speak the command but thought it. There came a slight loosening in the skintight membrane, a shift perhaps, not much, but enough to spur him on, *Please! Please, mercy!*

"We are not merciful."

He detected annoyance in the reply. Its grip, python-like, tightened again; it felt like it was seeping into his very pores.

Why are you doing this? His skin tingled, burned. *I was just trying to help.*

"Your compassion is your undoing, as it has been with every planet."

His nerves sizzled like chopped onions in a skillet. He was being dissolved, that's how it felt. He was being digested.

Please! He tried to wiggle, but he was wrapped so tightly he couldn't even twitch a toe. Mummified, the sizzling increased to a searing and he screamed mentally. *Please don't do this! I only tried to help you!*

The pain stopped, but he remained encased. He waited, trapped in the slow yet manic crawl of suffocation.

Abrupt release, and he found himself expelled, laying on the ground, gasping for breath. The sunlight hurt his eyes, each blade of grass like a tiny knife poking his flesh, the collective aromas in the air overpowering, offensive. It was like his senses were working for the first time ever. Smoke or steam or some vapor rose from his exposed skin and he tingled everywhere, like each limb had fallen asleep. His clothes felt thinner, thread-bare; they'd lost some of their solidity while enveloped by her.

"So you did," came the buzzing voice, and Carl balked at the shimmering spill of color floating before him. He detected a hint of remorse in that electric

hum. *"It matters not. I shall get my fill elsewhere. I may spare you, but others of my ilk won't."* It began to rise. *"Perhaps if the gardener can spare a spider, a spider can spare a fly?"* And it was gone, fluttering straight up into the sky it came from.

Carl lost sight of it immediately.

On his feet, he trudged towards the house, snatching glances up as if it'd change its mind and descend upon him again, or, as it had warned, one of its *ilk*. Inside, he moved through the rooms to the telephone. He didn't pick it up. Instead, he stared out the big bay window at the northern horizon, at a vibrant rainbow band appearing low, like the final moments of sunset.

There were so many of them. Enough to take over the horizon.

The rest of the northern sky rumbled with darkness, crackling with green lighting. He wondered what the clouds and lighting were about. A new atmosphere, perhaps, or maybe a means of defense.

He doubted he'd ever get an answer.

After a while, Carl went and sat down in front of the TV. His body still stung, his flesh sore and sensitive. He felt chewed up and spit out. The voices and faces on the TV filed by as he watched on.

"…angels from heaven, clearly, and any doubters only need to look at attempts from us meager mortal sinners to make contact with their holy personage as evidence of that fact."

Click.

"…makes absolutely no sense. There is no precedent for something like this. You understand? There is nothing we can look at to help us come to grips with the sheer absurdity of these people, walking around in the sky like—"

Click.

"…indoors if you can, or a safe location. Do not go outside if you can help it. Stay with us here on this channel as we await further developments—"

Click.

"…my whole family. I'm devastated."

"And how did you survive?"

"Well, I, uh, saw what they were doing to my wife and kids… The kids had already been… I mean… well, I ran—"

Click.

THE PROPHECY OF GULLS

HANNAH BIRSS

Along the coast of Nova Scotia lies the small harbour town of Aggie's Cove. Known for its picturesque seaside homes and large granite rocks that line the coast like the weathered bones of some ancient and enormous creatures that crawled out of the Atlantic Ocean to die, the small fishing community can be found only a short drive away from the capital city of Halifax. Just outside of town, perched upon a great white rock, sits its famous lighthouse. Its weather-beaten white boards jut upwards like a broken tooth, and its blood-red top and bright lantern has signaled to the seafarers and visitors of Aggie's Cove the same message for over a hundred years: "here lies death".

Indeed, there have been a remarkable number of deaths at the lighthouse. The bulk of them are tourists who do not understand the ruthlessness of the sea and the way she reaches for the uneducated and unaware, so that she may fertilize her waters. Despite the salt-encrusted signs begging them to act otherwise, people regularly descend the rocks to the slippery portion of the

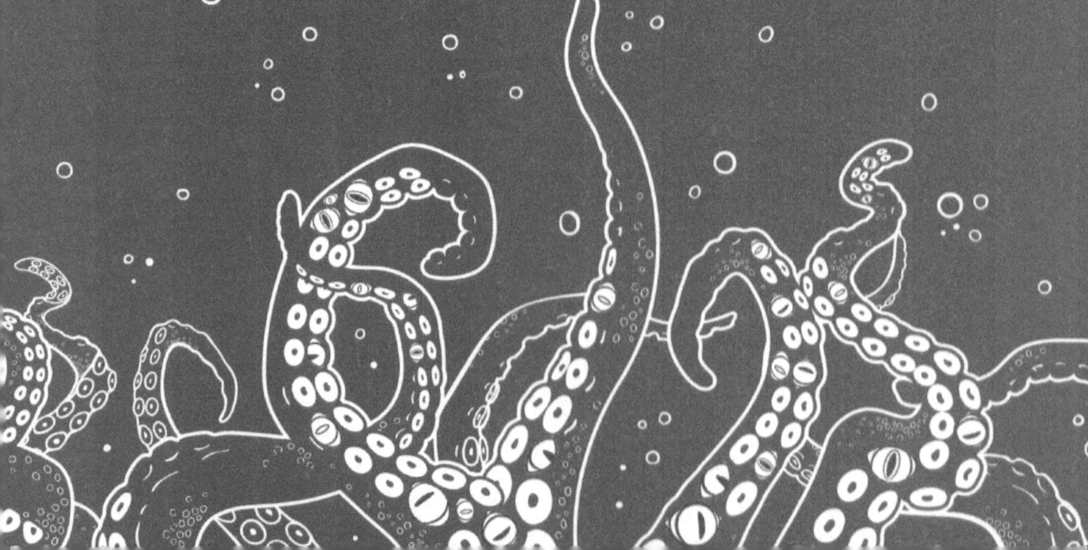

shore coloured black by the churning waters of the Atlantic Ocean. There, they are swept away to a watery death, or slammed repeatedly against the rocks by the educating waves until nothing remains but a smear of red and the echo of water-logged screams. No one ever dared to jump in and attempt a rescue of those who did not heed the warning and the hunger of the greedy ocean—it was not tempting death to brave the waters, but assuring it.

It was here in Aggie's Cove that Felix Hodgson lived and made his living. He was technically by definition an artist, painting mediocre watercolours that he sold to the tourists who flocked to the shore—different angles of the rocks, perspectives of the lighthouse, the boats in the harbour, and the saltbox houses that lined the streets. Despite his lack of true talent or imagination, his depictions of fishing life and portraits of old sailors sold well to people who also lacked imagination. He was content with this; as long as he could retire to his own cottage at the end of the day with a fire in the grate and a bottle of decent whiskey, he was happy to continue on in how he always had.

He was a regular fixture in the streets, his neatly trimmed salt-and-pepper beard and red Wellington boots stomping down the neatly paved roads, as he moved from gift shop to gift shop, restocking the plastic-wrapped prints and picking up the dwindling cheques and envelopes of cash. As of late, the amount of money (more truly, the lack thereof) was becoming too much to ignore and Felix was growing concerned.

"They aren't selling like they used to," Clark said from behind the counter of his store down by the docks. His was a small and cramped gift shop, the shelves overflowing with images of lobsters and trinkets and Nova Scotian delicacies such as dulse and barley candy.

Felix scowled. "Maybe you aren't pushing them hard enough. Put them up front and centre. See what happens." He had been wandering around while Clark sold a magnet to a businessman from New York and, while waiting for his turn at the counter, found his prints haphazardly crammed onto a single shelf near the back door. They were tinted red from the emergency exit sign that glowed next to them and looked entirely unappealing.

Clark gave him a long look. "The prints aren't selling any more, Felix. They're nothing new—the locals have all seen or collected them, and they don't really appeal to the younger crowd of tourists we've started to get. Gone are the days where simple leached landscapes sell. You're going to have to come up with a new angle."

"They've always done well. You just ain't selling them right," Felix said stubbornly.

Clark sighed and brushed a long brown lock of hair off of his forehead and behind an ear. Felix privately thought that the longer hairstyle, so popular among the younger folks these days, looked unkempt. Despite all his flaws, he had always prided himself on his salty-dog-yet-manicured appearance.

"Look, I get that it's hard for a leopard to change its spots, and don't get me wrong, you've sold well in the past," Clark said. "But we can't keep on like this. You barely made twenty dollars this past pay period. I can't keep you here on consignment if you aren't actually making me money. I'm better off at this point having that old biddy Betty from church and the little crocheted lobsters she keeps shoving in my face every Sunday. At least those could be great for kids."

"Are you kicking me out?" Felix felt a sense of outrage. His paintings were in almost every single gift shop—as a local "artist" he was accustomed to having a lot of space and sales afforded to him.

Clark put his hands up in surrender. "No, Felix. I'm not. At least, not yet, anyway. I'm just giving you adequate warning."

"What am I supposed to do?" Felix grumped. His house had belonged to his father and was owned outright, but he still needed money for booze and bills.

Clark shrugged and pushed his thick dark glasses up his nose. "Look, you haven't added anything exciting to your wares in the past few years. An injection of new works might be enough to get your sails unstuck. When was the last time you even had your paints out? Maybe try something new."

Felix just grunted at the suggestion, nodded curtly in goodbye, and left the store to continue his route through the town's gift shops and booths, the small stack of bills in his coat pocket quickly becoming a depressing call to create.

After finishing his rounds and returning home, Felix stood for a moment in his cold and outdated kitchen before going to the corner where his old easel was leaning against the wall. It was thickly coated in dust, and when he opened his tins of paints to check on them, they were all shrunken and cracked. Several had broken into pieces. He stared at them, wondering if he even remembered how to paint.

It had been two years since Felix had picked up a paintbrush. Art had never been a true love of his—it was always a means to an end, a whiskey bottle waiting to happen. He'd discovered a mediocre aptitude for it in his early twenties. While his friends had left the fishing town after high school in the search of better ports, Felix had never truly been one for schooling and had no desire to chase higher education. He'd bummed around town for a year or two working odd jobs before deciding to sign on to various fishing and research vessels. He'd gotten bored one night while out at sea and started sketching on a napkin.

He hadn't felt anything about it other than it was a somewhat productive way to stave off ennui, but the rest of the crew members had been impressed and the first mate had commissioned a piece for his sweetie. That was the start of his art career. Within a few years, he'd built up a big enough portfolio and had enough sales that he was able to quit seafaring. When his father finally died of liver failure, he had left an empty house and his empty seat at the local pub. Felix had been more than happy to take up both spots, entertaining the tourists and annoying the bartenders.

In a blink, thirty years had passed, and while he wasn't necessarily an old man now, he certainly wasn't a young one. He had painted less and less, coasting on commissions, and now he had to start working again, apparently.

He picked up the foldaway-easel. The cloud of dust it brought with it had him sneezing. Once the fit stopped, he rummaged through boxes, looking for the rest of his art supplies.

He found that he still had a stack of watercolour paper in his linen cupboard, which contained no actual linens. The corners of the paper were curling a bit. He would have to order new ones, but they were still good enough for Felix to do some colour and light studies. He supposed there was no time like the present to get started.

He grabbed the rest of his equipment, snapping up brushes that were sitting in a jar with a ring of dried up paint water on the bottom on the kitchen windowsill above the sink. He took a collapsible stool out from underneath the bathroom sink, put some water in an empty soda bottle, and slipped a half-crushed granola bar still in the wrapper into his pants pocket. He didn't bother locking the door behind him when he left.

Felix wandered up and down the streets, wondering blearily to himself what scene he should paint. The worn houses, the rows of shops with the hanging pub sign in view, or perhaps the harbour with its collection of boats with punny names? He could do a floral piece, or a painting of old rubber boots sitting outside a door. What would summarize life by the sea? What generic picture would people want in their bathroom or front entrance to commemorate their trip to the Atlantic Ocean?

Though they were his bread and butter, Felix was not a fan of tourists, and he didn't think that would change anytime soon. He liked his routines and was set in his ways. Small towns have a habit of making you xenophobic—you were either from there, meaning you had a long family history with the town going back generations, or you were from *away*. The tourists, with their soft hands and round faces and cries of "how quaint!" and "look, a whale!", made Felix resent them even more as he tromped through the streets, his small easel held under one arm. First, they had the gall to invade his space, and now they weren't even paying enough to afford him a proper living.

As he wandered, his head began aching—there must be a storm front moving in, he thought to himself. That, or he needed a drink. He could feel a tremor in his hands, and when he stopped for a moment to rearrange the old plastic bag that carried his supplies across his arm, he looked up and saw the lighthouse.

He had painted the lighthouse before from a dozen different angles. Its red-and-white shape was the symbol of Aggie's Cove—its likeness graced the walls of every residence, and the bulk of cheap merchandise meant for tourists had its familiar silhouette plastered onto them. It was the mascot of the town, if an inanimate thing could be one. He moved towards it, deciding that it wouldn't hurt to paint the rough, worn boards and white rocks as he remembered his craft again. With any luck, it would be just like riding a bicycle.

When he arrived at the rocks, there was someone else sketching there. It was a high school student, peering up at the old lighthouse and making hesitant lines in her dark sketchbook. Felix ignored her and set up his workstation, far back from where the tumultuous waves were reaching up the stone towards him.

The sky was grey, and the ocean dark and choppy. Perhaps he would paint a stormy sea then, a swirling vortex of shadowy clouds in the sky above it. All of his prints were of sunny days, with blue skies and bright streams of silver shimmering in the water; it would be good to offer another, darker angle of the unfeeling ocean for the moody young.

He started with a light wash on the paper, and while it was drying, he took out the small silver flask that was forever nestled in his coat pocket. His hands were already cold—the wind coming in off the water was sharp and frigid like a sheet of ice. The whiskey burned his tongue and slid down his throat with a comforting heat. The high school student watched him out of the corner of her eye, and when he turned to look at her with his flask still in hand, she gathered up her belongings and scurried off. A few tourists still milled about, but the sullen sky and lashing waves did not inspire them to linger and soon he was alone on the rocks.

He stared out at the sea, trying to muster the desire to keep painting and ignoring the call of the well-worn chair he kept before his fireplace, when there was a sudden gust of wind against his face, and the largest seagull he'd ever seen landed at his feet.

It was strangely mottled, as if it were still a juvenile. Spots of black and dark grey dappled its back and instead of the usual yellow and orange, its beak was as black at night. It was huge. Later, from the safety of his living room, Felix would remember it as being as large as a wild turkey, with wide wings edged in slate-grey feathers and a cruel beak to rival even the largest eagle. It cocked its head up at him with intelligent and unfathomable eyes.

"Shoo," he said, and kicked out at it. It flapped its wings and jumped back a step, but kept its black and beady eyes upon him.

He picked up his paintbrush again and dipped it in the water before he swirled it in a deep blue. He had applied a single stroke to the paper when the gull hopped closer to him.

"I don't have any food," he grumbled at it and kicked out again.

This time, the gull took no notice of his boot, and instead it opened its black beak. The inside of its throat bulged as it began to disgorge something, and he watched transfixed as the beak opened wider and wider and wider, until it seemed like the mouth of the gull had been wrenched so wide that the two halves of its beak would snap off its face entirely.

From out of its mouth came something dark and slithering that reminded Felix of a starfish crossed with a squid. At first he thought the gull was merely vomiting out some foul creature it had snatched from a tide-pool, but as the tentacles began to move, he realized that whatever it was—it was disgustingly alive. The gull seemed unbothered by it and continued to stare at Felix as the protuberances wiggled through the air like snakes, reaching towards him.

Felix scrambled back, knocking over his small stool and scraping his palms bloody along the rock. The gull hopped forward and stood over him. A noise came from its throat. It was coarse and garbled, and it took him several seconds to realize that it was not some strange avian call, but a word.

"COMING," the gull said over, and over, and over again. "COMING."

Felix screamed. Another, smaller gull landed next to the large one, and another and another, until they crowded together, circling him like vultures around a dead animal washed up on shore. For a brief moment, he wondered if he was actually dead. Perhaps he had slipped down the rocks and into the dark waters to drown, or his body was back in his small run-down home, facedown on the musty carpet and his eyes open and unseeing. This end was the punishment for his sins; a fearful and feathered hell awaited him.

As each gull landed and settled itself, their webbed feet slapping against the granite, they opened their beaks, and instead of their sharp and textured tongues something else arose, each mouth an individual horror. From them emerged stalks with blinking pale eyes attached to them, slimy tongues that were multi-headed like miniature hydras, probing tentacles, and skittering centipede-like limbs that thrashed as if they were trying to rip themselves from the gulls' mouths and escape. As each bird landed and exposed the horrors it had concealed within itself, the single word became a chant, a horde of gulls saying the same thing over, and over, and over again as they moved towards him. Felix scrambled backwards, clapping his hands to his ears as a cacophony of guttural cries and grating squawks assaulted him.

"COMING. COMING. COMING," they said as one. "COMING."

The large one spread his wings out even further, straining with the effort. It stood in front of the crowd of gulls, head fully thrown back like Christ on the cross, and from its eyes dripped tears of blood. Its voice rang louder than all the other gulls combined as it led them in the chant, the word reverberating down the rocks. The people that still wandered the shore and the harbours looked over at the noise as it echoed across the water.

Abandoning his easel and paints, Felix scrambled to his feet and fled for home, careening down the streets and knocking against offended tourists and confused locals. He sobbed openly as he made his way to his house, throwing open the crooked door and darting into the safety of the four familiar walls. Straight to his kitchen cupboard to grab the half-finished bottle of cheap whiskey stashed there. Flicking off the cap, he threw back his head and drank from it, the word "coming" flashing before his eyes and echoing in his ears. The alcohol hit him hard, and he staggered to bed and into the sweet embrace of a deep and wingless oblivion.

The next morning dawned even darker than the day before. There was a strange cast to the sky—a green haze, as if a tornado was imminent. However, there weren't tornadoes in this part of the world, so the most reaction it elicited was a few surprised comments from the locals and many snapping of photos from the visitors.

Felix stood in front of his kitchen window, staring out with dull, dead eyes at the approaching storm. The gas stovetop was on, and a small flame crackled underneath an old half-rusted out kettle that sat on one of the elements. His bloodshot eyes peered back at him from his faint reflection in the grime; he looked like a ghost in the dim light, and furthermore, he *felt* like one as well.

When the kettle started screaming, he broke out of his trance. He poured the hot water into an old chipped mug with two tablespoons of stale instant coffee and wrapped his hands around it while he sipped.

He needed to go back. He felt drawn to the lighthouse. When he had woken up, head throbbing, in the early hours of the morning, he'd stared up in the gloom at his water-stained ceiling, mulling over the events of the previous day, and came to the conclusion that he *had* to go back. Not only for his equipment, if it hadn't been stolen or blown into water by a nasty gust of wind, but to reassure himself that whatever he'd experienced was some sort of episode or breakdown. Whether stress or withdrawal that had brought on such a terrible hallucination was unknown, but the fact of the matter was the uniquely horrifying things he had seen could not be real. He needed it to not be real, and the only way to confirm that was to return to the lighthouse.

The coffee made his stomach churn in complaint, and he ate two plain slices of stale bread to quiet it. He donned a pair of jeans and an old sweater. After a moment's hesitation, he grabbed his father's old pistol from its spot at the back of his bedside drawer and shoved it into his coat pocket.

A woolen toque pulled down tight over his forehead, he made his way through the streets towards the lighthouse. Fearful anticipation coursed through his body, and he shoved his hands deep into his pockets to hide their tremble. He was sober—painfully sober at the moment—and he wished that he could take refuge in the familiar comfort of his flask. He knew, however, that if he was to return successfully to the lighthouse, he would need to do it under no other influence than his own and so he resentfully abstained.

The harbour was filled with people readying their boats for the coming storm. A few of them glanced nervously at the sky, but most seemed relatively unbothered. As he walked along, a few raised their hands in greeting, and Felix raised his back.

When he arrived at the lighthouse again, there was no one there. Locals were busy doing their preparations, and he had seen only a few tourists that morning milling around the streets, the majority having already taken shelter. His easel was still there, knocked to its side, one of the legs snapped off. The sheet of watercolor papers had been blown away, and there was no sign of his expensive paints or old paint brushes. His folding stool was also gone.

Felix snarled in frustration and kicked at the splinters of wood littered around the broken leg. One went flying, tumbling down to cut through the mist that crowded the edges of the rocks and land in the water with a small *plop*. He had lost all of his supplies, and he didn't have the cash to fill his rusted-out truck with gas and head into Halifax to replace them. He stared morosely out at the water.

Something made a noise behind him. When he whirled, the large gull stood there alone, staring at him. Felix stared back. His heart raced, his face quickly turning numb as he struggled to get his breathing under control. The gull slowly opened its beak, and instead of the thrashing limbs of yesterday, something stranger still began to happen. From its mouth a fountain poured, a liquid like thick and half-dried ink, staining the rock below the gull's feet.

"COMING," it garbled around the stream. "COMING."

Felix turned to run, screaming. He made it back to the road before he glanced back and saw once again that many more gulls were arriving. Several of them were caught up in the choppy wind and smashed to the ground to break legs and wings. It did not hinder them, and around their blood and broken bones, they took up the now-familiar cry.

"COMING," they screeched at him. Felix fled, hollering into the town and down the streets, John the Baptist in rubber boots.

"Something is coming, something is coming!" he shrieked. "Down by the lighthouse! The gulls! The gulls!"

People paused to stare. He ran faster still, frothing at the mouth, each gasping breath harsh and guttural, his mind and body spinning as he was overtaken by animalistic fear.

"You've been nippin' too much at the whiskey again, eh, Felix?" Someone called out to him.

"I'm telling you, something is going on!" Felix skidded to a stop and whirled to confront the startled man. "All the gulls are down by the lighthouse. Something's happened to them, something's wrong with the gulls!"

Overhead, the sky roiled, the very surface of it bubbling as if it was boiling. The sickly green cast of it tinged the harbour below in such a manner that the water seemed to glow as the churning waves sent up bright hurricane sprays against the rocks and the boats.

"What's this about the gulls?" someone else called out, and as they did, there came a great noise from above, and everyone looked up as one. Overhead, a thousand gulls flew in a massive flock, all of them winging towards the lighthouse with synchronized beats of their wings.

"See? The lighthouse! The storm! *Something is coming!*" Felix raved, spittle flying from his lips. "Go, see for yourselves."

Most people ignored him at first, but as he continued to shout, a few people followed after the gulls, heading down to the main road that led to the lighthouse. More followed, and soon a fairly large number of townsfolk and the tourists of Aggie's Cove had congregated, chattering amongst themselves. It was a strange procession—the people moving and twitching as their bodies mimicked the violent roiling of the sky above them, mirror images of one another that made Felix dizzy.

By the time these strange pilgrims had arrived at the rocks, the bulb of the lighthouse had been lit. The refractor began to slowly turn, the great beam of light cutting through the strange fog that now hung like a heavy blanket over the harbour.

People crowded together before the rocks of the lighthouse, standing only a few feet away from the hundreds of gulls that had congregated along the shoreline, the water practically lapping at their feet. At the head of them, a priest in feathered vestments, stood the large dark gull.

If it had seemed huge before, it was doubly so now, having grown to become the largest bird Felix had ever seen. The gulls shuffled, parting around the crowd like the red sea, as the mass of people began to make their way onto the outcropping of rocks, marveling at the birds and the ominous sky.

Felix hung behind, his stomach churning. His hand reached into his rain slicker, wrapped around the cold barrel of the pistol he had jammed in there. It soothed him, but he made no move to follow the rest of the crowd out onto the rocks.

The townsfolk moved down, closer to the churning water, murmuring to each other in fear and excitement. The gulls were silent, but then the large gull opened its mouth.

Wider and wider it stretched, and from its mouth unfurled long and thick worms dotted with strangely serrated suckers. They lashed at the rock below it with a scraping sound, like nails on a chalkboard. The people of Aggie's Cove shrank back in disgust and made to move off of the rocks.

From the back of the gull's throat came a single word. *"COMING."*

The spell was broken, and the hush over the coast ended. The crowd screamed, shoving against one another as they scrambled back towards the shore and away from the lighthouse.

As one, the massive flock of gulls moved. There was a flapping of wings, and they took off, a curtain drawing up and away from the bony rock. Behind them, a wall of black water rose a hundred feet in the air. The rogue wave was still for a moment, hanging suspended, and then it crashed down on the swell of sacrificial lambs that milled below. They barely had time to cry out before the white rock turned black under the onslaught of the water, and then the people were gone.

The wave had lapped them up like a cat does cream. No trace of them remained; no bodies beat against the rocks and no tortured cries rent the air. Their taking was abrupt, as if they had been entirely blinked out of existence.

Felix howled with desperation as he scrambled forward on the slippery rock, scanning the water. He stared out at the horizon, looking for a sign of any of the people who had stood there only seconds before.

The waves and clouds suddenly stopped mid-churn, as if in a blink they had been reduced to nothing more than a picture with a startling lack of depth. From just below the lighthouse out into the expanse of the horizon, nothing moved. It was as if one of his paintings had been brought to life, the canvas of it stretched out as far as the eye could see, a frozen snapshot of an empty world. All was painfully and terrifyingly still.

And then, movement. From the middle of the picture of the sky and the ocean, there was a bulge in the air. Space warping. Something pushing through, a hand through the curtain of an open window. His mind struggled to comprehend it. Petrified, Felix watched as the world came undone.

A crack opened up at the bulge—not so much a crack, he thought to himself in a faraway manner, as an unstitching, the sky coming apart at the seams. There was a sound as if air was being torn out of a pair of lungs, the sucking of a vacuum in the hollow echo of space. It was so loud that something deep in Felix's ears popped and liquid, hot and wet, trickled out of them and down his neck. The world became muffled.

Through the tear in the fabric of reality, a terrible eye peered out at Felix. It wasn't so much an eye as it was the idea of an eye, a great glistening and rolling thing that fell upon him and then careened away.

Felix raised the old pistol in his hand. He shot once, twice, a third time before it jammed, and then he threw it. The weapon did not get far; it clattered down against the stone to fall into the mute and unmoving ocean, the horrifyingly still waters folding around it as the gun sunk into the depths below the lighthouse. The bullets were absorbed into the monstrous not-eye with no acknowledgement of them—it did not blink, or even approximate a blink of shock and startle, much less pain.

Reminiscent of a spider upon another spider upon another spider, two hands, multi-legged and skittering, slithered through the gap to grip the edges. The hands began to widen it, pushing it with some immense strength as the thing behind the gap squeezed through the cosmic birth canal it had ripped open for itself. From behind him, those that had lingered in the town screamed, a chorus harmonizing, rising and falling as if conducted.

The thing that was as large as any star crawled through the tear from the terrible Elsewhere it had originated. Felix fell to his knees hard, his mouth slack and his eyes glazed. His kneecaps cracked against the granite, hobbling him. As a hand-that-was-not-a-hand reached down to steady itself, it turned the famous lighthouse into nothing but matchstick splinters. Another hand, and another hand, and another hand began to descend on Felix, and he knew he would soon be crushed, an ant beneath an unknowing boot.

As he waited dully for the oblivion that lowered itself towards him, a fierce wind began to blow as thousands of gulls appeared around the rift, moths circling a flame. Their beaks were open wide as things crawled and slithered and unrolled from their mouths, a single word cacophony that echoed across the harbour in their terrible excitement, and the last thing that Felix ever heard.

"HERE. HERE. HERE."

A PLACE CALLED OMLEY

A. J. LEWIS

THERE ARE MANY things I could place the blame on. Many things I *did* blame. The letter with my name—*Daniel Helquist*—written in cursive on the envelope. My colleague, Oscar, for delivering that letter to my desk. The storm that forced me to seek shelter.

But it does no good to speculate. What's done is done.

What matters is that in the dark of that early morning, I boarded the first train leaving the city. Four and a half hours later, I stepped out onto the platform at Droxsham, a town quaint, quintessential, idyllic—a place considered something of a rarity these days. I took in the clean country air, a great rousing lungful. Rain had fallen during the night and left freshness adrift on a breeze, fragrant and pleasant, a world-and-a-half apart from the acrid smog and sticky grime that clung to the city like an oil-soaked rag.

In Droxsham, people walked dogs and said hello to each other as they passed on cobbled streets. Children laughed and played in a small schoolyard. Thatched roofs sat atop crooked, white-washed walls with thick timber frame

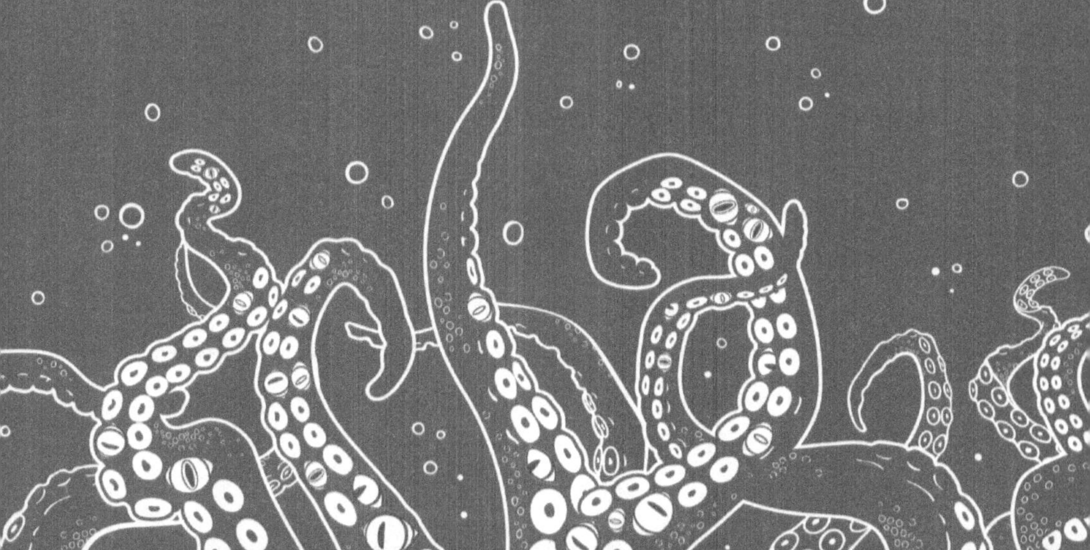

skeletons, while smoke rose lazily from chimneys. Wholesome somehow, when compared to the huge stacks that belched black smoke into the city skyline.

That was the very reason I'd been called to Droxsham, I supposed; to turn their small, stove-serving chimneys into something altogether mightier. To make them into behemoths of industry. My job was to broker the construction of such monstrosities, give them life, and see to it that their insatiable appetite for fuel never ceased to burn out.

The letter had invited me to speak to a man about the development of the town and surrounding countryside, though he'd held back on specifics. A mine and refinery, perhaps? The region was known for its mineral deposits; a wealth could be hiding right under their feet, just waiting to be pulled out like a coin from a purse. Or he might have wanted factories raised for manufacturing, giving jobs to farmers who'd seen their livelihoods diminish in the face of inexpensive imports. Whatever the town wanted, I would provide, all powered by smoke and fire. The tranquillity of the Droxsham idyll would come to an end. Perhaps not immediately, but over time—the damage coming on slowly enough to go unnoticed like cancer, lurking, waiting, growing until it was too late. And to begin with, the people of Droxsham wouldn't mind, they'd celebrate. They'd see the money rolling in and they'd rejoice. Their town would grow, prosper, become part of the modern world. It won't be until a decade or more, when their children are born in ill health and their water tasted foul, that they'd start to understand the true extent of what they'd brought on to themselves.

What I had delivered to them.

I knew it would happen. I'd seen it before in Stonebridge and Long Parish, in Farnbury and Livershall, places told apart from Droxsham only by the colour of the stone that made up the buildings. Communities poisoned by their need for progress.

Sickness seeded and spread, and my pockets became ever more lined.

In my hubris, I took it all in stride. The fate of such a town mattered little to me. Besides, someone from Droxsham had requested it. They wanted it. I simply answered the call.

However, the town's fate was not sealed that day. Maybe at some later date it was, progress being as inevitable as the turning of seasons, but not with any touch from my hands.

I found my way to the pub where we'd arranged to meet, *The Black Horse*, and there I waited out what little remained of the morning and all of the afternoon, for the man who'd sent the letter. I ate alone when I should have been talking business, making notes in preparation for the town's transformation. I asked the bar staff if they'd heard of him, figuring that in a town as small as Droxsham, everyone knew everyone else.

They had not.

So, a day wasted, then.

I angered. A joke at my expense? Orchestrated by Oscar back in the city? Not unlikely; he was always the fool, that one. He'd be laughing at me from the office, no doubt. Some joke, making me go so far out of my way…

There wasn't much time before the last train bound for home was scheduled to depart. Frustrated, and without the deal I'd been intent on, I left for the station. I looked back over my shoulder at the pub. Were my meeting to have gone as planned, a few years would see demand for lodgings outgrow the scant number of guest rooms it held upstairs, and it'd be demolished to make way for a large hotel with conference rooms. The tiny grocery store I'd passed by on a corner would be replaced by one much larger, capable of feeding an army. Instead of cottages and trees lining the roads, blocks of flats would rise up to house the workers who'd tend to the burgeoning industry.

And the sky would turn black with the choking smoke of progress.

It was just another of those things I could have blamed; the errant whisper that summoned me from the high-street and down into that alley. I had no good reason to follow, no special desire to investigate, but I did so all the same.

I could blame curiosity.

The indolent hum of the high-street subdued then silenced as I ventured further, like the town was left a mile behind me and the whisper was all that remained. I'll never understand how or why, but the air became cool at first, then dropped to frigid. Blades of ice pricked at my hands and cheeks; tiny shards stabbed bare skin over and over. The change in temperature proved only a harbinger of the fog that followed, descending abruptly from a blue-sky day. The walls of the alley retreated behind pale curtains. My arms looked as if they were dissipating into the nothing around me, evaporating from my body.

The sound that had pulled me into the alley seemed louder inside the quiet of the mist, ringing in my ears like tinnitus, static and cyclical. Footsteps—whether my own or another's—echoed and chipped off the unseen walls. I cautiously stumbled through the fog, not wanting to trip and fall. My hands met a surface, grainy, wooden, with a glass pane set higher up—a door. Pressing my face close to the window, I saw a sign that read, "Open".

My bones creaked from the cold. I grasped around for a doorknob, its touch freezing, turned, then pushed. A bell jangled overhead. Crossing the threshold, my face and fingers thawed in an immediate warmth. I was out of the blinding mist and into what appeared to be a shop. A scent of sour tobacco curdled with incense that emanated from censers fixed to walls. Deepest corners were shrouded in shadows darker than night, shadows that tried to reach out into the room while underpowered lightbulbs struggled to keep them at bay.

After my eyes adjusted to the gloom, I could see the room was stocked with trinkets and curiosities, pieces practical and decorative arranged by no apparent method: a typewriter, useless with no keys; jars of dried plant material and deceased animals suspended in formaldehyde; sculptures and ceramics from myriad collections and cultures.

Oddities certainly, all at home in a place that felt equal parts antique shop, apothecary, and sideshow. Somewhere that could only exist by being left undisturbed, neglected in an alley in a small town while the world around it moved towards the future.

I cast my eyes over a counter, thick with dust except for three small circles set in a triangular formation where something had recently been moved or sold. A wooden box carved with fantastical creatures sat beside a basket containing a dozen or so round, unlabelled tins. Humanoid figurines of ivory, jade, and onyx stood to attention, pieces crafted for a game whose rules were long forgotten. Value might be found in their materials, but who would buy these things? Behind the counter stood a bookcase crammed with leather-bound books, reams of yellowing parchment and old newspapers. I reached out and ran my fingers along the worn spines. No titles were visible, so I slid one of the books from the shelf and opened it. The pages were all blank.

The room was hazy; smoke caught in my eyes and rasped in my throat.

A hand—pale, bony, with small dots tattooed along the back of the index finger—came to rest on the open pages.

"Welcome."

I looked up at the man. His face was the same pallid grey as his hand, wrinkled and worn like the leather of the books. A wisp-thin moustache was drawn ghost-like above his lip.

He studied me through milky eyes. "Apologies, I didn't intend to startle you. Please, feel free to browse at your leisure, but take care when handling the artefacts you see on display. Many of them *might* be very old and from distant places, much like myself. We wouldn't want you to break any of them—" his slender lips pursed together into a brief but sinister smile, "—or them, you."

Artefacts belonged in museums, and judging by his dress, so did he. Bellboy met renaissance fair, with a measure of Eastern aesthetic; he held an air of the exotic and ancient. Both out of place and out of time.

I said I was sorry, told him I thought it was a shop, not a museum. I hastily closed the book and handed it to him.

"This was a shop. And it will be again," he said, his speech slanted by a dialect with which I was unfamiliar, as if he were learning to speak even as he spoke. "We have something for everyone, and the prices are very negotiable."

I asked if he was the shopkeeper.

"In a manner of speaking, yes, I am the Keeper. Though, it may be more accurate to say that the shop keeps me. I have seen you before, have I not?"

I was certain I'd never met him. I said I didn't think that was possible, that I'd never visited Droxsham.

Further riddles from the Keeper added to the sense of building unease that had settled in my stomach. "Neither have I, but I recognise your face, although I forget your name. It matters not. You're here now and that's the right way for it." As he spoke, he riffled carelessly through the pages of the book, kicking up a chalky cloud. It was a fast action and the light was low, but I could swear there were words and pictures on every one of those pages where before there were none. He snapped the book closed and returned it to its place, then turned to me.

"I know what you're here to see. Please, follow."

He led me further into that cave of decrepit relics. The room revealed itself to be of an unlikely shape. Corners formed where there were no walls. The ceiling rose and fell like it breathed. We passed by a display of colourful feathers from birds I'd never seen. Plumage of the Charb, the Keeper said.

I asked if he could help me, that I'd been looking for someone. I handed him the letter.

His milky eyes ran back and forth over the paper, then he said, "It seems your friend and I share a name."

I wanted to say that name to him, but I faltered.

He laughed. "There is no name on here, Mr Helquist. Other than your own, of course."

Snatching the letter back, I told him he was wrong, that the name was right there. It was—

He was right. Erased from the paper, just as it was gone from my memory.

"Don't look so lost. You may find it yet," the Keeper crowed.

Impossible, I thought…*wasn't it?*

Between two oaken bookcases, a hall branched off from the main room. The Keeper directed me to enter. Intrigue drove me to obey, even as trepidation held me back.

Doors along either side of the hallway led to spaces unknown. Wallpaper flaked and faded in weak light. The carpet under my feet felt heavy, saturated with dust. At the end of the hall, a sheet covered something hung on the wall. I approached cautiously, stopped at a comfortable distance and not an inch closer.

The Keeper took a fistful of sheet and tugged to unveil a gleaming mirror framed by hard, dark wood clumsily carved with whirling shapes and designs that followed no pattern. Gouges and peaks appeared to shift and turn at a lava-flow pace. Mounted on the four corners were contorted brass faces whose lips trembled and quaked—dared to speak but afraid to tell—their features stretched and melted as if made from wax, their eyes sunken and sullen and mournful. Then there was the glass itself, polished to a crystal sheen. Not a single imperfection tarnished its smooth surface. Incredible.

No speck of dust or fingerprint or smudge. Even in the twilight hallway, it radiated a glow, reflecting brilliance from some unseen source.

It was impossible to deny the beauty of the piece.

"Perhaps the name you seek will reveal itself, amongst other things. Please, take your time." The Keeper moved aside as I stepped toward the mirror, drawing closer so that I might see with greater clarity. I halted three feet away and watched intently. I saw movements in my body I couldn't be sure I was making: a faint grin I didn't know was on my mouth; a restlessness in my fingertips; an uncanny look in my eyes that I didn't quite care for. I was captivated. Never had I seen an image so clear, so precise and pure, as if for the first time in my life I could truly see myself for who I was, my thoughts unaltered by the lens of my own ego. But there was more on offer. More secrets and surprises.

And I wanted more, so much more. I surrendered.

A voice said to me, "You'll find that the mirror is very giving. Its generosity knows no bounds. It will show you yourself, should you wish to see."

The Keeper answered questions I'd never asked. Maybe it wasn't he; maybe it was the mirror that spoke.

Sounds emerged, like the ones that had drawn me into the alley. *Laughter*, I thought. Yes, in part. In some awful way. Soft as an echo chiming through distant hills. A lover's declaration of devotion whispered into a longing ear. How sweet it was! An aria heaven sent, beautiful and serene enough to tempt angels into giving up their wings to walk amongst mortals. I could have listened for eternities to those sounds which were not voices nor music nor laughter nor waves lapping at a golden shoreline. They were all those things and more besides, a dreamt dirge of perfection, a lullaby for and from the ages. Humankind's history written into an indecipherable song for my ears alone.

The more I listened, the deeper still I gazed. Hypnotists couldn't dream of such power.

Behind my reflection a darkness gathered. Ponderous. Black and unsettling. It was then that my reflected-self broke fully from the reality I'd known for a lifetime. I…he…smiled at me without subtlety. I reached to touch my mouth to check that I wasn't smiling too. The reflection then turned and walked away into the roiling dark clouds that had consumed the mirror.

Just as a shadow is uniquely one's own, a reflection is more-so. I felt the urge to stop myself and reached out. The letter I held in my hand was gone, my fingers dry and ashen. Without moving, I chased through the clouds, broke to the other side and came face to face with their source, savage and inconceivable, but right there before me.

Flames rose as tall as the highest mountains, roaring a ceaseless lion's roar loud enough to keep gods awake at night. Colossal walls of red, burning death fuelled with sorrow and rage, stoked by hands of pure hatred. Entire forests burned. The flames were alive. They moved and twisted with pained faces, each one telling a tale of unending suffering as they ebbed and flowed like a fiery tide.

I felt the Keeper close to me, but my eyes could not—*would not*—turn from the carnage in the mirror. He was so close his breath touched my neck, and I smelled a sweetness of exotic perfume mingle with the imagined ashes and choking soot.

Transfixed, I asked if what I saw was a vision of Hell. Could I see the place where sinful souls were sent to pay for their wicked lives with an eternity of torture?

The Keeper let out a chuckle. "Hell doesn't exist, Mr. Helquist. The mirror shows a reflection of the real, nothing more."

Heat radiated outwards, insurmountable. A real reality, reflected. My skin blistered and peeled, crisped and fell away. The flesh beneath cooked and melted, my bones roasted to charcoal. The fire burst from its confines of glass and wood and brass, and still I could not run.

No, I told the Keeper, it's no reflection—it's a nightmare.

"Nightmares aren't real, Mr. Helquist. Are you so sure that what you see is a fabrication? You see something few have ever seen. Something only for you. Does it scare you? It should!" Did he laugh then? "But you are not done yet. What the mirror shows you beyond that…even I cannot begin to fathom—" he sounded excited, giddy, "—I have never attempted to look so hard!"

I questioned that there could be anything beyond the tumult of fire. Such fierce, raw energy could leave nothing in its wake but scorched earth and corpses.

The Keeper rebuked, "You think this is the end? There is no end to anything, only beginnings, terrible and new."

Screaming bristled forth from where the angelic verse had lured me. In languages unknown, they pleaded, begged for salvation, prayed to and beseeched innumerable gods and demons, cursed and worshipped them in the bitter hope that they may be saved from the devastation that had been bestowed upon them.

There were people in there, I told the Keeper, I could see them! Hear them! All in tremendous pain. Such pain!

"You do not know pain until you feel it through someone else. Until you are amongst them, Mr. Helquist, truly amongst them, you will never know. Remember that."

I caught sight of my mirror-self as he dashed into the fire. My nerves were set aflame. *Agony.* He was gone, divorced from my body, a sliver of my mind loosed into the furnace like an arrow from a bowstring, and I knew the rest of me had been beckoned to follow. I stared over a precipice, ready to tumble into the unthinkable with no way of return, quivered, tensed, prepared to be totally consumed…and then the Keeper threw the sheet back over the mirror.

The vision was gone. Faded wallpaper and dim light. Tobacco and incense.

A dry lump sat rooted in my throat, coarse and itching, like I'd greedily drank down those phantom flames and parched my insides.

The Keeper said, "I can tell you have a certain affinity for this piece. I think it likes you, too."

Sweat layered cold on my forehead, ran under my arms and down my neck.

I spoke, and I lied. I apologised, said I had no money, made excuses to take my leave.

"That's quite all right. I believe that you've already paid in full."

I shouted at him that I didn't want it, that I'd never take it! I pushed past him and staggered haphazardly along the hallway, back to the shop floor and the door out into the alley.

"The mirror is yours now, Mr Helquist," he called after me, "but there are many other items that may interest you. Be sure to visit me again next time you're in Omley."

I burst out through the door, let it slam unceremoniously shut behind me. *Omley?*

The fog was gone, although a chill persisted. Blue skies reigned again, but I had no mood to enjoy them.

I walked, or ran, frantic, determined to leave the shop and the mirror and its tangle of chaos behind me. I tried not to think. I didn't think. Minutes passed. Hours. I couldn't tell, but one thing became apparent—I wasn't in Droxsham anymore.

I found myself adrift in a meadow. Tall grass reached up around my waist. Blooms waved in the wind that rushed down from the hills, and behind those hills the sun descended.

As if I had any other choice, I kept on walking.

Eventually, I came to a road and the road led me to a village. I asked a local how far it was to Droxsham and they told me it was miles away, twenty or more. My journey home would have to wait until morning. The village inn, *The Duck and Hare*, had a guest room available, so I paid for lodgings and food. I sat for my meal at the bar, where a few locals looked up at me from their jugs of bitter and muttered their thoughts on the stranger who came in from the dark. My thoughts were of the day. They pestered me as I ate. The shop. The Keeper. That damned mirror! It felt distant now, yet it lingered, like a dream so vivid that it couldn't be shaken. I was sure bad dreams would come in the night but hoped that in the morning, my sense would have returned.

The Keeper's parting word played on me.

Omley…

I thanked the landlord for my supper and asked if he'd ever heard of such a place.

"Omley? Now what d'you want t'know 'bout Omley for? You been out drinkin' with them ol' boys over in Rendholm? Ha! Thought you looked the worse for wear!"

I told the landlord that a man had mentioned it to me. I didn't elaborate on when or where, or the circumstances that led to it.

"Ha! Pullin' yer leg, 'e was. No Omley round 'ere, not fer long time. Me ol' grandma used to talk about it. She knew 'bout it from 'ers. Local legend, you might say. Story t' scare wee mites."

Curious, I asked of its fate.

He paused, said, "Gimme a second," then left the bar, returning a moment later with a small book.

"This 'ere's a collection o' folk stories. Fairy tales 'n the like. One of 'em were written by a chap from round 'ere, Reverend Silbaugh was 'is name. Story unto 'imself, that one. Long gone, now. If it's Omley you want t' know bout, give it a read b'fore bed."

I went up to my room, sat on the end of the bed, and opened the book. There was no mention of the mirror or its Keeper, nor the hell-scape I'd witnessed, but verse more akin to a children's nursery rhyme:

A village lies lit by the light of the moon.
The stars in the twilight they twinkled and shone,
And there in the churchyard with the Charbs and the trees,
Ghostly and pale it'll weaken your knees.
So, heed what I say if you go on your way,
And end up staying in Omley this day.

I yawned, stretched. Nonsense prose continued for a dozen pages. I was ready for sleep; the rest could be read over breakfast. I rose from the end of the bed and went to the bathroom, startled as I turned on the light. I was met by myself staring at me from another mirror.

I paused, half expecting to see myself smirk or shudder. The reflection only held the same pensive, quizzical expression I was certain I sported on my real face. I relaxed, stooped, washed in the sink below the mirror, then straightened up and looked at myself. I let out a laugh. Reflections were just that, I told myself, an identical image of something real, and this reflection was of a man who'd been scared half to death by...

Whispers found my ears.

The same soothing voices as from the shop mirror, from the alley. The same beautiful song.

No, it must be a couple in the room next-door, I told myself, or a radio somewhere turned up too loud. It...it didn't make sense. It couldn't be real. It just couldn't be!

The glass turned rosy, orange around the edges, inspired to life by heat from within, shimmering and dancing with me aghast in the centre. A crack loud like thunder. The mirror burst into flames, and the twisted faces issued forth again. My reflection began to hammer at the glass from inside, attempting to break free, screaming words that couldn't be heard above the demonic roaring of the fire.

I clasped my hands to my ears, wanting to block out the screeching. Flames reached around my reflection's shoulders and pulled him back, faded him from view until all that remained was broiling evil and the faces of those others who'd been consumed. I closed my eyes. Still, I could see. I felt something, another part torn from me and thrown as fuel for the furnace, like a single breath had been stolen from my lungs and captured in a bottle. That reflection of me was gone. It was one of them, in there with all the others, lost and afraid and trapped, relaying to me pain compressed and compounded by a million unfortunate souls.

Undeserving they were to be condemned to such a wretched fate. Their pain became mine. It burrowed into my bones as I toiled amongst them.

I turned away from the mirror, collapsed to the floor, and yelled for it to stop.

The commotion drew the attention of the Landlord.

He found me curled up on the bathroom floor, babbling, rabid, and utterly inconsolable.

Do you blame the weatherman when it rains?

Is it the person who made the mirror that I should harbour enmity for? Or the door of the shop for being right there when I needed shelter?

No. The fault is my own.

I cannot bear to face myself anymore. When confronted by a reflection, I run in fear. People say I'm irrational. They'd have no such words if they knew what I'd seen. No longer do I sell promises of a brighter future to those unknowing of the consequences. I hide myself away behind windows painted black. Steel and silver are banished from my home. Even the varnished sheen of my furniture has been sanded to matte.

There's a part of myself removed, burning away perpetually inside the mirror, caught there with no idea of how to escape, of how to return to my body where it belongs, imprisoned perhaps in the place the Keeper called Omley—or wherever else lay beyond those columns of fire.

He told me that I had paid for his mirror.

I have no reason to believe that to be anything but the truth.

THE SPLIT THROUGH THE SKY

LENA NG

AN EVIL HAS tainted my sleep. More than night terrors, what skin-crawling, defiled, and heaving abominations have come to plague me in my dreams. Body twitching and seizing until, in the dead of night, my eyes flung open, overstretched, to stare despairingly through my bedroom window into the endless, dark night canvas. Instead of stars, the pinpricks of light seemed as holes where an unknown, unfathomable voyeur was spying from the other side of the nocturnal sky, as through a camera obscura.

The second night, horrors most urgent bled from my ears. The insectoids scurried beneath the thread-bare blankets and scuttled over my skin. Nightmares made phantasmagoria crawled through my orbits to tattoo scarification patterns on the insides of my eyelids. The patterns mimicked the unsettling pattern of the stars.

The third night, a humanoid people in blasphemous tongues mutter-intoned in my sleep. They pointed at me and drew a star-shaped pattern in

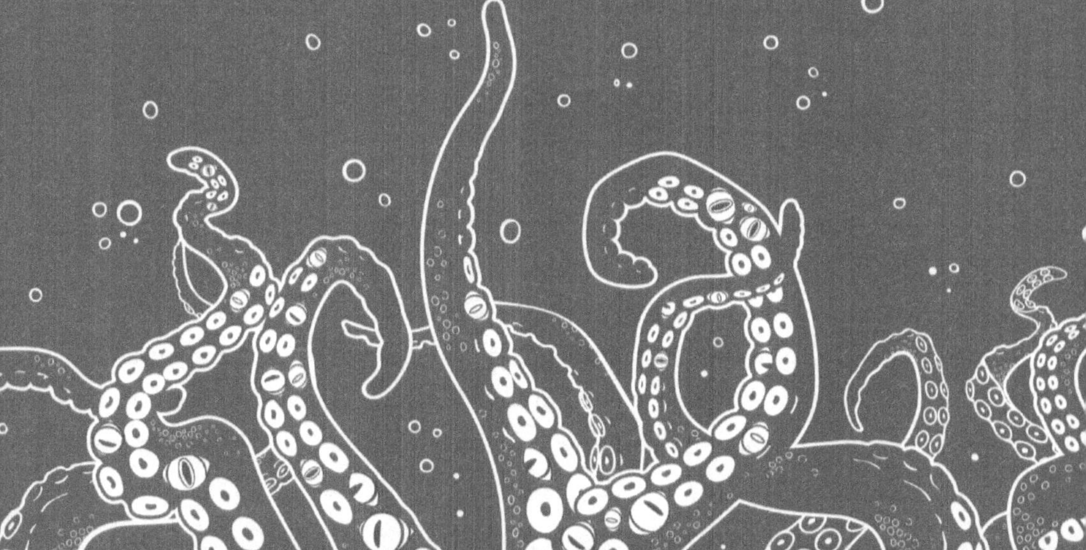

the dirt. Beyond their goatish eyes and snouts, some strange familiarity in their facial features; primordial ancestors in my reincarnated past danced and gestured an obscene beckoning to join them.

Before I had gone to bed on the first night of torments, I had noticed a disturbing alignment of stars. According to mathematics, stars and planets should follow a predictable elliptical path. But the planets of Versiveus, Kraelov, and Diaxon moved in enigmatic, unnerving voyages. Other stars crossed in horrendous formations, and I quaked at what such signs could mean. Though seers, prophets, and oracles read portents in tea leaves, in the scattering of bones, in the twist of lines on palm, I could read warnings in the positioning of outer planets, the fleeing of corrupted stars, and the burning of Azurrabed's comet, their bizarre and unpredictable movements in the black canvas of the cosmos not foreseeable by any astronomer or scientist.

Nor had my dreams contained the usual symbols and images of falling, fleeing, or flying. The fragmented glimpses of mesentery-moist, pulsing, flesh-like megacilia could mean a multitude of ambiguities and insinuations, and I fled to the Miskatonic University's underground libraries for answers. The cowled, tongueless monks accepted my body-pound, and I smelled the burning of my sacrifice as I followed the silent shroud of the monk deeper into the labyrinth of tunnels. He performed the crucial signs, sang the voiceless canticle, and the vault doors to the Deep Room, notched with protective rites, clanked open.

Frantically, feverishly, I delved into the delirium-inducing *Mortemordis*, poured through the curse-riddled *Gorgonology* using antidote-laced gloves, and studied the abhorrent *Maledictory*. Even locking myself in a fetid room with the *Necronomicon*, the poison book of the dead, could not answer my questions. I left when I began to weep blood.

Back in my studio, page after page I flung to the floor as I drew diagrams, scribbled equations, created derivatives and reductions of the movement of the stars—knowing the patterns of the celestial formation must be part of a grander design. Not the math of this world but the math of the parallel: non-Newtonian geometry, Fortunado's topology, octrine trigonometry. Not even the black calculus of Crucerbus could decipher the malevolent pattern.

After weeks of haunted nights, tired and with a suffocating blanket of dense depression which ground down my bones, I paid a visit to my great-uncle, my only living relative—though I had not spoken a word to him since I had finished my studies. Both my parents had died when I was a child, and this secluded great-uncle funded my upbringing and education. He was a grey, morbid man, his skin a pool of wrinkles, his frame seemingly stirred by a thread of will which animated his body like a puppet. I told him of the primeval people who beckoned me to join them, the foreboding alignment of the stars, the flash of animal-human hybrids that mutilated their fleshy forms in profane ways. When I spoke of these horrors, his face blanched as though he had seen the unnamed visions, the impure inferno, the contaminated images conjured before him.

He knew this day would come, he had told me. He had read the signs. He had heard it in the crow's screech, saw it in the psoriatic cirrocumulus clouds, and he trembled beneath the ominous stratocumulus sky.

He arose from his sunken chair, and from a gold chain around his neck he pulled forth a twisted key like that of a skeletal finger. He used this key to unlock a metal box, carved patterns on its sides like a demonic, hellish puzzle box. From his box, he took out a yellowed, ugly leathery papyrus that I came to realize was made from human skin.

"Here," he said as he thrust those papers away from him into my hands, "your real name."

As I opened the dried wrinkled skin paper, the unclean hieroglyphics undulated on the page, no letters in any human language decipherable. With this unpronounceable name came papers outlining my adoption at birth. This explained the remoteness of the parents I had known, Fabien and Magdalene Vigilius, so distant growing up, so lacking in warmth and parental affection. They were instead my gatekeepers, my guardians, my family of strangers. I played alone, ate alone as my parents watched as distant, silent observers. However, my true ancestors, the ancestors of my dreams, called to me.

Upon retrieving the documents, my great-uncle sank back into his chair. He said, "You were adopted through the Gentrocide agency in Blackheart, New England. They may have more revelations for you." After he uttered these words, it was as though his purpose had been completed and he collapsed, shrunken into a desiccated corpse before my eyes.

Blackheart, New England. From my research, a barren hamlet with abandoned, decrepit buildings set like battered teeth on salted, charred earth. Once a rural village in the late seventeenth century, it had been surrounded by crops of squash, beans, and corn before a Puritan offshoot religion grew more extremist. Medieval extraction techniques such as foot roasting, hamstringing, and de-nailing led to confessions of the practice of blood sorcery. The accused were executed by hanging, burning, and drowning.

So much innocent blood was spilled on the land that it had ruined the earth, and guilt and insanity drove out the remaining settlers. Over the years, new colonists—looking to return to the old ways in a fundamentalist folly—would try to settle the land for another rebirth of the village. But the befouled land could not sustain the population, and the settlement would eventually die again. It was during one of these resettlements that the Gentrocide Orphanage came into existence.

Before undertaking a trip to this sinister locale, I decided to investigate other methods to delve into my twisted, enigmatic roots. I swabbed my cheek to give samples to genealogy decoders, to find if I could unravel my family tree through the secrets within the coding of my cells. They mapped out my genes. Long strands of deoxyribonucleic acid formed helical patterns of adenine, thymine, guanine, and cytosine. But shockingly, other nitrogen bases, non-human ones, were also identified: dendrosine, parnadrine, lytonine, and monomotomine.

The scientific methods could not determine my heritage. Long segments were marked as inconclusive, or nonhuman, but no explanation could be ascertained. Twenty-nine percent unknown ancestry. No relatives traced on the cyber genealogy tree.

If I am not fully human, then what am I? Resurrected through recombinant gene-splicing? Hybridal chimera, part-human, part-nightmare?

By plane, by train, and by foot, I made my journey; my driver was quick to surrender me alone to the thick forest when he read a road sign citing "The Path of Righteousness". By compass and coordinates, I would find my way to Blackheart. The shivering woods were gloomy, dark, and deep, and the crows screeched themselves hoarse against me in the descending light. The scuffle of my feet on dead leaves sounded as though I were a monster stalking the woods.

My knapsack weighed heavier on my shoulders the longer I trudged through the woods. Despite the thickness of the forest canopy, without urban light, I saw clearer the unexplained calibration of the stars and felt naked beneath them.

It was close to dawn when I reached the outskirts of an outcropping of a dozen buildings, the decaying village of Blackheart. Nature had reclaimed the land. Vines of ivy tangled an insidious stranglehold over the crumbling stone buildings. The makeshift roads were empty and long weeds pushed through the crumbling paving. The silence was empty, and it seemed to be everywhere.

A copper-green plaque by the door alerted me to the Gentrocide Orphanage. The orphanage looked as though built as an old brick church, a morose, lachrymosal building. Four windows with faded black shutters stood guard on either side of a black-painted door. The door creaked as I opened it. The interior of the building seemed colder than the exterior, a psychic as well as physical cold, and breath transformed into apparitions. Charcoal shadows seemed burnt into the walls, as though an atomic bomb had detonated and blasted the shadows from the occupants. When I listened closely, I could hear a faint scratching emanating from behind the aging plaster. Likely rats or other vermin, and I had no desire to discover its inhabitants.

In a logical manner, I would start from the second storey of the building and work my way downward. Vile moisture ran down the walls like a sickly sweat. The breathy sounds of scurrying centipedes under watchful spider eyes. Glowing disembodied stares seemed to follow my every move as I wound my way up the rickety staircase to the upper level.

The door to the first room already stood open. It was a large rectangular room with three rows of empty cribs. The walls were painted a cloying green, peeling in some spots, large lace-like splashes of mould on others. The suffering of the prior inhabitants infused the walls, the atmosphere. My imagination—or at least I hoped it was only the imagination—heard the ghostly crying of children.

The next room held hole-ridden, rotting furniture where termites and wood-borers feasted. A writing desk, a splintered chair, and five filing cabinets set against the mould-splashed walls that sent up clouds of rancid dust as I went through their contents. The wood broke as I yanked the locked desk drawer open. A box, which I dashed upon the floor, contained yellowed leathery papers with slash-marked hieroglyphics.

When I touched these papers, the house creaked. A loud wailing swept through the house, and the floor beneath my feet began to shudder. The walls bulged rhythmically, as though a giant wormy heart had awoken within the plaster.

I fled the building as though a pack of demons pursued me.

I felt as though I had brought home a curse. The slash marks danced on its yellowed skin, and no matter where I was in my house, I felt its malignant presence. At night, it whispered venomous secrets that crept on the edge of consciousness. The mutterings infected my dreams. In my night's visions, the stars grew brighter, larger, and seemed to sprout teeth.

I sought an audience with the highest professors of the Occult University, linguistic savants of the opaque, unspeakable languages. The University, a brutalist monolith, was hewn from stone and ornamented with petrified blackwood. The rooms were star-shaped, and through the bending of the other dimensions, there were an infinite number of them. The mosaic flooring resembled the waves of the ocean, burgeoned with unnamed creatures, and the ceiling was patterned with stars.

The twelve monks grew silent as I brought forth the yellowed page. They burned cleansing herbs and chanted obsessively in an infrasonic language before touching the document; even then there were no guarantees of protection.

Finally, after much consultation through incantations and incense, oratory, and arguments, they referred me to High Priestess Narinka, a cleric who lived in the ruins of an Oracular temple in southern Notambishi. She had foreseen the death of the New Redeemer, the outbreak of the white pestilence, and the first wave of the Third Coming—the horrors from which had struck her blind. But her sight with the third eye, the eye which sensed the reality beyond, grew exponentially more powerful. A sense that had grown more acute from the loss of another. She had no age; she was as old as time. She suffered no fools, however. Many fortune hunters, if they had not perished in the journey, had been driven mad in her presence. Four monks, having reached the upper echelons of euphorical meditation and armed with binding amulets, agreed to take me to the site.

Seven days we spent climbing up the mountainside where the air was thin and altitude sickness had us bent and gasping. Seven days bitten by insects the size of our palms, leaving eye-sized welts. One monk developed a sweating sickness and died after convulsing. Another disappeared one night, deep in the middle of Mandire's Forest, presumably abandoning the journey.

At last, we reached the stone steps at the mountain's peak leading to her temple. I joined hands with the remaining monks and repeated their incantations before we took the first step. They continued their chanting until we reached the top of the stairs, blanketed by fog. The red columns of the temple were engraved with prayers.

The High Priestess's face was round and smooth, with a cupid-bow mouth, mask-like in its serene perfection, with a cluster of eyes that took up much of her forehead.

The two remaining monks' droning chant rose in volume. I took out the yellowed document from my bag, prostrated onto my knees, and pushed the paper towards her. The eye cluster glowed with a pearly sheen. She brushed the tip of her foreleg against the leathery paper. She split her mouth open and lightly tapped me with her mandibles, which had extruded from within. I tried not to tremble under her arachnid caress. A thin, curved fang pushed out and pierced me through my cheek. She tasted the drop of blood using a long pink tongue.

"Yesss," she hissed, "so now is the time." The eyes turned upward to the sky. "You are the catalyst, the key to the door. Go to the place of your birth. Follow the River Aox until you find its source."

She watched me as I stood. I backed away from her until I reached the start of the stairs before I fled. The blood had whetted her appetite, and she took one monk as an offering.

The place of my birth. The River Aox—a holy river where local people believed that bathing in its waters would free them from the cycle of life and death—grew narrow and more winding as the last monk and I followed it upstream. The thick forest gave way to long grasses and tangled, rope-like vines the width of my wrist. Finally, we were met with an abattoirial circular stone inscribed with hieroglyphics.

As the monk stepped onto this formation, the atmosphere grew oppressive and bristled with warning. A slicing sound cut through the air. The monstrous vegetation, with its tendrils, lashed around the final monk until he looked spooled as a ball of twine. The living jungle pulled him by the limbs into the sky. In a whiplash, the vines retracted, the speed of which cut into his skin. He fell onto the stone and bled to death before me, a death by thousands of cuts, the stone absorbing the blood.

I ran but there was no need to pursue me. The tendrils snapped around and dragged me to the circular stone. From there the vines retracted and from the lashes flowed my blood. Instead of crimson, the fluid glowed with an ominous phosphorescence. At its taste, the stone beneath me splintered, the sound thundering in my ears.

Above, the dark sky cracked open, and from this eggshell split, an unnatural infernal octrine light, a vomitus yellow-green from the deep outer infinity of the cosmos, shone through. Masses of squirming, pink-fleshed appendages, glistening moist from the universe's mucosal lining, thrashed their way twisting through the split, like an eruption of monstrous worms in a radiation pit. Cup-shaped mouthparts rhythmically suctioned open and shut while hordes of giant tick-like parasites scuttled over the organ-raw mass.

My eyes couldn't encompass the horrific imageries. The vitreous liquid contained within my eyes boiled, and from the toxicity of the visions, the eyeballs burst within the sockets, scorching the scarification tattoos beneath my eyelids. I should have been blind, but the octrine-vile light opened my third eye, the eye which allows us to see into the multiplicity of dimensions and I was cursed with a hideous knowledge.

The translated letter described how I was meant for slaughter. The code lay in my cells, my blood, the key pattern to opening this hell-world with the proper alignment of the stars. I was born to be sacrificed to the Ancient Ones under a bleeding moon in the centre of pentagonating stars but was snatched away by the remnants of a fundamentalist missionary sect.

Now, with the stars above once again in formation, the spilling of my blood the key, I saw the gibbering slave-priests, my dream-kin who had called to me in the unconscious nether realm, grovelling in eternal madness to the gods Nyarlathotep, N'yog-Sothep, and Abholos. Commonly known as The Triumvalent, the Unhallowed Trinity, from whom our human concoction of Satan or the devil is but a weak facsimile, the true entities infinitely more evil, infinitely more conflicting; delighting in destruction and in everything which is in opposition to the good and righteous. Its spirit is encompassing, infecting all parts of human nature, so we ground down those already fallen into the dust. My blood ushered in the new world as I was tormented in hideous helplessness upon a fractured altar.

Above, an acidic sticky toxin rained down and burned raw holes in my body. The smell of sizzling flesh contaminated the air. Out poured forth from the widening split in the sky hailed vast monstrous creatures—deities—from the nether-dimensional realms. The flaming, long-toothed Snakehead…the chimeral, dual-tongued Lizardwalker… The hoofed, unbounded Goatman with the split, weeping eyes…

KISSING BUG DAY

J. NEIRA

Living in a swamp hadn't exactly been Oksana's first choice, nor her second or third. It hadn't been a choice at all, as she was born there, in a hut at the edge of a humid town full of sweaty yet laborious people.

Books were a rarity, and most tales were shared around a fire in the town's plaza by an old wise-man or woman. Oksana's duty was to write it down and then care for the records. If a tale changed with the passage of time, Oksana took note, and if a traveler brought back a different point of view, Oksana was there to put the new version on paper. She also kept a registry of trade arrangements, quantities, and prices. Most merchants had their own simpler system of keeping up with their stock, but Oksana's messy scribbles were much more detailed.

While there were other, capable adults in town and a clergyman with better writing skills than hers—as she hadn't had a formal education in either of the arts or sciences people of higher standing could afford—no one else seemed to care that much about the records themselves. Part of Oksana also

didn't, but this had been her father's life work. He'd scratched a piece of coal against paper until he drew his last breath, whispering one last request: for Oksana to continue with his duty. One day, when the world had moved on from them and there were none of their people to tell their own tales, the many notebooks containing their stories would remain, evidence that there once had been a town at the edge of a swamp, and that good people had lived in it.

Oksana rolled her shoulders and straightened her back. The chair on which she sat creaked with the movement, and her vision had to adjust through her glasses to focus again on the words she'd been scratching over an old piece of parchment.

She would have been fonder of this, if not for one thing.

The small, lovely town filled with good people that her father had cared for so much was riddled with a curse. One day every year, *they* came and rained torture among the villagers, indifferent to whether they were man or woman, elder or child, strong or weak. Their hungering maws knew only one thing, and that was biting.

Kissing bug day came once every year, and the medical specialists—three old women that had delved a bit too deep into alchemy and herb smoking— had advised the town to keep their windows and doors closed those days. It wasn't much of a sacrifice. One day trapped in the confines of one's home in exchange for being free of the itch and the possibility of prolonged sickness.

It had been two years since Oksana learned to seal the crevices of her hut, how to stop even the smallest whisper of wind coming from under her door or between her curtains with mud and fabric. Then she researched repellents and unguents that could make her undesirable to them, but their quick visits made it difficult to study what kissing bugs were disgusted by.

She wondered how such a disgusting thing could be disgusted by anything, as in her eyes, they were the worst of their kind. The mere thought of them, of their oval and almost flat bodies, of their many feet and twitching antennae, made her break the thin piece of carbon between her fingers.

In less than one day's time, they would be here. With that same rag, after draining the mud from it, she filled one of her hut's little crevices. Others, she pushed into the space between her door and the floor, and did the same with her windows, also drawing the curtains closed. There was enough dry meat and clean water in crystal bottles for her not to worry about two dinners, and the breakfast and lunch for the next day.

They were only small measures, nothing big, in exchange for avoiding them, and the curse they carried. She prepared several days early because while the kissing bugs had invaded the town the same day, year after year, who was to say that they wouldn't reach them early one time? Every few years, the calendar had to have one extra day added to it. Could the bugs keep track of that? If not, then nothing stopped them from an early arrival. And if so…

Then that showed a higher level of intelligence, a confirmation of the presence of judgment, that Oksana refused to delve too deeply into. After she was finished with her task and lit one meager wax candle on her desk, she resumed her work, writing down the latest version of the tale of the man who could control rats with his flute. In this retelling that a traveling merchant brought to them, the man was not man at all, but an angel given mortal form and a task to complete, to rid the kingdom of evil rodent men who could turn people into beings like them with a mere bite.

Sometimes, Oksana dared to accompany her records with crude drawings. It was something she enjoyed for herself and it made the town's children more interested in the written word, as now the books contained imagery for them to gawk at. For this one, she couldn't conjure any other images than the bugs and their bites, so she decided to call it a day, blow the candle out, skip dinner and simply sleep.

Sweat ran down her brow. No air ran in or out of her quaint hut, but she felt mostly safe and contained, and covered herself from head to toe in no less than three different sheets before laying down on her hardened cot. The night passed and thankfully her dreams were free of creepy-crawlies and twitching little feet. She dreamed of her mother, faceless and gone too soon, and of her father scribbling the days away, letting her draw senseless shapes on the edges of his books during the long summer nights that she missed so much.

The hours passed, and Oksana only realized that she was awake because someone was knocking on her door.

"Not today!" she cried from her bed, barely peeking her head out of her sheets. "I'm not going out today and whoever it is, you know it!"

The knocking continued.

"I said—"

"I know what you said!" came her best friend, Zari's, muffled voice from the other side. "And I don't care! Open this dreaded door or I'll kick it down!"

Oksana leaped from her cot and ran to the door, opening it just a bit, enough to look out with one eye. Her vision was blurry as she had left her glasses on her desk, but her best friend's shape was unmistakable. She seemed to be already wearing her new gown. "You can barely work your weaving machine, and you think you can kick my door down?"

"Of course not," said Zari, trying to push her way through the opening that Oksana had created, "but I got you to open this door, didn't I?" She flashed a toothy smile. "It's early. Like, really early, the sun's in the middle of waking up, but I need you to come out."

"For *what* reason?" Oksana asked for her friend's sake, knowing that there would be no way she'd put one foot out of the safety of her house.

Zari tried to force her entry into Oksana's place, but the two friends were equally matched, and the door refused to move even an inch. "Aw, c'mon. There's a party tonight, you know that!" She raised a finger. "Yes, yes, I know it's kissing bug day, too, but they *just* bite. It's not worse than dealing with mosquitoes and they stay here all year round."

At that, Oksana sighed, grabbed Zari's forearm and pulled her inside, closing and locking the door once the both of them were in the barely lit darkness of Oksana's hut.

"Watch out for the dress, it's one of a kind," Zari muttered her complaint as she patted the skirt back into an orderly state. Her words went ignored.

"Just bites? Are you serious, Zari? People have gone mad from them!"

At that, Zari huffed harder, and her huffs became a short-lived laugh. "Now *I'm* asking if you're serious. No one goes mad from a teeny tiny bug bite, Oksana. The things aren't bigger than my thumb, and I have small thumbs."

She was wrong. They were bigger than that, albeit not by much. Oksana kept the thought to herself.

"You've kept to yourself in this place on this day every year for long enough. This is a huge party, all the guys will be there, and I can't do this alone, Oksana," Zari implored. "I want my best friend with me, ogling cute boys with me, drinking herself silly with me, possibly meeting my future husband with me." A short pause. Zari bit her lower lip. "Don't you?"

Oksana did.

But she couldn't.

She started shaking her head slowly. Her heart broke when Zari's expression fell. "It's not safe." She reached for Zari's hands. "Please, stay. I'll throw you a party tomorrow, after I help old Tarmont document his order. I'll have him forge the prettiest necklace and bracelets for you to go with all your dresses, but tomorrow. *Not today.* Please, today, stay with me. Here." Here, where it was safe and secure and controlled, free of kissing bugs. Here, she could protect herself and maybe her friend, too.

With an exasperated groan, Zari forced her hands free of Oksana's soft hold. "I can't believe you." Her frown turned into a facade of mockery. "You're one of the smartest women in town, almost no one can keep track of your mind and your numbers and your letters… Still, you hole yourself up because of some miserable insects that do more damage to you with all that fear," she tapped the side of her head, "than with their actual bite. The real monster is in your head, but you simply won't let it go, won't you, Oksana? Is it because…"

Oksana briefly prayed that she wouldn't mention it. That she wouldn't lower herself to that level of ridiculing her.

"Your dad told you that they killed your mother? Because my mother remembers; she went crazy because your father drove her crazy with his stupid books."

Something inside Oksana broke. Before she realized it, her fist was raining down onto her table, crashing on it with a loud crack. Zari screamed. Oksana was not known for having a temper—at least not publicly.

"You know what?" Oksana growled. "Go, then. Go crazy for all I care." As soon as she said those words, she regretted them. She was about to apologize for them and for her lack of self-control when the sight of Zari's watery eyes shut her up.

"Ugh!" Zari stomped on the ground, cheeks inflated and battling to contain the tears. "You're impossible! And just for rumors of insanity! It's more likely that a lightning bolt falls twice on your head than to be bitten and driven mad for a day or two by a freaking kissing bug, Oksana!"

She began to leave, completely ignoring Oksana's whispered, "Don't go." Zari fumbled with the lock and closed the door with a loud bang as soon as she was out of the hut. The lonely woman hugged herself, broken and furious, disheartened. This fear of hers, this sensation that they were already here, all over town, waiting to strike, was driving her mad already. It was driving her away from the people she cared about.

Maybe Zari hadn't been wrong in saying it was all in her head. Even if it wasn't her place to comment on the rumors about her mother's demise. She'd noticed how Zari had seemed to regret saying that, too. The both of them had been driven to one another because of relating to the stubbornness they saw reflected in the other. It made sense that it would eventually cause problems.

Nonetheless, it was done. It was kissing bug day, and the encounter had dislodged some of Oksana's rags and other materials she'd put in place to keep her hut hermetically sealed. She fixed them up, putting more space between the world outside and herself. At some point, she stopped hearing from beyond her walls and wondered for a second if the world had disappeared altogether.

Then it came.

The twitching. The flapping. The buzzing against her ears, inside her head. The deafening silence turned into static that turned into an infinite amount of diminutive feet crawling all over her house.

Oksana surrounded herself with her covers and sat on a chair in the middle of her hut, waiting, trembling, agonizing. Hours passed, maybe even an eternity, and she barely had the fortitude to remember to sip some water and munch on a strip of dry meat. Eventually, day turned to night. Even in the nothingness of the outside, Oksana knew that the sun had fallen; she'd always been good at keeping track of the time. Her eyelids felt heavy and her shoulders kept falling. Her body stunk and she undressed and donned a white pajama tank top and pants; the clothing was soft and comfortable against her thin frame. She was so tired that she couldn't sustain her fear for much longer, and like that, Oksana made her way to her bed and laid down.

The day passed.

It was over.

She fell asleep within minutes, ignoring her roaring stomach and the ache at the back of her throat. That night, she again dreamed of nothing easily describable, and if a recognizable image appeared before her sleeping eyes, she forgot it by the time she woke up the next morning.

It was the series of soft knocks on her door that fully roused her. Still in her pajamas, Oksana went to open it, too tired yet to inquire who could be visiting this early in the day. Opening the door revealed a Zari with heavy bags under her eyes.

"Oh my," Oksana coughed out. Her throat was raw. "You look awful," she added as she ushered her friend inside and closed the door. The kissing bug day had passed, and Zari needed her. Who could care about the words exchanged the previous day?

Oksana served Zari and herself twin glasses of water, and she noticed her friend had trouble holding the glass on her own. Oksana guided it to her mouth and prompted her to drink. "Rough night, huh?" she said, gently. "Zari?"

Zari looked back at her, eyes glassy and unfocused. Oksana started to inquire further about what had happened the previous night when Zari stood and ran to Oksana's bedroom, throwing herself at the closed window. Oksana called for her, but she'd been caught off-guard and recently awoken, so Zari reached the window and pulled it open.

To Oksana's horror, a dark cascade of minuscule bodies scurried in, crawling inside with an infernal pitter-patter that made her let out a scream of terror. They came in waves after waves after waves of shifting darkness, creeping closer, buzzing and flapping their wings, their feet clattering against all the wooden surfaces they walked over.

Panicking, Oksana grabbed her chair and brandished it as a weapon, swinging it around and trying to keep the bugs from placing their kiss on her skin. She swung and swung, and the kissing bugs that left only gave way for others to try to land on her. Through it all, she screamed and cried. *This can't be happening, it can't. The day has passed.*

She failed to notice that Zari, dizzy and slow, had closed the distance between them and clung to Oksana's back. "Let go of me!" Oksana barked out as she was dragged down by Zari's body, who simply hugged Oksana's neck and then hung limply from it. Oksana tripped over her own feet the moment she felt the tickling on the back of her foot, and the two women tumbled down onto the wood, in the middle of a sea of flapping insects.

She battled to free herself from Zari's hold as she shook and twisted, trying to keep the bugs at bay, away from her exposed skin, especially around the scoop of her pajama shirt neckline. Zari eventually seemed to regain some consciousness, but it was not to be in Oksana's favor. Her so-called friend, whose mind seemed to be beyond her reach, pulled Oksana in, aiming to turn her around and place her firmly on the ground.

Their limbs tangled together, with Oksana unable to win the confrontation in her state of fear and confusion. Zari's eyes remained glassy, but soon her hold turned into a clearer offensive, clawing into Oksana's skin and pulling on her hair. Then she started laughing. "They've come for you! Only for you!"

Oksana coughed and blinked repeatedly, wiping her tears away. She pushed against Zari, not wanting to actually hurt her. She was obviously not okay and not all there. With the kissing bugs climbing onto her body and with her failing to fully wipe them off, it was difficult to control her own movements. With one hand and fueled by adrenaline, she pulled on the back of Zari's dress, almost tearing it apart, and with her other hand, she batted the bugs off of her body. The chair, long forgotten in a corner of the room, was now covered in a layer of shifting insects.

Oksana called out her name repeatedly, trying to bring her friend back to reality. She'd noticed that parts of her skin showed small circular irritations, "kisses" so to speak.

"It is too late, Oksana!" Zari said. Oksana grew cold at the idea that Zari had read her thoughts somehow. "The era of the witch has come! It's too late to escape, it has come!" Then, Zari cackled, throwing her head back.

With the other distracted by her madness, Oksana got the upper hand and press Zari onto the ground, trapping her between her thighs with one trembling hand grasping her neck to keep her in place. There was little else to do as the bugs assaulted them both, climbing and crawling, climbing and crawling and creeping and...

Oksana roared and kept using her free hand to slap them away not only from her own body but from Zari's, as the insects tried to crawl inside her gaping mouth. "Wake up, Zari! This is not you, come back to me!" she called. "Zari! Wake up! I need you!" Tears bunched up at the edges of her vision. "Think of...of your dress! It's going to be all ruined now, but you can tailor yourself another, no?" she said through coughs and sniffles, breathing quickly and growing exhausted. "You're the best tailor in town, and the town needs its best tailor. I..." Oksana groaned as she punched one particular kissing bug and mashed it between her thin fingers, feeling bile rise up her throat. "I—I need my best friend with me, please!"

Zari's mad cackling became a scream of scorching pain and panic, her expression reflecting that she had become even more confused and lost in the situation.

"Help!" she called, clawing at Oksana's arm. "*Help!*" She struggled in Oksana's hold, forcing the other to increase the force being imposed on her friend. A bit more, and she would be causing actual harm. Oksana felt the ridges of Zari's esophagus beneath the layers of muscle and skin.

"I'm trying to help you! It's the bugs, Zari! You have to snap out of it!"

"Help!"

"Zari!"

It was a leap of faith, but if they kept struggling, Oksana would lose control to the panic and then she'd lose her best friend and herself to the bugs. So, she simply let go of Zari's neck, sitting back and allowing the other to crawl back. Zari was still screaming, now not at her friend, but at the piles of insects that had climbed all over her body.

Oksana grabbed some of her water kept in sealed containers and threw an entire jug over her body, aiming to, if not drown the bugs, at least force them to slide off of her. Then she grabbed another container and threw its contents all over Zari, washing her in the liquid and casting most of the kissing bugs off.

"What's going on?" a still-panicking Zari asked.

"Kissing bugs!" replied a frustrated but not quite afraid anymore Oksana. "What else?"

Together, they grabbed Oksana's broom and mop and started to wipe the kissing bugs away, using the cleaning tools as weapons whenever they dared to fly too close to them. "You were saying something about a witch," said Oksana as she crushed half a dozen kissing bugs under the weight of her broom.

Zari gave her a look that told her it was not the time to ask questions. "I have absolutely no idea what you're talking about!" She huffed as she kept mopping and wiping. Her body swayed, not completely free of the dizziness. "The last thing I can remember is you, on me, trying to kill me."

"You brought these into my house!" *Wipe. Crush. Wipe. Crush.* It was easy to fall into a rhythm. She needed it in order to keep both of them safe and secure.

Deep inside herself, Oksana knew she would never feel completely and utterly safe again, not inside this hut that had seen her grow. Possibly nowhere outside, not even in the most impenetrable of fortresses.

It was all because she believed Zari. All because she'd known this was the curse that they carried, and that her closest friend had fallen victim to it, albeit momentarily, and that it almost brought the both of them down. Oksana had lowered her guard once; it wouldn't happen a second time. It simply couldn't. She was tempted to say that she'd told Zari so, but seeing her own terror reflected in her friend's eyes had sobered Oksana to their situation.

Tomorrow, once things had passed, would be the time for bickering and pointing fingers.

If things passed.

HE WHO LIVES BELOW

MEL HARLAN

THE FIRST THING I saw was slithering. Writhing, sinuous, and coated in a milky viscous substance. For the sake of admitting nothing, we could say it happened to a friend of a friend. Or even a friend of a friend's extended family member, far enough removed that it wouldn't even feel like it had happened to me.

But I'm getting ahead of myself.

"Would you rather…" Ashley said to me as she scanned a bottle of merlot, "go on an all-expenses paid vacation to the Caribbean…"

Mid-question, Ashley's customer held out her credit card, ready to swipe and escape our loud conversation across the checkout lanes. The woman's Designer Shoe Warehouse flats squeaked on the linoleum as she shifted again in impatience.

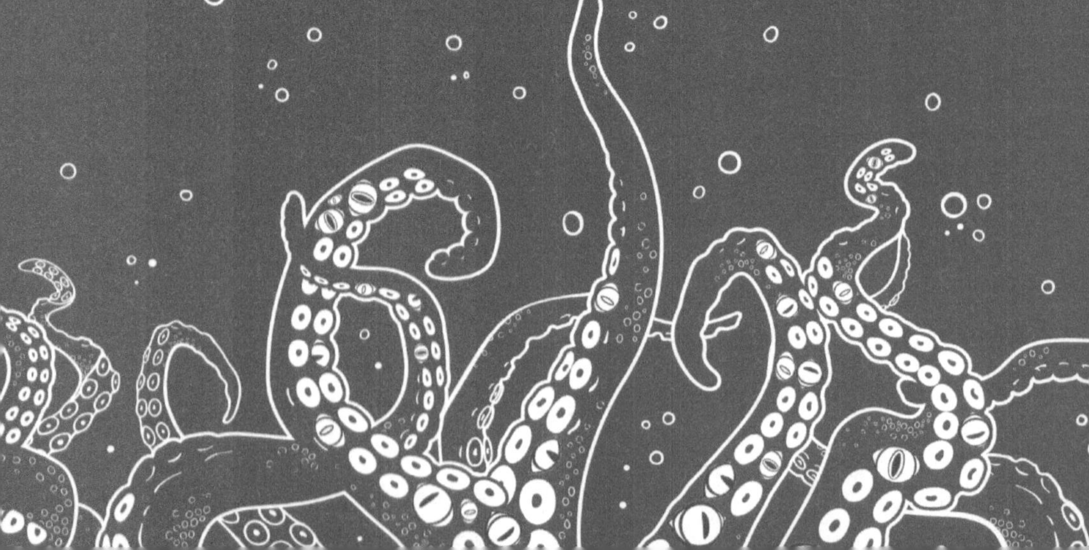

"Or…would you rather get a job where you could save for a year and go on a less cool vacation to a place of your choice?" Ashley scanned another bottle of wine, this time a cabernet. The register's pinging sound was the soundtrack to our relationship, Ashley being the bagger to my cashier up until two weeks ago, when Marlene quit. No matter how pleasant the ding, another moment was gone.

"Ask me a harder one," I said, crossing my arms.

"You're not even a little tempted?" Ashley craned her neck to look back at me, nose ring winking. The "mistake" she had made earlier this week fell across her eye, and she blew the stray bangs out of her face. The hair fell back where she didn't want it.

Ashley propped open a paper bag, filling it quickly with the woman's atrocious house decorations, like signs that said "Wine Time" or "Live Life Uncorked" or "Rosé the Day Away". Today it was "I don't care whether my glass is half full or half empty. I need a refill." Anyone who stayed in Coral Palms long enough felt compelled to shove their brain full of positive sayings like "Live Laugh Love" where the Is were wine glasses.

"I'd rather go where I want, rather than end up like…" I made wide eyes at the customer, offering the woman a practiced smile that hid my gums. I subtly waited until she rolled her cart out of the store to gesture at her back.

"She looks happy," Ashley said with the same look that came to her face when she considered a new boy-toy, a new hairstyle, a new future. Ashley *wanted*—more than anyone I'd ever met. I wanted Ashley to want the world, not just a piece of it to call her own.

Ashley hid the look she thought I'd missed, instead offering a cheeky half-smile before busying herself with restocking her lane. With no one in either line—Tuesday afternoons were the slowest—I joined Ashley in the tight cubbyhole behind her register, our hips bumping as I gave her a quick hug from behind. Her hands didn't leave the plastic bags as she refilled them on the metal rack for the next customer.

"Speaking of being out in the world," I said, shaking her shoulders. I didn't want to fight with only three months until we left Coral Palms. "How would you like to go to a party tonight? I got a text from Marlene inviting us to something by the water."

"Wouldn't you rather hang out?" Ashley bit her lip.

Before today, Marlene had texted me only for shift coverage, so a party invitation was a welcome change from our summer routine. We would watch another of Ashley's favorite rom-coms, her soft sweatshirt pressed against my cheek and both of us wrapped around a tub of popcorn. She'd tempt me with salty kernels to be still, although a few times her salty kisses had kept me appeased. Nothing too serious for Ashley, who whiled the hours away, and I was happy to oblige. Like a kite on the wind, she floated on her own, carried off in any direction.

I wanted that direction to be mine.

I was worried if we didn't go, Ashley would stay in Coral Palms. She'd become part of her couch, part of the fabric of the town like her own parents and theirs before them. I started talking, knocking down her forthcoming excuses like ducks at a shooting gallery.

"I'll pick you up and drive and everything." I could swing by Cypress Grove Mobile Home Park after begging my cousin for their ride.

"You can skip class tonight and won't get behind." Ashley's mom cleaned at the community college, allowing her to take free classes. She hadn't declared a major yet.

"If you hate it, we can always leave and go back to your place for sweatpants and *Sweet Home Alabama*." I could tell Ashley was weakening and went for the closer.

"She said to dress fancy," I sing-songed. "Which means no flip-flops." A fancy party was just another excuse to go, in a time when an excuse was all I needed to do anything.

Ashley blew a raspberry at me, as excited as I was to dress up. The closest we'd come was our high school prom, one night of sparkles and disco glitter that had not satisfied our need for glamor. We needed a spotlight on our lives, and we would find one.

With a slightly off-kilter smile on her naturally blemish-free face, she gave me her decision.

My own face always broke out at the chin and forehead no matter how much I moisturized or toned or tried the miracle solution As Seen on TV, but I still smiled back, returning to my register and awaiting the party—I know now—I shouldn't have attended.

As a true Floridian, I breathed easily in high humidity, glistening with an ever-present light sweat, but shriveled the moment the temperature fell below sixty. That night, it was fifty-eight and balmy. Wind whipped off the waves and chilled me through my flimsy blue dress as I exited the truck I'd managed to borrow for tonight. I rubbed my bare shoulder with a numb finger that had already frozen into a dry, pink icicle.

Blocking the wind only slightly, the faded white mansion jutted into the darkness like a jagged tooth. Only one streetlight illuminated our approach, the other houses farther down the winding road. Ashley looked back at the Chevy, her black dress shiny in the headlights. When the beams clicked off a moment later, she linked her arm in mine for shelter against the cool dark.

"We're going to have fun." I held out my pinky and linked it with hers, intertwined for what would become the final time. We had pinky promised only a few times over the years. At age five, we promised to always be best friends. In eighth grade, we promised to never leave the other behind. At an eleventh-grade house party, we promised to leave Coral Palms together.

All those promises are broken now.

We walked up the circular driveway, her strappy high-heeled sandals ticking on the concrete as they showed off her delicate ankles. I'd worn my best dress sneakers and done a swift updo that turned my brown, frizzy hair into something chic, collected, and highly flammable, given the sheer amount of hair spray holding it in place.

Looking back, this is how I remember her: half-smiling at me in the overhead light of the porch, winking as we heard someone approach the door, then nudging a return smile out of me. My teeth felt too low in my mouth, my smile all gums, but Ashley never seemed to mind. It was one of the things I'd loved most about her: her easy acceptance.

The front door swung open slowly, revealing a man in a tuxedo.

"We're looking for Marlene," I said hesitantly.

The house numbers said we'd found the right address, but there was no way the small-town cashier could afford this place. If this wasn't Marlene's house, then where did she send us?

"Mister Porter does not attend to interlopers, only those with an invitation." The butler started to shut the door as I fumbled for my phone.

"Marlene sent me a photo…"

The door halted, half-closed, when I found the photo of the invitation she'd sent while I drove. The only other party invitations I'd ever received were covered in balloons, a formality for special occasions like birthdays. I hadn't even opened it, assuming it was how she'd channeled her hosting excitement and hours unemployed.

I showed him the invitation. Despite the photo's grainy quality, the thickness of the paper and the deep swirl of the name "Porter" embossed in cursive script clearly stood out. In a smaller script below the name, it had some antiquated language about requesting our presence. The butler received it with an upturned nose, begrudgingly stepping aside.

As we entered, he directed us to a large book waiting at the bottom of a curved staircase. It smelled like an old wine cellar, or what I imagined one might smell like, musky with a hint of old water and grapes. Sour and rich.

Ashley picked up the pen, looked at the butler's expectant expression, and then signed her name. The flouncy script bubbled across the page, a youthful statement of ignorance. She handed the pen to me and I flipped the pages, finding them full of signatures with dates next to each. There was something every seven years before it. 2014. 2007. 2000.

A septennial party. *Cute.* I signed my name next to tonight's date—May 3, 2021— as my cashier's brain automatically added the numbers together. My fingers itched, reaching to turn the pages back to see if the other dates also combined to the same number.

Many years later, when I saw the book again, I found my signature from that night and traced the loops, wishing I'd paused to remember what America's Next Top Model had taught me. *Always look before you sign.*

Afterwards, the butler said, "Follow me," and we ascended the marble stairs.

The main room was dazzling. A chandelier nearly as large as the room dripped crystals in a graceful spiral. An astounding number of people filled the space, swirling in their finest dresses and suit jackets worn over three hundred-dollar jeans. The attire, the room, looked like it all belonged out of a movie set far away from Coral Palms.

Our best full faces of makeup and Macy's discount dresses looked shabby in that room. Awestruck, Ashley took a quick, forceful step back, nearly stepping on me. If I'd been too slow to move, her spiked heel would have driven clean through my foot.

To her credit, Ashley recovered first. She carved a jaded look on her face as she snagged one of the champagne flutes floating past on a nearby tray, sipping like she always drank champagne on Tuesdays. I knew she was channeling *The Devil Wears Prada,* our movie of choice this summer.

I crossed my arms, cold with an unshakeable feeling that we should leave. *We don't belong here.* Deftly snatching another glass, Ashley handed it to me. It felt ethereal in my hands but did little to ease my anxiety. I tried to tell her we should go, that the car was just outside, that we hadn't been noticed yet, when her hand on my shoulder steadied me. Calmed me enough to stay when she linked our fingers together.

If we were going to at least do a lap around the room, I navigated us to the one thing that would help make tonight worth the trouble. The table of snacks held an assortment of meat slices, cheeses, and fruit spread across a linen tablecloth.

My fingers hovered above the salami when a woman said, "What are you doing here?"

I jerked my hand away.

The woman was older, full-figured. A coiled snake pendant dangled between her breasts, which were hauled up by a strong bodice, still nearly spilling out of her top. Her gaudy jewelry couldn't have come from Claire's.

When I met her brown eyes, something clicked. "Marlene?"

She didn't look like the Marlene I knew, the one who wore too much eye makeup to hide her exhaustion and never went without her orthopedic shoes on her swollen feet. This woman was too well composed in her designer gown and with her tastefully manicured nails. Not a single strand of dyed blonde hair out of place from chasing teen shoplifters.

"You came," Marlene said too loudly as she pressed her hand to her stomach. A ruby twinkled on her finger.

She sounded almost afraid, but that didn't seem right. She'd invited us to this party, after all. Calm logic erased the sureness in my heart.

"Something wrong?" A man mingling nearby joined us, wearing a practiced smile and placing a gentle hand on Marlene's shoulder. I later learned his name was Toby, Mister Porter's lawyer.

Something odd crossed her eyes, even though she smiled and said, "Everything's fine." I should have recognized that peculiar tone. Every cashier used it when you were alone in your lane and something was about to happen. You prayed your voice would stop whatever was coming. It was both hope and submission laid bare.

"Are they here for Mister Porter?" Toby asked.

Marlene looked like she wanted to say something that might have come out in that same peculiar voice I would have recognized if I'd heard it a second time, if only I hadn't said, "Of course."

Marlene smoothed her dress, fixing nary a wrinkle, while Toby's smile turned from contemplative to sharp. "We're glad to have you, especially Mister Porter."

"Will we meet him?" Ashley said, standing up taller, like a kid in a candy store.

"Only if he wishes it," I said with a pointed look at Ashley.

She fell back into her relaxed repose, sipping the nearly empty flute of bubbles.

"Exactly," Toby said and tucked Ashley's arm in the crook of his elbow. I trailed behind them, frowning at their back. An immediate third wheel in my own relationship.

"I think Mister Porter would love to meet you," Toby said to Ashley, and I watched the blush creep up her back. She always blushed when she was nervous: barely a hint of color on her face, the flush creeping up her shoulders instead, her entire body hot. I'd traced it once, wondering how far down it went, until she had giggled and turned over.

"Really?" Ashley said.

"Oh, yes," Toby said. He realized I still walked behind them when he looked back at me, the flicker of annoyance on his face making my stomach twist.

An overwhelming feeling of wrongness overcame me. The gala was too glittering, too bright. I touched Ashley's shoulder and drew her to me, close enough so Toby couldn't hear.

"I don't think this is a good idea after all." I took her hand. Her pink glitter nail polish was already chipped from when I had painted it earlier that week.

"We just got here," Ashley said rationally. With a secret smile, she added, "Besides, I could use a sugar daddy."

I knew that look. My kite drifted, following a new lead wherever it would take her.

"You were promoted the other week. You don't need to—"

"I'm seeing where this goes," Ashley said. Her arm sparkled, her body glitter reflecting in the candlelight and transforming her into a mirage.

"Alright," I said slowly, releasing her hand. "But in fifteen minutes, we're leaving."

I wished I'd held out my pinky and made her promise, even if we had already done it earlier that night. I held a childish hope that a pinky promise could transcend what would come.

Toby looked impatient.

"She'll be well taken care of," he said, encircling her arm once more and leading her upstairs. She didn't look back.

Nervous for a reason I couldn't name, I wandered back to the snack table and gobbled a piece of cheese. Bubbles burned my throat as I finished my drink, setting it down on a tray held by an anonymous caterer, only to grab another. While we often drank at house parties, nothing had made me feel like my tongue buzzed.

This must be the good stuff.

Standing against the wall, I set a phone alarm for exactly fifteen minutes. *Only* fifteen minutes. I swigged from the second glass, warmth spreading across my limbs. Noticing Marlene across the room, I almost left my helm when we made eye contact. I had taken only a half-step when she imperceptibly shook her head and lost herself in the crowd.

My cell phone buzzed. Fifteen minutes had already passed and Ashley had not returned. I acted like I belonged at the gala while my stomach cramped with anxiety, weaving my way through guests towards the stairs. There was only one face I wanted to see.

I stumbled up the steps and picked a direction, throwing open the doors of room after room after room. Tumbling through the door at the end of the hallway, I found the master bedroom.

There was no *Taken*-style circular bed in the center of the room, only a king-sized one made up with fluffy white pillows. Scouring for signs of Ashley, I yanked open the closet doors, only to find a plethora of large men's suits and one giant velvet robe that I touched distastefully with two fingers. I shuddered and set it back, then opened the drawers to the built-in closet shelves.

The first drawer opened on a smooth track, revealing a multitude of black jewelry boxes. Curious, I opened one, then another. And another. My heart lurched, and I threw the boxes on the floor. Each one revealed a red ruby ring, but in different sizes and styles.

I wobbled back across the bedroom toward the bathroom, but plopped onto the bed instead, suddenly tired. I wished I'd never accepted Marlene's invitation. If Ashley and I had stayed home, we might be on the couch right now. Sweatpants sounded heavenly as my dress clung to the sweat between my thighs.

The room tilted, and suddenly my cheek was on the plush comforter. I could stay here. Maybe Ashley would eventually find me.

I was wrong: I was the one untethered without some place to run to, without someone to catch me.

Blinking slowly, my eyes landed on the heavy brocade curtains at the other side of the room. A sliver of something gleamed underneath. Squinting, I forced myself to stand, and the room righted itself. Another flash of silver glinted beneath the fabric. Pushing back the curtain, I discovered a hidden elevator. I pushed the call button and the elevator whirred.

When the doors opened, I stepped inside, hoping to find *my* Ashley.

When the doors reopened several floors below, I stepped into the den of something old and wanting and waiting.

It must be said, dear reader, that at this point, I no longer have words to describe what I saw that captures the horror which entered my heart that night, never to leave. So much so that, for my own sake and at the urging of my very expensive therapist, I wrote it all down from another perspective entirely.

In fact, my personal account became a bestselling horror short story in my first collection. Names were changed—Ashley became the unnamed sacrifice; I couldn't even type her name—and the whole thing was repackaged into an urban legend for the fictional cult I'd invented.

Mister Porter loved it. He came to my first book signing at Barnes and Noble. My hands shook when I took a freshly printed copy from him.

"Wonderful work you've done here," Mister Porter said. His jowls trembled with pleasure.

"In His name," I said begrudgingly, and he bowed his head.

"Hiding in plain sight," he said, half to me and half to himself. "Absolutely genius."

While Ashley had always been the master of blending in, my manuscript gave Mister Porter and He Who Lives Below that gift over tenfold. After all, once people sell merch for a story you've created, it's hard to say if it's real anymore.

And no one ever asked for the truth. In press interviews, they seemed to ask everything else.

Where did your inspiration come from? My experience.

Then they'd laugh and tell me about the first time they'd read it. *My favorite part is where the sacrifice gets the worst of it.* Why? *Because it felt so visceral.*

Why did you choose a male pen name? I had no other words, other than someone else's.

Can you believe that you've sold one million copies? I thought it was too popular.

They loved that answer.

Sometimes I wondered if my story—which I refused to read out loud at book signings, no matter how many times people asked—was popular because of my writing talent or because of what had happened. I had a feeling it was the latter when I thought too hard about it. Then, yet another person would tell me how much they'd loved it and I'd let myself forget all over again.

AN EXCERPT FROM *THE SERPENT MASTER* BY NORMAN KING:

The entire crowd writhed like a court of snakes. On stage, the Serpent Master called, "In His Name," from beneath a white half-mask. The congregation answered, their mouths moving beneath their own masks. Then the room hushed, a silent thrum of tension vibrating deep in their bones.

It happened only every seven years, this opportunity to appease their God. Their congregation met where He could reach them easiest: at the edge of the ocean. Behind the curtain, the back of the theater opened to a rocky cove. At this point in the year, the tide was lowest, opening up the cavern so He could easily reach their sacrificial bed.

"Welcome all," the Serpent Master said. "I thank you for your presence in my home and for your support as we enjoy this bountiful harvest."

He was a portly man, his chin doubling as he bowed his head. "Long May we live in His image. Long may the spirit of He Who Lives Below continue to inspire us and drive us to new heights. We only thrive with His blessing. In His name, in His honor, we have conquered the worlds of business, agriculture, and pharmaceuticals. We have netted billions between our members, and I thank you for your continued support and appreciation. We are a strong congregation, and He thanks you for your sacrifice."

A couple in the back row whispered to one another, loud enough to cut through the murmuring din but low enough where the Serpent Master wouldn't hear. The woman's neck glittered, diamonds dangling into her dress's plunging neckline. Her husband was well-kempt, his mustache oiled behind his white mask.

The husband said, "I forgot how over-the-top Davidson gets when he talks about He Who Lives Below."

His wife Marjorie covered her mouth and said, "Yeah, but if I were him I'd lay it on thick. You don't want to get on His bad side. Don't you remember the Hendersons?"

Her husband had met the Hendersons through his work, who introduced them to a friend of friend, a daisy chain of influence that led them to their first night in this same room.

"They never proved anything," her husband whispered.

"Did they need to? They disappeared and then their house mysteriously burned down. I wouldn't wish Him on anyone." Marjorie shook her head, pulled a cigarette from her custom Tiffany case, and tapped it along the side. Her husband had gifted it to her after the first time she attended this... display.

The man hushed his wife as the sacrifice was brought to the stage. She was young and willing, always willing, to be part of the ceremony to receive His bounty. In her fine gown, she settled on the gilded iron bed frame soldered to the stage. It was both beautiful and sturdy, for their God's presence was large.

The Serpent Master called, "Arise!"

The crowd stood for their God's arrival. The Serpent Master gestured, and the sacrifice disrobed, shedding her clothing in front of all. The woman offered her arms and was chained to the bed.

Marjorie's ruby ring blinked in the candlelight as she clasped her hands, hoping they could steady her where her husband could not. As loyal members, in trust and fear, they had waited for their bounty. Small windfalls blew in, enough to keep them comfortable, but not enough for retirement dreams. She'd convinced him this was the only way.

"Where did you find her?" her husband asked.

She knew the girl from work. Marjorie had sent the invitation late, only hours before the party. She'd given an address of a house almost an hour from town. She'd been prepared for her not to come, for there to be no sacrifice tonight. But the girl had found a way.

"Someone is always desperate enough to change their circumstances."

Her eyes burned at her handiwork. She had almost told the girl to leave, to run, to get as far away as possible. There had been only a moment where she could have stopped this, and she had faltered. There was nothing she could do now but live with it.

"We all do something for Him, but to be His sacrifice—better her than us." Her husband rubbed the back of his neck, readjusting his mask.

Marjorie had vomited after the first time she'd witnessed their Lord's process. She knew of other women who had been through it, who spoke of the rapture He bestowed upon them. Who willingly offered themselves again and again, but she still couldn't imagine...

And she didn't have to. He Who Lives Below had arrived. Her fingers trembled and her acrylic nails dug bloody half-moons into the backs of her hands. Marjorie knew the woman wanted to scream at the sight of her Lord, because she did, too. He was overwhelming.

His dark head emerged first from the curtain. Fresh from the ocean, the flickering candlelight highlighted each of his scales. He was large, dark, thick, and glorious. The top of his head could reach the ceiling if He wished, but He hung low to the ground as He slowly slithered forth.

As he backed away, the Serpent Master held out his arms in welcome, gesturing to their sacrifice. He Who Lives Below hovered above the woman, who—like all the others—realized her folly seconds before the coupling began. She tried to escape, but her hands were tied to the bed. The woman writhed in fear…and then pain.

Marjorie wanted to run for her, her own heart skittering and searching for somewhere dark, faraway to hide.

"In His Name," the Serpent Master cried.

The crowd answered.

Hours later, when their Lord and the woman were spent, His belly scraped as He glided along the stone floors, back behind the curtain, back to the ocean. Marjorie sighed in relief as their sacrifice was taken away.

She hated returning to this place every seven years. Technically, twice in seven years. In twenty-eight to forty-five days after the ceremony, everyone returned to witness the sacrificial woman scream and cry and birth His progeny. The first time Marjorie had seen it, she couldn't eat for a week. Every time she patted her stomach, she worried that something within might move. That His influence had reached her from the stage.

Marjorie went outside, lighting her smoke and puffing into the breeze. She wondered if He was watching her. If He was already headed towards the other congregation along the East coast. If her husband's next gift would help the memory of Him fade.

I still see Ashley sometimes when I make my pilgrimage to Coral Palms. Usually, I run into her at McMann's. Shopping instead of selling, of course. She looks well taken care of. We exchange pleasantries about something like the weather, her eyes glazed and unfocused.

Last time I saw her, she wore the finest of brands, nails lacquered and shiny under the fluorescents. It was the Lord's second night of return. We'd never spoken about what had happened, what we'd seen, and likely never would. It hung over every interaction like a dirge.

"How are the kids?" I asked. Ashley had married Mister Preston and gave him three beautiful children. They had her smile, the one she'd have on movie nights when she tried to sneak extra kernels without me catching her. Outside of the book events I was obligated to attend, I never saw Mister Porter and hoped Ashley somehow lived free of his influence. I pictured her alone with both men in a house by the water. She hadn't even told me she was going to marry Mister Preston—I'd already left by then, couldn't bear to look at what I'd done to my friend, so I couldn't entirely blame her—and once I found out, it was long too late.

She smiled, her eyes clearing for a moment, and said, "It's good to see you. How are you?"

Standing in McMann's, I could almost pretend it was all those years ago, and we'd been asked to open the store, clearing carts out of aisles. Time collapsed for a moment and I could see Ashley—*my* Ashley—underneath this version's spray tan and rootless highlights and silicone expression.

Unable to answer, I shook my head and said, "How about you?"

"Blessed." She shifted, and I noticed her swollen belly. I had trained myself not to flinch when she rubbed it. I knew that it wasn't—that it couldn't be, not again—but I wanted to run like I had all those years ago. I'd wanted to be there, but I couldn't watch—keep watching—what He had done to her.

Time reset itself and I knew, whether we spoke about it or not, I was never getting my Ashley back. A sign in her cart read, "Always Wine Time When Life's A Beach."

The ruby signet ring fit too tightly on my finger, bloated from the humid Florida morning like a beached carcass.

My smile hid my gums as I replied, "In His name."

DUST

RED CHARLES

OUR HOUSE WAS made of dirt. Big strips of dirt that Pa and Papa and Uncle Thomas cut out of the ground and piled up. There was even still grass on the top. When Papa could hear, Ma said I should call it "sod". But when he was out in the field or off hunting, we laughed together about how it was just dirt.

There was a small window through the eastern wall. I knew it was the eastern side, because the sun shone through in the morning and I could watch floating bits of dirt and dust glitter in the air as I got out of bed. Ma and Pa would both already be up by then—Ma making breakfast and baking bread, Pa out working with Uncle Thomas (and Papa, when he felt well enough). My grandma died before I was born; died on the ship before it got to Boston. Then Aunt Sarah died of a fever on the trip here. I was born then, but just a baby. That's all to say that Ma made breakfast and bread for everybody.

Sometimes, when Ma was busy kneading dough or peeling potatoes or scrubbing a pot, I would stand up on a chair and look out the window. I wasn't supposed to do that—I was supposed to be helping Ma, or maybe practicing my letters on my slate—but I liked watching Pa and Uncle Thomas handle the mules as they broke the dirt around the house. Sometimes it would make

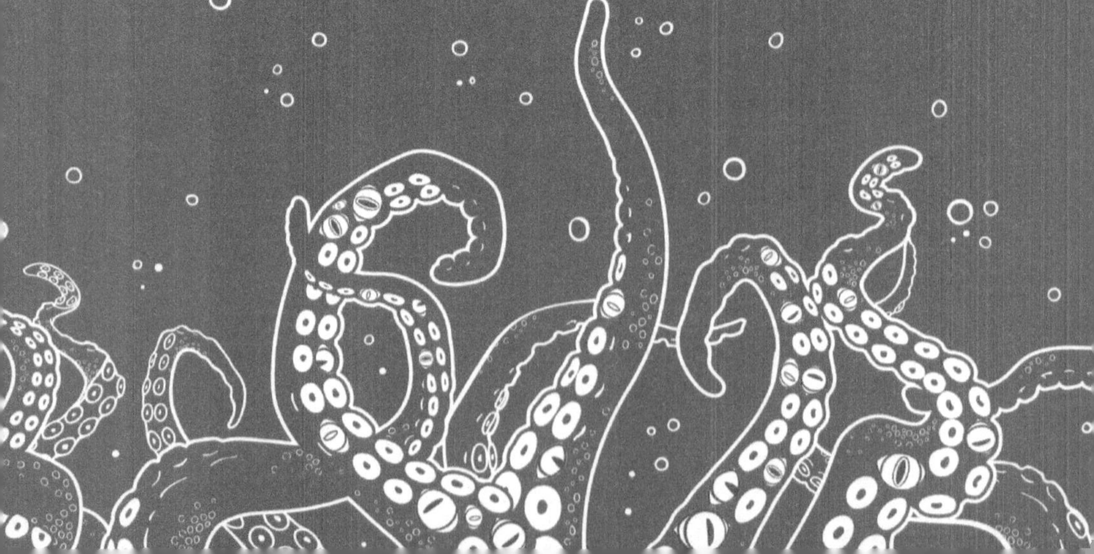

me think of the mule walking straight up our dirt walls and busting them with the plow. Then I would giggle and Ma would look at me and I'd get shushed and told to get down and get back to work. But that wasn't bad, either, because whenever I got to giggling and Ma would scold me, she'd only be pretending to be angry. She was never really angry when I got the giggles.

That was especially true when Uncle Thomas made me giggle. Ma told me once that he was real sad for a while after Aunt Sarah died—that's when she taught me to spell the word "melancholy", which I could barely fit on my slate—but for as long as I could remember, he'd been the one trying to get me giggling.

Sometimes he would just make funny faces at me. Or come up behind me and tickle my sides or pick me way up over his head and swing me around. One time, he carried me out to the barn and let one of the mules snuffle at my face. Those things were fun.

But the best times were when he'd tell me something to say or write on my slate that made Ma or Pa laugh or turn red. The best one was when he told me to ask Papa to have the upcoming Sunday's bible lesson on Ezekiel Chapter 23. I even wrote it on my slate so I wouldn't forget. Uncle Thomas said that's the best part of the Bible to learn about horses and donkeys. But when I asked Ma and Pa if we could read that part, Pa just laughed and Ma got all flustered like she does sometimes. Then she sent me outside while she yelled at Pa and Uncle Thomas. I couldn't hear what she said, but Uncle Thomas brought me a piece of licorice back from town on his next trip and said I'd done a good job. We still haven't had Bible study about the horses and donkeys, though.

Most of the time when I wasn't helping Ma or Pa with work, I liked to draw on my slate. Pa made sure I always had lots of chalk, and Ma made me a felt eraser that she attached to the slate on a length of cordage. My favorite thing to draw was horses. Sometimes real ones—like our riding horse Ferd—and sometimes ones I made up. When I filled up the slate, I'd wipe it clean with the eraser and then knock the chalk off on the edge of the table or chair. Ma would fuss at me for leaving dust on the floor of the house. I never really understood why, though, because our house was made of dirt.

We found out about the Johanssons when Pa went to town to buy some supplies and pick up that year's Farmer's Almanac. I wasn't supposed to know, but I listened to Pa tell Ma and Uncle Thomas about it after supper while I was supposed to be asleep in my bed. It was warm that night, warmer than it usually would have been in early spring, but I pulled all the blankets over me anyway to make it easier to pretend to be sleeping.

"The Johanssons are gone," Pa said, speaking quietly. He and Ma and Uncle Thomas sat around the table. Ma darned a pair of Papa's socks while they talked. Uncle Thomas tried to fix one of the buckles on Ferd's bridle that had bent out of shape. Everybody was always working, even when they weren't.

"I thought they were doing well," Ma said, also quietly. "And Ingrid just had the new baby not six months ago."

"They were doing well," Uncle Thomas said. He was a little less quiet. "I was behind Erik at the bank last month and heard him make his deposit. They were doing just fine. There's no reason they would have pulled up stakes and gone back East."

"I'm not saying they gave up and went back," Pa said. I couldn't see him, but I knew from the way he said it that he was shaking his head when he talked. Pa spoke slowly, just like Papa, and Ma and Uncle Thomas were always racing off in front of him when they talked. He always shook his head when they ran off in a direction that wasn't where he was going.

Pa continued: "I mean, maybe they *did*, but it's not just that. Tom Hollister at the store told me they left, and not only that, but their whole homestead was just…not there. I asked him to explain, but that's all he could really say about it. So I went by their place on my way back from town. And, just like he said, the homestead is gone. The house and barn and fence and everything is gone. It looks like virgin prairie. Like they were never there." It took Pa a long time to get all of that out. He sounded scared. I'd only heard him sound like that one other time—the first time a tornado came by the farmstead.

"You got lost," Uncle Thomas said, laughing. "You were so wound up by Hollister that you missed the Johanssons' place and ended up somewhere out on an unclaimed parcel."

"No," Pa said. "I wasn't lost. Remember how the Johanssons built their place right between that low hill with the flat top where they had their dugout and that sharp bend in Early Creek? And the old man told Erik he'd regret building there if the creek ever overtopped? That's right where I was."

The old man was what Pa and Uncle Thomas called Papa when he wasn't around. He had gone right back to the house that he and Uncle Thomas shared after dinner to go to bed. Most nights, he went to bed even earlier than I did! But then he got up a long time before the sun rose most of the time. Sometimes, he'd wake me up working on things in the barn in the middle of the night.

"Why would they pull the barn and fences down?" Ma asked.

"I didn't say they pulled them down," Pa said. "That's what I thought at first: maybe they'd pulled the buildings down and sold the lumber. Or that maybe they'd burned. So I went over to look. Those buildings weren't just pulled down or burned. Not unless somebody filled in the foundations and the root cellar and then replanted the grass that would have been under the floors. And filled in every fence post hole. I'm telling you, it looked like virgin prairie. Like how this place did when we first got here."

"And there was nothing left?" Ma asked.

"No. The ground was sort of dusty, like it gets when it hasn't rained for a while. But at the tops of the grass. It's been a rainy spring, though."

"You got lost," Uncle Thomas said again. "I'll ride over to the Johanssons' tomorrow. Maybe I'll take the buckboard and the old man. He could stand to get away from here for a bit."

"You do what you want," Pa said. "I'll be here working."

Uncle Thomas and Papa left before I got up, but I was in the kitchen helping Ma scrub out the stove when they got back. Ma had just told me, "I don't know if we've gotten the stove any cleaner, but we've definitely made you dirtier!" and wiped some of the soot off my nose when I heard the buckboard rattle into the yard.

Ma heard it too, of course, and said, "Stay inside for now. I'll be back in a few minutes and we'll get you in the bath." She gave me a soft pat on the head and went out to talk to Papa and Uncle Thomas. Pa must have seen them coming from a ways off, because he had already walked back over from the barn by then. I stood right next to the door—Ma had left it open a little like she usually did, to help the air flow through—and tried to listen as the four of them hung by the buckboard and talked.

Papa said something in German. I didn't really know much of it. Ma and Pa always said that we lived in America now, so we should speak like Americans. But Papa still spoke it most of the time when I wasn't around and Ma wouldn't fuss at him about it. He said something about the Johansson's farm being dirty. But everything here was dirty; our house was made of dirt.

"Yes," Uncle Thomas said, then he spoke to Pa. "But you were wrong about it being dust. Whatever that was all over the place wasn't dust. I mean, it *was* dust, but it wasn't the dirt that blows off the plowed fields when it's dry. It's more like ash."

"So you think the Johanssons' place burned?" Ma asked. She almost sounded relieved. It would have been a relief, had that been the explanation. Fire was always a danger to the barn.

"A sod house doesn't burn. Not down to nothing. And a fire doesn't fill in fence post holes or the outhouse pit," Pa said.

Papa said something in German that sounded like agreement. Then he spoke low and slow for a long time. I couldn't hear him very well, and I didn't understand very much of what I did hear. But nobody else said anything for what felt like ages after Papa finished.

"I will go into town on Sunday," Pa said. "We should find out if anyone else knows anything about the Johanssons. Or if this has happened to any of the other farms. Sunday will be the best day. People will be in town for church."

I begged Pa to let me go with him, but he said no. He gave me three licks with the strap, too, for eavesdropping. Not hard, though—just enough to let me know I broke the rules. It was worth it for the chance to try to go into town. I almost never got to go, but sometimes if I was lucky, Pa would take me with him when he went to the bank or the store. But this time, he told me I couldn't go; he said Ma needed me to stay with her. He promised to bring me some rock candy from the store, though. I liked that even better than licorice.

Pa didn't make it back from town on Sunday. Nobody said anything where I could hear, but I could tell that Papa and Uncle Thomas and Ma were all worried. Papa and Uncle Thomas even stayed in our house with us that night. It wasn't the first time somebody hadn't made it back from town the day they left, of course—it wasn't safe to ride back home after dark, so we stayed in town if we hadn't left to come back by late afternoon. But with whatever had happened with the Johanssons, it seemed like everybody was worried. It was quiet in the house after supper; nobody talked much. I just drew horses and flowers on my slate. Uncle Thomas and Ma both found little bits of work to do inside. Papa sat at the window, looking out across the fields. He had the Bible open on his lap and a lantern lit next to him, but I never saw him turn a page.

Thankfully, Pa made it home the next morning. He must have left town early and rode Ferd pretty hard, because it wasn't long after breakfast when we heard him clopping toward the house on the hard-packed earth. I had been practicing my letters enough that I'd worn down my chalk and there was a little pile of dust under my feet at the table.

We all scrambled out of the door to check on Pa. He looked tired and trail-worn. His shirt was dark with sweat even though the morning was still cool. There were splashes of mud on Ferd's gray haunches and belly and sweat on his chest. Pa almost never worked our horse that hard, so he must have been in a real hurry to get home.

He dropped out of the saddle as we got close to him and said straight out, "It's not just the Johanssons." Then he seemed to notice I was there, standing next to Ma and reaching out to pet Ferd's foreleg. He started talking in German; talking very fast for Pa. I couldn't understand most of it. I caught the name "Heinrich". Mr. Jobst was a friend of our family. We'd been in the same group coming out here, and his family and ours had been members of the same church back before we came to America.

Ma looked surprised at what Pa said, and then worried.

Uncle Thomas said something back to Pa then. Something fast and almost angry. Pa started to respond. Then Papa spoke. Not loudly, but I understood the word *enkelin*, which was what he called me sometimes before Ma would scold him. Uncle Thomas and Pa stopped arguing.

Ma took the worry off of her face and then turned to me and said, "Go into the barn and fetch up some water and a brush for Ferd. He's hot and he'll need to be brushed down. Your Pa will be with you in a few minutes and you can help him. Go. Go."

I went.

It seemed like a lot more than a few minutes before Pa walked Ferd into the barn. He had a smile on his face then. And he had a big piece of rock candy on a string for me. The smile wasn't real, but the candy was.

Uncle Thomas and Papa must have loaded the buckboard while Pa and I were brushing Ferd, because when we walked out of the barn, it was loaded with our things. Not everything—we didn't have the big wagon that we'd come in anymore, and we'd gotten some new things since we moved here—but with our clothes and the strongbox and Papa's writing desk.

I looked up at Pa and asked, "Are we going somewhere?"

"Yes," Pa said. He knelt down next to me and looked me in the face. He still smiled, but his voice was serious. "I don't want you to be scared, but something has gone wrong around here, and until we know how to stop it or avoid it, we're going to leave. It won't be forever. We're not giving up on the farm. But until we can know what is happening, we're going to go somewhere else. Do you understand?"

I didn't. But I said, "Sure, Pa, I understand. Can I bring my slate when we leave? And what about Ferd?"

Pa smiled. I hadn't realized how fake his smile had been until he showed me his real one. "Of course. You need to practice your letters! And Ferd will be with us the whole way. We wouldn't leave him behind." He put his hand on my shoulder; it was huge and heavy and warm and a little sweaty. "Now go climb up on the buckboard. You can sit in the middle and help me drive." I knew they really made me sit in the middle so Ma wouldn't worry about me falling out, but it was fun to help Pa drive anyway, so I didn't complain.

I sat on the bench seat and drew on my slate while Pa and Uncle Thomas finished packing the buckboard. Ma was in the kitchen fixing us some food for the trip. Papa was hooking the oxen up to pull the buckboard. They were all working fast.

It was just a little after noon when we left the farm, headed back East.

We saw strange things as we traveled.

The first was the railroad tracks. They traveled along the old wagon road for many miles, so we rode next to them on the buckboard for most of the afternoon. Before it was dark, when the sun was still low in the sky, we came to a place where the tracks stopped. The mound of dirt and crushed stone and steel rails and wooden ties just…stopped. Then there was a space maybe three times as long as our wagon where there was just ground. After that space, the tracks started up again, with only grass and flat ground in between, like the railroad tracks had never been there. The ground and grass in between the two ends of the railroad tracks was lightly covered in dust: finer than dirt and a gray that almost seemed like no color at all.

"We should warn them when we get to Placerville," Uncle Thomas said, staring at the empty space. "Otherwise the next train might derail."

"What does derail mean?" I asked, looking up at Pa.

He said something slow but angry in German to Uncle Thomas. They argued back and forth for a few minutes, then Ma said something and they stopped.

Nobody said anything else for a long time.

We didn't make it to Placerville that night. By the time the sun had set, we were still several hours' travel away. Pa saw a farmstead a little ways ahead down the cart road, though, so we headed there. We didn't know them, but most people out here on the prairie would allow a family of travelers to sleep in the barn for a night, so long as they didn't look too desperate. I didn't think we did.

From a distance, the farm looked a lot like ours—a dugout house on a small hillside with a barn and outhouse not too far away. The outhouse was bigger than ours, though. It must have had at least two seats. Maybe more people lived on this farm. And they grew wheat, just like we did; I could tell from the fields.

As we got closer, though, I could also tell that their house looked a little strange. It just sort of stopped a few feet out from the side of the hill. The fence around their pigpen had a big hole in it, too. The rails ended at one point, then there was a gap that our wagon could have driven through, then they started up again. The fence rails dipped a bit where they were at loose ends instead of connected to a post like they should have been.

Pa stopped the buckboard a good distance away from the house. It was too far and too dark to see any details about the house; the people inside must have been asleep and did not have their lanterns lit.

Pa looked at Uncle Thomas, and then the two of them hopped off the buckboard. Papa got down from his seat in the back and pulled the shotgun out from its hiding spot. He stood next to the buckboard while Pa and Uncle Thomas walked up to the house, with Uncle Thomas carrying a lantern. They stood there for a minute, and then I saw Uncle Thomas put his hand on Pa's shoulder. The two stood there like that for a little bit more, and then turned around and slowly walked back to the buckboard. Uncle Thomas wiped his face a lot as they walked.

"Let's keep going," Pa said when he and Uncle Thomas got back to the buckboard. "We'll just be careful on the cart road. The oxen will be alright. And they're not too tired." He patted one of them on the shoulder.

Ma just looked at him.

I said, "But I'm tired, Pa. Won't they let us stay in their barn? We've done that for people." I was tired, and my rear end hurt from the buckboard seat.

"No," Pa said. Uncle Thomas had walked over to say something to Papa in German, so it was just the three of us talking. "It's not good for us to stay here tonight. We'll push on. You can make it just a little farther. Then we'll stop in town, or maybe find a different farm." He pulled himself up in the buckboard seat.

As we passed the house, I looked down. Ma tried to catch my head and turn it before I could see, but even in the dark, I saw. The house just sort of stopped somewhere in the kitchen. In the moonlight, I saw the timbers that helped hold up the roof come to a smooth end. The dirt on top was hard-packed, like ours, and still sat on top. Just little dribbles of dirt fell down off of the end.

I looked down from the roof and saw a pair of legs. Like the roof beams, they just stopped smoothly at the knees. Past the legs was just dusty grass, with a dark puddle slowly spreading out from the ends of the legs. Something else next to the legs had also caused a puddle, something that maybe had the shape of half a person cut lengthwise, but Ma's hand closed over my face before I could make out exactly what it was.

"Look at your slate," she said. "Do not look up until I tell you." Ma wasn't truly angry with me very often, but she was then. I looked down and concentrated on drawing Ferd. Ferd with wings like a butterfly, but Ferd. It helped me forget about the legs and the other shape, too, which was good.

I wasn't sure exactly when we stopped that night. Eventually, even the pain in my backside and the noise of the wagon wheels couldn't keep me awake, and I fell asleep with my head on Ma's lap. I woke up when Pa picked me up to carry me into a different barn. This one was just at the edge of town in Placerville. I'd never been here before, but I knew this was where we were going. It wasn't quite daytime yet, but I saw some light on the horizon.

Ma and Pa and Uncle Thomas had beds made up for themselves already—blankets on top of piles of hay. They had one for me, too. Papa didn't have one. He stayed up and stood by the buckboard, looking back down the cart road the way we had come.

I couldn't get back to sleep, so I pulled my slate into my lap. There was just enough dawn light to see by. My slate was full of pictures of Ferd with wings, but I was ready to draw something new. I took my eraser and wiped off Ferd and his wings. Then I knocked the eraser against the side of my slate, trying not to make too much noise.

Papa looked over at me and saw the dust falling from the eraser to cover the dirt floor of the barn.

I started drawing something new.

He stared down at the dust for a long time.

THE DAUGHTER THAT WAS

SIOBHAN GALLAGHER

THE RED LIGHT was too slow, and Trish couldn't wait any longer. It had been a long, *long* month and nine days, waiting and waiting for that call. Hundreds of thousands of moments of agony, dread, and remorse. How they ate and ate at her sanity.

She sliced through the intersection. The speedometer struck sixty, seventy, eighty.

A mystery how she made it to the hospital without a wreck.

She abandoned her car to three parking spots, burst through the front entrance, smacked into the receptionist's desk, wheezed, "McMullen."

Again, the wait.

Room number in mind, she slipped into the elevator just as the doors closed, jostling interns. They could rudely stare until their eyes fell out.

On the third floor, the door numbers raced past her. 1B, 2B, 3B, 4B, 5B. Stopped in her tracks at the sight of Jake and Sheriff Robsin in front of her daughter's room.

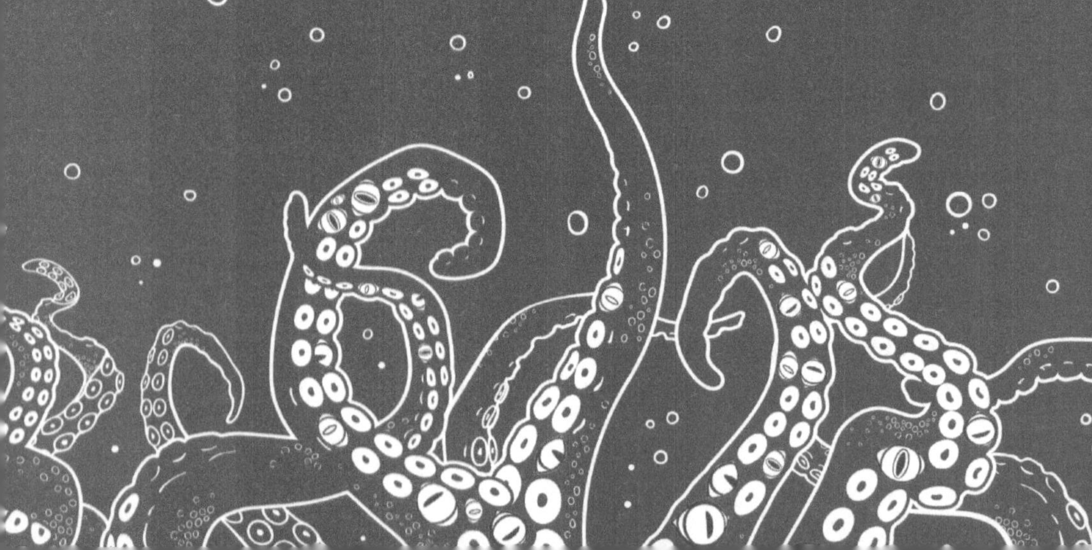

How did Jake manage to beat her here? Did they call him first? Called *him* first while she had tirelessly searched every place she knew, had fallen asleep each night with the phone clutched in her hands? All he did was take a week off.

Jake looked up from his conversation with Sheriff Robsin, ran to her with tears, tightly hugged her. She softened, face growing hot and wet.

"Is she…?" She could barely breathe. Relief was pouring out of her so fast, her whole body shook. Jake's embrace kept her standing.

"They're still examining her," Jake said, voice muffled by emotion. "But I mean, from what the sheriff said…"

"What did he say?" She looked to the sheriff, who stood at a respectful distance.

"Let me start from the beginning," said Sheriff Robsin, smiling for both of them. "Joey Carmon was the one who found your daughter, about two miles north of town. He was out hunting, called us up, said she was sound asleep on a bed of moss. And that's how we found her. She screamed bloody murder when we woke her, and, well…" His smile faded.

"What?" she insisted.

"Maybe she was hallucinating or something, because she didn't want to go with us. She screamed and cried and flailed. Gave Andy a broken nose." A brief, uneasy smile. "Anyway, glad she's safe and sound."

"Thank you," Jake said, and she nodded.

A nurse poked her head out from 5B and said, "Mr. and Mrs. McMullen?"

She rushed to the door. "Yes, is she all right?"

The nurse stepped out, closed the door behind her. "She's in good health. No signs of dehydration, malnutrition, or trauma. She does seem to be in shock, which could be—"

"Let me see her," Trish said, about ready to shove the little nurse aside.

Jake placed a hand on her shoulder, but she shrugged him off. *Enough waiting already!* They could tell her all this over the phone.

Wide-eyed, the nurse let her through.

Her heart punched a hole through her chest at the sight of her daughter. Cynthia sat on the edge of the bed in a hospital gown, her shaggy layered hair and long bangs masking her face. Another nurse was there, putting away some sort of kit. A rape kit? *Oh god!*

She flung her arms around her daughter, squeezed and squeezed. All her warmth, all her love into that embrace, and Cynthia was as stiff as could be.

She knelt, brushed the bangs aside, and made eye contact. "How do you feel, sweetie?"

"Violated." Cynthia stared coldly at the nurse.

The nurse smiled nervously.

"She can come home with us, right?" Trish asked the nurse.

"Of course. We'll call you in a week about the blood work."

She squeezed Cynthia once more before allowing Jake his turn. Cynthia remained rigid and unresponsive.

"Oh, here." From her tote purse, she brought forth a cute long-sleeved dress that Jake's mother had gotten Cynthia, a pair of flip-flops and fresh underwear.

Cynthia accepted the clothing casually, without a hint of recognition.

"I still have my school uniform," Cynthia said, "but okay. May I change in peace, without watching eyes?"

"Oh, yes. Yes, of course," Trish said hurriedly. She took several steps back and turned to face the door.

Jake gave her a sidelong glance, touched her hand. She smiled, rubbed at the soreness in her chest. Everything was right in the world; their family was back together, and they could go back to their normal, everyday lives.

Her poor Cynthia didn't sleep the first night back at home. Trish knew this because *she* didn't sleep either. She stayed awake in the living room, drinking orange pekoe tea and catching up on Netflix shows. Every so often, she'd pass by Cynthia's door to check if her daughter needed something, and every time, Cynthia could be heard mumbling words that didn't sound quite right, words scraped from the back of the throat. If they were words at all.

Listening too long made her head…cluttered, heavy. Motes swimming in the dark hallway. Breathing in her own ears, Jake's snoring, crickets chittering outside.

Step back, shake herself. Gone, all gone. The mumbling now mute whispers. Yet from brainstem to tailbone, a chill remained.

All those nights staying up and worrying had caught herself a cold—yes, an oncoming cold.

Around 5:30 a.m., exhaustion caught up with her. She set the alarm to wake her in three hours and passed out next to Jake.

At breakfast, Cynthia behaved as she had at dinner, avoided eye contact and spoke the bare minimum. She nibbled on plain toast while Jake tried to entice her into going to the movies or to the ice park.

Halfway through her coffee and still not feeling the effects, Trish said, "What would *you* like to do, sweetie?"

"Go to the woods," Cynthia said, her voice too quiet.

Coffee jolt shock. That had to be a joke. Cynthia always made smartass remarks.

"Okay, kiddo." Jake chuckled, reassuring her that it was indeed a joke. "When you decide what you want to do today, let me know."

Trish said, "Do you want to know what your friends have been up to?"

"No," Cynthia said.

"Really? They've been so worried about you."

"At first, they were concerned, but they've adjusted to life without me. I am a mere echo in their social circle."

"I don't think that's true."

"Choose to believe what you wish." Cynthia stood, having hardly made a dent in her toast. "I'm going to bed now."

"Oh, okay, sweetie. Sleep well."

Jake added, "Sleep tight, kiddo. We'll plan something tomorrow."

Cynthia left without further words.

For a long moment, Trish and Jake exchanged looks, unable to put into words what had just happened.

"I don't understand," Jake said. "I feel like we've done something wrong."

"She's been through a lot. Let's just give her some time." Though in the back of her mind, she was recounting the digits of the psychiatrist's number the hospital had given her.

Every meal where Cynthia sat with them was a repeat of breakfast. Rarely did Cynthia step outside her room. The mumbles heard from behind her door started to sound like prayers.

Sheriff Robsin showed up the day after Cynthia's return and asked if he could speak with her. Forensics had found no evidence on Cynthia's school uniform, nor in the area where the police had found her.

In her worse thoughts, Trish feared that maybe, just maybe, there wasn't a kidnapper.

She knocked on Cynthia's door. "Sweetie, the sheriff is here. He'd like to speak with you."

No answer.

No mumbling, either. Perhaps Cynthia was asleep at three in the afternoon.

She cracked the door open, peeked inside. The bed was empty. Where had that girl gone to? She hadn't seen Cynthia leave her room.

She checked the bathroom, checked the kitchen, then returned to the room to give it another look. The bed was still empty, and Cynthia wasn't at her desk.

From the closet came the softest of sighs, like the rustling of a mouse.

Trish flung the closet door open to find Cynthia sitting with her knees drawn up. Cynthia looked up at her with bleary eyes, her hair matted and wet as if she'd washed it in the sink, and she still wore yesterday's nightshirt.

On the walls inside the closet were odd marks, maybe symbols, but none she recognized. What had possessed Cynthia to do *that*? This wasn't her house, she didn't have a right to vandalize it.

She took a moment to breathe out her frustration. Nothing that couldn't be painted over; in fact, she'd do it tomorrow. Looking at those symbols made her eyes want to roll back.

She said, "What are you doing in here?"

"Thinking," Cynthia said, annoyed.

"In the closet?"

"Yes."

"Come, put some pants on. The sheriff is waiting downstairs."

Trish quickly dug through the dresser drawers, produced a long skirt instead. After Cynthia was properly dressed, she marched her downstairs.

The three of them sat at the kitchen table. Jake was out shopping since he knew how much it meant to her to stay home with their daughter. Sheriff Robsin was friendly and gentle with his questioning. *Did you see someone suspicious outside of school or at the bus stop? Did you speak to anyone that was unknown to you or your family? Did a stranger give you anything to eat or drink?*

Cynthia, who'd up to this point answered in head shakes, sharply cut him off to say, "I was not kidnapped, nor did I run away. I followed the song, the song of…"

Cynthia recited strange, unintelligible words which slid off Trish's eardrums. Never sticking, never penetrating her mind. And when the flow of words stopped, she felt much more at ease, as if she'd just survived the passing of a great storm.

Cynthia continued, "A name for every age. Sometimes Ages or Ages Thyssu."

Trying to fill the emptiness left by Cynthia's words, Trish said, "Why don't I make some coffee?"

A moment longer before Sheriff Robsin answered, as if he had to shake himself wake.

"Oh, no. That's all right. I have a lot of work back at the station." He stood hastily, nearly tipping over his chair. "Maybe I'll come back another time."

She made the coffee anyway. Drank it black, alone in the kitchen.

The hospital called a day later than expected to say there was nothing unusual in Cynthia's blood.

"Nothing," Trish repeated to herself as she ended the call. It was almost disappointing.

The following week, Cynthia had a late-morning appointment with Dr. Lily Abeck. Trish wasn't allowed to attend, but Dr. Abeck would record and pass along each session.

The first session was copied onto a CD, and Trish tucked it securely into her purse. As soon as she was home, she locked herself in the den, popped the CD into her laptop, and put on headphones. Her body shook, excited and nervous. What had Dr. Abeck discovered about her daughter's situation?

"I heard you were gone for a while," Dr. Abeck said after Trish got through introductions and pleasantries. "Do you mind taking me through that day on June 29th?"

"I'd have to take you through June 28th first," Cynthia said flatly.

"Please, I'd like to hear it."

"As I was going to the bus stop that day, I heard the most…*wonderful*, magnificent song. I couldn't believe it existed. It was too perfect. And it came from the woods.

"I continued to hear the song while riding the bus, and it was with me at school. I asked my friends at lunch if they heard it, and they all shook their heads. The song was there when I returned home, there as I fell asleep, and it was even in my dreams. When I awoke, it was still there. I alone could hear this song and knew it must be for me."

Trish paused the recording, tried to remember if there was a particular song playing that day on the radio, one that might have gotten stuck in Cynthia's head. Nothing came to mind, or maybe she'd been listening to the wrong stations (usually classic rock). She resumed listening.

"On the 29th, I had resolved that I'd find the source of this song. After I got off the bus, I went into the woods. I spent *hours*. The day was long, so I had plenty of light. But suddenly the sky darkened.

"I was afraid, but I didn't actually know what fear was. It didn't matter. I was cared for, even…*loved*." Cynthia sighed as if she were an old woman remembering a long-ago romance.

"What happened next, after this…?"

The audio gave out. Trish cursed, checked the CD for scratches. Maybe the recording equipment had malfunctioned. The audio returned ten minutes after Dr. Abeck's question.

"…It's natural to reciprocate, desirable," Cynthia said.

"Oh…" Dr. Abeck sounded off, as if she suddenly had a head cold. "How exactly did you reciprocate?"

Silence.

"That's okay, you don't have to answer," Dr. Abeck said. "Do you think you could sing or hum this song for me?"

"Impossible."

"Do you believe it's an angel's song?"

"No."

"Can you hear the song now?"

"No."

"Why do you think that is?"

"That's like asking why our galaxy, the solar system, and earth formed from the primordial chaos. Why did any of it begin?"

Abruptly, the session was declared over. Dr. Abeck said her goodbyes, adding that she looked forward to their next session in two weeks.

Trish sat there for several minutes, the glow of the laptop's screen burning her eyes. That person Dr. Abeck had spoken to didn't even *sound* like her daughter. It was…*alien*.

Alien? What was *wrong* with herself? What was… Never mind. It was going to be okay. It was going. To. Be. Okay.

Found her teeth grinding and hands clenching. Found herself unable to move until Jake arrived home.

Dr. Abeck arrived at the coffee shop on a motorbike, wearing a brown leather jacket and skinny jeans on a figure Trish yearned to have again. Funny, without glasses, Dr. Abeck looked ten years younger, though no doubt the pixie haircut helped.

After ordering a cappuccino, Dr. Abeck sat with her, and insisted she be called Lily.

"I believe Cynthia has created this alternate reality," Dr. Abeck said, "an attempt to distance herself from the trauma. I think if she gets out a bit more, maybe nature walks, that may help her engage in the world again. Natural light is also good. You can buy lamps online or maybe encourage her to spend mornings in the backyard."

Trish typed all the advice into her phone. It seemed so obvious now. She shouldn't have let Cynthia stay cooped up in her room all this time.

"Most importantly, to stay patient. This is a difficult time for her, and you never want her to feel as if she's at fault. Always remain a positive force in her life. If you feel you need to take a moment, take a moment."

"What about the song she mentioned?" Trish said, unable to hide her worry.

"It might be a symptom of schizophrenia, though you say there isn't a history of mental health issues in either your family or your husband's. So, for now, we'll just observe."

Before Dr. Abeck left, she promised to provide another copy of the first session, as well as double-check her recording equipment.

Trish slowly sipped her warm apple cider; of late, she'd been drinking too much coffee and tea. She was glad for the discussion, glad for the context. Schizophrenia didn't scare her as much as, well—

She caught herself staring at an empty glass. *Huh, funny.*

The autumn morning air was crisp but not too chilly. They ditched the scarves, mitts, and hats for their walk. Jake also joined, saying he could use the exercise.

They walked around the neighborhood, startling stray cats and remarking on early Halloween decorations. They followed the bike trail, which led them out of their neighborhood and into another—older, less densely packed. The bike trail continued, running along the woods for several miles, where it would end in the local park.

Trish had no plans to go as far as the park, but maybe it would be a goal for them in the future.

Except Cynthia left the trail.

She caught Cynthia's shoulder, but the girl wiggled out of her grasp. Cynthia might have actually gotten away had Jake not lunged and grabbed her.

"Just let me go," Cynthia said, her voice breaking.

"Are you…" Trish bit her tongue to keep from saying *crazy*. It wouldn't help to say that.

Nor would it help to ask about the woods. Likely, the answer would make her brain swim in a vat of wine.

Cynthia ceased her struggle, head hanging in defeat. There were no tears, just a longing gaze at the woods as they held her in their iron grips.

She passed Aaron's art gallery on the way to pick up school notes from one of Cynthia's friends. She missed the gallery. Aaron had been so kind to let her have all the time off she needed, but now she wondered if that had been a disservice. Jake had his job to keep him occupied while she was stuck all day with a stranger. There were days when she wanted to grab and shake this stranger, demanding to know what had happened to her daughter.

Maybe she should go back to work. Something could be worked out where Jake went in late, and she left early, so Cynthia was never left unsupervised.

But when she proposed this to Jake, he gave her the briefest look of horror, and said he couldn't do it because he'd already taken too much time off. How was it that her boss allowed time off and not his? He couldn't answer.

She went up the stairs, knocked on Cynthia's door.

"I have your school notes," she said.

Cynthia opened the door, handed her the pile of homework she'd picked up this morning.

"Wait, you finished it?" That was at least two weeks' worth of homework. "All of it?"

"Yes."

They exchanged papers, and Cynthia briefly, almost mockingly, looked over her friend's notes. She was wearing the same heavy sweater from this morning, despite that the day had warmed considerably. A light jacket would have been more fitting.

"You want me to turn on the heater?"

"I'm fine."

"Well, would you like to go over this homework?"

"You may if you wish. It will be found satisfactory." Cynthia was about to close the door but stopped. "May I go outside?"

"Only to go to school."

"I'm going to take a nap." The door closed.

Trish turned around and sighed. At least Cynthia still cared about her academics. Maybe there was still hope.

Cynthia had always been a middling student, getting Bs, sometimes As, the occasional C. So, Trish was shocked to see not a single answer was incorrect, and the handwriting was clean and neat. *Well, okay, Cynthia is now a genius.*

She erased some of the answers, replaced them with incorrect ones. As far as anyone outside this family and Dr. Abeck would know, Cynthia was still Cynthia.

Trish wasn't sure about this Dr. Abeck. Not only was that first session's audio never fully restored, but no progress had been made in the three months since they started. It was Dr. Abeck asking the same question, five different ways, and Cynthia pointing this out.

The latest session started with Dr. Abeck saying, "You look well today."

"You mean I look fat," Cynthia said.

Dr. Abeck stammered a denial. The whole exchange could be mistaken for a comedy routine.

What was she paying three-hundred dollars a session for? And that was with a discount!

Though she did agree, Cynthia was gaining weight. When Cynthia had regained her appetite, Trish was simply glad that her daughter wasn't going to starve. But the second helpings, snacks, and lack of exercise were adding up.

After she replaced the snacks with grapes and carrot sticks, she caught Cynthia rummaging through the kitchen cabinets. When she pointed out the healthier snacks, Cynthia grumbled, "Not enough calories," and made a bowl of cereal instead.

Over dinner, she and Jake conversed normally, as Dr. Abeck recommended, specifically about helping organize a garage sale for Jake's sister.

"Do you have anything to sell?" she said to Cynthia.

Cynthia scooped the last of her meal into her mouth, chewed slowly, and swallowed.

"I can refill your plate for you," she said, grabbing Cynthia's plate. "I was about to get up, anyway."

Cynthia didn't protest, just looked at her with a bored expression.

She got the skinniest pork chop, and only a spoonful of mashed potatoes and green beans. Then put the leftovers away, so there wouldn't be thirds.

That night, she locked the fridge to prevent midnight snacking.

The leftovers were gone the next morning.

Jake, that idiot man. He must've forgotten to relock the fridge after getting a beer. Or he had undermined her.

She found Jake in the den, closed the doors behind her. He gave her the dumbest look, as if he didn't know what the hell was going on.

When she left the den, she was drained of all emotion. Her voice hoarse, her face burning hot.

After another argument, Jake suddenly had to fill in at a conference. Apparently, she was the only one who cared about their daughter.

The day passed slowly without Jake around. Trish picked weeds, reorganized the bookcase, tried out her new teas, watched Netflix shows, made sandwiches, and still the clock hadn't struck noon.

Cynthia absconded with the remaining sandwiches, but by that time she'd remembered the bottle of red wine buried in the pantry.

She awoke from the couch to darkness and running water. Temples throbbing, mouth full of sticky sourness. She had a vague memory of Cynthia cooking steak in a pan and herself not giving a damn.

Where was that water coming from? Oh, a shower. A shower? At 3:00 a.m.? What was *wrong* with that girl?

She sluggishly stomped to the bathroom.

A girlish giggle.

She blinked, tried to comprehend what she had just heard. A giggle, really? Not strange mutters or throat-scraping words?

Steam burst through the open doorway. A glow came from behind the shower curtains. She slammed the lights on, ripped the curtains back.

Her cry tangled in a scream.

Cynthia shielded her belly, five or six months pregnant. Black ichor ran down the inside of her thigh.

Trish was too weak to grab support, too weak to stand. She crumpled to the floor as Cynthia fled.

This…this had to be a nightmare. It wasn't possible. The hospital would have told her.

She curled up like a child, buried her face in her knees, and heaved mountainous sobs.

A thousand times she thought about calling the hospital and screaming until her lungs were raw. But then they would know. And she didn't want anyone to know.

She *had* to do something. She had to help her daughter.

There was Samantha, who worked at and was part-owner of an OB/GYN clinic. She'd known Samantha for many years, who loved art as much as she did, but lacked the training to know what to look for in a piece. Samantha wouldn't gossip to others about her poor Cynthia.

She scheduled an appointment the very next day at the earliest time available.

Cynthia had locked herself in her room and, apparently, had taken provisions because the peanut butter and box of crackers were gone. She apologized, pleaded, and tried to bribe Cynthia to open the door.

All day it was like this. *All* day. Cynthia was beyond reason, too sick to understand what was going on with herself. Trish was forced to use a screwdriver to dismantle the doorknob.

"You can't come in here," Cynthia said, trying to block the doorway with her desk chair.

"It's my house. I can come in if I want."

She grabbed the chair from Cynthia, who gave up willingly. Cynthia retreated to her bed, used a giant pillow to guard herself.

"You need to see a doctor," she said.

"I'm not getting an ultrasound."

"You're getting what you need." Though an ultrasound was *exactly* what she was thinking. "Don't you understand?"

"Only that you wish to imprison me at your own expense."

The last of her patience flew out the window.

"You're fifteen years old! You're not old enough to make adult decisions. Don't you want to go back to school? Hang out with your friends? You haven't even been to a prom. How will you go to the prom if you have it?"

"*He*," Cynthia said. "The baby is a boy."

She threw her hands up. "How can you possibly know that?"

"I know," Cynthia said icily. "Just like I know you had an abortion when you were twenty."

Smack!

Cynthia held her face. Her palm burned.

"Oh god, I'm so sorry." The words tumbled from her lips in a single breath. She had never, ever, ever, *ever* raised her hand toward Cynthia. Not even to spank her! "I'm sorry, sweetie. Do you need some ice?"

"It's nothing. A phantom memory." Cynthia's hand fell from her face, her gaze far off. "I've said my goodbyes ages past. I've not missed anyone since."

Though she still felt awful, Cynthia's response made it less objectionable.

"I'll get you some ice." She backed away. "And we're leaving 6:30 a.m. tomorrow," she said with finality.

Surprisingly, Cynthia didn't put up a struggle. She was even properly dressed, wearing a heavy sweater (which hid the pregnancy), knee-length skirt, stockings, and jogging sneakers.

The car ride to the clinic was full of silence. The horizon was barely lit, the air cold, the sky dark.

At the tail end of the South Central Plaza, next to an imported dishware shop, was the clinic. The parking lot had been expanded quite a bit since the last time Trish was here; this wasn't her go-to place to shop. Though just beyond the parking lot was the woods. She parked close as possible to the clinic, kept the back seat doors locked until she opened the door for Cynthia, then maintained an iron grip on her daughter.

No one else was in the waiting area, which eased some of her tension. The fewer people who knew, the better. She quickly filled out the paperwork, and when called, she ushered Cynthia into Samantha's office.

Samantha was in her early fifties, lots of gray blending into her sandy blonde hair, which she kept in a tight ponytail. Her face expressed shock, but she quickly masked it with a smile.

"Thank you for seeing us so soon," Trish said, smiling apologetically. "I'd like to do this discreetly."

"We can do that. Have a seat, you two." Samantha indicated to a couple of chairs against the wall, then dragged her swivel chair comfortably close.

"Do you think we could go ahead and do the ultrasound?" Trish continued to stand.

"Only reason we're here is because the abortion clinic is five hours away," Cynthia said, also standing.

Samantha looked both appalled and confused.

Trish chuckled nervously. "It's a joke. She's developed this bizarre sense of humor. We're going to put it up for adoption."

"*He*—and no." Cynthia's icy tone returned.

"What do you mean '*no*'?" She said, voice heated and rising. "You don't know what kind of decision you're making."

"Okay, okay. Let's calm down," Samantha said. "Here, I've got something."

From the large desk drawer, Samantha removed a radio-looking device with a trumpet style stethoscope attached by a cord, and another skinny cord ending in an earpiece.

"Take a seat, Cynthia, please." Samantha held up the device. "Do you know what this is?"

"A baby heartbeat monitor," Cynthia said, sitting.

"Impressive." Samantha smiled. "Would you like to listen to your baby's heartbeat? This isn't as intense as an ultrasound, if that concerns you."

"I can already hear his heartbeat. But since you asked nicely." Cynthia lifted the sweater and shirt underneath to reveal a round abdomen. Trish looked away.

"You're pretty far along," Samantha said, applying the device's stethoscope. "Sit straight, please."

All Trish could do was seethe in silent discontent. She didn't come here for Cynthia to be coddled and reassured in her delusion. Where were the facts on teenage mothers?

"Ah, found it," Samantha said, listened for a moment. "A strong, healthy heartbeat." She removed the earpiece. "I'll get you a new one."

Samantha instructed Cynthia on how to hold the stethoscope and carefully placed the device on Cynthia's lap. For the first time since Cynthia returned home, her daughter smiled.

"I'm going to speak with your mom for a bit," Samantha said, stood, and took Trish aside.

In a hushed voice, Samantha said, "What's going on with you two?"

"Look, I only found out yesterday. She's been hiding it from me."

"Well, I can see why."

"If those hospital nurses had just done *their job* properly, we wouldn't be in this position." She wanted to cry and pull her hair out. None of this was fair; she shouldn't have to defend herself. "Can you just…please perform the ultrasound."

"Your daughter doesn't want to."

"It doesn't matter!" She took a deep breath, forcing her voice low. "She hasn't been well for a while now."

"Arguing about it is only going to lead to more stress. I think we should—"

Darkness. Total and complete darkness.

Shouts outside the office. She and Samantha bumped heads. Trish reached out, trying to find Cynthia, her heart pounding in her ears.

Somehow, deep down, she knew Cynthia was no longer in the room.

She felt for the door, followed the walls to the waiting area, and out the glass entrance door. Cynthia's silhouette passed behind the trees at the edge of the parking lot.

Trish ran straight into the woods.

The ground was slick with icy dew, and several times she missed her footing and lost sight of Cynthia. She kicked off her slip-on dress shoes, sprinted to catch up. Socks soaked, bone-chilling cold, her ears ached like frostbite.

Cynthia stumbled, cried out, and clutched her abdomen.

"Stop!" Trish's mouth, nose, throat, and lungs burned; she could barely speak. "You're going to hurt yourself!"

The trees grew thick around her. The morning light dimmed. Left, right, straight, it all looked the same. Could they make it out of here?

Cynthia slowed down, leaned heavily on a tree. If she could just get a little closer…

The trees backed away—no, a clearing. Cynthia fell to her knees. Finally! She could catch her daughter and—

High above the trees, a tower of black smoke swirled.

A strong gust swept smoke into the woods, obscuring the ground, the surrounding tree trunks, and Cynthia herself.

"Cynthia!" She heard herself yell. "Cynthia!"

It was growing darker, darker, darker than a moonless night, darker than the space between stars. Each time she repeated Cynthia's name, her voice grew softer, softer, softer…

Warmth. Surrounding, comforting. Cynthia uncurled and opened her eyes. Pillows? Oh, a bed. *Her* bed.

But not her room.

Her bed was in the middle of an ever-expanding body of mist; shadows carpeted the floor. The mist formed wispy gray membranes with gaping, drooping pores. The pores continuously collapsed and reformed, each time hinting at other lands, other worlds that lay eons away.

No soreness as she sat up. No scraped or bruised shins from a dozen stumbles. She ran her fingers over a nightgown she'd never donned. Where they rested on her belly, the baby kicked joyfully, making her smile. Safe. They were both safe.

"I'm so glad," she whispered breathlessly. "It was all just a terrible dream."

Sweet, wonderful relief! A laugh escaped, flew high, high, higher. Crackling electricity coursed through the mist, and the song—oh, the song!—arose all around and within herself.

She shuddered, held herself as every emotion tumbled and swirled, danced and clashed. The baby had calmed down; sucking his thumb, he listened intently.

The melody stung her eyes, the harmony embraced and shied away, the rhythm shook worlds.

Yet something was new, different. She dug through a labyrinth of layers, pushed notes aside, filtered out thousands-upon-thousands of echoes to find one that repeatedly and persistently called out her name. An echo from a familiar voice.

How perfect! How wonderfully perfect! The addition was just so right—a simple touch of endearment, passion, and angst.

She wiped away tears, nestled into her pillows. Hopefully, in time, her baby would become just as musical.

ABOUT THE AUTHORS

A Place Called Omley – A.J. Lewis

instagram.com/ajlewisfiction

A. J. Lewis is from the South of England. He mostly writes sci-fi and horror but dabbles in romance from time to time.

Berry Juice – BJ Thoray

linktr.ee/bjthoray

BJ Thoray is a writer/editor active in the nonprofit space. BJ is currently shopping their short story collection *gaslightbulb* and finishing a novel.

Bluefish – Doug Brunell

dougbrunell.wixsite.com/writerofdepravity

Doug Brunell lives in Northern California, the land of earthquakes and the Wicked Woman of the Woods. His latest book is *Broken Bones*.

Dark Waters To Nowhere – Rekha Valliappan

silicasun.wordpress.com

Rekha Valliappan is an award-winning multi-genre writer and poet. Her credits include Best Small Fictions 2025, Pushcart, Best of the Net nominations, publications in *Penumbric, Lackington, Aphelion*, others.

Darla's Monster – Cassondra Windwalker

polymathpress.com/products/ghost-girls-and-rabbits-by-cassondra-windwalker

Writing full-time from the Colorado Front Range, Cassondra Windwalker is the author of the indigenous horror *Ghost Girls and Rabbits*, her ninth novel.

Descendent – Bryson Richard

Bryson Richard is a writer from the Black Swamp region of Ohio.

Desert Silver Blue – Jay Kang Romanus

jaykangromanus.com

Jay is a queer, disabled, mixed Asian-American author whose work runs the entire gamut of speculative fiction.

Dossier #KR-042: The Veil Cantors – Subham Rai

subham6.bsky.social

Subham Rai, from Kolkata, India, creates captivating sci-fi stories, exploring cosmic puzzles and human courage with richly drawn characters and intricate narratives.

Dust – Red Charles

Red Charles is the handsome, dashing alter ego of a new horror author who by day is a practicing attorney in the southeastern United States.

Eldritch Moon – JG Faherty

jgfaherty.com

JG Faherty is a multi-award-nominated writer and a relative of Mary Shelley. He is the author of 25 books, 4 collections, and 95 short stories.

Finder's Fee – Edward Ahern

Ed Ahern's had over 550 stories and poems published so far, and twelve books. He also squats on the editorial board at *Bewildering Stories*.

From Black Clouds – Amanda M. Blake

amandamblake.com

Amanda M. Blake is author of *Question Not My Salt, Deep Down, Drift,* dark poetry collection *Dead Ends,* and the *Thorns* fairytale mash-up series.

He Who Lives Below – Mel Harlan

stillprettystudio.com

Mel Harlan is a writer and consultant in Houston, TX. Her short fiction has appeared in Allegory, Graveside Press, and Thirteen Podcast.

Her Sister, In Starlight – Devan Barlow

devanbarlow.com

Devan Barlow writes the *Curses & Curtains* series of fairytales-meet-musicals fantasies, among many other works. She's usually hanging out with her dog.

In Extremis – J.J. Smith

J.J. Smith is an Ojibwa and journalist living in the Washington, D.C. area where he spends his daylight hours covering Congress and the federal government.

Intrusive Thoughts That Are Not Your Own – TT Madden

linktr.ee/ttmaddenwrites

TT Madden (they/them) is a genderfluid, mixed-race horror writer who refuses to leave "politics" out of their writing.

It Feasts – Harold B Hoss

haroldhosshorror.wordpress.com

Harold Blake Hoss is a writer, filmmaker, and attorney whose horror fiction and films explore the line between reality and nightmare. He lives in New York.

Kissing Bug Day – J Neira

jneiraauthor.bsky.social

J. Neira is a cozy horror author & a slushie for GRADEside (Graveside Press's middle grade line). They have a young adult novel coming out with Graveside Press next year!

Northern Lights, Too Far South – Michael Kellichner

facebook.com/authormichaelkellichner

Michael Kellichner is a poet and writer who grew up in central Pennsylvania, but has settled in South Korea.

Piexe Vampiro – Terry Campbell

alittlewestofweird.com

Terry Campbell enjoys writing cosmic horror, folk horror, western horror…and sometimes, just plain horror.

Summoning Caleb – Margo Pecha

notmargopecha.bsky.social

Margo Pecha lives in southwest Washington state. When she's not reading or writing, she's working in her gardens.

The Harvest – Hannah Rebekah Graves

creepshannah.carrd.co

Hannah Rebekah Graves is an AuDHD ball of nerves and chaos. Her special interests are horror and Anne Boleyn. She lives in the redwoods with her wife and a cockatiel named Bananakin. Voted "Most Likely to Join a Cult Someday".

The Book of Howard – Alex Hunter

alexhunterwrites.com

Alex Hunter is a weaver of nightmares, sending them out from his London home. His debut novel, *The Harvest*, was published in January 2025.

The Daughter That Was – Siobhan Gallagher

siobhangallagherauthor.com

The Fairy Field – R. Wren

twitter.com/ro_wren

R. Wren (they/she) is an Irish writer of weird tales. They write because they don't believe in ghosts, but wish that they could.

The Gorge – Tom Blicq

tomblicq.jimdofree.com

Tom Blicq is an author hailing from Winnipeg, Manitoba. His education includes a BSc in biology, with a minor in English literature and creative writing.

The Prophecy of Gulls – Hannah Birss

hannahbirsswrites.carrd.co

Hannah Birss (she/her) is a writer and aspiring magpie based out of Ontario. She can usually be found in a nest constructed of books, writing journals, and shiny trinkets.

The Split Through the Sky – Lena Ng

isfdb.org/cgi-bin/ea.cgi?248172

Lena Ng lurks around Toronto, Canada. She has creepies published in tomes such as *Amazing Stories.* " *Under an Autumn Moon* " is her short story collection.

Travel Package – Clay McLeod Chapman

claymcleodchapman.com

Clay McLeod Chapman writes books, comic books, middle-grade and YA books, as well as for film and television.

CONTENT WARNINGS

Please note: it should be assumed that basic horror tropes will apply. These include death, gore, and violence.

Berry Juice – ableism, bullying of a neurodivergent character

Darla's Monster – domestic violence, child endangerment, loss of a child

Desert Silver Blue – homophobic and racial slurs, animal death, body horror

From Black Clouds – homophobia, transphobia, animal death

He Who Lives Below – sexual assault, forced pregnancy and childbirth

Intrusive Thoughts That Are Not Your Own – racism, suicide

Kissing Bug Day – insects

Northern Lights, Too Far South – depictions of dead and mutilated animals

The Harvest – arachnids, mild body horror

The Book of Howard – body horror, mentions of incest

The Daughter That Was – mentions of off-screen abortion

The Fairy Field – animal death

The Gorge – child death

The Prophecy of Gulls – mutilated animals

The Split Through the Sky – insects, arachnids

Thank you for supporting Graveside Press and our authors.

One of the biggest ways you can help is to leave a star rating or a

review wherever you purchased your copy!

Stay spooky.

graveside-press.com